Praise for
FADE TO RED

"Castillo is pushing the envelope. And she is doing a very convincing and, yes, disturbingly good job . . . This is not a book for the faint-hearted . . . If you like nothing better than an adrenaline rush and a hero and heroine possessing multiple character layers, then be assured that *Fade to Red* will be exactly what you are looking for and so much more."
—*A Romance Review*

"A throwback to the old days of romantic suspense . . . chilling . . . Great character development, an ability to totally immerse the reader into the sleazy underbelly of porn and cause a shiver or two." —*Romance Reviews Today*

"Enlightening and original." —*The Romance Reader*

"Chillingly graphic—romantic suspense at its best."
—*The Best Reviews*

THE SHADOW SIDE

"An electrifying chiller rife with action and passion . . . splendid." —*The Dallas Morning News*

continued . . .

Depth
Perception

Linda Castillo

BERKLEY SENSATION, NEW YORK

THE BERKLEY PUBLISHING GROUP
Published by the Penguin Group
Penguin Group (USA) Inc.
375 Hudson Street, New York, New York 10014, USA
Penguin Group (Canada), 10 Alcorn Avenue, Toronto, Ontario M4V 3B2, Canada
(a division of Pearson Penguin Canada Inc.)
Penguin Books Ltd., 80 Strand, London WC2R 0RL, England
Penguin Group Ireland, 25 St. Stephen's Green, Dublin 2, Ireland (a division of Penguin Books Ltd.)
Penguin Group (Australia), 250 Camberwell Road, Camberwell, Victoria 3124, Australia
(a division of Pearson Australia Group Pty. Ltd.)
Penguin Books India Pvt. Ltd., 11 Community Centre, Panchsheel Park, New Delhi—110 017, India
Penguin Group (NZ), Cnr. Airborne and Rosedale Roads, Albany, Auckland 1310, New Zealand
(a division of Pearson New Zealand Ltd.)
Penguin Books (South Africa) (Pty.) Ltd., 24 Sturdee Avenue, Rosebank, Johannesburg 2196, South
Africa

Penguin Books Ltd., Registered Offices: 80 Strand, London WC2R 0RL, England

This is a work of fiction. Names, characters, places, and incidents either are the product of the author's imagination or are used fictitiously, and any resemblance to actual persons, living or dead, business establishments, events, or locales is entirely coincidental.

DEPTH PERCEPTION

A Berkley Sensation Book / published by arrangement with the author

PRINTING HISTORY
Berkley Sensation edition / February 2005

ISBN: 0-425-20109-0

BERKLEY® SENSATION
Berkley Sensation Books are published by The Berkley Publishing Group,
a division of Penguin Group (USA) Inc.,
375 Hudson Street, New York, New York 10014.
BERKLEY SENSATION and the "B" design are trademarks belonging to Penguin Group (USA)
Inc.

PRINTED IN THE UNITED STATES OF AMERICA

10 9 8 7 6 5 4 3 2 1

ACKNOWLEDGMENTS

This book was not easy to write, and I have a few people to thank either for helping me through the process or for so generously sharing their time and expertise.

To Doris Whitworth, Investigator for the City of Allen, Texas Police Department, thank you for sharing your knowledge and for understanding why I ask the questions I do.

To Kim Lionetti, friend and literary agent extraordinaire, thank you for helping me find the magic that made this book so special. You'll never know how much I appreciated your phone call that night in New York.

To my editor Cindy Hwang, thank you for having such an open mind and for doing what you do so very well. You are very much appreciated.

As always, to Catherine Spangler, Jenna Mills, and Vickie Taylor, you're the best friends a girl could have.

And lastly, to my husband, Ernest, my real life hero, I love you always.

"Let the dead Past bury its dead."

—Henry Wadsworth Longfellow
A Psalm of Life

chapter
1

NICK BASTILLE STEPPED OFF THE GREYHOUND BUS, hefted the duffel onto his shoulder, and pulled in a deep breath of air that reeked of stagnant water, sun-baked foliage, and day-old armadillo roadkill. He'd been breathing free air for three hours and fourteen minutes, and no matter how badly it stank, he still couldn't get enough into his lungs.

The October sun beat down on him like a hot cast iron skillet as he started down the narrow stretch of asphalt. His shirt clung wetly to his back, but he barely noticed the Louisiana heat mingling with the stench of his own sweat. Returning to Bellerose after eighteen years was like entering a time warp and traveling back in time.

The gas station out on Parish Road 53 still had only one full-service pump that didn't accept credit cards. Old man Pelletier still grew cotton and sugarcane and drove that rusty old John Deere tractor. The shotgun shacks that sprang out of the mud like cattails on the south side of town were still just a nail or two away from sliding into the black water of the bayou with the alligators and water moccasins.

But while the town of Bellerose hadn't changed, its wayward son had. Eighteen years ago an ambitious and idealistic Nick had left this muddy little hellhole for the dazzle of New Orleans and the promise of a better life. At seventeen, he'd been

on a mission to conquer the world and willing to take on any
army to do it. He might have been born the son of a cotton
farmer, but Fate had cursed him with a proclivity for big
dreams. He'd been just enough of a gambler to pursue those
dreams with the blind ambition of a reckless fool.

But Nick had soon learned that Fate was a fickle bitch with
a penchant for cruelty and little compassion for ambitious
young fools. He'd learned that dreams didn't come without a
price. That hard work and a willingness to go the distance
weren't always enough. That love was a fallacy and trust was
an illusion believed only by those who were too naïve to see
the truth.

In the end his dream had cost him six years of his life. Six
hellish years that had ripped the last of his humanity from his
soul. It should have bothered him that he was no longer even
human enough to mourn its loss. But he'd long since stopped
grieving over things that could never be resurrected.

Now, Bellerose's farm boy-turned-restaurateur had nothing
to his name but the clothes on his back and a hundred dollars
in the pockets of his prison-issue trousers. Standing in the hot
Louisiana sun with the smell of swamp mud in his nostrils and
a thousand regrets in his heart, he found the irony as black and
endless as the bayou itself.

At the edge of town, where the cattails and alligator grass
met the crushed-shell road, he stopped outside the not-so-august
portals of The Blue Gator, Bellerose's only drinking establish-
ment. Eighteen years ago, the place had been an escape from
the endless work of the farm and the heavy hand of his father. A
place to dream and dazzle the pretty women who drove in from
all over rural St. Tammany Parish. Back then, the one-story
clapboard structure hadn't seemed quite so derelict.

But The Blue Gator was as dilapidated as a place could be
and still be standing. The front porch drooped like a swayback
nag. The weathered wood was as warped and gray as sun
bleached bones. The neon Beer on Tap sign looked incongruous
behind the smeared glass of the single ancient window.

It was the kind of place that wouldn't last a week in New Orleans, where the health inspectors made it their mission in life
to hassle restaurant and bar owners, and maybe even make a
little cash on the side from the ones who could afford to avoid

the aggravation of citations. But The Blue Gator was exactly the kind of place that wouldn't think twice about hiring an ex-con.

Holding that thought, Nick swung open the door and entered the dimly lit interior. The bar reeked of spilled whiskey, old cigarette smoke, and the musty redolence of rotting wood. Slowly, his eyes adjusted to the semidarkness, and he was surprised by the quick jolt of familiarity. The same dented jukebox huddled against the wall next to the men's room door. A battered pool table sat at the rear of the room, its green felt surface scarred by decades of misuse and cigarette burns. Mike Pequinot, a man he'd gone to high school with a lifetime ago, stood behind the bar with a broom in his hand. Pequinot was an ex-biker with a fondness for Harley-Davidsons, blondes in black leather, and Saturday night specials—as long as the serial number was filed off. He'd lost a leg in a motorcycle accident right before Nick left for New Orleans. He'd never bothered with a prosthesis, but it didn't look like the missing limb had slowed him down.

Pequinot stopped sweeping and looked at Nick. *"Mais, gardez dont sa."* Well, just look at that. He said the words in fluent Cajun French. "If it ain't my favorite con."

"Ex-con," Nick corrected and walked to the bar. *"Il n'a in bon boute."* It's been a good while.

"When did you get sprung?"

"Cet avant midi." This morning.

Leaning on the broom, Pequinot turned and snagged two shot glasses and a bottle of dark rum from the shelf. The good stuff he saved for special occasions. He set the glasses on the bar and proceeded to break the seal and pour.

"I've been saving this for you, Nicky." Pequinot's biceps were the size of cypress trunks and just as hard. His brown hair was receding slightly, but he'd slicked it back and pulled it into a neat ponytail that reached halfway down his back. He wore a black leather vest with silver studs, faded blue jeans with a big silver buckle, and a steel-toed biker boot.

"Welcome back to bumfuck, my man." He slid a shot glass to Nick. "This one's on the house."

Nick looked down at the glass. "I'm on parole, Mike."

"Fuck the Louisiana Department of Corrections. I sure as hell ain't going to tell them."

Nick didn't mention that he would be driving down to New

Orleans to piss in a cup once a week for the next five years. But he knew that by the time next week rolled around, the alcohol would be long gone from his system, so he picked up the glass. "To new beginnings."

"And old friends." Pequinot downed the double in one swallow.

Nick did the same, shuddering when the rum burned all the way to his belly. He watched a heavyset woman in tight jeans and a black halter top feed quarters into the jukebox. An instant later, an old Stevie Ray Vaughan song blared from mammoth speakers situated on either side of the bar.

"That your wife?" Nick asked.

"Rita." Pequinot refilled his glass. "We tied the knot last year. She's mean as a hornet but keeps me out of trouble."

Not wanting to get into the subject of wives and trouble, Nick didn't comment. "You seen Dutch around?" he asked, referring to his father.

"He doesn't come in much anymore. I saw him at the diner last week." Pequinot grimaced. "Damn shame about the Alzheimer's."

"Knowing Dutch, I imagine he's taking it pretty hard."

Pequinot shot him a questioning look. "He keep in touch with you? Drive up to see you?"

Nick shook his head. "I told him not to," he lied.

Stevie Ray Vaughan yielded to a lively zydeco number and, with the alcohol beginning to hum through his veins and the music pounding in his ears, the place didn't seem quite so derelict, his life not quite so bleak.

"I see that ex-wife of yours around plenty, though."

Because Nick didn't want to talk about Tanya, he shrugged. "We're divorced."

"Never should have married that one, Nicky. Pretty and crazy. That's a bad combination."

"Yeah, well, you know what they say about hindsight." Nick considered himself an expert on the subject.

"Divorcing you like that. It's a fucked up thing to do to a guy when he's doin' time."

Because the divorce had had nothing to do with his being incarcerated, Nick looked away. "It was a mutual thing, Mike."

Nick had spent four years of his life married to Tanya Chantal. Back then, she'd been a pretty farm girl caught up in an abusive family. Like some lovesick fool, Nick had rushed in to save her. The consummate rescuer, he'd fought for her and won. In the end, he'd confused lust with love, and it had cost him more than he could ever have imagined.

"She's in here just about every night, getting shit-faced and handing it out to whoever wants it. I swear to Christ, I'd rather stick my dick in a Tasmanian devil. She's fucking nuts. Been on a downward spiral ever since—" Pequinot cut his words short, looked down at the scarred surface of the bar. *"Le Bon Dieu mait la main."* God help.

Nick tried not to react, but he felt the recoil deep inside. He tried to cover it by sliding his glass across the bar for a refill. But his hand was shaking.

It had been two years since Nick's son drowned, but the grief still cut. Some days it cut so deep, he thought he might just bleed out and die.

"Look," Pequinot began, refilling his glass, "six years is a long time for a man to be without a woman. I can set you up. On the house for you . . ."

Though the idea of sex appealed greatly, Nick figured the last thing he needed in his life was a woman. Especially a hooker—on the house or not. He was smart enough to know when he was better off alone, and this just happened to be one of those times.

"I was actually wondering about the job, Mike. I saw the Help Wanted sign out front." He rolled his shoulder. "I thought I might apply."

Pequinot looked amused. "This dump's a far cry from that highfalutin place you had yourself down in the Big Easy."

"Highfalutin is overrated." Nick grinned, but it felt tight on his face, as if his facial muscles no longer remembered how. "Alcohol's the same no matter what kind of glass you serve it in."

"You want the job, it's yours."

Relief shuddered through Nick. Once upon a time he would have laughed at the notion of working in a dive like The Blue Gator. Funny what a little desperation did to a man's pride. "Thanks . . ."

Pequinot waved off his gratitude. "I figured you'd want to spend some time getting the farm back into shape. I hear Dutch has pretty much let everything go to shit."

"I'll work the farm during the day." Nick finished the last of the rum and picked up his duffel. "Spend my nights here."

"Ain't you going to ask me how much the job pays?"

Nick shook his head. "It doesn't matter. When do I start?"

"How about tomorrow night? We do a good business on Fridays. Shift at the mill ends at four o'clock. Guys come in thirsty. I'll need you till we close at one A.M."

"I'll be here."

Pequinot stuck out his hand. "Welcome home, Nicky."

Nick shook the other man's hand. "Thanks," he said and wished like hell he could say he was glad to be back.

NAT JENNINGS WAS GOING TO HAVE TO STOP FOR gas. The Mustang had been running on fumes for the last twenty miles. She'd planned on stopping at the Citgo station on the highway only to find the windows boarded up, the pumps gone, and knee-high weeds sticking out of the concrete. Now, unless she wanted to backtrack all the way to the interstate, she was going to have to fill up in Bellerose.

"So much for anonymity," she muttered as she drove slowly down Main Street, past the courthouse on the square, Boudreaux's Corner Drug Store, and Jenny Lee's Five and Dime.

She tried hard not to notice the double takes and shocked expressions of the people who recognized her. But then she'd known before ever coming back that the upstanding citizens of Bellerose had long memories when it came to murder.

Ray's Sunoco was located on the bayou side of town. The service station had only one pump and hadn't yet made the technological quantum leap of accepting credit cards. Nat slid out of the car, careful to keep her back to the highway, and pumped the gas in record time.

Once the tank was full, she grabbed her purse and went inside to pay. A teenage boy wearing a dirty work shirt and a sour expression sat behind the counter, eyeing her with unconcealed curiosity. A pregnant woman in a bright green maternity top was eyeballing the candy bar display.

Nat smiled at the boy. "Take a check?"

"'Slong as you have a driver's license."

Tugging her checkbook from her bag, she crossed to the counter.

"Sixteen fifty-three," he said.

Nat began making out the check. She could hear the low hum of the RC Cola machine out front. The hiss of the occasional car as it passed on the highway. Behind the counter, wooden shelves with peeling white paint displayed cans of 10W-40 motor oil and filters and various sizes of engine belts. One of the cans was rattling, blending with the buzz of a fly trapped against the window.

The dizziness struck her like a sledgehammer. Too late she realized the buzzing wasn't from the soda machine or the can of oil or even the fly in the window. The high-frequency hum was inside her head, as powerful as a jet engine, the vibrations jolting her body all the way to her bones. Dread and alarm coiled inside her as the warm shock of energy penetrated her brain. Sensations and thoughts and images flew at her in dark, undulating waves.

Dear God, not now, was all she could think.

She tried to finish writing the check, but her hand fumbled the pen. Her arms drooped as if they were paralyzed. It was a terrifying sensation to be trapped inside her own body and unable to control her limbs. She was aware of her left hand grappling for the pen. Her nails cutting into her palm. Her knuckles going white as her hand swept across the check.

"Lady, are you okay?"

She heard the words as if from a great distance. Vaguely, she was aware of the boy looking at her strangely. She wanted to answer, to reassure him that she was fine. But the breath had been sucked from her lungs. Words and thoughts tumbled disjointedly inside her head. She tried to focus, but his face kept fading in and out of her vision.

An instant later her legs buckled. Her knees hit the floor with a hollow *thump!*

"Oh, good Lord!"

Nat heard alarm in the pregnant woman's voice. She heard the shuffle of shoes against the floor. Felt a gentle hand against her shoulder. "Honey, are you all right?"

Slowly, she became aware of cool wood against her cheek. She was lying on her side, still gripping the pen. She wanted to get up, but she was dizzy and disoriented and an inch away from throwing up all over the woman's Nikes.

"Ma'am, are you sick?" came the boy's voice.

Bracing her hand against the floor, Nat pushed herself to a sitting position and shoved her hair from her face. "I'm okay," she heard herself say.

Her checkbook lay on the floor next to her. She picked it up, saw that her hand was trembling violently.

"You need me to call Doc Ratcliffe for you?" the woman asked.

Nat shook her head. "I'm fine. Really, I just . . . got a little dizzy."

Shaken and embarrassed, she rose unsteadily to her feet and brushed at her jeans. The vibrations had quieted, but her thoughts remained fuzzy and disjointed. She felt as if she'd just stumbled off some wild amusement park ride and had yet to regain her equilibrium. She glanced at the boy behind the counter to see him staring fixedly at the check, his expression perplexed.

"What's that?" he asked.

bad man take ricky. kill again. hurry.

Gasping, Nat snatched the check off the counter. "Nothing," she muttered.

The woman shot her a wary look. "It said something about killing."

Unwilling to explain—not sure she could, even if she knew what to say—Nat shook her head. "I just . . . must have gotten confused for a second, right before I blacked out." She tried to smile, but was too shaken to manage. "I have epilepsy."

"Oh." But the woman didn't look appeased.

Nat knew it the instant the woman recognized her. Her eyes widened, then she took a step back, as if she'd ventured too close to something dangerous. "You're Nat Jennings."

Sliding the ruined check into the pocket of her jeans, Nat began writing a second one. She had wanted anonymity for her return home. She should have known that was the one luxury she would never have in a town the size of Bellerose. "That's right," she said.

The clerk and the pregnant woman exchanged startled looks. Nat did her best to ignore them, but her hand was shaking when she tore off the check and handed it to the clerk. "Thanks for the gas."

"If I'da known who you was, I never would have let you pump here," the clerk muttered.

"Yeah, well, it's too late to do anything about it now." Nat started toward the door.

"Bitch," he said to her back.

Nat felt the word as keenly as if he'd thrown a rock at her. She'd known her return would be met with hostility, but she wasn't going to let that keep her from doing what she'd come here to do. She'd waited three unbearable years for this moment.

Once in her car, she pulled the note from her pocket and read it again.

bad man take ricky. kill again. hurry.

A chill passed through her as she studied the child-like scrawl. Aside from seeing that justice was done, there was nothing she could do for the ones who were already gone. Nat knew all too well that the dead could not be resurrected. But if she could prevent the death of a single child, whatever she faced in the coming days would be worth it.

Staring at the note, she set a trembling finger beneath the words.

kill again.

"Not if I can help it, you son of a bitch," she whispered and jammed the car into gear.

chapter
2

MELTED ASPHALT STUCK TO THE SOLES OF NICK'S boots like hot chewing gum as he made his way down the narrow road toward his father's farm. Stopping at the mailbox, he let the sight of the ancient live oaks and sweet gums arching over the white gravel lane sink into his brain. Growing up, he'd never seen the farm as anything except an endless hellhole of backbreaking work and a combat zone for him and his father to do battle. Now, even though the place was by no stretch of the imagination picturesque, there was a primal beauty in the way the hundred-year-old farm embraced the land.

The lane curved like a capricious river for a quarter of a mile. When the old house loomed into view, it was like seeing an old friend to whom the years hadn't been kind. The two-story frame had a wide front porch and tall, narrow windows. It had been built at the turn of the century and added onto a dozen times over the decades, giving it the haphazard look of a structure that had been thrown together. The house had never been pretty. Neglect had made it downright unsightly. The wood siding that had once been as white as winter frost was weathered gray and warped from the elements. The windows were grimy and dull with neglect. The shingles on the roof curled like palsied fingers.

Nick wondered if his father had fared any better. If the

years had been kinder, the storms of his life gentler. If the Alzheimer's was as bad as Mike Pequinot had intimated.

On either side of the lane, fields that had yielded a hundred years of sugarcane and cotton stood barren and overgrown with weeds as tall as a man. The Ford tractor Dutch had bought used twenty years ago sat in the side yard at a cockeyed angle, its right rear tire as flat as the Louisiana countryside.

"Home sweet home," he muttered as he took the concrete steps to the porch. The wooden planks creaked as he crossed to the front door. Setting the duffel at his feet, he knocked and tried hard to convince himself he'd done the right thing by coming back.

A minute ticked by before the door groaned and slowly opened. An instant later he found himself looking at a man who was far too old to be his father.

Eyes as dark as molasses swept down to his boots, then back to his face to glare. *"T'as du gout."* You've got a lot of nerve.

The years had been as brutal to Dutch Bastille as they had the house. Eyes that had once been as sharp as a cane knife were rheumy and bloodshot. Skin that had once lain like fine leather over strongly boned features now sagged from jutting cheekbones. Hair that had once been as black as a raven's breast had faded to a sallow color that was part gray, part yellow. With a two days' growth of white beard, he looked washed out and pissed off and none too pleased to see his only son.

"Hello to you, too, Pop."

Dutch made a sound that was part growl, part disgust. "I was wondering when you were going to show up."

Nick stared at him, not sure if he was more taken aback by his father's appearance or the rancor in his voice. He hadn't expected a warm welcome, but he hadn't expected open hostility either. At least not right off the bat. "The bus ride took a while," he said. "A lot of stops along the way."

"You look like a goddamn convict."

Nick looked away, focused on the overgrown fields. "I guess I do."

Dutch's eyes landed on his forearms. "Why the hell did you go and get yourself tattooed like that? You think anyone's going to hire you with your arms tattooed like some carnival freak?"

"Just passing time."

"I guess you figure you haven't already embarrassed me enough, huh?"

"Nobody's trying to embarrass you, Pop."

Dutch cackled, the sound of a bitter old man. "You've been an embarrassment to me since the day you took a match to that fancy restaurant of yours. You finally get a break, a chance to make something of yourself, and you fuck it up. Don't that sound familiar?" he said sarcastically. "I guess you've always been your mama's boy, though, haven't you?"

Nick met his gaze, felt a flare of what he could only describe as hatred burn deep in his chest. Of all the emotions he was feeling at the moment, that he could hate his own father when he hadn't seen him in eighteen years hurt a lot more than he wanted to admit. "I might be guilty of a lot of things, but arson isn't one of them."

"I lost my job at the mill because of that stunt you pulled."

Nick looked at him closely, wondering how much of the bitterness had to do with honest disappointment and how much was a result of the Alzheimer's disease. "You lost your job because of your memory, Pop."

"That's bullshit. My memory's as good as it ever was. This is all political. Those bastards wanted my job. Thanks to you, I got the boot."

Suddenly feeling very tired, Nick lowered his head and pinched the bridge of his nose between his thumb and forefinger. "I'm not going to argue with you about your job, Pop. If you want me to leave, just say so. There's a halfway house in New Orleans I can go to. I just thought . . . after eighteen years, you might want to . . ." For the life of him, he couldn't find the words to finish the sentence.

Growling like an old bear, Dutch swung open the door and stepped aside. "You may as well stay here. Just don't think you're going to sit on your ass while I work my tail off around this dump."

Nick picked up his duffel. "Wouldn't dream of it," he said and stepped inside.

SHERYL CROW WAS BELTING OUT A TUNE ABOUT leaving Las Vegas when Nat took the Mustang across the old steel bridge that spanned the muddy water of the Bellerose River. She slowed for a curve in the road, then made a quick left onto the gravel driveway. The two-story Victorian hadn't changed in the three years she'd been away, and the utter sameness of it shook her. The wraparound front porch still beckoned one to sit on the swing and sip sweet tea. At the dormer window, she could see the frilly curtains she'd hung a lifetime ago. In the front yard, the magnolia she'd planted the year Kyle was born was still in bloom, and it shocked her anew that the tree had outlived her son.

In the last six months Nat had made this pilgrimage a thousand times in her mind. She'd seen the house as it stood now, as Southern and pretty as a belle. A snazzy For Sale sign in the front yard touted the word *Reduced* in big red letters. The house had been on the market for over a year now. According to the real estate agent, lots of people had looked, but not a single offer had been made. She supposed people just couldn't get comfortable with the idea of living in a house where a brutal double murder had taken place. Especially when the killer had never been caught . . .

Trying not to think about that, she parked the Mustang and slid from the car. She felt as if she were walking through a void as she crossed to the porch and took the steps to the door. She knew it would be locked but tried the knob anyway, found it secure. Leaving the porch, she took the flagstone walkway to the rear of the house. The backyard was mostly wooded. At one time, there had been a path through the trees that led to the river a quarter mile away. She and Ward and Kyle had walked that path countless times—for swimming or fishing or just to watch the water meander through the forest. Nat could still make out the mouth of the path, but the trail itself was overgrown with tall grass, wild honeysuckle, and tangled kudzu.

She crossed to the French doors. Standing on her tiptoes, she reached for the key in the porch light, exactly where the realtor had said he would leave it. He'd been more curious than disappointed when Nat had taken the place off the market. The realtor had asked about her plans, but Nat hadn't elaborated. She figured the less people knew about why she was back, the better off she'd be.

The house smelled of stale air and mildew. Hardwood floors

that had once been glossy and waxed were now coated with dust. To her right was the kitchen with its speckled granite countertops, glossy oak cabinets, and stainless steel appliances. Straight ahead the living room stood in the shadows of late afternoon.

Nat hadn't set foot in the house since the night her life had been torn apart by violence, and it was bizarre being back now. She'd almost expected to see the place as it had been three years ago. Full of laughter and life and the dreams of people who'd been utterly certain the future held good things for them. But the house was as silent and hollow as her heart.

Dr. Pettigrew had warned her against returning so soon. He'd told her that while her physical recovery had progressed better than expected, her psychological recovery could take longer. He'd told her that pushing herself too hard, too soon, could set her back. But Nat had already lost three years of her life. She'd lost her family. Her heart. She'd nearly lost her mind.

Her legs were shaking when she entered the living room. Someone had draped the furniture with sheets, and for a moment the room seemed to be filled with ghosts. Annoyed with herself for letting her imagination run amok, she walked quickly through the room, yanking the sheets from each piece of furniture as she passed. Dust motes exploded as the sofa and chair and occasional tables appeared. She crossed to the foyer and jerked the sheet from the console table. She stared down at the glass top where some kind soul had placed the framed photographs facedown. And even though Nat knew better than to look, she remembered each photograph with startling clarity, as if she'd placed them on that table just yesterday. Kyle on his rocking horse when he was three years old. She and Ward on their wedding day, their faces young and beaming with happiness. Ward and Kyle in his fishing boat for Kyle's first fishing expedition. He'd been six years old and so kindhearted he hadn't been able to bait the hook. . . .

For a full minute she stood there, aware that her heart was beating too fast. Not wanting to shatter the equanimity she had struggled so hard to achieve, she left the photographs facedown and backed away from the table. Behind her were the stairs. Turning, she took the steps two at a time to the second level.

Four doors opened to the hall. She started down the hall at a determined clip, opening doors as she went. In the bathroom, she strode across the tile floor and flung open the window. The house needed air and light and life. She could feel the memories pressing down on her as she crossed to the guest room and did the same. She tried hard to shut out the ghosts, but they were powerful and encroached on her like an invading army.

In her mind's eye she saw Kyle running down the hall, his bare feet slapping against the wood floor. His sweet voice echoing in the hall, "Mommy! Daddy's home!"

Nat paused at the door to the room she and Ward had once shared. The place where they'd talked and laughed and made a child together. Not giving herself time to think, she shoved open the door. Ghosts scurried out of sight, but she knew they were there. She could feel their presence as surely as she felt the hot slash of grief.

The room was vacant and sullen, the mattress bare. A layer of dust had collected atop the dresser and chest. From where she stood, she could see into the bathroom. Same off-white tile. Same etched-glass shower door. Everything was the same, less the souls of the people who'd once made the house a home.

She left the master bedroom and crossed the hall to Kyle's room. She shoved open the door and for an instant saw the room as it had been three years ago. A twin bed draped with Spiderman sheets and piled high with stuffed animals. The antique desk that had once been Ward's. A toy box in the shape of a boat. The scent of cedar from the hamster cage . . .

The sudden pang of grief took her breath. Some days she still couldn't believe he was gone. Couldn't believe the merciful God she'd always known would be so cruel as to take him away from her. The child she'd loved more than her own life. But Nat knew it hadn't been the Lord who'd taken him from her. The thought gave her the strength she needed to blink back tears she was determined not to cry. No, she thought darkly, she hadn't come back here to cry. She'd done enough grieving in the last three years to last a lifetime. Nat had returned to Bellerose to find a killer.

Taking a steadying breath, she walked over to the window

that looked out over the backyard. It was open a couple of
inches, probably by the realtor in an attempt to circulate air.
Nat could hear the crickets chirping, the incessant buzz of the
cicadas, and the song of a lone mockingbird. Signs of life that
she badly needed to hear at that moment.

Spreading the curtains, she knelt and opened the window
the rest of the way. Her eyes went immediately to the screen.
The police report indicated the screen had been cut. Sure
enough, just above the latch, a neat four-inch slit had been cut
into the screen. She studied the curved edges of the hole, realized it was just big enough for a hand to reach inside and un-
latch the lock.

She ran her fingertip along the edge of the slit. "How did
you cut the screen from the inside, you son of a bitch?" she
whispered.

Straightening, she left the bedroom and went downstairs
and out the front door. She unloaded her suitcase from the
trunk, snagged her purse and briefcase off the seat, and lugged
everything inside. She set the suitcase by the stairs, then carried her bag and briefcase to the dining room table. Pulling
out the manila folder, she opened it and looked down at the
notes written in a painfully familiar childlike scrawl.

Mommy.
bad man came in ar house n hurted me an daddy.
Kill Branden to . . .
gona hurt more kidz
Make him stop.
hell hurt you to
monster in the woods
bad man take ricky. kill again. hurry.

Nat studied the third note she'd received. It had taken quite
a bit of research, but she'd finally figured out the note was referring to Brandon Bastille, a little boy who'd drowned two
years earlier. His death had been ruled an accident by the
parish coroner's office. But Nat knew it was no accident.

The problem was going to be proving it.

chapter
3

THE BASTILLE PLACE SAT ON RIVER BOTTOMLAND AT the north end of the bayou where the soil was as black and rich as Texas oil. Nat stopped the Mustang at the end of the lane and stared at the faded letters on the battered mailbox, trying hard to convince herself she was doing the right thing.

She'd spent the last six months planning every detail of her trip back to Bellerose. Thanks to the Internet and news-paper archives, researching Brandon Bastille's so-called ac-cidental drowning had been relatively easy. Having grown up in Bellerose, Nat knew of Nick Bastille. She knew he'd grown up poor. Knew his father was a cotton farmer and they still spoke Cajun French. But she and Nick hadn't run in the same circles. He'd left Bellerose for New Orleans some eighteen years ago, and their paths had never crossed.

It had been front-page news when he'd been sent to Angola State Prison. It had also made the front page when he'd been released just two days ago. A phone call to the local police de-partment had confirmed that he was returning to Bellerose. People had a right to know if there was going to be an ex-con in their midst, after all. And so Nat had timed her pilgrimage back to coincide with his.

God help us both, she thought and turned the Mustang into the lane.

When she'd been safe in her room at the River Oaks Convalescent Home in Baton Rouge, approaching Nick Bastille had seemed like the most logical place to begin. Now that she was here, the nerves she'd been feeling all day had edged into a very bad case of uncertainty. It wasn't going to be easy convincing a man his son—a child whose death had been ruled accidental by the parish coroner—had been murdered.

A plume of white dust billowed as she sped toward the house. The place looked like the dozens of other farms in the area that had fallen upon hard times. The rail fence was badly in need of paint. The fields on either side of the lane were barren and riddled with milkweed and thistle and a hundred other weed varieties she couldn't name. A few scraggly stalks of last year's sugarcane quivered in the breeze.

The lane curved, and a moment later a two-story frame house loomed into view. It had once been white, but the paint had long since fallen victim to the elements. Nat spotted the Chevy pickup near the barn, and the reality of what she was about to do sent another jolt of uncertainty through her. Not giving herself time to rethink her decision to do this, she parked next to the truck and started toward the house. She'd rehearsed her lines a thousand times in the last weeks. She'd drilled them into her brain along with the knowledge that if she was going to get the job done she would have to keep her emotions out of it.

But as she took the crumbling steps and crossed to the door, all of her carefully rehearsed lines stuck in her throat like shards of glass. Her heart was beating hard and fast against her ribs as she rapped on the screen door with her knuckles. The urge to hightail it back to her car was powerful, but Nat had long since given up on the idea of running away.

She'd just rallied the nerve to knock a second time when the door swung open, and she found herself staring at Nick Bastille. Wearing nothing more than a pair of low-rise jeans and a snarl, he was the epitome of primal male beauty. His piercing gaze was a lot more hostile than friendly. Heavy brows rode low over eyes that were as dark and mysterious as the bayou at midnight. His cheekbones were high, the planes of his face sharply angled. His jaw sported a day's growth of black stubble. He looked as hard and chiseled as a man could be and not be carved from stone.

As if of their own accord, her eyes did a quick sweep down the front of him. He was well over six feet tall, but for the effect he was having on her he might as well been the size of a mountain. His bare chest revealed pectorals that were rounded with muscle and sprinkled generously with black hair. His abdomen was as hard and flat as a frozen pond in winter. Fully developed arms were etched with the green-blue ink of intricate tattoos, reminding her that he was an ex-con, that she should be careful when dealing with him.

Still, something inside her stirred at the utter maleness of him. A rousing that was as unfamiliar as it was unwelcome. Nat had never been one to ogle men. She'd never been impressed by such topical things as physical attributes. But she wasn't so dead inside that she didn't acknowledge the fact that this man oozed sex appeal. That her body had noticed. And that a wave of heat was slowly making its way up her body and into her face.

That she was capable of feeling anything at all stunned her. Up until this moment, she'd thought that part of her was dead. Torn from her heart by grief and the loss of the only man she had ever loved.

"You lost, little girl?"

The smooth-as-whiskey drawl seemed incongruous with the rest of him, but Nat knew better than to be taken in by the refined voice. This man was about as refined as a pack of wild dogs. "Are you Nick Bastille?"

Folding his arms across his bare chest, he leaned against the jamb, looking amused. "You selling something?"

"No. I just . . . need to speak to him."

"You mind if I ask what about?"

"It's . . . a personal matter."

His eyes raked down the front of her, and she felt every inch of his perusal as if he'd peeled away her clothes and touched her flesh with his fingertips.

"Personal, huh?" One side of his mouth quirked, but Nat couldn't tell if it was a smile or if he had a bad taste in his mouth. "Look, *chere,* if Mike sent you, this probably isn't a good time. . . ."

She didn't know anyone by the name of Mike and had no idea what he was talking about. "Nobody sent me."

His eyes did another slow, dangerous sweep of her, his expression telling her his initial surprise had given way to curiosity. "I'm Nick Bastille. What's this about?"

"I'm Nat Jennings." She stuck out her hand, hoping he didn't notice her wet palm or recognize her name.

Never taking his eyes from hers, he accepted her hand. His palm was calloused and rough. Even though his grip was gentle, she sensed the power behind it. If he'd recognized her name, he gave no indication.

He released her hand and opened the door wider. Her heart pinged hard against her ribs when he stepped onto the porch. Nat wasn't exactly short at five feet five inches, but Nick Bastille towered over her, and she amended her initial estimation of his height. The man was at least six four.

"The house is hot as an oven," he said in a slow Cajun drawl. "Air conditioner's on the fritz. More comfortable out here on the porch." He strode to one of two columns, looked out over the barren field for a moment, then turned to face her. "I've got to leave for work in a few minutes, so you might want to tell me what brought you all the way out here when I can see this is the last place you want to be."

At some point her heart had begun to pound. All of her carefully rehearsed lines left her mind the instant his eyes met hers. Within their depths she saw the glint of amusement, but it was hard and unpleasant now and played on her nerves like the hot strike of a match on gunpowder.

"I want to talk to you about your son," she blurted.

His eyes went cold and brittle, like liquid steel plunged into ice water. "I don't have a son."

"I'm talking about Brandon."

"My boy died two years ago."

"I know." She tried to swallow, but her mouth had gone talc dry. "I'm sorry. I know how difficult it is to lose a child."

"Do you?"

She met his gaze in kind, angered even though she knew he probably didn't know what she'd gone through in the last three years. "Yes."

He didn't ask her to elaborate, didn't even look interested.

He simply gazed at her with an expression that was so cold it brought gooseflesh to her arms.

"My son died, too," she said. "Three years ago. He was . . . murdered. In our home. My husband, Ward Ratcliffe, was killed, too."

"What does that have to do with me?"

Nat crossed to him on shaking legs, close enough for her to see the questions in his eyes, the hostility burning just beneath the surface, the underlying traces of pain a parent never recovered from. "I don't know how to tell you this, so I'm just going to say it. Brandon's death was not an accident, Mr. Bastille."

Shock registered in his eyes, and then his mouth pulled back into what she could only describe as a snarl. "What the hell are you talking about?"

"He didn't drown in that pond alone."

He came off the column like a puppet jerked to attention by an overzealous puppeteer. "What is this? Some kind of sick fucking joke?"

"N-no."

His lips peeled back to reveal straight white teeth that were clenched in fury. "What are you saying?"

Nat took a quick step back. "I'm sorry I have to tell you this, but your son was murdered."

"Murdered?" His laugh was a terrible sound, but the look in his eyes was worse. "Where do you get off telling me something like that?"

"I know this is difficult to hear—"

"Difficult is not the right word, you crazy bitch. Who the hell are you?"

"I don't blame you for being angry a-and confused. If you'll just let me ex—"

"Lady I'm a hell of a lot more than angry and confused. I'm fucking furious and an inch away from showing you exactly what a furious man can do. If you had a brain inside that pretty head of yours, you'd get in your car and get the hell out of my sight before I do something we're both going to regret."

The temptation to run was strong, but Nat resisted. She was shaking, but in a quiet place deep inside she knew there was nothing this man could do to her that could be any worse than what she had already endured. It was a twisted way to bolster her courage she knew, but it worked.

"At least hear me out," she said. "Please. It's important."

He stared at her as if he wanted to kill her. Nat could see his jaws bunching as he ground his teeth. His hands clenching at his sides. Lips peeling back as if he were a fanged creature about to take a chunk out of her. Black temper burning in his eyes.

"Who the hell do you think you are, coming here and telling me some bullshit story about my son being murdered?" he ground out.

"I'm the woman who can help you find the bastard who did it."

IT TOOK SEVERAL SECONDS FOR HER WORDS TO PENE-
trate the black cloak of fury. Nick had never been a violent man; he'd never touched a woman in any way she didn't want to be touched. But for an interminable moment, he feared he might cross a line and do something he would be sorry for later.

The death of his son was an open wound on his heart. An agonizing wound that had festered and bled every second of every day he'd been locked away. To have that wound prodded so thoughtlessly enraged him.

He stared down at her, shocked that the lovely creature looking up at him could say something so utterly brutal and still have such a pretty face. He searched her eyes for the lie he didn't understand, but her expression was as guileless as a child's.

"Look, Mr. Bastille, I know you don't want to hear this," she said. "I know it's ugly and painful and difficult to under-stand, but you have to listen to me."

He was upon her before he could stop himself. His hands on her shoulders, fingers digging into soft flesh. She tried to twist away, but he tightened his grip and muscled her backward.

"I don't know what kind of twisted game you're playing, lady, but you just fucked with the wrong guy."

She made a sound when her back hit the wall. "You're hurt-ing me," she gasped.

He saw fear in her eyes. He wanted to believe that was satisfying because there was a small, mean part of him that
wanted to hurt her. But there was nothing satisfying in the way
her face went pale or in the way she winced when he squeezed
her shoulders.

Shamed that he'd touched her in anger, he loosened his
grip and gave himself a hard mental shake. "Where the hell do
you get off telling me something like that about my son?"

"I know this is a shock. Just . . . listen to me. I have information."

"You have two seconds to state your case."

"The man who murdered my son is the same monster who
murdered yours."

"My son's death was an accident."

"I'm sorry, but it wasn't."

"My son drowned!"

"He may have drowned, but it wasn't an accident."

Furious that she would say something so heinous, he
slapped his palms against the siding just a few inches from her
face hard enough to make her jolt. "The police investigated,"
he snarled. "The parish coroner—" His voice broke at the
memory. "There was an autopsy, for God's sake."

"The coroner was wrong."

Nick ground his teeth. Having lost Brandon in a cruel accident was bad enough. But to have this woman present him
with the possibility that his son had spent his last minutes
knowing evil existed was simply too much to bear.

Afraid he was about to snap, he shoved away from her. He
could feel his heart raging beneath his ribs, his breaths tearing
raggedly from his lungs, pain slicing like a knife. When he
raised his hand and shoved his finger in her face, he was surprised to see it shaking. "Get the hell out of here."

Watching him with dark, frightened eyes, she pushed away
from the wall and backed toward the porch steps. "I'm not
wrong about this."

A strand of hair had fallen into her face. When she lifted
her hand to tuck it behind her ear, he spotted the scars on the
underside of her wrists. Another emotion that was part anger,
part disgust coursed through him. Before even realizing he
was going to move, he snagged her wrists, yanked her toward

him, then turned both arms wrist side up so that the bright pink scars were visible to both of them.

His gaze drilled into hers. "You think these scars give you some kind of license to hurt people, or are you just fucking nuts?"

"It's not my intent to hurt you."

She tried to tug her wrists from his grasp, but he didn't let her. He didn't give a damn if she was ashamed of the scars. "Yeah, and I think you need to get back on whatever medication you're taking."

He looked down at her wrists with a sneer. The scars were ugly, even though the wounds had long since healed. He could see stitch marks where some emergency room doctor had closed what must have been hideous wounds. He could only assume they were self-inflicted. One thing he knew for certain was that she hadn't hesitated. These wounds hadn't been a cry for help. She'd been totally focused on finding the most expeditious way to the radial artery and severe bloodletting. *Jesus Christ.*

"Let go of me," she said.

He looked away from the scars and met her gaze. Her eyes were the color of Arizona turquoise, large and fragile and fringed with sooty lashes. They were the kind of eyes a man could get lost in if he looked too long. He wondered what could have been terrible enough to make this pretty young woman think that death was a better alternative than life.

He released her with a tad too much force, sending her stumbling back. "If you're not off this porch in the next ten seconds, I'm going to call the cops and have you arrested for trespassing."

"I'll go," she said. "But I don't see how you can think that burying your head in the sand and letting your son's killer go free is a better alternative than the truth."

"Give me one reason why I ought to believe you."

"Because the man who took our children from us is going to kill again if someone doesn't stop him."

Nick stared at her, incredulous and shocked speechless. "How do you know that?"

"I know. And I know we don't have much time to stop him."

"Does this nameless, faceless monster have a name?" he

asked. "An address? Hell, maybe you've got his home phone number?"

"I don't have a name."

"That's convenient as hell." Sighing tiredly, he scrubbed his hand over his jaw, realized she'd given him a headache. "Go tell the police what you know and leave me the hell out of it."

"The police won't believe me."

"You think maybe that might be because your theory is total bullshit?"

She looked fierce standing there on his porch with her eyes flashing and her chin jutting defiantly. But he could see clearly that she wasn't nearly as impervious as she wanted him to believe. Her entire body was shaking, from her hands and shoulders all the way down to her knees. He told himself that didn't bother him. But Nick had always had a weakness for vulnerable, troubled women, and this one fit the mold to a T.

"Three years ago my son was murdered," she said in a shaking voice. "The murderer was never apprehended. Your son drowned under suspicious circumstances a year later."

"The only suspicious circumstance related to my son's death was that my ex-wife was passed out in the house." Even after all this time, the thought twisted him into knots.

"I have nothing to gain by lying to you," she said.

"Yeah, maybe you're having some kind of psychotic episode." Nick wasn't sure why he was still listening to her. The last thing he needed was some woman making wild claims about an incident that had come within an inch of destroying him.

"Do you have any evidence to support anything you've said?" he asked.

"I have—" She bit off the words abruptly and flushed.

Something niggled at the back of his neck. "You have what?"

When she didn't say anything, he crossed to her, took her arm, and muscled her down the steps. "You've had your say, *chere*. Now I want you off my property."

"Mr. Bastille . . ."

"For the life of me I can't figure why you'd make up a wild story like this and drive all the way out here."

"The only thing I have to gain is justice for my son."

He could feel her shaking within his grasp, but he didn't let go. Not for the first time it entered his mind that she was emotionally unstable and in need of some kind of psychiatric care. But Nick didn't care. He'd long since considered himself a compassionate human being.

She put up a fight as he forced her through the high grass, but she was small and he handled her with ease. When they reached the driveway, he released her and shoved her toward her car. "Get in the goddamn car."

"Mr. Bastille . . ."

When she made no move to obey, he opened the door. "Get in or I swear to Christ I'll throw you in."

She slid behind the wheel. "What's it going to take to convince you?"

Nick thought about it for a moment. "An eyewitness," he said and slammed the door.

chapter
4

NAT WAS STILL TREMBLING WHEN SHE PARKED THE
Mustang outside the Bellerose Police Department and shut
down the engine. For a full minute she sat behind the wheel
and tried to convince herself her encounter with Nick Bastille
hadn't shaken her badly.

But the ex-con with the dark eyes and snarling mouth had
shaken her up plenty. Nat had expected anger and disbelief
from him; she'd been prepared. What she hadn't anticipated
was the threat of violence. She'd been looking directly into
his eyes when she'd told him about his son. She'd never seen a
man look so dangerous and so utterly broken at the same time.
Nick Bastille may not realize it, but he was still grieving for
the loss of his boy, and that grief was as dark and bottomless
as the soul of the man who'd killed him.

Shoving thoughts of Nick Bastille aside, she looked through
the windshield and studied the red brick facade, telling herself
she wasn't terrified of walking inside. Nat hadn't set foot inside the Bellerose Police Department since that terrible night
three years ago. She knew there were a host of unpleasant memories waiting for her. Memories made exponentially worse by
a hostile police force that believed she'd gotten away with
murder.

Her heart knocked hard against her ribs as she got out of

the car and started toward the entrance. Shoving open one of
the double glass doors, she strode purposefully into the
building. The public utilities department where people could
walk in and pay their water bill was to the left. Nat took a
right and crossed to the reception desk, where a bored-
looking strawberry blonde was flipping through a glossy magazine.

"I'd like to see Chief Martin," Nat said.

The strawberry blonde glanced at her over the tops of her
bifocals, sizing her up. Recognition kicked in and the woman's
mascara-ringed eyes widened to the size of silver dollars.
"Oh, you're . . . uh, Nat Jennings?"

Nat nodded, mentally noting that the woman's expression
was more curious than hostile. "I just need a few minutes of
his time."

The woman closed the magazine and sat up straighter. "Do
you have an appointment?" She fumbled with an appointment
book that, Nat noticed, was mostly blank.

"No." She'd known that if she'd called ahead, the chief
would have found an excuse not to see her. Better to catch him
off guard.

"I'll let him know you're here." She punched numbers on
the switchboard with a long, red fingernail. "Chief Martin?
Nat Jennings is here to see you."

The chief's office was down the hall, close enough for Nat
to hear his exclamation of *"What?"*

The woman tapped her pencil against the magazine for a
moment, then hung up the phone and pursed her lips. "I'm
sorry, Ms. Jennings, but the chief is tied up this afternoon.
Town council stuff. If you'll leave a number, he'll call you as
soon as he's free."

Nat had known before walking in that Alcee Martin wasn't
going to be happy to see her. Hell, if she were in his shoes, *she*
wouldn't be happy to see her. But she'd been hoping he would
at least give her the respect of going through the motions. That
he wouldn't even give her that made her realize she wasn't going to be able to do this the nice way.

The receptionist was peering at her curiously over the tops
of her bifocals, the way a kid might after prodding a nasty-
looking bug. Nat had pegged the woman as a gossipmonger

and found herself wondering how fast she could dial with those long nails. It wouldn't take much to get the tongues wagging in this town once the word was out that Nat Jennings was back and sniffing around the police department.

"Thanks for your help," she said and started for the chief's office.

"Ms. Jennings . . . you can't go back there."

Nat heard the woman's chair scrape against the tile floor, but she didn't stop. She might have found the whole thing amusing if there wasn't so much riding on this initial meeting.

She stopped outside the door labeled Alcee Martin, Chief of Police. She heard the receptionist's swift steps behind her and, taking a deep breath, shoved open the door.

Alcee Martin was a tall, lanky man with intelligent brown eyes and skin the color of dark roast coffee. He had the dubious honor of being Bellerose's first African American police officer, and he had a chip on his shoulder the size of Lake Pontchartrain to prove it. He was standing with his back to the door, looking out the window through the miniblinds at the parking lot beyond. His shirt was crisp and white as snow. His navy slacks were snug with a precision crease down the front. He was as neat as a man could be without looking like a mannequin.

"She gone?" he asked upon hearing the door open.

"No," Nat said.

He turned slowly. His eyes went flat when they landed on Nat.

"I'm sorry, Chief," the receptionist's voice sounded from behind her. "I tried to stop her."

"It's all right, Charlene." Shaking his head, he sighed tiredly. "Just close the door behind you."

Nat heard the door close and tried hard to ignore the quiver of nerves that ran through her when he gave her a hard look. "I would have called you tomorrow," he said.

"I didn't want to wait."

He motioned toward the chair opposite his desk. "Since you're here you may as well have a seat. I've got a few minutes."

Taking the chair, Nat pressed her hands against her thighs, not sure if she was doing it to keep them from shaking or to keep him from noticing.

He settled into the chair behind his desk. "I'll hand it to you, Nat, it took a lot of nerve for you to walk in here."

She wasn't feeling particularly brave at the moment, but she didn't correct him. She figured the less Alcee Martin knew about her frame of mind, the easier this would be.

"How are you feeling?" he asked.

If the circumstances had been different, she might have smiled. Southern good manners had taken precedence over that tough-cop facade Martin was so good at. He had a reputation for being by-the-book. In terms of his being top cop, that was probably a good thing. In terms of what she needed from him, she wasn't so sure.

"I'm fine," she said.

"How long have you . . ." He looked uncomfortable for a moment. "You know . . ."

"Been back in the land of the living?"

He cleared his throat.

Nat did smile then, but it was wry. "About six months now."

"When did you leave the . . . hospital?"

She didn't want to answer, but didn't see a way to hedge. "Yesterday."

He looked pained. "You sure you ought to be here? I mean, so soon?"

"I was born and raised in this town, Alcee. Why wouldn't I come back?"

Niceties out of the way, he slipped back into cop mode. "Because you're smart enough to know there are some people in this town who don't want you here. A few who might even try to do something about it."

"I can't control what other people think or do."

"I don't want any trouble, Nat."

"I have every right to be here."

Martin leaned back in his chair and studied her as if she were a mongrel dog that had surprised him with an impressive trick despite its scruffy appearance. "What did you want to talk to me about?"

She rolled her shoulder, her eyes never leaving his. "I want to know how the case is progressing."

"The case is cold. I have a detective assigned. He's working it."

"Do you have any new leads?"

"We're pursuing any and all leads."

"That's a canned answer, Alcee."

"That's all you're going to get."

"What about suspects?"

"Nat, I'm not going to have this conversation with you."

"You owe me, Alcee."

Something she couldn't quite read flickered in his eyes an instant before he masked it with an indignant scowl, and Nat knew she'd scored a hit. "I don't owe you a damn thing," he snapped. "It's an open case. I'm not obliged to share information with you. If you want to know what the status is, read the goddamn newspaper."

"The only thing I've read in the newspaper is your bullshit story about the transient that came through here about the same time they were killed."

"And disappeared that same night," he shot back.

"That transient didn't do it."

"Nat, I've got two witnesses who saw him ride in on the railway car the day before. Joe Rossi was fishing in the river and saw him under the bridge just a mile from your place."

"What was his motive?" she asked. "He didn't steal anything."

"I don't know what his motive was. As far as we know he could have been watching the place. He could be a child predator or rapist. If he did intend to rob, maybe Ward came downstairs and surprised him. He panicked, picked up the knife." As if realizing he was getting into details best left alone, he sighed. "We won't know what happened until we get him."

Blinking back images she couldn't let herself dwell on now, Nat took a deep breath and went to the next point she wanted to make. "I think the man who murdered them is still here in Bellerose."

Martin groaned. "Nat, you need to be concentrating on getting your life back. Getting yourself healthy again. Not digging into things that are only going to drag this tragedy out."

"What I need is justice."

He came forward in his chair, his expression fierce. "Half of the people in this town think you murdered your husband

and son. How do you think they're going to react once word gets around that you're back?"

"I don't give a damn what they think."

"Maybe you should." He tugged on his shirtsleeve and glanced at his watch. "I have to go over to city hall."

"The bastard is here in Bellerose, Alcee. Living right under your nose."

"You don't know that!"

Nat did know, but there was no way she was going to convince Alcee Martin in the next five minutes, so she said what she had come here to say. "I think Ward was having an affair," she blurted.

"An affair?" he said. "With whom?"

"Sara Wiley."

"Sara Wiley?" Martin looked to the heavens as if to ask for patience. "Now how do you know?

"I found some letters. I was going through his things." Nat reached into her bag and pulled out the manila folder. "I made copies."

Alcee grimaced at the sight of her shaking hands, but he didn't say anything as he took the folder and opened it. His expression remained impassive as he read, then he raised his gaze to hers. "There are two letters here, and they're not signed."

"It's her handwriting. I recognize it. They worked together for four years."

"That doesn't mean they were having an affair. He was a minister, for God's sake."

"I'm not laying blame, Alcee. I'm just . . . trying to work through this as best I can."

"Nat . . ."

"It's a possibility and you know it. Ward and Sara were close. Add Reno's temper to the mix, and you have a viable suspect."

"Those are some powerful charges, Nat. Reno and Sara Wiley are upstanding citizens." But for the first time since she'd set foot in his office, he wasn't looking at her as if she were some mental case who'd escaped the local institution. He was looking at her like she had something important to say, even if it was something he didn't want to hear.

"Are you telling me you believe Reno Wiley flew into a jealous rage and murdered your husband and son?"

She closed her eyes briefly at the mention of her son. "I'm saying it's a possibility you should consider."

"I think it's one hell of a stretch. I've known Reno since high school."

"Will you at least look into it? See if he has an alibi?"

"I'll do what I can." But he didn't look happy about it.

Feeling drained, Nat rose on legs that weren't quite steady and started toward the door.

"Nat?"

She turned and looked at him over her shoulder.

"Do me a favor and stay out of trouble, will you?"

"I'll do what I can," she said and walked out.

chapter
5

WEST HILL EPISCOPALIAN CEMETERY WAS LOCATED on a two-lane parish road a few miles from Interstate 12. Nat made the thirty-mile trip from Bellerose in half an hour, her thoughts twisting between her conversation with Alcee Martin and her confrontation with Nick Bastille. By the time she drove through the wrought iron gates, her stomach was in knots.

The uncertainty that had been eating at her for weeks now had succeeded in putting a hole in her conviction that she was going to be able to find the person responsible for murdering her husband and son. That she would be able to keep him from killing again. She'd known before leaving Baton Rouge that the task would be difficult. Three years had passed since the murders and, as Alcee had pointed out, the case was cold. Facing the suspicion of a hostile town, she couldn't count on a single soul to help her.

But Nat was as adept at overcoming obstacles as she was at beating the odds. If it was the last thing she did, she was going to hunt down the son of a bitch and make him pay.

Light rain fell from an angry sky as she followed the curved road to the rear of the grounds. Fingers of steam rose off the hot asphalt and hovered like ghosts in the shadows. Beyond, massive live oaks and magnolias stood like sentinels sent from heaven to watch over the dead.

She had wanted Ward and Kyle to be buried in the tiny cemetery behind Saint George's Catholic Church in Bellerose, where her father and grandparents were buried. But Ward's father, retired evangelist Elliott Ratcliffe, wouldn't hear of his son being buried in a Catholic cemetery and, despite Nat's wishes, he'd buried his son and grandson here. Nat had been in no condition to argue. By the time the parish coroner had finished the autopsies and released the bodies, the grief had swallowed her whole. Her mother, Analise, had driven up from New Orleans, but Nat barely remembered her mother's presence. She had almost no recollection of the double funeral. To this day she didn't know how she got through the ordeal. She'd been like the walking dead herself. The viewing. The funeral. The wake. Somehow, she'd survived. Then when it was over and her husband and son were in the ground for eternity, Alcee Martin and his star detective Norm Pelletier had come into her home and arrested her for murder.

Shaking off the memories, Nat left the car and started down the stone path. It was so quiet she could hear the raindrops striking the leaves of the magnolia as she passed by it. West Hill was lovely as far as cemeteries went. But the knowledge that these grounds housed the dead never left her as she made her way to the Ratcliffe family plot.

The gate squeaked as she opened it. A tall statue of Jesus Christ, His face serene, His arms open, stood in welcome. A dozen aboveground crypts bore the Ratcliffe name. The letters had been worn down by the years and elements, but Nat could still make out a few of the names: Edwin Ratcliffe, born 1826, died 1878; Marie Ratcliffe, born 1837, died 1857.

Kyle's and Ward's crypts were smaller and set in the rear. Their names were etched into sparkling gray granite. Ward Edwin Ratcliffe July 17, 1967–July 20, 2002. Kyle Alan Ratcliffe December 9, 1995–July 20, 2002.

Gripping the bouquet of magnolia blossoms she'd picked up at the florist, Nat went to her knees and set the flowers on the ground in front of the crypts. Her hand trembled when she leaned forward and brushed her fingers over her son's name. "Kyle . . . I've missed you so much."

The grief came with the force of physical pain and was so powerful a sound of pure agony escaped her. Covering her mouth, Nat doubled over and waited for the worst of it to pass. When she could finally breathe, she lifted her head, then set her hand against Ward's name.

"I know you'll take good care of him," she said.

She barely noticed when the skies opened up. Sitting back on her heels, she watched the water cascade over the crypts. And as the rain mingled with her tears, she made a silent promise to her dead son and husband. It was a promise she would keep, no matter what the cost, because she had absolutely nothing else left to lose.

NAT HAD JUST STEPPED OUT OF THE SHOWER WHEN the doorbell jangled. Uneasiness rippled through her at the thought of a visitor. Only a few people in the entire town knew she was back, but she knew word would spread quickly. Still raw from her trip to the cemetery, she wasn't sure she was up to a confrontation.

Wrapping her hair in a towel, she grabbed her robe and took the steps to the living room. In the foyer she checked the peephole. A quiver of uncertainty went through her when she saw Faye Townsend standing on the porch, a brown paper bag in one arm, a bottle of wine in the other. Nat stepped back, feeling gut punched by the sight of the woman she'd once considered her best friend. For an instant, she contemplated not answering the door. But she knew that sooner or later she would have to deal with her. Better to get it over with now.

Taking a deep breath, Nat opened the door. For several long moments the two women simply stared at each other, two deer caught in the headlights of a speeding eighteen-wheeler, too stunned to flee what would surely be a deadly collision.

Then with her usual vivacity, Faye pushed past her and walked into the foyer, her orange sarong and purple shawl swishing around her like a flamenco dancer's skirts. "You could have told me you were back in town," she said airily.

Nat smelled sandalwood and lavender and wondered how a woman who claimed to be so in tune with everyone's energy could be blind enough to miss the fact that she was not welcome.

"What are you doing here?" Nat didn't close the door.

Faye spun to face her. "Making things right, since evidently you're not going to."

"There are some things that can't be made right."

"We've known each other too long to let this be one of them."

Because it hurt to think about it that way, because Nat was sick and damn tired of hurting, she went for something generic. "This isn't a good time."

"Well, then get dressed. I don't mind waiting."

"That isn't what I mean."

Faye lifted the bag, which appeared to be groceries, and the bottle of wine. "Is there someplace I can put this stuff?"

Nat ignored the question and continued holding the door open.

Faye contemplated her the way a teacher would a willful child. "Don't give me that look."

"What look?"

"The one telling me I'm not welcome here."

"You're not." A moth flew inside. Muttering a curse, Nat swatted at it, missed, then slammed the door. "How did you know I was back?"

Faye rolled her eyes. "Who *doesn't* know you're back?"

"If I wanted to see you, I would have called. I didn't."

"That would be fine and dandy if the world revolved around what you want, Natty. But it doesn't. You should know that by now."

Natty. Of all the weapons she could have used to inflict pain, the endearment was the most brutal. Faye had been calling her that since their first day of kindergarten when Mrs. Skelding put them at the front of the class for talking when they were supposed to be napping. Their friendship had survived grade school and high school, first dates and weddings, Faye's struggle with infertility and her ensuing divorce. The night Kyle and Ward had died, it had been Faye who held her while she'd sobbed and raged and weathered the violent storm of grief.

But it had also been Faye who'd later told the police that Nat's marriage had been a troubled one. Of all the betrayals that had taken place during those black, terrible days, that her best friend would turn on her when she'd needed her so desperately hurt the most.

"It's been a long day, Faye. I'm tired. I don't want to deal with you right now."

"Yeah? Well I have a few things to get off my chest." Turning away from her, Faye started for the kitchen.

"If it's an apology, don't bother." Nat followed, the anger inside her grabbing a foothold and digging in.

"I don't have anything to apologize for."

"How can you say that? Thanks to you, I just about went to trial for something I didn't do."

Faye set the bag of groceries and the bottle on the counter. "I told the truth."

"Ward and I were getting along fine. Our marriage wasn't perfect, but—"

"You were having problems, Nat. For God's sake, you told me he hadn't made love to you in over a year. When the police asked me about your relationship, I told them the truth. I had no way of knowing the prosecutor was going to twist my words around and use them against you."

Nat could feel the emotions building inside her. A tempest of fury and grief that had lain dormant for three years. "Ward and I were working through our problems, Faye. You could have mentioned that."

"I did, Natty, but the police didn't care. That detective wanted the person responsible for those murders, and he had his sights set on you. He honestly believed you had done it. And for that, honey, I'm sorry."

Stunned because she was on the verge of tears, Nat turned away and walked into the dining room. At the table, she gripped the back of a chair and leaned. The logical side of her brain knew there had been other factors involved that had resulted in her arrest and the ensuing grand jury proceedings. Flimsy circumstantial evidence, mostly. Nat's fingerprints had been on the bloody knife that had killed her son. The bedroom window screen had been cut as if someone had gained access to the house that way. Later, evidence had revealed the screen had been cut from the *inside*. The emergency room doctor testified that Nat's wounds could have been self-inflicted. But Faye's statement had been damaging. She'd given the police a motive.

"When the police asked me if you were having marital problems," Faye began, "I mentioned your suspicions about

Ward having an affair. I thought maybe the detective would look at the *other* woman. I could never have foreseen them using that information against you."

Nat would never forget the stab of pain when she'd learned that her best friend had helped the police build their case against her. "Yeah, well, evidently they did."

Faye shook her head. "What they didn't take into account was my telling him there was no way in hell you did it."

Because she wasn't yet ready to forgive, Nat walked to the French doors to stare out at the gathering darkness beyond.

"I need to put these groceries away," Faye said, digging into the bag.

"I don't want them." Nat glared at her.

"It's just a few staples."

Nat held her ground at the French door while Faye clanked things around in the kitchen. After several minutes, Nat turned to her. "That's not where the cereal goes," she said crossly.

"You're being a bitch, Nat."

Crossing to the kitchen, Nat took the cereal box from Faye and walked to the built-in pantry and opened the door. The dozen or so shelves were completely barren, so she set the sole box of cereal on the center one, face out. She knew it was stupid, but for some reason the sight of that bare pantry reminded her of her life—stark and achingly empty when it should have been full—and for several uncomfortable moments she had to blink back tears.

Faye must have sensed her inner turmoil, because she came up behind her and set her hand on her shoulder. "It'll get easier, honey."

"That's what everyone keeps saying." Nat squeezed her eyes closed, fought back tears. She was thinking too much, feeling too much. If only she could turn off her emotions.

"This is your first day back," Faye said. "Give yourself time."

"Ward was a minister, Faye. He wasn't supposed to have an affair." But in her heart of hearts, she'd known something wasn't right. She'd seen it in the way he looked at her. The chasm between them. During the last year of their marriage, Ward had suffered from impotency. He hadn't made love to her in more than a year. . . .

"Ministers are human," Faye said gently. "They make mistakes."

"I think he was seeing Sara Wiley." Nat me the other woman's gaze. "Was he?"

"Honey, knowing isn't going to help anything. You need to try to put this behind you and get on with your life."

"You knew, didn't you? The whole town knew." Nat choked out a laugh, but she felt like a fool. How could she have been so blind?

Faye raised her hands, a conductor quieting a symphony that had gotten too loud. "Let it go, Nat. Please don't do anything stupid."

"Oh, for God's sake, Faye, you don't think I'm going to stomp over to her house and yank out her hair, do you?"

Faye didn't smile. "If it's any consolation, I didn't find out it was her until just a few months ago."

The confirmation of something she'd already suspected shouldn't have hurt, but it did. How could she have been so naïve? She'd had Sara over to the house for dinner. Sara had watched Kyle a dozen times. Ward had talked about her a little too often, a little too fondly. "How did you find out?" she heard herself ask.

"I ran into Sara at The Blue Gator. We had a couple of beers, and she just started laying it on me. She was half drunk. Crying and telling me she'd loved him. I think she had a guilty conscience."

Nat's mind was reeling. "Did anyone bother to tell the police?"

"I told Alcee Martin. I heard later that Norm Pelletier talked to her. But nothing ever came of it." Her gaze met Nat's. "I know what you're thinking, honey, but you're wrong. Reno Wiley might be a mean-spirited jerk, but he's not a killer."

Nat thought of her meeting with Alcee Martin earlier in the day and felt a rise of anger because he hadn't bothered to mention Reno had already been considered and eliminated as a suspect. "I guess all the suspicion in this town was reserved for me."

"Some people just want to believe the worst. The people who know better are the ones who count." Faye reached out to touch her. "In case you haven't figured it out by now, that in-cludes me."

Nat walked to the dining room table and sank into a chair. "What a mess."

"Honey, you're shaking." Faye set the bottle of wine on the table between them and took the chair across from her. "Are you okay?"

She nodded but figured both women knew she was a long way from being okay.

"How's your mama?" Faye asked. "She still living in New Orleans?"

Nat's smile was sardonic. "She's good at pretending every-thing is all right. I think she's in denial. She doesn't talk about it." Analise Jennings was the quintessential southern belle. Appearances were everything, and she worked hard to main-tain them, sometimes at the cost of facing reality.

"People deal with grief in different ways," Faye said. "She lost a grandson. She almost lost you." She paused. "Does she know you're here?"

"No." Nat gave her a hard look. "I want to keep it that way."

"Why *are* you here, Natty? Of all the places you could have gone, why did you come back to a place that holds so much pain?"

To find a killer.

The words flitted through her mind, but Nat didn't voice them. She didn't trust Faye enough to tell her the truth. She figured the less people knew about why she was back, the bet-ter her chances of succeeding. "I just . . . needed to face some old demons so I can put this behind me and move on with my life."

Faye nodded, but Nat didn't miss the instant of hesitation, and she knew the other woman suspected there was more to her arrival in Bellerose than the need for closure.

Because she didn't want the conversation to go in that di-rection, Nat moved quickly to change the subject. "Do you know Nick Bastille?"

Faye looked startled by the question. "I know enough about him to know he's trouble."

"How so?"

"Well, he's an ex-con, for one. A shame, considering he's

so damn good to look at. Talk about a waste of man-flesh. I saw him pumping gas the other day out at Ray's Sunoco, and he really is something to look at, if you like the dangerous type, anyway. Emma down at the diner told me he took a job at The Blue Gator."

"I wonder why he came back to Bellerose," Nat said, thinking aloud. "I mean, there aren't many opportunities here, especially for an ex-con."

"Maybe he didn't have anywhere else to go." Faye's eyes narrowed. "Any particular reason you're asking about Nick Bastille?"

Nat lifted her shoulder, let it fall. "I had a run-in with him earlier," she said vaguely. "He was rude."

"Yeah, well, from what I hear, he's not the kind of guy you want to piss off. He went to prison for murder, you know." She lowered her voice. "Jenny Lee told me he has all sorts of shady friends down in New Orleans. He might even have ties to the Mob. You definitely don't want to run into him in a dark alley. When Nick Bastille showed back up, folks around here started locking their doors."

But Nat knew all too well about small towns and gossip. She knew how a story got bigger and more vicious every time it was told. And because she herself had been a favorite topic among Bellerose's gossipmongers, she resolved not to pass judgment on Nick Bastille.

"I drove up to see you a few times when you were in the hospital, you know," Faye said after a moment.

Nat didn't even try to hide her surprise. "I didn't know."

"You were still in a coma."

"If I hadn't been, I probably would have told you to leave."

Faye smiled, but it looked sad on her face. "The first time was a week or so after . . . you went in. At that point, the doctors didn't know if you were going to come back."

Some days Nat still couldn't believe she'd spent over two years in a coma. Months that had passed in the blink of an eye and were lost forever. She didn't remember much about the night she'd tried to commit suicide. Ward and Kyle had been dead for a week and life had seemed too bleak to bear. Nat had been sitting in a jail cell, and it had seemed as if her very soul had been ripped from her body. Her heart torn to bits and trod upon. She knew slitting her wrists had been a cowardly thing to do, but at the time she'd been too shattered inside to care. . . .

"I read to you mostly," Faye said.

Nat contemplated her, wondering if they could ever go back to being friends. "What did you read?"

"Whatever I was reading at the time. You seemed to enjoy *Fanny Hill*," she said deadpan.

Nat made a sound that was half laugh, half sob. "For God's sake, Faye, you don't read erotica to someone who's in a coma."

"You moved your hand that night, Natty. You knew I was there."

Nat didn't know what to say and for a moment all she could do was blink back tears. How very like Faye to do something so utterly unorthodox. And so selfless and kind, a little voice added.

Because she didn't want to cry, Nat took a deep breath and focused on the bottle Faye had set on the table. "What kind of wine is that?"

"Blackberry. From my own patch. I thought you might appreciate some about now."

"I hate your blackberry wine."

"That was peach cognac you tried, spoilsport. And for your information, I've refined my wine-making skills since you last tried it."

Rising, Nat walked into the kitchen and snagged two wineglasses from the cabinet. At the bar, Faye uncorked the bottle. "I like to let this breathe for a minute or two."

Nat met her at the bar and set down the glasses. Faye looked at her, her expression sober. "It hurt when you refused to see me after you came out of the coma."

"I was a mess, Faye. Physically. Emotionally."

"You were angry."

"I was a lot of things, and none of them were good."

"Considering what you've been through, you have a very positive energy, Nat." A smile whispered across Faye's features. "You look damn good for a woman who's spent the last two and a half years sleeping."

Nat thought of the months of grueling physical rehabilitation and grimaced. "It was tough, Faye. Even though I'd had quite a bit of physical therapy, my muscles had atrophied. I couldn't walk. I couldn't even sit up. It's taken me six months to get my strength back."

"Any lingering effects from the stroke?"

After her suicide attempt, Nat had gone into hypovolemic shock and suffered a minor stroke from blood loss. "I had some memory problems early on and some minor paralysis on my left side." She raised her left hand and flexed her fingers. "My left hand is a little awkward, but since I'm right-handed, it's not a problem."

"That's good." Faye studied her face. "You look a little tired. A lot sad."

"I am. Both."

"But your energy is strong." The other woman's eyes narrowed. "Different somehow. Powerful. But good. That's the most important thing."

Nat had always been a skeptic when it came to things like personal energy and the woo-woo mumbo jumbo Faye subscribed to. The last six months had changed her view dramatically.

Faye raised her glass. "To the healing energy of friendship," she said.

And the sweet promise of justice, Nat silently added, and clinked her glass against Faye's.

chapter
6

THE BLUE GATOR WAS HOPPING. THE SHIFT AT THE
lumber mill had ended at four o'clock, and by four-fifteen half
of Bobby O'Malley's crew were at the bar, their minds set on
putting a dent in Mike Pequinot's supply of booze. A lively
zydeco number blasted from the jukebox. Even though it was
still early, several couples were already kicking up sawdust on
the matchbox-size dance floor.

The boisterous atmosphere of The Blue Gator was a far cry
from the jazzy elegance of the restaurant Nick had owned in
New Orleans. The Tropics had been dark wood and candle-
light, smooth jazz, Dominican cigars, and top-shelf liquor. But
atmosphere was a relative thing, and Nick was in his element,
no matter which bar he stood behind.

He'd always believed one of the things that made him good
at what he did was his willingness to roll up his sleeves. Even
back when he'd been wearing two thousand dollar suits, if a
table needed busing, he jumped in and did it himself. Even after he'd had the money to hire the best bartenders in the city,
he'd made it a point on occasion to elbow his way to the bar
and serve up shots and drafts or whatever alcoholic concoc-
tion his customers wanted.

It seemed like a lifetime ago that he'd been bursting with
dreams and ambition and the utter certainty that he was going

to succeed if only by the sheer force of his will. Nick might have grown up poor, but he damn well hadn't liked it, and that discontent had bred ambition into his blood. At twenty, there had been no doubt in his mind that he would one day own a restaurant the same caliber as Arnaud's or Commander's Palace, and there wasn't a soul on this sweet earth big enough or strong enough to stop him. He hadn't counted on hooking up with a scheming partner and a two-timing woman. . . .

Trying hard not to think of what a blind fool he'd been, Nick twirled the shot glass, slammed it onto the scarred bar, and filled it to overflowing with cheap rum and a thick wedge of lemon. "Dark rum with a twist. Two bucks."

Someone shoved three dollars at him. Nick stuffed the tip into his fanny pack, placed the other two in the cash register. He glanced up to see a sunburned man wearing a muscle shirt and Tabasco cap ask for a draft. Nick snagged a mug from the ice machine, shoved it beneath the nozzle, and filled it to the rim.

It was his first day on the job, and the place was as hectic as Bourbon Street on Fat Tuesday. But once Nick had settled down and found his rhythm, his years of experience had come pouring back. He was good at the bar. He knew his drinks, knew how to hustle. He enjoyed the contact with people. And if he closed his eyes, he could almost make himself believe he was back at The Tropics. . . .

"You keep up that shit, and I'm going to fire all my help and turn this joint over to you."

Nick looked up to see Mike Pequinot lift the pass-through door and limp behind the bar. "Hell of a business you do here," Nick said.

"Helps that we're the only bar in town." Pequinot poured dark rum from a bottle of top-shelf stuff he kept hidden for his personal use and slammed it back. "Tanya came in a couple of minutes ago."

Nick didn't let himself react at the mention of his ex-wife, but he felt the quick rise of tension. She was the one person in Bellerose he didn't want to see. Especially if she was fueled up on cheap booze and God only knew what else.

"I'll watch my back," he said.

Pequinot slapped him on the back. "And your front."

For a few minutes Nick concentrated on his customers. A draft. A hurricane. Change the keg. Replenish the ice. Another shot of bourbon. Change for a ten dollar bill.

But his thoughts kept going back to Tanya, and they were troubled. The last time he'd seen her was the day she'd walked out of the prison visitor's room after telling him she was filing for divorce. She'd been gripping little Brandon's hand so hard the boy's fingers were white. His son had looked at him over his shoulder and waved. Nick hadn't been able to do anything but stand there and let them go. He'd had no way of knowing it would be the last time he saw his son.

In the two years since, he'd been able to forgive her for walking out on him. As desperately as he'd needed those visits, he'd known prison was no place for a little boy. Nick had been able to forgive her for sleeping with his business partner. He'd even been able to forgive her for testifying against him and helping to convict him of a crime he hadn't committed. But the one thing Nick hadn't been able to forgive her for was letting their son die. For letting a little boy wander into the bayou and drown in a deep pool of water. He knew that wasn't fair; he knew sometimes bad things happened, no matter how careful a parent was. But right or wrong, he blamed her. He would never forgive her. And in some small corner of his mind, he hated her for it.

"I never thought I'd see Nick Bastille behind the bar at The Blue Gator serving up Mike Pequinot's cheap booze."

Dread snapped through him at the sound of his ex-wife's drawl. Nick glanced up to see her standing at the bar directly opposite him, and an emotion he couldn't quite identify rushed through him like a shot of bad whiskey. Tanya Bastille had once been beautiful, with vivid blue eyes, a sensuous mouth, and yards of blond hair that fell like silk halfway down her back. She was tall and slender with the kind of body that could drive a man just a little bit insane if he wasn't careful. Looking at her now, he barely recognized the young woman who'd once held his heart in the palm of her hand.

The years had not been kind to her. Skin that had once glowed with health had gone sallow and sagged like cheap leather from her high cheekbones. The heavy makeup did little to accentuate eyes that had gone hard with bitterness. Her hair was still long, but she'd bleached it platinum, and it looked as brittle as her smile.

Nick knew the lines etched into her face were not from age. Grief gave a person a distinctive look that was hard to describe. He recognized it because he saw the same thing when he looked in the mirror. He knew firsthand how grief hollowed a person out. How it could age a person before their time. If not on the outside, then on the inside where the scars were visible only to those who shared them.

Tanya hadn't yet seen her thirtieth birthday, but she looked a decade older. There was a falseness to a smile that had once been guileless and engaging. A hard edge to a face that had once been soft. Eyes that had once been pretty were glassy with the effects of alcohol or whatever drug she used to get through the day. He could tell from the size of her pupils that even though it wasn't yet six o'clock, she was already well on her way to oblivion.

"You got anything stronger than alcohol back there?" she drawled.

"Just the usual legal stuff," he said with the same easy tone he used with all the customers.

"You always did make the best hurricanes, Nicky. Why don't you mix me up one like you used to?"

"You look like maybe you've had enough."

"Honey, I'm just getting warmed up." She smiled a too-bright smile. "Make it a double, will you?"

Turning away from her, Nick reached for a tall glass and began to mix, taking it easy on the alcohol. He knew from experience that even a sober Tanya could spell trouble. An intoxicated Tanya could make a tornado look like a Sunday picnic.

"So, how long you been out?" she asked.

"Two days."

"Hmmm. How long's it been, Nicky? A couple of years?"

Nick knew exactly how long it had been, right down to the hour. Some days he could still feel that internal clock ticking silently inside him, counting out the seconds to freedom.

He slid the tall glass across the bar. Never taking her eyes from his, she picked it up, puckered her lips around the straw, and drank deeply. "Ah, that's good. You still got the touch, don't you?"

Nick didn't say anything, but he could tell from the look in her eyes that she wasn't going to go away. "That's three bucks," he said.

"How have you been?" she asked, digging into the tiny purse slung over her shoulder.

"I think you know how I've been."

"You're still angry."

"Look, we're busy as hell tonight—"

"Too busy for your ex-wife, huh?"

"That's three bucks for the drink," he repeated.

She smiled, but it was the smile of a piranha with evil things on its mind. She'd zipped the purse, and he knew she had no intention of paying. He figured three dollars was a small price to pay to get her the hell out of there. But he had the sinking feeling it wasn't going to be that easy.

"I didn't even know you were in town until Jo Nell Jenkins over at the bank told me you'd come in to straighten out Dutch's accounts." She suckled the straw. "I can't believe you let me hear it from a complete stranger."

"I didn't come back to Bellerose for you, Tanya. In case you've forgotten, we're divorced."

"We may not be married legally, but we've still got that bond, you know? I mean, come on, you were my first. We had a good time, Nicky. We had a son together."

A wave of fury swept through him at the mention of Brandon. He didn't want to talk about his son. He didn't want her to speak his name. Especially not in a place like this when she was drunk and needy, and his patience were wire thin.

"There is no bond," he said curtly. "Not anymore."

"You're angry because I walked out on you."

Nick was a hell of a lot more than angry. He was furious, but it didn't have a damn thing to do with her walking out on him. "Tanya . . ."

"I had a little boy to think of, Nicky."

Because in the four years they were married she had never thought of anyone but herself, Nick ignored the statement. "This isn't the place to discuss this."

"Why not?" She made a sweeping motion to encompass the bar and all its patrons. "It's not like what happened in New Orleans is a huge secret in this town."

"What happened is between us."

"You're being an uppity prick just like you always were."

Nick knew he was a fool for engaging her. Even more of a fool for letting her get to him. He was playing into her hands, giving her exactly what she wanted. But she'd always known which buttons to push, and tonight she was pushing those buttons with the proficiency of a master hacker.

"If you don't like the company, maybe you ought to take your drink and go." Grabbing the towel he'd slung over his shoulder, he began to wipe down the bar, hating it that he was so angry that he was shaking inside.

Tanya watched him, sipping her drink, a sleek cat playing with a mouse. "It's hard coming back to a place like this after living the high life, isn't it?"

Doing his utmost to ignore her, he bent to retrieve a tray of freshly rinsed glasses and began to towel them dry.

"Well, now you have a taste of what I've had to contend with the last six years. I went from a four-bedroom house in the Garden District to this dump." Gesturing at the hodgepodge of patrons, she threw her head back and laughed. "How's that for irony?"

He wanted to point out that their losing the house in New Orleans had more to do with her and his scheming partner framing him, but he knew she'd probably already justified her actions in her mind, so he didn't bother. Tanya was the kind of person who, if she heard her own lies often enough, would believe them.

"I think it's a pretty fitting irony," he said.

"Don't get nasty with me, Nicky."

A burly man in faded coveralls asked for a beer. Nick gave him a nod, snagged a frozen mug, and filled it.

"You showed me how the other half lives, then you get yourself thrown into prison and left me and little Brandon with nothing."

Nick closed his eyes briefly at the mention of his son. "I've got to work, Tanya."

"Don't be such a prick. You can spare a minute for me."

"I've nothing to say to you." He slid the mug to the man in coveralls and collected two dollars. "If you don't hit the road, I'm going to have Mike show you the door."

"Mike won't throw me out. I'm his best customer." Her lips curved. "Did I ever tell you he fucked me in the men's room once? Bent me over the sink and stuck it in and started grunting and sweating like some fat three-legged pig."

Needing to put some distance between them before he lost his temper, Nick turned away and began stacking mugs on the shelf below the bar.

"Don't turn you back on me, you self-righteous son of a bitch."

Sighing in resignation, he turned to her, gave her a hard look. "This isn't the place for one of your tantrums."

"That's where you're wrong, Nicky." Tossing her head, she looked around, made a sweeping motion with her arms. "This is the perfect place for a knock-down-drag-out. Half the people in this dump would pay a week's salary to see us go a round or two."

"I'm not interested in going a round with you."

Her smile sharpened to a razor's edge. "Oh, honey, going a round with me is the one thing you could never resist."

"You overestimate your charms. You always have."

An ugly emotion he couldn't quite identify flared in her eyes. "You think you had it rough in prison? Do you think it's been easy for me being back here all by myself and having to start all over again? I had no money. No job. No place to live except that goddamn trailer."

Realizing the situation was getting out of control, Nick straightened and looked around for Mike Pequinot.

"Let me tell you how it's been," she said with sudden emotion. "I've spent the last six years working in that shit-hole motel on the interstate. My salary and tips barely make the rent. I use food stamps. My car is a piece of shit. I need new tires—"

"Maybe you ought to stop spending your money on booze."

She went on as if she hadn't heard him, her voice cracking. "I miss my baby so much I can't stand it, Nicky. Nothing has been the same for me since Brandon . . ."

Just hearing the name hurt. Pain that was bright red in intensity and so bone deep that it took his breath. "Don't bring him into this," Nick ground out.

An emotion he could only describe as hatred flared hotly in her eyes. "Oh, I forgot. That's how you deal with problems. Don't talk about them, and *poof!* they disappear. God, Nick, if you could put that in a bottle and sell it, you'd be rich."

"Tanya, you're drunk."

"I may be be drunk, but at least I'm alive. At least I'm not dead inside like you."

"Why don't you go home and sleep it off?"

"You've always been a holier-than-thou-art son of a bitch, and you still are. I guess those years behind bars didn't do a damn thing for that high-and-mighty attitude of yours. Even broke you still look at everyone down your nose.

"Well, look at you now, Nicky. You're nothing but a second-rate loser ex-con working in a shit hole, just like me. You're broke. Back on the farm and living with your crazy old man. You always thought you were better than me, didn't you? Now I guess everyone in this town knows you're not."

Several people standing at the bar had noticed the exchange and were staring, their eyes alight in anticipation of a brewing fight. "Take your drink and go," he said.

She ignored him. "The last time I saw you, you weren't quite so high and mighty, were you, Nicky? You remember that day, don't you?"

"Shut your goddamn mouth."

"If my memory serves me, I'm pretty sure you got down on your knees and begged me to stay, didn't you?"

Nick wished he could dispute her words, but he couldn't and the wash of humiliation burned. He'd never begged for anything in his life. But that day in the prison visitor room when she'd told him she was filing for divorce and wouldn't be back, Nick's knees had hit the deck. Not because he'd loved her, but because he'd loved his son, and when it came to his little boy, pride hadn't mattered. Nick had known she was incapable of caring for a child. He'd known his son would be in danger if he let her go.

"Maybe you even cried a little," she teased. "That's a pathetic thing for a man to do."

"Get out, Tanya. Take your delusions with you."

"Oh, that burns, doesn't it, Nicky?" Her mouth twisted into

a smile. "High-and-mighty Nick Bastille begging his little trailer trash wife not to leave him to rot in prison."

"You're making a fool of yourself."

"I'm making a fool of *you,* and you don't like it. Well, here's a newsflash for you, Nicky. The world doesn't revolve around what you do and do not like. You're a *nothing* with a capital N. A big fat zero. A loser ex-con with a record who will never amount to anything, just like your old man."

Nick could feel the rage building inside him, a storm cloud heavy with violence. "Someone get her out of here."

A man tried to take her arm. "Come on, Tanny, leave him be. Let's get some air."

Tanya jerked away from him, her furious gaze on Nick. "You didn't know how to be a husband and you sure as hell didn't know how to be a father. All you cared about was that fucking restaurant. You put it above me. Above Brandon."

"Leave him out of this."

She choked out a sound that was half laugh, half sob. "And now you have the gall to stand there and look at me as if what happened to him was all my fault, you son of a bitch. You might like to think otherwise, but you played a role, too."

"He was in your care."

"If you hadn't been in prison, he never would have died! You had as much a hand in his death as I did. So don't stand there and judge me!"

Nick's temper snapped with the violence of a gunshot. One moment he was standing a few feet from the bar, the next he was leaning over it with his hands around her biceps. "You let a little child run wild in the swamp unsupervised!"

For a moment, she looked startled. She opened her mouth. Blinked several times as if trying to bring him into focus. Then her lips peeled back. "You son of a *bitch!*" she snarled. An instant later she drew back and threw her drink in his face.

Nick jolted with the shock of cold. He tasted rum and fury, felt the burn of alcohol in his eyes, and for the first time in his life he wanted to do physical harm to a woman.

"I didn't know he could unlock the door!" she cried. "He was so smart! I swear! He opened two locks. *Two,* for God's sake! He'd never done it before! He wasn't supposed to do that!"

"You were passed out from being drunk the night before!"

A sound that was half sob, half scream tore from her throat. "You *bastard*!" She launched herself at him. The first blow caught his left temple, hard enough to snap his head back. Another grazed off his shoulder.

Nick staggered back, but she held onto him, and he dragged her halfway over the bar. "Get off me," he growled.

"I wasn't drunk!" she screamed. "I swear to God I wasn't!"

A big woman in leather pants tried to pull her back, but Tanya fought her like a wildcat. She was lying across the bar, holding onto Nick's sleeve with one hand, hitting him with the other. "It wasn't my fault!" she cried. "He died because you weren't there, you motherfucker!"

Nick disengaged himself from her and stumbled back. Vaguely he was aware of the throng of people that had gathered around the bar. He jolted when a heavy hand landed on his shoulder. He turned, ready to defend himself, and was relieved to see Mike Pequinot come up beside him. "Why don't you go out back and have a smoke?"

Nick barely heard the words over the jackhammer rhythm of his heart. He could feel his control peeling away. He looked across the bar at the woman he'd once loved. The woman who'd borne his only child. The woman who'd ripped that child from his arms and then let him die like an animal. . . .

The urge to put his fist through something was strong, but he held on to his control. "Keep her away from me." Shaking with rage, he tossed the towel onto the bar and started for the door to the kitchen.

"You had no right to say those things to me!" Tanya screamed to his back. "He was my baby, too! Goddamn you! I loved him! It was an accident! You can't blame me for what happened!"

Nick didn't look back. He was too furious. He wasn't sure what he would say to her. He wasn't sure what he would do if she pushed him any farther.

He hit the swinging doors with both hands. They flew open and banged hard against the walls. Pequinot's wife looked up from the steaming pot she was stirring, but she was an astute enough woman to realize he couldn't be talked down.

Nick didn't stop until he reached the back door. He shoved

it open hard and stepped into the sultry night. He could still hear the drum of the music beating in time with his heart. He could still feel the rage flowing through him in a swift and dangerous current. He was keenly aware of the ugliness of the emotions inside him. Hatred and grief and a rage that never seemed to leave him, no matter how hard he tried to exorcise it.

He sat down hard on the step and put his face in his hands. of all the terrible things he had endured in the last six years, losing his son was the one that had gutted him. The day they'd taken him into an interview room and told him his innocent little boy had drowned, something inside Nick had died. A piece of his humanity. A chunk of his heart. It was as if a giant hand had plunged into his body and torn out his soul.

At least I'm not dead inside like you.

"Jesus Christ," he muttered and scrubbed his hands over his face.

But when he closed his eyes, it was his son's face he saw. Sweet, innocent Brandon with his bright blue eyes and hair as dark as midnight. He'd had a smile that could light up the darkest of nights. A face that could warm the coldest of hearts. A presence that could banish the deep ache of loneliness. He'd been purity and goodness, and Nick had always looked upon him in reverence, unable to understand how he and Tanya could have created something so utterly perfect.

He'd loved that child in a way he'd never loved anything else on this earth. In a way he would never love again in his lifetime. Brandon had represented everything innocent and good in a world where such things were rare and many times false.

"You look like you could use this."

Nick started at the sound of the husky female voice. He looked up to see Pequinot's wife Rita standing at the door, offering a lit cigarette. He hadn't touched any kind of tobacco for going on a year, but he needed that vice now with the desperation of a man in the throes of withdrawal.

"Thanks." He took the cigarette, drew hard on it.

"She comes in here all the time," Rita said.

"Yeah, Mike told me."

"She's an alcoholic."

"She's a spiteful bitch."

"Grief can do that to person, Nick. I'm not making excuses for her, but she hasn't been the same since your boy died."

Surprised that she would touch on the subject of his son, Nick looked up at her. Rita Pequinot stared back at him with the shrewd eyes of a woman who wasn't afraid to speak her mind. She was a substantial woman. Not only in size, Nick thought, but in character, too.

"Nobody's ever the same after something like that," he said.

"She was out of line. I'll tell Mike to keep her out of the bar."

Realizing he'd left Mike at the bar alone in the midst of a rush, Nick said, "Tell him I'll be right there." But when he looked up, Rita was already gone.

chapter
7

NAT HAD NEVER BEEN A GOOD SLEEPER. EVEN BE-
fore that terrible night three years ago, she'd been prone to in-
somnia. Dr. Pettigrew had prescribed sleeping pills, but they
made her groggy the next day, so she rarely took them. Herbs
seemed to help her relax. Reading kept her mind from grinding. Driving helped when she was restless. Tonight, with the
walls and memories closing in, she opted for a drive.

She'd spent much of the evening rehashing her disastrous
meeting with Nick Bastille. To say he hadn't believed her was
a gross understatement. His reaction had been volatile. She'd
seen his hands clenched at his sides, the fury in his eyes. The
man had wanted to do physical violence to her.

She wasn't going to let it keep her from what she needed to
do. Nick Bastille might be hot-tempered and unpredictable
and maybe even a little dangerous. But while any one of those
things was reason enough for her not to approach him again,
Nat knew they were also her best hope of getting him to listen.

On the outskirts of town, she turned onto Pelican Island
Road. The narrow road was shrouded with high weeds and
overhanging branches webbed with Spanish moss and kudzu.
Her headlights cut twin beams through the utter darkness, and
she felt as if she were a diver spelunking in an underwater cave.

The Blue Gator sat at the dead end of the road, a neon oasis surrounded by swamp. Nat wasn't surprised to find the lot packed with vehicles. She located Nick Bastille's truck at the rear and parked next to it. Trying not to think of all the reasons why she shouldn't be walking into a roughneck bar like The Blue Gator to try to convince an ex-con of something he didn't want to be convinced of, she started for the entrance.

She knew broaching the subject of his son again so soon would be like thumping a beehive with a stick. She knew she was probably going to get stung. But Nat had known since the day she'd wakened from the coma and found her life in tatters that the task ahead of her wasn't going to be easy.

Shoving her uncertainties aside, she pushed through the front door and entered the bar. Lou Reed's "Sweet Jane" blasted from mammoth speakers loud enough to rattle the nails right out of the roof. A group of men and a tall blonde in black leather hovered around a pool table at the rear. Two bikers eyed her, but there was no hostility on their faces, no whispers behind her back. An odd sense of relief flitted through her that inside this most disreputable of establishments, she'd found the one place in Bellerose that did not shun her.

She elbowed her way through the throng of bodies toward the bar. An unexpected frisson of tension went through her when she spotted Bastille. He was wearing a white shirt with the sleeves rolled up to the elbow, revealing muscled forearms. His button-down jeans were faded nearly white and hugged his lean hips with the perfection of custom trousers. Nat sidled up to the bar and slid unobtrusively onto a stool.

For several minutes she watched him work unnoticed. He seemed completely at ease behind the bar and served up drinks with the finesse of a man who'd done it many times before. She thought about Faye's assertion that he was attractive and realized she'd been right, though Nat had long since ceased to put any weight in such superficialities.

Even so, she couldn't help but notice his smile. It was the smile of a man who enjoyed what he did. A man who enjoyed being around people. A smile like that was a dangerous thing in a man like Nick Bastille, and she quickly reminded herself that he'd spent six years in prison for murder. . . .

"Well if it isn't the minister's wife come to gloat."

The words went through her like an ice pick stabbed into

her back, and Nat felt every inch of it all the way to her spine. Slowly, she turned. Cold dread spread through her when she found herself facing Ward's brother, Hunter Ratcliffe. He was standing less than a foot away from her. So close she could smell the whiskey on his breath, see the mean glint in his eyes.

Her heart began to pound. "Hunt . . ."

"I gotta hand it to you, Nat-a-lie, you have some nerve showing your face around here after what you did to my brother."

She felt the words like a punch, but didn't allow herself to react. "I didn't do anything to Ward or Kyle." She glanced over his shoulder to see the two men behind him, watching her, their eyes glassy with alcohol and malice. "I don't want any trouble."

"Sugar, you invited trouble the day you put a bullet in my brother's heart."

For an instant, she was so shocked by the ugly words and his open hostility that she didn't know what to say. Then she looked down at the beer bottle in his hand, realized he was drunk, and shock gave way to anger. "You have no right to speak to me that way," she said, hating it that her voice was quavering.

"You deserve a hell of a lot worse than anything I could say to you. You ought to be in prison instead of sitting pretty on that barstool."

Hunt Ratcliffe was slightly built, but he had a mean streak that more than made up for what he lacked in stature. She'd seen it in the years she and Ward had been married. Hunt never had the guts to turn that meanness on her—Ward never would have tolerated it—but she'd always known he had a dark side. Judging from the look in his eyes, she was going to get a taste of it tonight.

"What the hell are you trying to prove by coming back?" he asked. "Do you think the people in this town are going to forgive and forget? Do you actually think they're going to welcome you back?"

"You know I didn't hurt Kyle or Ward."

He smiled, but it was the kind of smile designed to hide something ugly slithering just beneath the surface. "Me and a lot of other people in this town think you did a hell of a lot worse than hurt them."

"You're wrong."

"Was the evidence wrong, Nat-a-lie?"

"I wasn't indicted, Hunt."

"Goddamn bleeding hearts let you go because you were laid up in the hospital. The rest of us think justice would have been served if you'd succeeded when you cut your wrists and bled to death right there on the jailhouse floor that night."

She winced inwardly at the cruelty of his words, but she didn't let the hurt stop her. "Hunt, listen to me. I didn't do it. You have to believe that."

"Jesus, you're good, aren't you?"

"Whoever killed Ward and Kyle is still out there."

His expression turned incredulous. "You just don't stop, do you? Do you have any idea how many lives you've ruined? How many people you've hurt?"

"I know people were hurt. I was hurt, too. Hunt, I lost my family that night."

"You were a lying bitch three years ago, and you're a lying bitch now. If it's the last thing I do, I swear to Christ I'm going to make you pay for what you did."

Nat looked around, aware of the eyes turning their way, hating it that she was shaking inside. That she was embarrassed and hurt and deeply ashamed when she had nothing to be ashamed of.

"Your fingerprints were on the knife that slashed my nephew's throat," he said. "You were covered in their blood. You cut yourself to make it look as if you'd been attacked."

"Stop it, Hunt. I can't . . . talk about it. Not here."

"You afraid you'll get caught in a lie?"

"It's too painful," she snapped.

"Too painful? Oh, for crying out loud, that's rich." Laughing, he pressed his hand to his chest. When he leaned close to her, his eyes were as cold and hard as ice. "Let me tell you something, Nat-a-lie. People in these parts don't take kindly to women who kill their children."

"I didn't," she said breathlessly. "You know I couldn't do something like that."

"What I know is that you received a big life insurance check. More money than you would have seen in your lifetime if you hadn't hooked up with Ward. That's an awful lot of motive for a little swamp rat like you. Marrying into the Ratcliffe family wasn't enough, was it?"

Nat knew defending herself was useless. He was drunk. Her own emotions were beginning to spiral. A volatile situation that was only going to get worse if she didn't get the hell out of there pronto.

She started to slide off the barstool, but he reached out and stopped her by grasping her arm. "I'm not finished with you. I've been waiting three years to say this. The least you can do is listen."

"I don't have to listen to you. You're so blinded by hatred and blame that you're incapable of seeing the truth."

"And what truth is that?"

"That someone in this town got away with murder."

He shook his head, gave her that ugly smile again. "They say if you hear a lie often enough, people will start to believe it. I think you actually believe what you're saying," He leaned close to her. "But rest assured, Nat-a-lie, I will not forget. This town will not forget. We're not going to let you get away with it."

That he could believe she'd done something so heinous made her feel sick. She simply couldn't fathom how anyone could believe she was capable of murdering her own husband and child.

"I have to go." Shaking off his hand, she slid from the stool and started for the door. She'd only taken a couple of steps when strong fingers bit into her shoulder and spun her around. She caught a glimpse of Hunt's lips drawn back, his teeth clamped and grinding.

"Did you know my father hired a private detective?" he asked. "From what I hear this guy's a real pit bull. He's going to get you, Nat-a-lie. No matter how long it takes. No matter how far you run or how many lies you tell. He's going to take you down."

"He's looking at the wrong person," she said.

"I'll be sure to tell him that, but somehow I don't think he'll believe it any more than I do. You see, Natalie, while you were in the hospital, playing possum all those months, he was already hard at work. You'd be amazed at all the stuff he dug up."

She stared at him, vaguely aware that her breaths were rushing in and out. That she was shaking all over. She looked around, saw the dozens of people that had gathered to watch, and suddenly knew what it was like to be a rabbit surrounded by a pack of wild dogs.

He leaned so close his breath ruffled her hair as he whispered into her ear. "We know about Ward's lover. I didn't think my brother had it in him to go after that hot little secretary of his. But he was fucking her brains out every chance he got, wasn't he? Combine that with a five hundred thousand dollar life insurance policy, and we have one hell of a motive for murder."

"I'm not going to listen to this."

She tried to slap his hand off her shoulder, but he grabbed her wrist and gave it a twist. "You found out about Ward and Sara Wiley and flew into a jealous rage, didn't you?"

"No!"

"Kyle is the one I could never figure, Natalie. A seven-year-old little kid. Jesus Christ, that is sick. It took me a while, but I finally figured why you did it. He saw you shoot his daddy, didn't he?"

Something terrible glinted in his eyes, and with a sense of horror, she realized he truly believed what he was saying. He thought she was capable of cold-blooded murder.

Fury and grief tangled inside her, two storms colliding with a violence that made her legs go weak. "I didn't, damn you."

Hunt's teeth pulled back in a snarl. "You might be able to fool some hick jury, but you can't fool me, you money-grabbing piece of trash. Gold-digging bitch. Baby-killing whore."

"Stop it."

"You're not going to get away with killing them, you cold-hearted bitch. How could you do something like that?"

Nat jerked away, broke his grip on her arm. The urge to run out the door was strong, but she didn't. She held her ground, met his gaze. "Stay away from me, Hunt. I mean it."

"Or what?" he mocked. "What are you going to do? Shoot me? Cut my throat? Slit your wrists so everyone will feel sorry for you?"

Dizzy with fury and adrenaline and a terrible agony that

never seemed to leave her, Nat turned away, pushed through the crowd and headed toward the door. Her entire body was vibrating. She could feel the sobs bubbling in her throat, but she didn't cry. She wouldn't give them the satisfaction of seeing her break. Damn them all.

She'd been wrong to come here tonight. She'd been wrong to come back to Bellerose. She'd been crazy to believe she could do this. There was too much hatred. Too much pain. Too many memories. All of those things stood like a mountain before her, and at the top lay the truth, as out of reach as the sky.

She was midway to the door when a hand clamped down on her arm. Surprise and the first real jab of fear assailed her when she was spun around. She caught a glimpse of Hunt, his lips pulled back in a snarl.

"Don't you walk away from me, you little bitch." His fingers dug into her arm. "You came in here, throwing what you did in my face. Gloating because you got away with it."

"Let go of me."

He shook her with enough force to knock her off balance. "Now you can take what you got coming."

Before she even realized what she was doing, she drew back her free arm and slapped him hard across the cheek. Surprise flickered in his eyes. Even in the dim light she saw his face redden, the vein at his temple begin to pulse.

She knew better than to fight violence with violence; she knew it was a fight she would lose. He was fueled up on alcohol and hatred, and the situation was an inch away from spiraling out of control. But Nat had had all the bullying she could take. Her own emotions were like a raging river, overflowing its banks, threatening to drown her.

His hand shot out so quickly she didn't have time to react. His knuckles connected with her left cheekbone hard enough to snap her head back. She heard her teeth clack together. The sound of a jet engine roaring in her ears. Pain radiated from her jaw to her temple. Then she was reeling backward into space.

An unexpected shove from someone in the crowd sent her sideways. She lost her balance and went down hard on her hands and knees. Vaguely, she was aware of the dozens of people around her. The din of voices coming from all directions.

"Killed her own child . . ."

"Slit that little boy's throat like a butchered cow . . ."

"Her husband was a minister . . ."

"Serves her right . . ."

She couldn't believe this was happening. That the people she'd grown up with, gone to school with, lived among her entire life, could hate her so much. The knowledge wounded her terribly. She'd told herself it didn't matter what they thought of her. But it did. This was her home. She was innocent.

"Get up." Rough hands closed like talons over her right biceps. Nat tried to lunge away, but Hunt was stronger and yanked her to her feet, forced her around to face him.

"Get your hands off me." She tried to make her voice sound authoritative, but it was shaking like a piano wire. Her entire body was trembling. And for the first time, she was truly afraid that he was going to harm her. That not a soul in the crowd would step forward to stop him.

He shook her hard enough to whip her head back. "No one murders their own kid and gets away with it." Spittle flew from his lips as he snarled at her. "Not in this town."

"Get your hands off of her. *Now!*"

Nat looked over to see Nick Bastille drill through the crowd like an icebreaker cutting through a frozen sea. She caught a glimpse of eyes that were black with fury. A mouth that was pulled into a nasty snarl. Hands that were clenched into fists. He didn't bother with a second warning. One instant Hunt was shaking her hard enough to jar her teeth, the next he was lying on the floor, blood pulsing from his nose. Nick pointed at him with a steady hand. "If you want to walk out of here under your own power, don't get up."

chapter
8

THERE WERE A WHOLE SLEW OF REASONS WHY NICK shouldn't get into a barroom brawl, the most pressing being his status as a parolee. One wrong move, and his ass would be back in Angola faster than he could call his lawyer. Hunt Ratcliffe had been drinking half the night. God only knew what else he'd been doing to arrive at the altered state he'd achieved. People got stupid when they were pumped up on adrenaline and booze, especially wealthy jackasses who didn't have the good sense to know when to quit.

But there was no way Nick could stand by and do nothing while some juiced-up bully pounded on a woman half his size.

Ratcliffe scrambled to his feet. "You jailbird son of a bitch. Do you have any idea who you're fucking with?"

"I know exactly who I'm fucking with, and I'll put you on the floor if you so much as lay a hand on a woman in this place again. You getting the gist of what I'm telling you, Hunt?"

"You don't know what you're getting in the middle of." Ratcliffe blotted the blood from his nose with his sleeve. "You're protecting a murderer."

"Touch her again, and I'll make you regret it," Nick said.

"That bitch came in here looking for trouble."

"You appear to be the one looking for a fight."

"She murdered my brother." He gave Nat a killing look. "Murdered her own kid."

A murmur went through the crowd. Nick hadn't been expecting him to say that. He sure as hell wasn't expecting Nat Jennings to go on the offensive. But one minute she was standing quietly, the next she was launching herself at Ratcliffe.

"That's a lie!" she cried.

Nick managed to snag her around the waist an instant before Ratcliffe would have nailed her with his fist. "Cut it out," he growled, pulling her back and shoving her away so that she was out of reach of the other man. "Stay put."

He swung around to face Ratcliffe in time to see the other man throw a punch. Nick tried to duck, but he wasn't fast enough and a hard-as-steel fist slammed into his jaw. He heard bone crack, found himself hoping it was Ratcliffe's knuckles and not his own teeth. Pain zinged from his jaw to his sinuses.

Shaking off dizziness, Nick went into a boxer's stance, keeping his weight on the balls of his feet, his fists high and loose. Ratcliffe threw another punch, but Nick was ready and went in low. He landed a quick uppercut to the chin. A neat jab to the jaw. Ratcliffe threw another wild punch. Nick lurched back, felt the *whoosh* of air, then followed up with a power punch to the stomach. Ratcliffe doubled over, retched, went to his knees, and spewed vomit.

The sharp crack of electricity silenced the crowd. "*C'est assez!* That's enough!"

Nick looked up to see Mike Pequinot hobble to the outer perimeter of the crowd, a souped-up cattle prod in one hand, an aluminum bat in the other. "The next man who throws a punch loses his teeth." His gaze landed on Ratcliffe. "Hit the road."

Looking thoroughly humiliated, Ratcliffe spat blood on the floor and struggled to his feet. He glared at Nick for an instant, then cast a final look at Nat before heading for the door. "This isn't over," he muttered.

Pequinot raised the bat. "It is tonight, rich boy." He motioned toward the door. "Unless you want us to carry you out, I suggest you make use of the door."

The crowd began to disperse. Someone fed coins into the jukebox, and a popular Cajun number began to rattle the speakers. Nick looked around to see Pequinot limp back to the bar with the bat and cattle prod in hand. A few feet away, Nat Jennings had sunk into a chair, looking shell-shocked.

Nick found it odd that not a single man in the bar had gone to her aid when Ratcliffe slugged her. Even among drunks in the most disreputable of establishments, there was an unwritten code of honor that precluded a man hitting a woman—even if the woman had it coming. Considering Ratcliffe's accusations—the murder of her husband and son—Nick wondered if maybe Nat Jennings had had this coming.

But even after the crazy, hurtful things she'd said to him earlier in the day, some smidgen of decency wouldn't let him walk away without making sure she was all right. Scooping her purse off the floor, he crossed to her. "Did anyone ever tell you, you have a real penchant for pissing people off?"

"It's a gift," she muttered.

He held out the bag. "I think you dropped this."

She looked up at him, and for the first time he noticed the bruise on her cheekbone. It hadn't yet bloomed, but he could tell it was going to be a doozy when it did. Damn, he hated seeing a pretty face like hers messed up.

Rising, she looped the bag over her shoulder. "I guess I should thank you for stepping in."

Nick shrugged. "Ratcliffe is a mean drunk."

"He's mean when he's sober."

"You want me to call the cops?"

She shook her head, keeping her bruised cheek turned away, as if hoping he wouldn't notice. "No thanks."

"That cheek is going to swell if you don't ice it."

"I'm fine. I just . . . want to go home."

He was nearly a foot taller than she was and found himself tilting his head in an effort to get a better look at her face. She wasn't making it easy, so he reached out and gently put his fingers beneath her chin. "Let me have a look."

Closing her eyes briefly, she allowed him to lift her chin and tilt her head toward the light. The flesh was just beginning to color. An abrasion the size of a quarter stood out in stark red against her pale complexion. Nick growled low in his throat. "You ought to press charges against that jackass."

"I threw the first punch."

"It doesn't matter. You're a woman. He outweighs you by eighty pounds."

She eased from his grip, then stepped back. "I don't think that matters when your last name is Ratcliffe."

Nick couldn't argue with that. The Ratcliffes were Bellerose's wealthiest residents. Elliott Ratcliffe had made millions on the televangelist circuit. He had three sons, Hunter, Travis, and Ward. From what Nick had gathered, this woman was Ward Ratcliffe's widow, and evidently the family made no bones about blaming her for his death.

"Besides, the cops hate me in this town," she said.

"You, too, huh?" He smiled.

She didn't smile back. "Look, thanks for helping me out. I'm sure it didn't earn you any points. But I've got to go."

"Not everyone in this town gives a damn about points."

She just shook her head, and started for the door.

Nick knew he should let her go. Judging from what he'd seen and heard, Nat Jennings was not a woman he wanted to know. But something he'd seen in the depths of her eyes wouldn't let him allow her to walk away. Not when she was trembling and bruised and trying her damnedest to look unaffected.

"Wait," he heard himself say. "I'll make an ice pack."

She stopped and glanced at him over her shoulder, her expression perplexed. "You don't have to be nice to me."

"No one ever accused me of being nice, *chere*."

For an instant he thought she might smile, but she only continued to stare at him with those sad, haunted eyes. She had the kind of eyes that told a man things. The kind of eyes that wouldn't lie even if she wanted them to. Right now those eyes were telling him she desperately needed someone to be kind to her. Nick didn't think he was the man for the job; he wasn't even sure he remembered how. But it didn't look like anyone else was going to step forward, so he motioned toward the kitchen.

"Come on." Taking her arm, he guided her past the bar and pushed through the double doors, keenly aware of the eyes following their retreat.

The kitchen was a galley-style room with a single greasy window, a porcelain stove circa 1950, a refrigerator with a crease marring its facade, and a stainless steel sink that leaked like a sieve. There was no place to sit, very little room to turn around, but the lighting was good.

Nick cleared a small section of the scuffed Formica counter, wiped it down with his towel, and patted it. "Up you go."

"This really isn't necessary."

"Sure it is."

"It's just a bruise."

"On a very pretty face."

She looked away, but not before he saw that he'd embarrassed her, and for some inexplicable reason that charmed the hell out of him.

When she made no move to heft herself onto the counter, he put his hands beneath her armpits and lifted her. She was amazingly light and not for the first time he realized how slightly she was built, how soft she was, how good she smelled.

Then she was at eye level, and beneath the bright light he got his first good look at her up close and personal. Her gaze met his, and for an instant he felt it like the whisper touch of skin against skin. She had large, fragile eyes that made him think of high-grade turquoise. A deep bluish green that was as bright as the Gulf of Mexico on a sunny day. Within the depths of her gaze, he saw the remnants of a dozen emotions, each tempered by the resolve not to let a single one escape her control.

Realizing he was staring, Nick shook himself and stepped back, taken aback by his reaction to her. He wanted to believe his heart rate was up because it had been six long years since he'd been this close to a woman. But the hard tug he felt low in his gut was more complex than simple attraction, and it went deeper than lust.

He walked to the freezer and proceeded to put crushed ice into a plastic bag. "So what are you doing at The Blue Gator all by yourself on a Friday night, *chere*?"

"I was looking for you, actually."

"Must be my lucky night," he said dryly.

"I guess that depends on how you feel about what I told you earlier today."

Remembering, he felt a stir of anger. "If it has anything to do with my son, I'll take a pass." He wrapped the bag in a clean towel and walked over to her. "Tilt your head back."

When she didn't acquiesce, he put his fingertips beneath her chin and angled her head toward him. She winced when he set the bag of ice against her cheek. "Hurt?"

"What do you think?"

"You know, *chere,* for such a little thing, you have one hell of a right jab. You been taking lessons from Mike Tyson, or what?"

Her mouth twitched, and Nick felt the knot of tension at the base of his neck begin to loosen. It was the first time he'd seen her smile, and the simple beauty of it touched a place inside him that hadn't been touched for what seemed like an eternity. Her lips were full and looked very soft. He wanted to touch them with his fingertips. Maybe lean forward and set his mouth against hers . . .

"I hope he doesn't press charges," she said.

"Bellerose is a small Southern town. He'll be a laughing stock if he does."

"That's a double standard."

"Life is full of double standards. On the rare occasion when one works in your favor, take advantage of it."

"I'll try to remember that next time I get the urge to slug someone."

He thought about the things he'd heard between her and Ratcliffe, the things he'd heard from others in the crowd, the things she'd said to him earlier in the day, and for the life of him he couldn't reconcile any of them with the woman sitting on the counter looking like she didn't have a friend in the world.

"So why does Ratcliffe hate you so much?" he asked.

She closed her eyes briefly. When she opened them, the sadness was back. "I'm his brother's widow."

"Being a widow is hardly your fault." He was still holding the ice to her cheek. His other hand was beneath her jaw, and he could feel her tightening up.

"Ward . . . was killed three years ago. Murdered. Along with . . . my son."

He could feel her trembling now. Minute tremors he wouldn't have been aware of had he not been touching her. Her breathing had quickened ever so slightly. He could tell she was trying very hard to control her reaction. But Nick knew enough about people to see how profoundly the subject had upset her.

"Hunt thinks I did it," she finished.

"Why does he think that?"

"Because I was there. The night it happened."

"That doesn't make you guilty."

"It made me a suspect."

"Officially? Or in the eyes of the Ratcliffes?"

"I was arrested, so I guess that would make it official."

Surprise rippled through him. Simultaneously, a voice in the back of his head reminded him that he didn't want to know this woman. That she could very well be guilty of what she'd been accused of. But Nick knew firsthand that Lady Justice didn't always get it right. "So there was evidence against you? What?"

"My prints were on the knife. . . ." She looked everywhere but into his eyes. "I can't talk about this."

Nick didn't press her. The last thing he wanted to contend with on top of that pretty face and curvy body was tears. She was too close. Too sad. Far too soft. And he'd always had a weakness for troubled, vulnerable women. . . .

When her gaze finally met his, her expression was fierce. "I didn't do it."

"But the Ratcliffes already tried and convicted you," he said.

"They need someone to blame."

"And the rest of the town?"

"I think you already know the answer to that."

Nick knew narrow-mindedness wasn't reserved for small towns. But he'd lived in Bellerose long enough to know people liked to label other people. He knew a label had been put on him. A label that didn't fit any better than the ones he'd heard thrown at this woman tonight.

"This town isn't exactly Mayberry for you," he said. "Why did you come back?"

Her gaze met his. "Because the bastard who murdered my husband and son got away with murder. Because he's still in this town."

Not wanting the subject of his own son to arise again, Nick raised his hand. "I've heard enough."

"I don't think you have."

He removed the ice from her face, set it on the counter and stepped back. "You can take the ice pack with you."

"Mr. Bastille, please listen to me."

Turning away from her, he started toward the door. He wasn't sure where he was going. Away from her. Away from those sad, haunting eyes. A body he wanted to touch. And words he didn't want to hear.

"You said you'd listen to me if I found a witness," she called out.

He stopped. For an interminable moment he stood there, facing the doors that would take him back to the bar and away from words he knew would only rip open a wound that had barely begun to heal. Slowly he turned and strode toward her, stopping halfway there. "Let me give you some advice, *chere*," he ground out. "Don't fuck with me about my son."

She slid from the counter and started toward him. Her eyes were fierce and direct. Not the eyes of a liar, he thought, and that scared him. To consider the possibility that his son had been murdered was simply unthinkable. . . .

"I have a witness," she said.

"I don't believe you."

"Let me prove it to you." She stopped a foot away from him, her eyes clear and beseeching.

"Are you trying to tell me someone saw . . . what happened to Brandon?"

"That's exactly what I'm telling you."

"Why the hell didn't they come forward? Why didn't they talk to the police?"

"I can't answer that."

He choked out a sound of incredulity and frustration. "Can't or won't?"

"Look, you said you would listen to me if I came up with a witness."

He stared hard at her, trying to read her, trying even harder to understand what she could possibly hope to accomplish by lying. "What the hell do you want from me?"

"Come to my house. Tomorrow morning."

"I'll meet with you on one condition."

"What condition?"

"I want to talk to this witness one on one. No games. No fucking around. You got that?"

"I got it."

For several interminable seconds they stared at each other. Then, as if realizing her business was finished here, she brushed by him and started toward the door.

He watched her walk away, aware that his heart was pounding, that her words had upset him despite his efforts not to let them. And like a fool, he was already looking forward to seeing her again.

HE WATCHES HER FROM THE SHADOWS BENEATH THE stand of live oaks at the edge of the bayou. He is as silent and deadly as the alligators that slither along the murky river bottom and mud flats. He is patient, but the bloodlust torments him. A hunger that drives him to commit unspeakable acts. Acts he has been able to conceal through cunning and brilliance and a conscience that has ceased to exist since long before he made his first kill.

He can't believe the bitch is back. He can't believe she's asking questions and opening old wounds just when they'd started to heal. What can she possibly hope to accomplish after all this time?

The answer eludes him. But he knows Nat Jennings is a threat. A threat that must be dealt with swiftly and permanently and without raising suspicion. He has worked too hard to risk having his secret uncovered now.

The parking lot is nearly empty as she crosses to her car. He watches her, taking in the long strides, liking the way she moves. Stupid, crazy bitch. He could have the knife buried in her throat before she even hears his approach. Before she can scream. She would be helpless against the knife. And his troubles would be over forever.

He imagines the dark spray of blood. The warmth of it on his hands. The copper smell in his nostrils. The terror on her face. Her energy pouring into him. The thought of killing her arouses him. His senses heighten to a fever pitch. The rush of blood to his groin is intense. His sex grows heavy and full and the hunger becomes an unbearable pain.

Come to me. . . .

The night throbs with the symphony of the bayou. The rhythmic chirp of crickets and frogs, the lap of dark water against ancient cypress trunks, the quick slide of a reptilian body over mud. Music as primal as death.

His heart is pounding, a mix of hunger and rage and dark anticipation he feels all the way to his bowels. Sweating, he slaps at the mosquitoes. Feeling the stickiness of blood on his fingers, he brings them to his mouth and suckles, enjoying the salty tang. The heady rush of energy.

He watches her climb into the car, the taste of blood metallic on his tongue. He imagines her blood in his mouth. The thought excites him. And even though the night is muggy and hot, he begins to shake.

He wants to believe it is anticipation making his muscles quiver and twitch. But deep inside he feels the fear encroaching, stealing his enjoyment, his power, and he hates her for it. Fear is the one emotion he cannot allow, the one thing he will not tolerate. Fear equals weakness, and he has sworn that he will never be weak or helpless or humiliated again. He has power now. And the power is the only thing that will save him.

He watches the taillights of her car fade into the night, and the hunger is alive inside him. Removing the pocketknife from its sheath, he opens the blade and sets it against the underside of his forearm where no one will notice a cut. Just one, he promises himself. He slices the flesh and watches the black spread of blood. The pain arouses him. His mouth waters as the metallic smell fills his nostrils. He sets his mouth against the wound and begins to lap.

Nat Jennings has no idea with whom she's dealing. He will stop her. Only this time, he will stop her for good.

chapter
9

NICK KNEW BETTER THAN TO PASS THE TIME THINK-
ing about Nat Jennings. The woman was trouble any way you
cut it. She had it written all over that curvy little body of hers
in big, bold letters. A more cautious man might have heeded
the warning. But Nick had never claimed to be cautious, especially when it came to women.

He wanted to believe his interest in her was purely physical
in nature. After all, he was a red-blooded American male and
hadn't been with a woman for six long years. That was more
than enough time to wear down a man's resolve to stay the
hell away from trouble. But that resolve hadn't kept him from
looking. It hadn't kept him from liking what he saw. It sure as
hell hadn't kept him from wanting to do a lot more than just
look. . . .

But while he couldn't deny the hard tug of lust every time
he laid eyes on her, he knew he wasn't going to do anything
about it. Nick had enough personal baggage of his own without taking on someone else's. Nat Jennings was lugging
around a ton of it. The last thing he needed in his life was a
troubled, sexy-as-sin female with a boatload of demons to
slay. He could barely handle his own these days.

"Hell of a night, eh?"

Nick looked up to see Mike Pequinot limp to the cash

register and remove a thick wad of bills. "Not bad for a dive a stone's throw from the bayou."

It was almost midnight, and The Blue Gator had been winding down for the last hour. Two men were still at the back, shooting pool. Another man in faded coveralls was slumped at a table smoking a hand-rolled cigarette and nursing a beer. A haunting Peter Gabriel tune keened from the speakers.

"Must have been your night for crazy women," Pequinot said with a grin. "First that polecat ex-wife of yours, then the Jennings girl."

Nick ignored the reference to Tanya. "What's Nat Jennings's story?"

Pequinot shot him a knowing look. "She might be good to look at, but you don't want to get tangled up with her."

"I'm not going to get tangled up with anyone."

"If it's a woman you're wantin', I can hook you up—"

"I don't want a hooker, Mike."

"Just askin'."

"So are you going to tell me about Nat Jennings, or am I going to have to ask someone else?"

"Ti parele! Si! Laisee mon te dire!" Talk about. "She's been a favorite topic down at the diner ever since it happened."

"She kill them, or what?" Nick asked.

Pequinot rolled a giant shoulder. "Folks say she did. But I don't know. You know, people like to talk. But she don't look like no killer to me." He laughed. "Man killer, maybe."

"So what happened?"

"Murders happened about three years ago. Cops get a 911 call in the wee hours. Deputy arrives to find her husband the minister shot dead and her seven-year-old son's throat slashed. From what I hear it was a hell of a goddamn scene. Cops puking and what not. That girl was hysterical and covered with blood. She'd been cut, too, but not like them. She claimed she heard something, went downstairs and found them in the kitchen. That the intruder jumped her.

"But the cops strung together a different version. They suspected she orchestrated the whole thing. Turns out her minister husband was having an affair with his secretary. Nat Jennings was in line for a five-hundred-thousand-dollar life insurance policy. Cops had motive. They had her fingerprints on the knife. They got a doc out of 'Nawlins to say her wounds could have been self-inflicted. She claimed the intruder had come in through her son's bedroom window. But the knife that had been used to cut the screen was her own. And the screen had been cut from the inside, not the outside."

"Pretty damning evidence," Nick said.

"I'll say. Whole damn town was divided. I mean, you see that sweet face of hers and you think she couldn't possibly have done it. But you look at the evidence, and you're not so sure."

"So how did she get out of it?"

"She didn't, really. Alcee Martin arrested her the day they put her husband and baby in the ground. Cops pounded her all day and half the night. When they finally put her in a cage, she took a piece of tile and cut her wrists. Got the artery, too. Almost died, that one. Poor Alcee found her, carried her to his car, and drove her to the hospital hisself. But she lost so much blood she had some kind of stroke and went into a coma. I swear, Alcee ain't been the same since. He went above and beyond to make things right when he testified 'fore the grand jury."

It was the first time Nick had heard the story, and it shocked him. "Jesus."

"Can't figure why she's back, though. If I was her, Bellerose is the last place I'd want to be."

Nick thought about that. For a moment he considered confiding in Pequinot about the alleged witness she claimed to have with regard to his own son's death, but decided against it.

"If you want to go on home, Rita and I can close up."

Nick *was* tired. He'd been working nights at the bar and getting up at dawn, trying to work the farm back into shape. There was hay to be cut and baled, but the baler was on its last leg. He'd be lucky if he could get the damn thing running. . . .

He'd just stepped out from behind the bar when the door swung open. A quiver of uneasiness went through him when Chief of Police Alcee Martin strode in looking like someone had just killed his dog. His uniform was military neat. His boots polished to a high sheen. His Glock tucked neatly into its glossy leather holster.

His gaze swept the room, stopping on Pequinot, who'd stopped counting cash and looked up. "Mike."

"Alcee," Pequinot drawled. "Get you a beer?"

"Not tonight." Martin looked around the bar, his gaze lingering on Nick an instant too long before going back to Pequinot. "I got a missing child on my hands. I wanted to let y'all know. We're putting together search parties. We can use all the help we can get."

Pequinot came around the bar, his expression concerned. "Whose kid?"

"Becky and Jim Arnaud's boy. Ricky. I think he's their oldest, seven or eight years old."

"Le Bon Dieu mait la main." God help. "How long's he been gone?"

"Since about eight o'clock this evenin'. He was visiting little Jamie Beckett. Usually cuts through old man Gray's cornfield on the way home. Mama says he's always home before dark. But he never made it." Martin's gaze landed on Nick. "Gray's place is right next to your daddy's farm."

Another wave of uneasiness swept through Nick. Six years ago he would have laughed at the suspicion on Alcee Martin's face. But experience had taught him that Lady Justice was not only blind, but cruel.

"Can you account for your whereabouts this evening?" Martin asked.

Pequinot put his hand down hard on the bar. *"C'est tout du dregaille."* That's all trash.

Martin looked uncomfortable. "I gotta ask, Mike. He's an ex-con. People are going to want to know."

Fury swept through Nick at the implication, a blowtorch burning him from the inside out. *A child. Christ.* "You know I didn't have a damn thing to do with that boy's disappearance."

"For chrissake, Alcee, Nick was here behind the bar all night."

Martin stared hard at him. Nick stared back, aware that his blood was pumping hard. A lost child. How could anyone think he had anything to do with that?

The chief looked away first. "A couple of my deputies are setting up a grid search. Bob Boulee is going to bring in his bloodhound. We got one four-wheeler. Yancy is firing up the airboat for the swamp. A couple of guys on horseback are already out. The more people we have looking for that boy, the better our chances of finding him."

"The bayou is no place for a kid," Pequinot said.

Nick knew firsthand just how dangerous the bayou could be for a little boy. The pain of that never left him. It haunted his dreams, dominated his thoughts when he was alone. Some days the loss was more than he could bear.

"I know the bayou." Nick shot Martin a hard look. "Unless you have a problem with me, I'd like to help."

Martin stared at him. "You got ten minutes to get over to the police department 'fore we head out."

Alcee Martin tipped his hat and walked out.

"See you tomorrow, Mike." Nick tossed his towel on the bar and followed.

chapter
10

THE BELLEROSE POLICE DEPARTMENT WAS LIT UP like a football stadium when Nick arrived. A dozen four-wheel drive trucks were lined up on the street. Two men on horseback chatted with a police officer, the horses' steel shoes clanging against the asphalt. In the bed of a pickup truck, a saggy-faced bloodhound bayed at a three-quarter moon.

The people of Bellerose had turned out in force to look for little Ricky Arnaud. The boy's parents were well liked. Jim worked at the mill. Becky was a high school teacher in nearby Covington. As Nick took the sidewalk to the front door, he found himself thinking about another lost little boy and wondered if as many of the townsfolk had turned out for him.

He shoved open the doors and walked into the building. Heads turned toward him, but there were no greetings. Nick didn't care. When it came to finding a lost child, even the outcasts were expected to help.

Someone had taped a terrain map to the display board next to the reception desk. Beside it, the picture of a little boy with fat cheeks and freckles smiled impishly at the crowd of people who would be searching for him.

A hushed silence fell as Alcee Martin stepped up to the desk. "I want to thank all of you for turning out tonight to help us find Ricky Arnaud." Picking up a ruler, he used it to point out the photograph of the little boy. "Ricky is eight years old. Brown hair. About four feet, two inches tall. He was last seen wearing a purple T-shirt, blue jeans, and red sneakers."

He slid the tip of the ruler to the map. "The search area is marked in yellow." He turned to his audience. "Danny Lee?"

A hand went up in the crowd. "Right here."

"I want y'all on horseback to take the trail along Dove Creek. Becky was telling me Ricky liked to stop off at the creek occasionally to cool off."

"Gotcha, Alcee." A man in a western hat and boots sauntered out the door.

Martin scanned the crowd. "Where's Bob Boulee?"

Another hand shot up. "Yup."

"Bob, a couple of officers are going to take you out to old man Gray's property. Becky brought us one of Ricky's socks so you can scent your hound."

"We're on it."

Martin turned his attention back to the map. "If the rest of you want to help, you'll need to stay away from the area marked here in orange. We don't want to mess up the scent trail. My deputy Matt Duncan is going to set up a loose grid search on the other side of Dove Creek. We don't think Ricky ventured too far, but the more ground we can cover, the better."

He turned and set his pen against the map. "I want everyone to park at the Dove Creek Bridge here. Take the path to the water, and spread out from there on the west side of the creek. We've got a couple of dozen people. Stay within shouting distance of each other. Take at least one flashlight and insect repellent if you have it. Those damn skeeters are as big as crows down by the water. I don't have to remind anyone that time is of the essence."

The impromptu meeting ended abruptly with the sound of a woman's anguished keening. Nick looked over to see Becky Arnaud standing next to her husband, looking as if she were about to collapse. Her face was blotchy and red and wet with tears. "Please find my baby," she sobbed. "He's out there all by himself. He's afraid of the dark. Please help us find him."

"He's afraid of the dark."

The words slashed with unexpected ferocity, and made Nick think of his own little boy. Brandon had been just two years old when Nick went to prison. He'd been only five when he'd drowned. That Nick hadn't been there to protect him tormented him every hour of every day. How terribly frightened Brand must have been when he'd realized he'd ventured into deep water. . . .

Suddenly, Nat Jennings's words danced in the back of his mind:

"Brandon's death wasn't an accident. . . . your son was murdered. . . . the man who took our children from us is going to kill again if someone doesn't stop him."

Even though the room was plenty cool, Nick felt a cold sweat break out on the back of his neck. Had Brand's death been an accident? Or was there some merit to her assertions? Had little Ricky Arnaud become lost? Or was something more sinister in the works?

The unspeakable questions taunted him with agonizing possibilities . . . possibilities he knew he could no longer ignore. As much as it destroyed him to consider it, Nick was going to have to talk to Nat about his son. He was going to have to find out what she knew, if anything. Then he was going to have to decide what to do about it.

Holding that thought, he turned away from the picture of the little boy and started for the door.

THE NIGHTMARE CAME TO HER WITH THE VIOLENCE of the storm. Rain lashed at the windows as she made her way down the hall toward her son's room. Lightning flashed like a strobe as she pushed open the door and peered inside. A frisson of uneasiness went through her when she found the bed empty, the Spiderman coverlet turned down. A few feet away the curtains billowed in the breeze coming in through the window.

Aware that her heart was beating too fast, she took the stairs to the darkened living room. Thunder crashed as she crossed the living room and peered into the kitchen. She saw the outline of glossy oak cabinets. Polished granite countertops. The curtains fluttering in the window above the sink.

Her heart slammed hard against her ribs when she spotted Kyle lying motionless on the floor. For the span of several heartbeats she stared at her son's form, unable to get her mind around the picture of her seven-year-old little boy lying silent and still on the cold tile in his teddy bear pajamas.

"Kyle?"

She smelled the blood before she saw it. Coppery and warm and as black as melted tar in the semidarkness. Horror and disbelief screamed through her. She could feel it tearing through her body with the violence of a hollow point bullet.

Her vision tunneled on her son, so tiny and pale and bleeding out right before her eyes. The pool of blood seemed to cover half of the floor. In a distant corner of her mind she wondered how such a little body could bleed so much. . . .

"Kyle!"

Then she was rushing to her child, her breaths bursting from her throat in ragged gasps. In her peripheral vision she saw Ward sprawled near the cooking island. Another wave of horror exploded in her brain when she saw that his pajamas were covered with blood.

"Ward! Ohmigod! Ohmigod!"

She dropped to her knees beside her son's prone form, her brain stumbling through basic first aid, knowing deep inside that it was already too late. "Kyle! Oh, baby, talk to mommy!"

She heard movement behind her. A brutal punch of terror took her breath when she realized whomever had done this was still in the house. Nat didn't know how she got to her feet, but the next thing she knew she was standing, shaking, dizzy with horror. She could hear herself breathing hard. The razor edge of panic cutting her. Her pulse roaring like a tornado in her ears. Every beat of her heart was like a fist pounding her chest.

The intruder moved toward her. She saw dark clothes. A ski mask. Light from the window flittered like blue ice on something in his hand, and she realized he had a knife.

He's going to kill me, she thought and the terror of that paralyzed her.

"Bitch," he snarled and lunged.

Nat snapped out of her stupor just as the blade came down. Screaming, she raised her arms to protect herself. But at the last instant he changed tactics and went in low, slashing from left to right. She tried to get out of the way, but wasn't fast enough and the blade sliced across her belly. An animal sound tore from her throat as the shock of pain registered. The sensation of heat just below her ribs. The realization that he'd cut her.

Reeling backward, she crashed against the counter. "Get away from me!"

The knife went up. Nat reached behind her, grabbed the coffeemaker, dragged it across the counter and flung it at him. The carafe flew from its nest and hit the stove. Glass shattered. The coffeemaker clattered to the floor.

She lunged toward the phone on the built-in desk, but he beat her to it and ripped the cord from the wall. Remembering her cell phone recharging on the counter, she bolted past him. He tried to grab her, she felt the scrape of his fingertips on her arm, heard her robe tear as he snagged the fabric, but she broke free and raced to the counter.

Shock punched her at the sight of Ward's revolver. She pounced on the gun. The wood grip was cold and rough against her palm. She brought it up as she swung it around, leveled it at the figure standing in the doorway.

Choking out animal sounds, she pulled the trigger. Once. Twice. But the only sound that met her was the hollow click of the hammer against the firing pin.

"No!" She hurled the pistol at him and darted toward the cell phone. Before she'd gone two steps, vise-like fingers closed around her right biceps, jerked her around to face him. The knife arced, the blade glinting blue. White-hot pain flashed from her left breast to her navel.

The knowledge that she'd been cut shocked and horrified. She felt the warmth of blood on her tee shirt. The material clinging wetly to her. The metallic stench filling her nostrils.

Oh, dear God, he's going to hack me to death . . . !

She tried to fight, but for the first time in her life she was paralyzed with fear. The knife came down again, and she felt the numbing pain of a razor slash on her belly. She tried to use her knee, but her bare foot slipped in her own blood, and then she was falling. . . .

Nat screamed in horror and rage as she went down. She

couldn't believe this was happening. Violent crime didn't happen in Bellerose. . . .

Then she was on her hands and knees, crawling away from her attacker. Whimpering like a beaten dog, she made it to the cooking island and used the cabinet door to pull herself to her feet. She looked around, expecting him to rush her at any moment. But the kitchen was empty and silent.

"Oh, God. Oh, God!" Choking back sobs, Nat stumbled to the phone and punched 911.

Taking the phone with her, she dropped to her knees at her son's side, touched his shoulder. "Kyle," she whispered. "Oh, baby. Mama's here. I'm here." Gently, she turned her son onto his back. "Please, God, oh, please let him be all right. . . ."

Kyle's eyes were open, and for a moment Nat expected him to look up at her and smile the way he'd done a thousand times before. But when she pressed her fingers to the carotid artery, there was no pulse.

She heard a voice on the other end of the phone.

And then Nat Jennings began to scream.

Nat woke to her own scream. It was a terrible sound in the silence of the house. She found herself standing in total darkness, sobbing and breathless, her body slicked with sweat. She was cold to the bone and trembling violently. She could still feel the tight grip of terror. The ache of grief that never seemed to leave her.

"Just a dream," she whispered.

Pressing her hand against her wildly pounding heart, she stumbled in the darkness, bumped into a wall, found a light switch, flipped it on. She blinked, momentarily blinded. She was standing in the dining room. The quilt she'd dragged from the sofa lay in a heap at her feet. A magic marker was clutched in her left hand. She stared at it, dread whipping through her. Then she slowly raised her eyes to the wall.

Monster has ricky. Wood house

A sob escaped her as she stumbled back. The marker clattered to the floor. Nat stared at the words, wanting desperately to believe she hadn't written them. But she knew there was no one else in the house.

Monster has ricky. Wood house

The childlike scrawl was stark and black against the white paint. She didn't know who Ricky was, but she knew he was in danger. She knew the killer had him. . . .

Blinking back tears, she glanced at the clock on the stove to see that it was not yet four A.M. The dead of night, she thought and suddenly felt very alone and very much afraid.

"I'm going to stop you," she whispered, trying hard to ignore the little voice in her head telling her she couldn't, that she wasn't strong enough, that no one would believe her. And for the first time since leaving the hospital, she thought about giving up. She could go to New Orleans and let her mother take care of her. She could leave this town and the horrors of that hellish night behind and never look back.

But Nat knew there was a killer out there. She knew he was going to kill again. There was no way she could turn her back. Or let the son of a bitch get away with what he'd done.

Pulling out a dining room chair, she collapsed into it and put her face in her hands. She would get through this. She'd gotten through other tough nights.

"You're going to be okay," she whispered.

Raising her head, she looked at the words scrawled on the wall.

Monster has ricky. Wood house

It wasn't the first time she'd sleepwalked, but the experience never ceased to frighten her. Waking to a nightmare was bad enough. Waking to find that you'd written a message from the dead was infinitely more terrifying.

Rising, she rose and scooped the quilt from the floor, and carried it to the sofa. The pillow she'd been using was on the floor, so she picked it up and sank onto the sofa, curling her legs beneath her.

Nat nearly jumped out of her skin when the doorbell rang. Alarmed, she crossed to the foyer and checked the peephole.

Surprise flashed at the sight of Nick Bastille standing on her porch.

Stepping away from the door, she pressed her hand to her stomach, her mind racing. What was he doing on her porch at four o'clock in the morning? Had the anger she'd seen earlier in the day reached its flash point, and he'd come to take it out on her?

But in some small corner of her mind it registered that he didn't look angry or out of control or even particularly dangerous at the moment. And on some elemental level, she knew why he'd come to her in the middle of the night. She knew he wanted information about his son. And she knew she was going to open the door and let him in, despite the alarms blaring in her head.

Quickly, she wiped the tears from her cheeks, then glanced down at the faded denim shirt and boxer shorts she wore. The ensemble looked like hell, but it was decent enough to answer the door, considering the hour. Taking a deep breath to steady herself, she opened the door. His gaze met hers with an intensity that unnerved her immediately. "I was driving by and saw the light."

She didn't believe him, but she didn't close the door. "What do you want?"

"You told me there's a witness who knows what happened to my boy. You can't drop a bomb like that and expect me to stay away."

She studied him, trying to gauge his frame of mind, but his expression was impossible to read as he stared back at her with shuttered eyes. "Come in."

He stepped into the foyer, and for the first time she noticed his appearance. A day's growth of whiskers darkened his jaw. His hair was mussed with a small twig tangled at the crown. He was wearing the same clothes from the night before. A white shirt with the sleeves rolled up and button-down jeans faded nearly white. Only now his clothes were rumpled and dirty. The shirt was torn at the sleeve and smeared with dirt. He looked haggard and wounded and tired to his bones.

An involuntary shudder moved through her when his eyes swept down the front of her. She felt his gaze like the caress of his fingertip against her skin. Suddenly painfully self-conscious, she folded her arms and stepped back. "You look like you've had a rough night."

"Looks like maybe I'm not the only one."

Nat could only imagine how she looked. Her face was blotchy from crying. Her hair was tangled and damp with sweat. The shirt was wrinkled. She told herself she didn't care. But even through the grief and turmoil of the last years, a tiny sliver of female vanity had survived.

"Did you get into a fight?" she asked, wondering if Hunt Ratcliffe had been waiting for him after he'd closed the bar.

"I was out with the search party."

"Search party?" The hairs at her nape prickled. "Who's missing?" she asked, but in some small corner of her mind, she already knew.

"Eight-year-old by the name of Ricky Arnaud. He disappeared while walking from his friend's farm back to his parents' place."

Ricky.

The name struck her like a punch, confirming her worst fear. Another child. Oh, dear God, no . . . Nausea climbed into her throat. Closing her eyes, Nat recalled Kyle's warning at the gas station the day before.

bad man take ricky. kill again. hurry.

The knowledge that she may have been able to prevent this was a crushing weight on her shoulders. Sick with fear for a child she'd never met, she pressed her hand to her stomach. She didn't even realize she'd stumbled back until her back met the wall. The impact snapped her back. When she opened her eyes, Nick was standing a couple of feet away, looking at her as if expecting her to collapse at any moment.

"Are you all right?"

Embarrassed, she nodded, but she was trembling inside. "Did you find the boy?" she asked.

He grimaced. "No."

She closed her eyes against the quick swipe of pain, terrified it was already too late for Ricky Arnaud.

"Maybe you ought to sit down," he said.

Because she didn't trust her voice, Nat turned away and started toward the kitchen. "I should have done something," she said. "I knew this could happen."

"What the hell are you talking about?"

"The boy," she snapped. "I should have found a way to stop it."

"Wait a minute. Are you telling me you know something about that missing boy?"

She heard him moving behind her, but she didn't stop. She was midway through the living room when the sight of the words written on the dining room wall stopped her cold. She stared at the heavy black letters against the crisp white paint, wondering how to explain them, wondering if he would believe her even if she could find the words.

"What the hell?"

Nat turned at the tone of his voice. He was staring at the words, his expression taut with shock. "Jesus." His gaze snapped to hers. "What the hell is that?"

She'd rehearsed this moment a thousand times in the last six months. Times when she stood in front of the mirror in her room at River Oaks Convalescent Home in Baton Rouge and explained to an open-minded and sympathetic Nick Bastille that since waking from a coma she had certain capabilities she hadn't had when she'd taken that jagged piece of tile to her wrists. But the man standing before her looked about as sympathetic as a gator right before it chomped down on an unsuspecting nutria.

"I was . . . sleepwalking. I wrote that just before you arrived."

"Sleepwalking?" His gaze flicked from the writing on the wall to her. "Why did you ask me the boy's name when, evidently, you already knew it? What the hell kind of twisted bullshit is this?"

"Nick, I didn't know his name. I swear."

"If you didn't know his name, how could you have written it on the wall?"

"I didn't write that," she stammered.

"You just told me you did."

"Yes, I wrote the words. Physically, I mean. But the message came from . . . somewhere else. From *someone* who's trying to help me." God, that sounded insane.

Incredulity filled his expression when his gaze shifted from the wall to her. "Look, I don't know what the hell's going on—"

"Sit down." She pulled out a chair, then rounded the dining room table and sank into the one across from it. "Please. We need to talk."

After an interminable moment, Nick took the chair. "Lady, my tolerance for bullshit is pretty low right now, so why don't you just tell me about that goddamn witness?"

Nat stared at him, her heart pounding. And suddenly she knew there was no way she could convince this man of what was happening to her simply by talking about it. An explanation wouldn't be enough. She was going to have to show him.

She'd never invited a trance writing session, and the prospect of inducing one now frightened her, particularly with Nick Bastille as her witness. The episodes were unsettling at best, terrifying if she wanted to be perfectly honest about it. When she entered a trance, even if it was only for a few seconds, she lost all sense of time and place and had no idea what was going on around her.

But if she wanted this man to believe her—if she wanted his help—she was going to have to convince him that his son's death had not been an accident. That there was a killer on the loose in Bellerose. That he had killed more than once. That he would kill again unless they stopped him . . .

Moving quickly, she rose and went to her briefcase on the counter where she removed a legal pad and pen. Behind her, she heard him sigh, an angry, impatient sound that told her he was losing patience. That she probably only had a couple of minutes before he got up and walked out.

"What the hell are you doing?" he asked.

"Do you believe in psychic phenomena, Mr. Bastille?"

"What?"

"I said, do you believe—"

"I heard you the first time," he snapped. "I just can't believe I'm hearing it."

"If you're skeptical—"

"Lady, I'm a hell of a lot more than skeptical. I think you're yanking my chain, and I'm an idiot for sitting here and letting you do it."

"I'm psychic," she said. "I've been psychic since emerging from a coma six months ago."

He was looking at her as if she were sprouting a second head right before his eyes. Then he surprised her by laughing. "Oh, for chrissake," he muttered.

"Hear me out."

Abruptly, he shoved away from the table and rose. "I've heard enough."

"You have to listen to me," she said.

"I don't have to do shit."

Panic descended when he started for the door. "Give me five minutes," she said. *"Please."*

Nick stopped, but didn't turn around. She saw impatience and fatigue in his stance. Then he slowly turned to face her, exasperation and puzzlement clear in his expression. Laughing harshly, he pinched the bridge of his nose between thumb and forefinger. "I don't believe this."

Nat took the chair. Her hand was shaking when she picked up the pen. She pulled in a deep, calming breath, then wrote: "What happened to Ricky Arnaud?"

"Jesus," he muttered.

Ignoring him, she wrote: "What happened to Brandon Bastille?"

Nick cursed. Out of the corner of her eye, she saw his hands clench into fists. She could feel the fury coming off him. It was like a storm, building into something awesome and dangerous. She closed her eyes, reaching, reaching . . .

But the uncertainties were interfering with her concentration. Maybe Kyle wouldn't come to her this time. Maybe she needed to be alone. Maybe this had been a very bad idea and she was a fool for trying. . . .

No, she thought, and conjured a mental image of Kyle. His sweet face, round and covered with freckles. A crooked haircut because he couldn't sit still in the barber's chair. The scrape on his nose from when he'd wrecked his bicycle in the driveway . . .

Vaguely, she was aware of Nick crossing to the door to leave. She was losing him. Damn. Damn. *Damn!* Desperation hammered at her, but she didn't open her eyes. She didn't break her focus. Something was starting to happen. She could feel the vibrations in the room. She could hear the buzz inside her head, a swarm of bees in a hive that was as big as a house. Then her peripheral vision turned to monochrome, as if she were looking through a black-and-white kaleidoscope. She heard Nick's voice but couldn't understand his words. She saw Kyle's face and a mother's joy overwhelmed her. She heard herself sob, felt the wetness of tears on her cheeks. Then his innocence and purity and love were inside her, soothing her shattered heart.

"Oh, sweet baby."

She wasn't sure if she'd spoken the words aloud or just thought them. But she knew Kyle had heard her because he smiled. She saw his little white teeth. Freckles on a turned-up nose. Her love for him was an ache deep inside. She wanted to squeeze him and kiss him, hold him tight and never let go. But even overcome with emotion, Nat knew she could not indulge, no matter how powerful the need.

I need your help.

I know, Mommy.

She was vaguely aware of her hand gripping the pen, the point moving across the pad, digging into the paper, tearing it.

Where is Ricky?

Heaven.

A sob choked out of her. *Where is his body?*

Bad man Took him.

Gatea mud.

She was blind and paralyzed now, her body gripped by a vacuum that was devoid of sound and sensation and light.

I need a sign from Brandon, sweetie.

Nothing.

Kyle?

Blue the one eyed bear.

What does that mean?

He'll know.

Honey, don't leave me. I miss you so much.

Be careful, Mommy.

Come back. . . .

She didn't want to let him go, fought to hold onto him. But as quickly as he'd come to her, Kyle was gone.

chapter
11

NICK HAD SEEN A LOT IN HIS THIRTY-FIVE YEARS. When he was in prison, he'd seen a fellow inmate have an epileptic seizure. One minute Danny "The Wolf " Parsons had been sitting at the lunchroom table cursing his girlfriend and complaining about the macaroni and cheese. The next minute he was lying on the floor with his eyes rolled back, his jaws clenched tight, his body as stiff as a board.

That hadn't been the only terrible thing Nick had seen while he'd been at the mercy of the state, and it took a lot to shake him up. The sight of Nat Jennings slumped in the chair with her eyes rolled back, her head lolling, and the pen clutched in her fist as if it were her lifeline to the world shook him up and then some.

Cursing under his breath, he dashed across the living room and set his hands gently on her shoulders. "Easy does it. Try to relax. I've got you."

He glanced down at the pad on the table. She was still clutching the pen with her left hand. Her hand moved across the paper as she scrawled crude words onto the page. Shock slammed through him when he saw that she was writing backward, from right to left. What the hell?

An instant later she went limp. She would have fallen out of the chair if he hadn't caught her beneath her arms and lowered her gently to the floor. "Easy. Jesus."

She wasn't convulsing, but he could feel the tremors ripping through her body. Not knowing what else to do, he knelt beside her and eased her onto her back. When she began to thrash, he pressed gently on her shoulders, holding her down.

"Nat? Can you hear me?"

After what seemed like an eternity, she stilled. She was breathing hard. Her forehead was slicked with sweat. He could feel the dampness coming through her shirt where he was touching her. Relief swept through him when her eyes fluttered open. They were glazed, but at least she was conscious.

"Just relax," he said. "You had a seizure."

"Not . . . a seizure."

"Just lay still. I'm going to call an ambulance."

She pushed his hands away. "No doctors."

"You had a seizure, for chrissake."

"I didn't have a seizure." She tried to sit up, but he gently pressed her back down.

"I don't think you have any idea what just happened."

"I know exactly what happened." Wiping tears from her cheeks with her sleeve, she slapped off his hands and struggled to a sitting position. "I've been videotaped, for God's sake."

"Videotaped?"

"My doctor did what's called video monitoring when I was in the hospital. I've been diagnosed with psychogenic epilepsy."

Even though he didn't have the slightest idea what psychogenic epilepsy was, Nick found himself inordinately relieved to hear there was a medical explanation for what had just happened.

"Are you okay?" he asked.

"I'm fine." Then, as if realizing the episode had alarmed him, she softened. "I'm sorry. I know it can be upsetting to witness. But I'm honestly okay."

She was sitting on the floor with her legs crossed, and for the first time he noticed her boxer shorts had ridden up, revealing the pretty flesh of her thighs. Nick stared at that dangerous stretch of skin. His response was primal and swift and inappropriate as hell.

Shifting to accommodate the heady rush of blood to his •
groin, he looked down at her, tried not to notice the way her
hair had fanned out over his hand. That her eyes were the color
of high-grade turquoise. That she wasn't wearing a bra . . .

"How often does this happen?" he asked.

"Depends. I'll go a week with nothing. Then it will happen
twice in one day."

"Don't you take medication?"

"There is no medication for what I have." Shaking off his
hands, she struggled to her feet, then used the chair back to
steady herself.

He stared at her, not quite sure how to help her or what to
do next.

She glanced at the legal pad on the table. "Give me the pad."

Baffled that she would want the pad at a moment like this,
Nick handed it to her. "I don't see what that has to do with—"

The words died in his throat when he spotted the words
scribbled on the paper. The first sentence was written in a
neat, slanted cursive. The remainder had been written in a
childlike scrawl.

Where is Ricky?

Heaven.
Bad man Took him.
Gatea mud.
Blue the one eyed bear

He stared at the last sentence, aware that his heart was
pounding, the hairs at his nape standing on end. Something
uncomfortable niggled at his brain, a warning telling him he
wasn't going to like what happened next.

She was looking down at the pad, her brows drawn together, then she raised her gaze to Nick's. "Did your son have
a pet or stuffed animal named Blue the one eyed bear?"

Something cold crept up the back of his neck. Something
deeper than a shiver. Something that shook him so hard inside
that for a moment he couldn't speak. "He had a hamster," Nick
said when he found his voice. "It had been born with only one
eye. Brand named it Blue." He cut her a hard look. "How did
you know that?"

"I didn't."

"You wrote that. How did you know about the goddamn hamster?"

"I didn't write that."

"You and I were the only people in the room, and I sure as hell didn't write it."

Intellectually, Nick knew there was no way his son had anything to do with what Nat had written. But he couldn't deny that it was very unlikely that she would know the name of Brand's first pet.

"My son wrote that," she said. "Through me."

He dragged his gaze away from the words to glare at her. "I don't know how the hell you managed this, but I don't believe that was written by some goddamn unholy intervention."

"This has been happening since I came out of the coma. It's called trance writing."

He stared at her. A pale beauty with turquoise eyes that reflected more pain than any human being should ever have to feel. He wondered if his own eyes reflected the same thing. If she recognized the kinship between them.

"I don't want any part of this," he said.

"You're already part of this."

"What the hell do you want from me?" he asked angrily.

The instant the words were out, he wished he hadn't said them. He knew what she was going to say. He knew it was something he didn't want to hear. But he also knew he wasn't going to refuse her.

"I need your help. I can't do this by myself."

"Do what?"

"Find the bastard who killed my son." Her nostrils flared. "Your son. And keep him from doing it again if we're not already too late."

Nick stared at her, disturbed by her words, incredulous that she believed them, downright alarmed because there was a part of him that was starting to believe her, too.

"I'm not buying this," he said. But the words held no conviction.

"You saw it with your own eyes, Nick."

"I saw you have a seizure."

She tapped her finger against the pad of paper. "This is my son's handwriting."

"That's bullshit. I saw you write it."

"He wrote it though me." Her expression turned fierce. "Before you write me off as insane, why don't you walk me through what you saw?"

"I don't know what you want me to say."

"Let's start with which hand I used."

"You used your left hand."

Nat tore off the top sheet. Holding the pen in her right hand, she wrote her name in a smooth, neat cursive. Next to it, she printed her name. Quickly, she switched hands and tried to do the same with her left hand. But the writing was barely legible. "I'm no more ambidextrous than you are," she said.

"I saw you write that with your left hand."

She raised her gaze to his. "Kyle was left-handed."

When he only continued to glare, she added. "What else did you see? Exactly how did I write those words? Left to right? Right to left? How?"

At the time, he'd been a hell of a lot more concerned about her seizure than that damn pad of paper. But he'd had the presence of mind to notice her hand moving across the page. That she'd been gripping the pen awkwardly, tightly, and that her hand had been moving from right to left.

"I wrote from right to left, didn't I?" she asked.

He wasn't going to agree. To accept any of what she was telling him was simply too far beyond his realm of believability. To consider the repercussions was unthinkable.

"Nick, I'm not trying to be cruel. I wouldn't do that to someone who's lost a child. I know what it's like to grieve. But you've got to believe me."

After a long moment, he touched the paper with his fingertips and looked at her. "Are you trying to tell me that your dead son has been in contact with you? You expect me to believe that?"

She held his gaze. "I know that's hard to grasp. I was a skeptic myself, believe me. I thought I was losing my mind. But over the last few months . . ." She shrugged. "I've come to believe."

"If you want me to believe you can communicate with the

dead, you're going to have to come up with something a hell of a lot better than this." Tearing the paper from the pad, he crumpled it and hurled it at the wastebasket.

Silence pressed down on them for several minutes, then she said, "I don't know how much you know about me or what happened three years ago."

"I've been in prison the last six years, *chere*. I didn't exactly keep up with the town gossip."

"You know my husband and son . . . were murdered." She took a moment to gather herself, then continued. "You know I was arrested."

"What does that have to do with your claim that you're psychic?"

"After their deaths I was . . . distraught. Seriously depressed." A breath shuddered out of her. "I tried to commit suicide."

"I don't think that's something you want to brag about."

"It was a stupid, self-destructive thing to do." Her gaze skittered away. "I'm not proud of what I did. I nearly died that night. I lost half my blood volume. They put me on life support, gave me transfusions, but I had already gone into hypovolemic shock. I suffered a stroke and lapsed into a coma."

Nick had already known most of what she'd just told him, but to look into her pretty eyes as she relayed such a horrific ordeal shocked him all over again.

"I was in a coma for two and a half years," she said.

He hadn't known that, and he was speechless.

"When I finally came out of it, I was a mess," she said. "Even though I'd had physical therapy, I was incredibly weak. The stroke was relatively minor, so I didn't have much paralysis, but I had some memory loss. I was still grieving." She lifted a shoulder, let it fall. "You see, I had no idea how much time had elapsed, and it came as a huge shock to learn that I'd lost two and a half years of my life.

"My doctor started me on an aggressive physical rehabilitation program. My muscles had atrophied, so it was tough at first. By the end of the first week, I could stand. By the second week I could walk with the help of a walker. That was when the sleepwalking began."

"Sleepwalking?"

She nodded. "At least that's what I thought it was, at first. It happened twice that second week. I'd never experienced anything like it in my life, and it was incredibly frightening. I mean, to wake up in a strange place was bad enough. But to see things written in my son's handwriting on the wall or the side of a box or tabletop . . ."

He motioned toward the black lettering on the dining room wall. "Notes like that one?"

"I was convinced I was having some sort of emotional breakdown."

"What did the doctors say?"

"My doctor brought in a neurologist from New Orleans. They did a battery of tests, including several electroencephalograms. He also ordered video monitoring for several days. They captured one of the so-called seizures on videotape, and at that point I was diagnosed with psychogenic epilepsy." She gave him a wry smile. "In case you're not up on your medical terminology, psychogenic epilepsy is psychological in origin as opposed to physical, which is the case with other forms of epilepsy."

"He thought it was all in your head?"

She nodded. "Don't get me wrong. Psychogenic epilepsy is a very real disorder that afflicts thousands and can be quite debilitating. But I knew he was wrong. I did not have epilepsy, and I knew the episodes were not a result of some emotional or physical trauma. Nor was it a manifestation of the grief that had been trapped inside me during the coma." Her eyes intensified. "It took me a while, but I finally realized my little boy was trying to communicate with me."

Nick raked his hand through his hair. "Jesus."

"The episodes were extremely frightening at first. Slowly, I began to recognize that afterward I had a very powerful sense of Kyle. I know it sounds crazy, but I could actually smell him. Once, when I was in the hospital library, I came upon a book about mediumship and trance writing. It was a stunning moment when I realized that's what had been happening. That Kyle had, indeed, been communicating with me. Once I accepted the possibility, the seizures weren't quite so terrifying. I stopped looking at the notes as the rantings of a crazy, grief-stricken woman. Instead, I opened my mind and saw them for what they were. Notes from a little boy who'd died a violent death long before his time."

Because Nick still wasn't ready to accept that, he side-stepped the statement. "Do you have the notes? Can I take a look at them?"

"Of course."

He watched her walk to the island in the kitchen where she dug into a thin leather briefcase, removed a tattered manila folder, and set it on the table in front of him. "They're in order by date."

He opened the folder and found himself looking down at a single, disturbing word scrawled in blue colored pencil.

Mommy.

"Keep going," she said.
He turned the page.

bad man came in ar house n hurted me an daddy.

When he didn't turn the pages fast enough, Nat leaned down and flipped through them, barely giving him time to read.

Kill Branden to . . .
gona hurt more kidz
Make him stop.
hell hurt you to
monster in the woods
bad man take ricky. kill again. hurry.

Nick scrubbed his hand over his face, not sure what to make of any of what she'd told him. His logical mind was telling him communicating with the dead was not possible and that this woman was dealing with some serious emotional is-sues. But in some small corner of his mind, he wondered if something extraordinary was happening.

"Did you see a shrink?" he asked.

"Three, actually. But Dr. Pettigrew was convinced the notes were a manifestation of my grief over losing my son. I mean, that makes sense when you take into consideration everything that happened. I'd lost my husband and son. I was in an unexplained coma for over two years. The grief was trapped inside me that entire time with no outlet. He thought the notes were my mind's way of releasing the grief."

Nick didn't know what to say. He definitely couldn't tell her he believed her, because there was a very big part of him that did not. But he couldn't deny that the case she'd just laid out was compelling.

As if reading his mind, she went back to her briefcase, pulled out a second manila folder and slapped it down on the table. "Okay. Then how do you explain this?"

Nick stared down at the childlike drawings. Most had been done in crayon. The Louisiana countryside with hills and trees and a single fat cow beneath a big yellow sun. The words "To Mommy" had been scrawled in the upper left-hand corner.

"Kyle gave that to me for my for my birthday." She flipped to the next drawing. "Look at the handwriting, Nick. Compare it to the handwriting of the notes."

But Nick had already made the comparison. He was no handwriting expert, but the two writings looked the same. "It's similar."

"No," she said adamantly. "Not similar. The handwriting is *exact*."

Nick had always thought of himself as having an open mind. But to believe this woman could somehow communicate with the dead was simply too far-fetched.

"My son is communicating with me," she said. "This has been going on for six months. I'm just now getting to the point where I can go into a trance without losing it afterward. The connection between Kyle and me is getting stronger every single time it happens."

The room fell silent. The window above the sink in the kitchen was open, and he could hear the night sounds of the forest creeping in. The opus of crickets and bullfrogs. The distant cry of a nutria as an alligator chomped down on its leg and dragged it into the black water to devour it.

Nick looked at the drawing. He looked at the words on the

dining room wall. As badly as he wanted to, he could not deny that the handwriting was the same.

Remembering the missing child, he shifted his gaze to Nat, felt a chill at the base of his spine. "Is Ricky Arnaud dead?"

"I don't know." Nat closed her eyes. "What I do know is that the killer has him. That he's in terrible danger. And that if we don't do something to help him, he's going to die."

Nick stared hard at her, wondering how she could possibly expect him to believe something so utterly unbelievable. "Jesus Christ."

"Someone is killing our children," she said in a shaking voice. "We have to stop him before he kills again."

Because he couldn't look at her and think about that, he studied the disturbing words on the wall.

Monster has ricky. Wood house

She picked up one of the notes. "I don't know what *gatea* is."

"If you sound it out, it could be Gautier Mud Flats," he said.

She shot him a startled look. "I've heard of it. The quicksand pits." Her eyes widened. "Do you think that's where he took Ricky?"

Nick sighed. "There's only one way to find out."

"We go to Gautier Mud Flats to see if we can find him," she said hollowly.

"Yeah," he said. "And hope like hell you're nuts and not right."

chapter
12

THERE WAS NO PLACE ON EARTH AS DARK AND FOR-
bidding as the south Louisiana woods at night. Twenty years
ago Nick had known every fishing hole, every bog and quicksand pit within a five-mile radius of the farm. He'd been able
to knock a crow out of the sky with his slingshot and a ball
bearing. He'd once caught a twenty-two-pound catfish in
Dove Creek using a bamboo pole and a homemade hook. He'd
swum the creek on a dare when it had been swollen with rain.

Tonight, he felt like an outsider in a hostile foreign land.

After a quick stop at the farm to check on Dutch and pick
up a battery-powered searchlight and some mosquito repellent, he and Nat rode in silence to the Dove Creek Bridge.
Two miles to the south, through swamp and grassy marsh and
cypress forest, lay the Gautier Mud Flats. The place was
named after the leader of a survey team that had disappeared
while mapping the area in 1918. Legend had it that Paul Willis
Gautier and his four-man team became lost and suffered horrific deaths in the quicksand pits that abounded in the area.
Nick wasn't sure how much of the story was legend and how
much was truth, but it had been enough to keep him very alert
as a boy.

Putting thoughts of the ill-fated survey team out of his
mind, he turned the truck onto a dirt road and parked. Mist

and insects swirled in the beams of the headlights. For a moment, he just sat there, staring into the utter blackness of the woods, his mind roiling with everything Nat had told him.

She'd made a convincing argument. The evidence was compelling. But it was going to take more to convince him she could communicate with the dead. Nick needed tangible proof before committing himself. He figured if she could lead them to Ricky Arnaud, he'd be well on his way to becoming a believer.

"Do you know the way?"

In the dim light coming off a pale three-quarter moon, he could make out the shape of her face. Her large, dark eyes. An impression of her mouth. Under different circumstances he might have liked the idea of being alone with a pretty woman on a dark night with the pulse of the bayou all around. But in truth, Nick didn't want to be here. He didn't want that little boy to be out wandering lost in the swamp—or God forbid, lying dead somewhere. The situation brought back too many memories, and his demons had come knocking with a vengeance.

"It's not an easy hike." He let his gaze skim down her body. She was wearing jeans and sneakers. Not exactly the kind of getup you wanted to wear in the swamp. Even in the darkness, he could see the alluring curve of her hip, the glint of gold off the tiny cross that hung between her breasts.

"I can do it," she said. "I'm in good shape."

The last thing he wanted to think about was her shape, so he looked away. "Yeah, and we're a couple of damn fools for coming out here without waders and a bass boat."

"All I care about is finding that boy."

"And convincing me you're psychic."

He felt her gaze on him, even through the thick blanket of darkness. "I can't do this alone," she said.

"Don't pin your hopes on me, *chere*. The only reason I'm here is to prove you wrong."

"For Ricky Arnaud's sake, I pray to God you can." She got out of the truck and slammed the door.

Sighing, Nick reached into the duffel behind his seat, withdrew mosquito repellent and the spotlight, and slid out of the truck. He spent another minute applying the repellent, then handed it to Nat. When she'd finished, he turned on the spotlight and started down a path, which was little more than a narrow slash in grass as high as his waist. They entered the tree line, and within minutes the darkness swallowed them.

The deep woods of south Louisiana was not a quiet place at night. The mosquitoes buzzed incessantly, blending with the symphony of crickets and frogs. Somewhere nearby a barred owl screeched. In the distance, a gator bellowed a warning.

The grass thinned as they penetrated the forest. Silver light from the moon filtered through the canopy to glitter on wet leaves, revealing a narrow path set into the soggy forest floor. They walked in silence for several minutes, the only sound coming from the mud sucking at their shoes and the breaking of reeds as Nick pushed forward down the trail.

After a while the path widened, and she came up beside him. Not close enough to touch, but he could smell the sweetness of her scent. "Tell me about these episodes of yours," he said.

"The fugue state I go into, combined with the writing, is referred to as *trance writing* or *automatic writing*. It's a form of channeling or mediumship."

"Communicating with the dead."

"In essence, yes."

"What happens to you when you go into a trance?"

"Right before an epileptic seizure, some patients report feeling what's known as an aura. In my case, that aura is more auditory. I hear buzzing. My vision is affected in strange ways. I lose my sense of depth perception, colors begin to bleed. I feel out of control. There is a sensation of paralysis. Sometimes I have nausea. I usually lose consciousness to a degree. Most of the time I come to on the floor, or slumped in a chair. If I'm sleepwalking, I wake up right where I'm standing." Her gaze met his. "But every time this has happened, I write something. On the wall. On a piece of paper. A magazine. Whatever's handy."

"I can't imagine living like that."

"It was extremely frightening at first. I thought I was either epileptic or crazy."

"Why is it happening?"

"I don't know." She shrugged. "I have some theories."

"Like what?"

"I've done quite a bit of research on psychic phenomena.

I've studied Edgar Cayce's philosophies. I educated myself on telepathy, precognition, clairvoyance, psychokinesis, and mediumship." She sighed. "I think something happened to me when I was in that coma. Something opened a channel that had been closed before. Combine that with the way Kyle died . . . Before his time. Violently. There's a lot of injustice in that."

"You think he's trying to make things right?"

"I think he's trying to help me solve his murder."

When he didn't say anything, she looked at him. "I was skeptical, too. Most people are skeptics, and should be. Throughout history, there have been people who've claimed to be psychic but were not. Con artists who preyed on the bereaved. Charlatans who would do anything for fifteen minutes of fame. But while there have been plenty of fakes over the years, there have also been documented cases of psychic phenomena."

He smiled. "John Edward?"

She smiled back, but it was small and wry. "Let's take the police, for example. They don't like to publicize it, but there have been times when law enforcement agencies have turned to psychics for help with difficult cases. In 1971 a man by the name of John List murdered his wife and three kids in Union County, New Jersey. It was a brutal crime that went unsolved for several years. Eventually, the police turned to Elizabeth Lerner, a woman who claimed to be psychic. While she didn't actually solve the case for them, after List was arrested, the detective noted that a lot of the information Lerner had given them was correct."

"Coincidence?" he asked.

"Who knows?" she said, and continued. "In 1982 three teenagers were murdered in what was dubbed the Lake Waco murders. Two women reported 'visions' to the police the same night. But they were disregarded because their claims sounded so crazy. Later, desperate for a break in the case, the police brought in John Catchings, a psychic. Even though the police had been skeptical about the two women's so-called visions, it is documented that a lot of the details the women gave the police were correct. Details right down to the kind of tattoo the killer had."

"It could have been a coincidence," Nick said.

"What most people don't understand is that psychic phe-nomena are not an exact science." She sighed. "That's one of the things that's making this so difficult."

Nick thought about that for a moment. "Have you consid-ered taking this to the police?"

"Of course I have. But, like I told you, I have a history with the police in this town. Alcee Martin might be a good cop, but there's no way he's going to believe me."

Nick saw her point. He still couldn't quite get his brain around the idea of her being psychic. "Did it ever occur to you that you could be wrong?"

"That possibility never leaves my mind. But when I think of the alternative . . ." She shrugged. "With or without your help, I'm going to find this guy. I'm going to stop him."

"All by yourself?"

"If I have to."

Her voice and stance were fierce, but he could see that she had begun to shake. A small warrior ready to take on an army single-handedly if she had to. And even though he wasn't one hundred percent sure he was buying into the psychic connec-tion theory, he found himself respecting her strength, her will-ingness to go the distance.

Turning away from her abruptly, he started down the path. Neither of them spoke as they descended a slope and entered a grassy marsh. The ground was muddy, and she was begin-ning to lag behind. But he didn't slow down.

"The mud flats aren't much farther," he said.

"I'm not tired."

He looked at her and frowned. Several strands of hair had come loose from her ponytail, the wisps framing her face. Considering that she'd spent the better part of the last three years in a hospital bed, she was in good physical condition. They'd covered over two miles of difficult terrain, and she hadn't voiced a single complaint. But he could see the sheen of sweat on her forehead, the strain on her face.

"You push yourself too hard, and you're not going to be any good to anyone, including yourself," he said.

"I know my limits."

"Yeah, well, I don't feel like carrying you all the way back to the truck."

Because he didn't want to think about what she might feel like in his arms, Nick raised the flashlight and illuminated the swamp ahead. "It's going to be a wet hike from here on out."

The beam swept over water as smooth as black glass. Fog rose like ghostly fingers, forming a mist that turned the swamp into a primordial world as silent and still as death. Spanish moss hung in tangled locks from ancient cypress. Knobby roots protruded from a watery carpet of duckweed like the arthritic knees of some long-dead explorer.

"What makes you think I can help you find this killer?" he asked after a moment. "What makes you think I want to?"

"You're the only person in Bellerose who has something at stake."

He thought about that a moment and wondered if she knew he was a convicted felon. "If it's credibility you're looking for, *chere*, you're looking in the wrong place. There are people in this town who will tell you I'm no better than the man you're looking for."

"I know you were in prison," she said. "I read the newspaper accounts of your trial."

Nick turned and gave her a hard look.

"You don't seem like the kind of man who would . . ."

"Kill someone?" He sneered.

Her eyes were wide and cautious and he thought if he made a sudden move she would turn and run. He knew it was stupid, but that pissed him off. "Or maybe now that we're out here in the swamp you're afraid I'll turn my criminal tendencies on you."

"I'm not afraid of you."

"Maybe you should be."

When she only continued to stare at him, he cursed. "In case you're wondering, I didn't kill anyone," he growled.

An uncomfortable silence descended. The volume of the swamp rose to a fever pitch. Her face was a pale oval in the darkness. He could make out the dark slash of her eyes. A smudge of dirt on her cheek. The pout of her full mouth. The swell of her breasts beneath her T-shirt . . .

As if realizing the direction his thoughts had taken, she

turned away and stepped into the knee-deep water. Nick set the beam on her ass and admired the view for a moment, all too aware that she was built just the way he liked, trim but with plenty of interesting curves.

"What the hell are you doing?" he muttered under his breath.

She stopped and looked at him over her shoulder. "What did you say?"

Cold sank into his feet and calves when he stepped into the water and started toward her. "I said we're damn fools for being out here in the swamp without proper gear."

"How much farther to the Gautier Mud Flats?" she asked.

"Not far. There used to be a duck blind just ahead," he said. "It'll be dry. We can rest there."

"You know this area?"

"I used to come here as a kid."

They slogged through the water for several minutes in silence. Around them, the bayou was transforming with dawn. Birdsong and the *kok-kok-kok* of the least bittern echoed through the forest. The reds and oranges of sunrise blazed like a distant fire on the eastern horizon. Ahead, Nick spotted the duck blind. Set four feet above the water's surface, it was constructed of weathered cypress planks. Directly below, an abandoned pirogue sat rotting in a foot of water, its flat bottom filled with duckweed and lily pads.

Stopping next to the blind, Nick cupped his mouth with his hands and shouted. "Ricky Arnaud! *Ricky!* Can you hear us, son?"

A great blue heron took flight at the sudden noise. For a full minute, they stood in the water and listened for an answer that didn't come.

"We should have brought a whistle," Nick said.

Nat brought her hands to her mouth. *"Ricky!"*

The hoarseness of her voice drew his gaze. She was soaked from the hips down. The smear of mud on her face was dark against her pale complexion. She looked cold and exhausted and an inch away from dropping where she stood.

"He's not here," he said after a moment.

Ignoring him, she walked a few feet away and called out again. "Ricky! Are you there? *Ricky!*"

"Nat, there's nobody here. We're wasting our time."

She shot him an incredulous look. "I didn't hike all the way out here just to turn around and leave."

"If he was here, he would have answered."

"Unless he's hurt or . . ." Letting her words trail, she started toward the blind. "I'm going to look around."

Nick put his hands on his hips and sighed. "Nat, we don't have gear. We don't have a map. We don't have a whistle or GPS for coordinates. We don't even know if he's in the area."

"He's here, damn it." She waded through knee-deep water, looking around as if she might spot the little boy at any moment. "I know you don't believe me, but I feel it, Nick. He's here."

Even from twenty feet away, Nick could see that she was trembling with cold. Watching her, he wondered if she was about to slide down some slippery slope. If maybe he was making things worse by encouraging her. Seeing the hope and determination in her eyes, he felt a sudden wave of sympathy for her. Was she out in this godforsaken swamp looking for Ricky Arnaud? Or was she really looking for her own little boy, who would never be coming back?

"Nat, we've been out in the swamp for two hours. We've given it our best shot. It's time to go."

She spun and started toward him, her eyes furious. "You agreed to do this, damn it. The least you could do is keep your word."

"You're wet and cold and exhausted." He gestured toward her clothes. "Look at you. You're shivering. This is crazy."

She stopped less than a foot away and got in his face. "I don't need you to finish this. My sense of direction is good. I can find my way back."

"I'm sure that's what Gautier was thinking back in 1918." Wishing he was anywhere but here, Nick stepped back and looked away. He did a quick double take upon spotting the patch of red.

Nat's gaze followed his. "What is it?"

But Nick had already started toward the speck of color. His heart rolled and began to drum when he realized it was a child's shoe. He heard her moving through the water behind him, but he didn't stop until he reached it.

The little high-top sneaker was lying on its side in the mud and duckweed near the pirogue, its sole facing him, the shoe-strings still tied. He stared at it, not wanting to believe the shoe belonged to Ricky Arnaud, knowing in his heart it did.

"Le Bon Dieu mait la main." God help.

She came up beside him. "It's his."

"It doesn't look like it's been here long," he said.

She leaned down as if to touch it, but he put his hand on her shoulder. "Don't touch it." He didn't voice what he was think-ing, but he knew this could be a crime scene.

Around them, the swamp had gone silent. Nick stood still, listening, his eyes scanning the area, trying in vain to penetrate the shadows playing hide-and-seek within the maze of trees and fog. After a moment, seeing nothing out of the ordinary, he raised his hands to cup his mouth. "Ricky! Ricky Arnaud!"

Next to him, Nat turned in a slow circle. *"Ricky!"*

They called out to the boy for five minutes. But Nick's mind had already jumped ahead to all the terrible things that could befall a little boy in the swamp. When he'd been a kid, Dutch had forbidden him to come here under the threat of his belt. Dutch had told him tales of alligators swallowing chil-dren whole and of mud pits sucking grown men to their deaths. But not even fear of his father's wrath had been enough to keep Nick away.

Wishing for a whistle, he waded through the water, skirting the outer perimeter of the clearing. "Ricky! Answer us, son!"

He circled around to where Nat stood and glanced down at the sneaker. It looked incredibly out of place lying in the duckweed and covered with mud. The image made him think of the terrible fate his own son had met just a few miles away.

Banking the brutal slash of pain, he glanced at Nat. She was staring at the sneaker as if trying to wrest the mystery from it by the sheer force of her will. "What was he doing out here all by himself?" she whispered.

"This isn't the kind of place an eight-year-old boy would go alone," Nick agreed.

"Unless he wasn't alone."

"You don't know that." But the hairs at his nape prickled nonetheless.

"What if someone lured him out here?"

A dozen arguments entered his mind. But Nick didn't voice them. He may not believe in psychic phenomena in general terms, but he didn't believe in coincidences, either. That put him squarely in a place he didn't want to be.

"I don't want to get into this with you right now," he said. "We need to call the police and let them handle this. Maybe they'll want to move their search to this area. Get a few guys out here in boats." He held out his hand. "Give me your phone."

She unclipped her cell from her belt and handed it to him.

He punched in numbers. "You know the cops are going to have some questions for us."

"We didn't do anything wrong."

"Yeah, well, here's a news flash for you: sometimes that doesn't matter." The bitterness in his voice surprised him. God, he sounded just like Dutch. Bitter and old and full of regrets. Sighing unhappily at the thought of ending up like his father, Nick turned his attention to the call and asked to be connected to the police department.

As he waited for the chief to come on the line, he watched Nat wander toward the blind a few yards away. Twenty years ago, hunters had used it to hunt wood duck and mallard. The wooden structure was mounted onto four cypress trees with nails. Over the years the floor of the structure had become tilted at a precarious angle. At some point, someone had added a primitive ladder by nailing strips of wood to one of the trunks, but most of the makeshift rungs had begun to rot.

When Chief Martin came on the line, Nick identified himself and asked, "Any luck finding the Arnaud boy?"

"We ain't found so much as a footprint." The chief sighed tiredly, and Nick got the impression he hadn't yet been to bed. "We got more volunteers and a fresh dog coming in from Covington. Hopefully, we'll get lucky today." The other man paused. "Any particular reason you're asking?"

"I'm out near Gautier Mud Flats south of town. I just came across a red sneaker. A child's sneaker. I thought you'd want to know."

Alcee Martin made a very coplike sound, then asked a very

coplike question. "What are you doing out at Gautier Mud Flats at the crack of dawn?"

The drawl was designed to make the question seem casual. Nick knew it was anything but. Cops always had questions, and those questions were never causal when it came to ex-cons. "I was picking oyster mushrooms for Dutch," he said. "He's going to boil up some crawfish tonight."

"Dutch has always had a knack with them crawfish."

"That he does." Nick watched Nat climb onto the blind.

"I'll send a deputy out there to meet you. Shouldn't take but half an hour or so if he takes his boat. You mind waiting around?"

"Not at all. I'll keep an eye out—"

A bloodcurdling scream cut off his words. Nick swung around to see Nat perched on the top rung of the makeshift ladder, staring into the duck blind.

A second scream split the air. *"Nick!"*

He hit End without explanation. Shoving the phone into his pocket, he sprinted toward the blind, praying to God their worst fears hadn't just become a reality.

chapter
13

NICK HAD HEARD PEOPLE SCREAM BEFORE. DURING his stint in Angola he'd heard grown men scream more times than he wanted to recall. He'd heard screams of agony. Of rage. Of terror. There had been times when he'd felt those same screams echoing inside his own head. But the scream that poured from Nat's throat was so filled with horror it was as if it had been ripped straight from her soul.

He ran toward her at a dangerous speed, hurtling over cypress knobs and submerged roots. "What is it?"

One instant she was clinging to the ladder staring into the blind. The next she was falling backward into space. Her back hit the water hard. He reached her an instant later, but she'd already lurched to her feet, dripping wet, choking out sobs, her face the color of dough. "He's there! Oh God. Oh *God!* The little boy."

"Easy." He grasped her upper arms, forced her gaze to his. "The Arnaud boy?"

She turned ravaged eyes on him. "He's dead. That sweet little boy." She was crying, choking out sobs, fat tears mixing with the water running down her face. She was soaking wet and cold to the touch. He could feel her trembling violently, but he knew the tremors racking her body were as much from shock as cold.

She made a halfhearted attempt to twist away, but he held onto her, gave her a small shake. "I need for you to calm down," he said. "I'm going to take a look."

She looked at him as if he'd spoken in a foreign language. Shock, he thought, and lifted his hand to cup the side of her face. She was as pale and cold as death. The circles beneath her eyes were dark and made her look as fragile as blown glass. But the eyes within those circles were haunted with knowledge. With grief. With the horror of what she'd seen in that blind.

"Stay put," he said. "Okay?"

Blinking back tears, she jerked her head. But he could tell she was holding it together by little more than a thread. Giving her arm a final squeeze, Nick turned to the blind. Dread pounded through him when he started up the ladder. Two steps and his eyes were at floor level. He saw sandy hair against pasty skin. Staring blue eyes and a small mouth that was open as if in a scream.

An electric shock of horror rippled through him. "Aw, God."

Anguish and outrage mixed with a deep well of grief. Vaguely, he was aware of the buzz of flies. For a moment he considered using his shirt to cover the body, to protect it. Then he remembered that this could be a crime scene.

His heart was heavy in his chest when he climbed down the ladder. Nat was standing where he'd left her, her arms wrapped around her body as if she were trying to hold herself together. "Please tell me that little boy is not dead," she whispered.

Nick couldn't speak. He could feel his entire body trembling as he crossed to her. He wasn't sure who reached for whom, but in the next instant she was in his arms. A keening sound tore from her throat when she fell against him. It was a sound so filled with anguish that he felt it echoing within the hollowed shell that was his own heart. She felt small and fragile in his arms, and he suddenly wanted to protect her from this. From the ugliness. From the pain.

Closing his eyes, he wrapped his arms more tightly around her. "It's going to be all right," he said in a rough voice.

"How could someone do that to a child?" she asked.

"Nat." He shoved her to arm's length. "Listen to me. We

don't know what happened to him. As far as we know, it could have been some sort of accident."

"It wasn't an accident," she said fiercely.

Looking into her eyes, he reminded himself that she was the one who'd led them here. A fact that left only one of two possibilities: Either Nat had harmed the boy herself, which Nick knew was an absolute impossibility. Or she was psychic.

He wasn't sure which scenario troubled him the most.

THE INTERVIEW ROOM AT THE BELLEROSE POLICE Department was as cold as a meat locker and smelled just as rank. Chief Martin had given Nat a blanket from the jail, but her clothes were still wet and she was cold to her bones. Every time she closed her eyes she saw Ricky Arnaud's body lying in that duck blind, as still and pale as a mannequin. It was a sight that would haunt her for the rest of her days.

Sitting across from her, Nick looked as if the world had just come down on top of him, and he was bearing every pound of it on those broad shoulders. He was leaning back in the chair with his arms crossed at his chest, staring at the table in front of him. While he looked calm on the outside, Nat had spent enough time with him in the last day to see the tension that was running through his body like a piano wire.

She wasn't sure what she would have done if he hadn't been there when she'd found that child's body. As much as she disliked the thought of needing anyone, his embrace had come at a moment when she'd desperately needed that small human contact. His arms had comforted her in a way nothing else could have. His touch had warmed her in a place she'd thought was frozen forever.

The interview room door swung open. A ripple of unease moved through her when Alcee Martin and Deputy Matt Duncan walked in. Alcee looked as if he'd spent the night in hell. His eyes were bloodshot. His shirt was wrinkled, with rings of sweat at his armpits. She figured he'd been the one to break the terrible news to Becky and Jim Arnaud. She knew firsthand what that first brutal punch of grief did to a person. She wouldn't wish it on her worst enemy. She sure as hell didn't envy Alcee his job.

Matt Duncan, on the other hand, looked as if he were enjoying the excitement. Setting his Coke on the table, he pulled out a chair and looked at her and Nick as if they'd just committed mass murder. Nat had known Matt since high school. Even back when he'd been star quarterback for the Fighting Trojans, she'd known he had a dark side. She'd found that out the hard way when she'd said no in the backseat of his jacked-up GTO. Matt had never let her forget it.

"Did you talk to Becky and Jim?" Nat asked.

Alcee seemed to age ten years right before her eyes. "God almighty, they took it hard."

Nick spoke to Chief Martin. "Any idea what happened to the boy?"

"Doc Ratcliffe did a cursory exam at the scene. He'll know more once he performs an autopsy, but he didn't find any signs of foul play. He thinks maybe hypothermia got him."

Nat set her hands on the table hard enough to draw the attention of all three men. *"Hypothermia?"*

Chief Martin gave her a curious look. "That boy had been lost in those woods for almost twelve hours. Even though it's been mild, the water is cold. Plus, he had some kind of childhood arthritis that made his joints hurt. Doc thinks he got wet and cold, started getting stiff, so he climbed into the blind to get out of the water. Hypothermia took him during the night. Course, an official autopsy will be performed, but Doc Ratcliffe doesn't think we're dealing with anything sinister." He sighed tiredly. "Just a terrible tragedy."

"Are you sure?" Ignoring the warning look from Nick, she looked from Duncan to Martin. "I mean, Gautier Mud Flats is an awful long way from his usual route, isn't it?"

"Kid that size can cover a lot of ground." Martin looked at Duncan. "How far is it, Matt? Two, three miles from where he was supposed to be?"

"But he would have had to travel through the swamp," she said. "That's rough terrain for a little boy."

Martin frowned at her. "What are you getting at, Nat?"

"Just that his death should be investigated thoroughly." She was *certain* Ricky Arnaud had met with foul play. Kyle's note had told her where to find the body. Had he been wrong? Or had she somehow misinterpreted and written the note incorrectly?

Was she so desperate to find the person responsible for her own son's murder that she interjected something of her own mind into the writing?

"I just told you Travis is going to do an autopsy," Alcee said. "There's no use speculating on what happened before he finishes his report."

Leaning back in his chair, Duncan folded his arms across his chest and gave her a superior look. "We got an interesting call from Elaina Wilbur about you, Nat."

"I don't know Elaina Wilbur," she said.

"She's a pregnant lady," Duncan said. "Said she was out at Ray's Sunoco the other day when you were gassing up. She said you wigged out and wrote some kind of strange note, and that you used the name Ricky. You want to explain to us what that was all about?"

Both Duncan and Martin were staring at her intently, their cop's eyes hard and suspicious. Nat stared back, her heart pounding. "I-I have epilepsy," she stammered. "I experienced a mild seizure while I was writing the check."

"Elaina said you wrote the name Ricky," Duncan insisted. "She was sure of it. And she was concerned about it enough to call us once she found out the boy was missing."

"She's mistaken," Nat said.

"Do you have the check?"

"I threw it away."

"Of course you did." Duncan's eyes were lit with an almost predatory gleam. "How is it that a dozen volunteers and two police agencies can look for a little boy all night and not find a trace? Then you two go picking mushrooms at six o'clock in the morning and find him right off the bat. Some people in this town might find that a little suspicious."

Nick growled something nasty and French beneath his breath. "If you've got something on your mind, why don't you just say it?"

"I think it's suspicious as hell that a convicted felon and a woman once suspected of murdering her own kid find a missing child the way you two did."

"Fuck you," Nick said.

Duncan's lips didn't move, but Nat saw the smile in his eyes.

Martin slapped a hand down on the table. "That's enough.

For chrissake, we're all tired. Let's let Travis do his job. If anything irregular comes of the autopsy, I'll deal with it then." His gaze moved from Nat to Nick. "In the interim, I don't want either of you leaving town."

Nick swore, but Alcee raised his hand. "And I suggest you two watch your backs. Matt's got a point in that there might be a few people in this town who think it's odd that you were the ones who found that boy."

"What's going to keep some yahoo from jumping to the wrong conclusion and trying to do something about it?" Nick punctuated the question with a pointed look at Nat.

"If anything comes up, call the police and let us handle it." Nick and Nat rose simultaneously.

"Oh, one more thing before you go," Martin said.

Nat stopped midway to the door and turned.

Martin looked directly at Nat. "You know what a hot-head Jim Arnaud is. When I told Jim and Becky about their son . . . well, Jim lashed out, started making all kinds of wild accusations."

"What kinds of accusations?" Nick asked, but Nat already knew.

Martin grimaced. "About Nat finding his boy. It was the pain talking. But Jim was looking for someone to hurt. I warned him not to do anything stupid, but he's half out of his mind with grief. If he lays into the booze, it's hard telling what he might do."

Nat felt Nick's stare, but she didn't look at him. She didn't expect him to understand that she wasn't afraid of Jim Arnaud. That in the last three years she'd faced down far worse than a drunken, grief-stricken father.

"If Jim shows up at your place," Martin said, "call us, and we'll send someone out to take him home."

"Sure." But as Nat turned and started toward the door, she wondered just how fast the Bellerose PD would show up if she needed them.

chapter
14

IT WAS NEARLY TWO P.M. WHEN NICK PARKED THE truck in Nat's driveway and shut down the engine. Beyond, the two-story Victorian sat on a manicured lot, looking as pretty as a chamber of commerce real estate ad. It was a beautiful piece of property, but he didn't think the woman sitting next to him even noticed. Since leaving the police station, she'd done nothing but stare blindly out the window.

When she made no move get out of the truck, he touched her arm. "We need to talk about what happened."

She blinked at him as if noticing him for the first time. "I don't want to talk about it." She glanced down at her muddy clothes. "I just . . . want to take a shower."

"Yeah, well, I hate to put a damper on your plans, but I've got some questions that aren't going to wait." When she didn't acquiesce, he added, "I didn't ask to get dragged into this."

"It's not like I'm a willing participant, either. I didn't ask for any of this to happen."

"I want the blanks filled in, Nat. All of them, including everything you know about my son's death." Hating those words, he scrubbed his hand over his face. "I want to know who's responsible and why it was ruled an accident. I want to know why the parish coroner thinks Ricky Arnaud died of natural causes, when you're claiming he was murdered."

"I don't know," she snapped. "Damn it, I don't have all the answers."

"I'm not going away until we talk about this."

Angrily, she flung open the door and started toward the house. Figuring it was as much encouragement as he was going to get, Nick followed her inside.

The interior of the house was an eye-pleasing mix of Victorian character and Southern charm. Bright and airy with spacious rooms, it was the kind of house where one would expect the smell of baking bread to be wafting from the big kitchen. Blues easing from a radio in the study. The blare of a TV in the living room. Shouts and laughter from boisterous children playing in the backyard.

But the house was as silent as a funeral when Nick paused in the foyer to remove his muddy boots. Nat did the same, then crossed the living room and headed toward the kitchen. He trailed her as far as the dining room, then stopped to watch as she pulled the carafe from the coffeemaker and filled it with water from the tap. Her back was to him, but he could see that her shoulders were rigid with tension.

A wave of compassion went through him when he saw her shiver. It wasn't cold inside the house, or outside for that matter, but she'd been wet for several hours. Combine that with the lack of sleep, lack of food, and the shock of seeing that dead child, and he figured he had one mentally and physically exhausted woman on his hands.

Crossing to her, he touched her gently on the arm. "You're shivering, *chere*. Why don't you take a hot shower? Get into some dry clothes."

She turned to him, and not for the first time Nick was taken aback by the simple beauty of her face. Porcelain skin. High cheekbones. A soft, pretty mouth. But she had the most haunted eyes he'd ever seen. The kind of eyes that could break a man's heart if he was fool enough to make the mistake of caring. Nick was no such fool.

"I'd rather just get this over with," she said.

"It'll keep for a few minutes."

When she didn't acquiesce, he eased the carafe from her hands, took her by the shoulders, and pointed her toward the living room. "Go. I'll finish the coffee."

She paused halfway to the living room and frowned at him over her shoulder. "I like my coffee strong."

"I'm Cajun. I don't know how to make it any other way."

He watched her walk away, liking what he saw, disturbed by what he felt, and stirred a hell of a lot more than he wanted to admit. *"Sa vaut pas la peine,"* he muttered. It's not worth it.

Shaking off thoughts he was a fool for entertaining, he finished making the coffee, then went to the refrigerator in search of food.

Ten minutes later, he was in the process of sliding omelets onto plates when Nat appeared in the doorway. "What are you doing?"

Pleasure quivered through him at the sound of her voice, then doubled back and did it again when his eyes swept over her. She shouldn't have looked good in a pair of faded jeans and a plain white T-shirt, but she did, and Nick drank in every inch of her like a thirsty man taking in water. He knew he was staring; he knew she'd noticed and that his scrutiny was making her uncomfortable. But there were some things that were as natural to a man as breathing and, having spent the last six years locked in a cage, taking the measure of a beautiful woman was one of them.

Realizing his body was responding—that it was going to be obvious if he didn't get a handle on things real quick—he turned back to the toast he'd been buttering. "I thought you might want some breakfast to go with that coffee."

"I'm not hungry."

"You haven't tasted my omelet yet." He plopped the toast onto plates and took them to the table. "Sit down."

"You didn't have to do this," she said as she lowered herself into the chair.

"I don't want you passing out on me."

"You don't even like me."

"I like you just fine, *chere*. It's those crazy ideas of yours that give me pause." Back at the counter, he poured coffee, then returned to the dining room and set one of the cups in front of her. "Be careful; it bites."

She sipped, then shot him a grateful look. "You're becoming more tolerable by the moment."

Nick laughed outright as he took the chair across from her. He dug into the omelet, but out of the corner of his eye he was watching her. When she finally picked up her fork and began to eat, he smiled inwardly.

For several minutes they ate in silence. Two people with a lot on their minds and absolutely no idea where to begin. Nat surprised him by asking the first question, the hardest question, one he still wasn't one hundred percent sure how to answer.

"Do you believe I'm psychic? That my son is communicating with me?"

Twenty-four hours earlier, he would have laughed himself into hysterics at the notion. But after witnessing the trance writing session—after finding Ricky Arnaud's body—there was only one answer he could give. "I believe you, *chere*."

She closed her eyes briefly, and for the first time he realized just how desperately she'd needed to hear him say that.

Nick chose his next words with care. "If your son can communicate with you and knows what happened the night he died, why doesn't he just tell you who the murderer is?"

"I pondered the same question," she said. "The fact that he couldn't tell me who was responsible was the main reason I doubted myself. I had no way of knowing if these notes were coming from my own subconscious or if my little boy was really communicating with me."

Nick waited.

"Then I started reading about psychic phenomena and learned that a spirit guide can forewarn—"

"Spirit guide?"

"A spirit guide is a being or entity or energy, if you will. A highly evolved spirit who has spent many incarnations on the earth and has grown in spirituality and purity."

Jesus Christ that sounded crazy. . . . "Kyle?" Nick asked.

She nodded. "Spirit guides will communicate when called upon, but are unable to reveal information that could conceivably change the future. It's left up to the living whether or not they want to try to change the course Fate has set for them."

"That seems a little convenient."

"Or maybe that's just the way it is." Setting down her fork, she rose and walked over to her briefcase, which was on the cooking island. Retrieving a folder, she walked back to the table and set it in front of him. "I was able to obtain this and a copy of the police report."

Nick hesitated an instant before opening the folder. A chill crept into his bones when he found himself looking at an autopsy report detailing the violent death of a child. A police report describing a horrific scene. "Jesus," he muttered.

Deeply disturbed by the clinical details, he put the report back in the folder without reading it. He could feel his heart beating heavily in his chest. Too fast. Too hard. He thought about his own son and shuddered inwardly.

Turning away from him, she walked over to her briefcase and pulled out a second manila folder. "I have the autopsy and police reports on your son's death, too."

Nick tried to deflect the quick blow of grief, but he didn't succeed. Losing his son was the most terrible thing he'd ever experienced in his life. But to read the details of what had happened, to consider the possibility that his precious child had been murdered was infinitely worse.

"Nat, goddamn it," he growled. "I don't want to see it."

"I know this is difficult," she said.

"This is a lot worse than difficult," he snapped.

"There's a discrepancy in your son's autopsy report."

He stared at her, knowing there was more coming, knowing it was going to be bad. "What discrepancy?"

Opening the folder she began paging through reports as if she was familiar with every horrific page. As if she'd done it a hundred times and knew exactly what she was looking for.

Nick watched her, aware that his pulse was hammering, that he was nauseous and sweating. He'd always considered himself a strong man, not only on a physical level, but emotionally as well. But he didn't think he could handle reading some clinical report detailing his son's death.

"The St. Tammany Parish Coroner ruled Brandon's death an accidental drowning. There was water in his lungs."

"I already know that."

"Did you know the first paramedic on the scene noted bruises on Brandon's neck and arms?"

Nick felt the words with the violence of a physical punch. "How do you know that?"

"I did a lot of research, Nick. The Freedom of Information

act requires the autopsy and the first page of the police report to become a matter of public record. Of course, autopsy photos remain sealed. Witness reports remain sealed as well."

"How the hell did you find out about the paramedic?"

"Bellerose is a small town. I made a few calls. Anonymously, since no one would talk to me. I got a name. Everyone knew Rusty Burke had been the first paramedic on the scene. I called him. Lied to him. Told him I was a reporter and wanted to do a story. He told me he'd seen those bruises with his own eyes." She took a deep breath. "He thought maybe your wife had . . . hurt him."

She may as well have plunged a knife into his heart for all the pain the words caused him. Nick knew Tanya hadn't been a good mother to his son. He'd tried to get the State of Louisiana and Child Protective Services involved. He'd made phone call after phone call after phone call. But the system was overloaded. Because Nick had been incarcerated, no one had taken him seriously enough to do anything about it.

"I want to talk to the paramedic," he heard himself say.

"That would be a good idea if he were alive."

Nick cut her a sharp look. *"What?"*

"Rusty Burke was killed in a car accident two weeks after your son's death."

His mind reeled with the implications of what she was saying. "Are you saying Rusty Burke was murdered?"

"I'm saying he's not around to tell us what he saw that day."

Nick shook his head, thinking about his son. "I don't see how the police could have overlooked murder. Alcee Martin is no dummy."

"Neither is the parish coroner. I know Travis Ratcliffe. He was my brother-in-law. Nick, he's a good doctor; he cares about people. I did some checking, and he doesn't have a single mistake on his record."

"If Brand was murdered, someone missed something."

"Unless maybe the killer knows how to make murder look like an accident."

"Killers have been trying to do that and failing since Abel and Cain."

"Maybe the cops weren't looking for evidence of murder."

"Cops always look for murder when a body shows up." His gaze met hers. "I think it's time I talked to Ratcliffe."

"I'll go with you."

Considering the ugliness he'd witnessed between her and Hunt the other night, he wondered if it would be wiser for her to stay behind. "You have a history with the Ratcliffes, *chere*. Might be more productive if I go alone."

"Travis is nothing like Hunter," she said. "He was the only Ratcliffe who stood up to his father, Elliott, when Ward and I were married."

Nick was still trying to get his brain around the idea of Elliott Ratcliffe disapproving of his son's marriage to this woman. "Why did the old man object to your marrying his son?"

"I think Elliott had some debutante in mind." She smiled wryly. "He got me."

"A homegrown girl."

"A farmer's daughter and a Catholic to boot."

"He could have done a hell of a lot worse." Their gazes held for an uncomfortable moment before she looked away.

"So the entire Ratcliffe clan turned on you after you lost your husband and son?" he asked.

She nodded.

"Surely they realized you weren't capable of something so heinous, didn't they?"

"I wish I could say yes to that, but I honestly don't know. I do believe that much of Elliott's lashing out at me was a reaction to grief. Everyone was so shocked, so incredibly sad. I think they needed someone to blame."

"And you were the cops' number one suspect."

"Ward left me with a generous life insurance policy."

"The cops figured that as a motive for murder?"

"There were other factors, too. Ward and I hadn't been getting along. There was some evidence in the house."

"What kind of evidence?"

"The most damning was a window screen in Kyle's room that had been cut. At first, the police thought the killer had climbed onto the roof, cut the screen, and entered the house through the window. But Alcee sent the screen to the State Police Crime Lab in Baton Rouge, and it was discovered that the screen had been cut from the *inside,* not the outside. It was also discovered that the knife used to cut the screen was mine. From the kitchen drawer. The murder weapon had my fingerprints on it."

"You picked up the knife?"

"Nick, I honestly don't remember." She looked down at her hands as if expecting to see blood on them. "That night is such a terrible jumble. I must have."

"What else?"

"I was stabbed that night. The cops called the wounds superficial even though it took over sixty stitches to close them. The emergency room doctor who examined me later testified that the wounds could have been self-inflicted."

Nick grimaced, not wanting to think of what a knife would do to soft skin. "It sounds like maybe someone tried to make you look guilty."

"That's the only explanation that makes sense."

"Any idea who? Do you have any enemies? Did Ward?"

She shook her head. "I've been wracking my brain but there's no one."

"Maybe someone believed you were guilty and decided to help the investigation along."

She met his gaze. "You mean the police?"

"I was thinking more along the lines of Elliott Ratcliffe."

"I can't believe he would do that."

"Maybe you should."

Nick knew it was counterproductive to feel too much when it came to this woman. Still, he couldn't deny the quick rise of outrage for what she'd been through. He knew firsthand how the police operated. He knew they had probably taken her into the interview room and hammered her with questions for hours. Ugly questions that would have ripped at her with all the violence of a knife. They hadn't let her rest or eat. Once they'd put her in a cell, grief-stricken and alone, she'd taken the only way out she could think of. . . .

"So why didn't the killer finish you off that night?" he asked after a moment.

"Because everything he did—cutting the screen, using one of my kitchen knives, even the injuries I sustained—was geared to make me look guilty."

"He wanted you to be suspect."

"And he gets off scot free."

Sighing, Nick rose. *"Le Bon Dieu mait la main,"* he muttered. *God help*.

Nat rose, too. "Where are you going?"

"I'm going to talk to Travis Ratcliffe."

"I'm going, too."

Her eyes met his, and a silent communication passed between them. This meant they would be working together. Nick didn't know how smart that was, considering the way he was reacting to her. But he figured this was one of those things he didn't have a choice about.

Reaching for the keys, he hoped the prickly sensation on the back of his neck didn't have anything to do with the little voice inside his head telling him to stay the hell away from the Ratcliffes.

chapter
15

THE RATCLIFFE ESTATE WAS AS MAGNIFICENT NOW as it had been 150 years ago when Henry Howard Ratcliffe completed construction in 1846, just before the Civil War. Situated between downtown Bellerose and the bayou, the antebellum mansion sat on 240 acres of fertile farmland where four generations of Ratcliffes had farmed cotton and sugarcane and rice.

Six grand white columns rose out of the concrete porch like massive aristocratic fingers to stretch forty feet up, past the second level balcony, to the widow's walk on the roof. Live oaks and magnolias and sweet gums crowded around the front of the house like a group of Southern belles fussing over a new baby.

Sitting in the passenger seat of Nick Bastille's ancient pickup, Nat was invariably taken aback by the timeless beauty of the old plantation house. It was hard to believe a place could remain so utterly the same over 150 years when her own life had been changed so drastically in only three.

She tried to remember the last time she'd been here but couldn't. Not since Ward's and Kyle's deaths. In the years she and Ward were married, it was tradition for the three of them to come here for dinner after church on Sunday. But the time she spent with the Ratcliffe men had rarely been pleasant. For

Ward's sake, she'd tried hard to fit in. But Nat was the daughter of a cotton farmer, and the Ratcliffes never let her forget it. Not that she wanted to. The expensive clothes Ward had insisted upon might have changed the way she looked on the outside, but those clothes hadn't changed who she was on the inside.

If it hadn't been for Ward's insistence—and the firm belief that Kyle deserved to know his grandfather and uncles—she wouldn't have subjected herself to those torturous Sunday dinners. But while Ward's two brothers were hostile to Nat, they had doted on Kyle. The moment Kyle came through the front door, Travis or Hunter would sweep him into their arms. Kyle would giggle, and the house would be filled with the sweet music of a child's laughter. . . .

"Are you sure you're up to this?"

Nat started at the sound of Nick's voice and realized she'd been daydreaming. She glanced at him, saw concern on his features, and wondered if she looked as strung out as she felt. "I'm sure."

"I can do this without you." He'd washed up before leaving her house, but it hadn't helped much. If the circumstances had been different, she might have smiled at the thought of Nick Bastille walking into the Ratcliffe estate with muddy boots, stained jeans, and a wrinkled shirt. She looked down at her own clothes and realized it had been such a long time since she cared about what she looked like, it hadn't even crossed her mind to change.

"I need to do this," she said.

"Let's get it over with," Nick said and opened his door.

They left the truck and went up the steps together. The afternoon was mild and humid, and the breeze felt good on her skin. A blue jay scolded them from atop the magnolia. As they crossed the porch to the door, Nat felt a moment of déjà vu. She'd walked this path a hundred times in the years she'd been married to Ward. Only now she was entering a world in which she no longer belonged. A world she'd never fit into. A hostile world she would not be welcomed back to.

She was keenly aware of Nick's presence beside her. She wasn't exactly sure when it had happened, but at some point he had become her ally. Two people working toward a common goal as a combined force. She wanted to believe that was all there was to it. But that didn't explain the way he looked at her sometimes. It didn't explain why every nerve in her body jumped to attention when he did.

They stopped outside the fourteen-foot cypress doors and he used the brass knocker to announce their presence. Nat waited, her heart pounding, one small corner of her brain hoping against hope that no one answered.

The door swung open, and Nat found herself looking at a young African American woman with pale caramel skin, bright blue eyes, and the cheekbones of a New York runway model. "Can I help you?" she asked with a thick Louisiana drawl.

"We're looking for Travis Ratcliffe," Nick said.

"Can I tell 'im who's callin'?"

"Nat Jennings."

The woman's eyes swept to Nat and narrowed. "Miz Ratcliffe?"

Nat forced a smile. "I go by Jennings now."

The woman looked uncomfortable for a moment, then opened the door wider and stepped back. "Y'all come on in. Wait here, and I'll fetch Dr. Ratcliffe."

The woman's black-and-white uniform swished around her knees as she turned and left the foyer.

"Nice place," Nick commented.

Nat had always loved the old mansion, even though she'd never been comfortable inside it. The foyer was grand with black and white marble tiles that swept to a massive mahogany staircase. At the apex of the twenty-eight foot ceiling, a Belgian crystal chandelier cast prisms of light onto delicate egg and dart moldings. Through the arched doorway to her left, she could see the marble fireplace and mural in the great room where she and Ward and Kyle had spent many a Sunday evening lingering over coffee and beignets. . . .

"Natalie?"

She looked up to see Travis striding toward them, his expression an odd mix of puzzlement and surprise. He was wearing his trademark Eddie Bauer polo and khakis. "My God, what are you doing here?" His gaze swept from her to Nick and back again. "What is he doing here?"

Nat might have smiled at his expression if she'd been there for any reason other than to ask him about the death of a child. "Surprised to see me?"

He stopped a few feet away and put his hands on his hips. "I don't think it's appropriate for you to be here."

Travis hadn't inherited the Ratcliffe good looks like his two brothers, but he was attractive in his own right. His sandy hair was swept back from a high forehead. His face wasn't classically handsome, but his features were interesting and well arranged. At an even six feet and a perfectly toned 180 pounds, he possessed the kind of charisma that could have landed him on the big screen if he'd so chosen. The elder Ratcliffe had wanted all three of his sons to follow in his lofty footsteps and join him in the televangelist circuit. Much to his father's chagrin, Travis had chosen medicine over the church and became a general practitioner with a small, but successful practice. Ten years ago, he'd been elected parish coroner. Hunt, on the other hand, had flunked out of college at Tulane and fallen into a job at the mill and spent most of his spare time at The Blue Gator. Nat had always suspected both sons were disappointments of varying degrees. Ward had been the only son to devote his life to the church. Elliott Ratcliffe's great hope. Maybe that was why he hated her so much. . . .

"We just want to ask you a few questions," she said.

Travis looked at her the way a man might look at a mongrel dog that was about to track mud all over his Persian carpet. "Questions about what?"

"I want to talk to you about my son," Nick said.

Travis shot him a decidedly unfriendly look. "You're Nick Bastille." It was an accusation more than a question, and he didn't bother extending his hand for a shake.

"I wasn't around when Brandon died." Nick grimaced. "But I saw the autopsy report, and I have some questions."

Travis rubbed his chin as if trying to decide what to make of the unexpected visit. "Mr. Bastille, it's highly inappropriate for you to come to my home about this matter."

"I found a discrepancy on the autopsy report," Nick said.

"*Discrepancy?*" Travis made no effort to hide his shock. "What are you talking about?"

"I'm talking about the paramedic who was first on the scene."

"Rusty Burke? What about him?"

"He said there were bruises on Brandon's neck."

Travis blinked rapidly, "If there was bruising on that child's neck, I would have indicated it on the report. It would have been indicated on the police report as well."

"It wasn't."

"Well, then, Rusty was mistaken."

"Or maybe there were some bruises you didn't notice or failed to note—"

"Look, I'm not saying I'm infallible, but when it comes to my work, I'm meticulous. There are check-and-balance systems in place. I don't have to tell you how thorough Alcee is."

Nat knew exactly how thorough the chief was. Three years ago, he and his lead detective had nearly nailed her for a crime she hadn't committed. "Is there any way someone could have missed something?" she asked.

"No way." Travis shook his head adamantly, then looked solemnly at Nick. "I know that's not easy to accept, and I'm sorry for your loss, but the investigation was thorough. Bellerose might be a small town, but Alcee Martin is a top-notch professional. He did his job, and so did I."

"Travis," Nat began, "can we take a look at the autopsy photographs?" Photos she'd been unable to obtain through the same channels she'd used to get her hands on the police and autopsy reports.

"Autopsy photos?" The doctor shot her an incredulous look. "Why in the name of God would you want to see those photos?"

"We think my son may have been murdered," Nick said evenly.

"Murdered?" Travis made a sound that that was part astonishment, part irritation. "There's no way in hell that boy's death was anything but an accident. I performed the autopsy myself. Alcee Martin investigated the scene. I know it's a terrible tragedy, but your boy drowned."

Nick looked away, his jaw working.

"We think someone may have tried to make Brandon's death look like an accident," Nat said. "Is that possible?"

"No, it's not possible. There would have been signs of a struggle. Bruising. Scratches—" Travis cut off the words abruptly, his eyes narrowing on Nick. "Is this about your ex-wife? You think she did something to that child?"

"This isn't about my ex-wife," Nick said.

"Look, I'm probably out of line for saying this, but if there's anyone who's at fault, Bastille, it's your ex-wife. Not because she's guilty of murder, but because she was negligent. She was in the trailer when it happened. The DA didn't pursue charges, but from all appearances, she'd been drinking. In my book that's at the very least neglect. At worst, child endangerment. Maybe you ought to be looking at her instead of autopsy photos that will do nothing but tear you up inside."

"What about Ricky Arnaud?" Nat asked. "Have you determined the cause of death yet?"

His gaze flicked from Nick to Nat. "What does this have to do with Ricky Arnaud?"

"We just want to know if there was any kind of foul play involved."

"Look, I'm not going to go into the details with you. Discussing a closed case is one thing. But the police are still investigating the Arnaud boy's death. As parish coroner, all I can say at this point is that I did a preliminary exam at the scene. From all appearances, it looks like he succumbed to hypothermia."

"Are you sure?" Nat asked.

"Of course I'm sure! There's no way to be positive before the autopsy and tox screen. But that's my preliminary find—" He cut the words short as if realizing he'd already said too much. Suspicion flickered in his eyes, as cold and hard as a January freeze. Nat had seen that look before, and she felt the weight of it pressing down on her, chilling her inside. "What the hell is going on here? Why all the questions about Brandon Bastille and Ricky Arnaud?"

There was a part of her that wanted to confide in him about their suspicions, but some inner warning stopped her. She and Travis might have been family once, but time and circumstance had driven a wedge between them. She felt that wedge now as clearly as she saw the suspicion in his eyes.

"When are you going to perform the autopsy?" she asked.

"I'm not going to answer that, Natalie. In fact, I think you should leave. If Dad comes downstairs and finds you here, things could get ugly. He hasn't been the same since . . ." His words trailed, then he sighed. "Since Ward and Kyle."

"None of us have been the same," she said.

As if realizing the conversation had strayed into territory best left alone, Nick spoke up. "Have there been any other suspicious deaths? Particularly of children?"

Travis's gaze cut to Nick. "Look, I don't know what you people are up to or what you think you know, but I don't like what I'm hearing. If either of you knows something you haven't told the police, I strongly suggest you do it now."

Regret swelled inside her when she realized they hadn't accomplished anything except, perhaps, arousing Travis Ratcliffe's suspicions. The last thing she and Nick needed was more suspicion.

"Our only involvement was finding that boy's body," Nat said. "Both of us have lost children, so it was a difficult, emotional thing to contend with. We just felt the need to follow up. That's all."

Travis didn't look convinced, but he nodded. "All right. You've followed up. Now I'm asking you to—"

"What is that woman doing in this house?"

Nat's heart did a single sickening roll at the sound of Elliott Ratcliffe's voice. She looked up to see the evangelist descend the stairs. He struck her with a glare so full of hatred that for an instant she thought he might forget who he was and follow through on the violence she saw in his eyes.

She took his measure as he crossed to them. At fifty-nine years of age, Elliott Ratcliffe was in his prime. He was tall and barrel-chested and carried himself with the self-assurance of a man who knew his place in society—a place that was at the very top. An almost tangible aura of power surrounded him, a force that radiated outward like heat from a fire. In the three years since Nat had last seen him, his hair had gone from salt and pepper gray to pure white. His bushy eyebrows were still black and rode low over eyes as hard and colorless as steel.

He entered the foyer, staring at her as if she were vermin. "How dare you come into my home."

Travis stepped forward. "Dad—"

The elder Ratcliffe cut off his son's attempt to intervene by slashing his hand through the air. But his glare never left Nat. "What ungodly business could you possibly have here?"

"We were just leaving," Nick said.

"Elliott, I just needed to speak with Travis," she said.

"My son has nothing to say to you. My family wants nothing to do with you." He looked at Travis. "I want this evil woman out of his house. *Now*."

Vaguely, she was aware of Nick stepping between them. The room had gone silent. Her own heartbeat was deafening. She could hear the roar of it in her ears, feel her blood pumping outrage and adrenaline through her veins. She knew better than to do battle with Elliott Ratcliffe. He hated her too much for her to ever convince him of her innocence. But knowing that he believed she was capable of something so heinous, that he blamed her for the very thing that had destroyed her life, inflamed her.

"You—" Choking on the emotion that had crowded into her throat, she raised her hand, pointed at him, and was surprised to see it shaking. "You have no right to blame me for what happened."

"You took my son from me," he said with barely concealed rage. "Now you have the nerve to walk into my home? You are not welcome here. You were never welcome here."

Nat's heart was beating so hard that for a moment she thought she might pass out. "You have no right to speak to me that way."

"This is my house, and I will speak to you in any fashion I see fit."

"Dad. Hey. Come on." Travis crossed to his father and gently took his arm. "She was just leaving."

"Get your hands off me." The elder Ratcliffe shook off his son's hand, but his eyes never left Nat. Eyes that shone bright and hot with a hatred that was so deep and black that it chilled her. "I didn't believe your lies three years ago, and I don't believe them now."

"That's a hateful, insane thing to say." She'd intended the words to come out strong, but her voice was shaking so badly she barely recognized it.

"You killed them for the insurance money. When the police

got too close, you tried to commit suicide, like the sinner you are."

Nat's breath left her lungs in a rush. Shadows crowded her peripheral vision until she saw only Elliott Ratcliffe's face. The hatred burning in his eyes, the bitterness etched into his face. The dark emotions gathering in her own heart.

"I'm not going to defend myself," she said in a shaking voice. "Not to you."

"You're not going to defend yourself because your actions are indefensible. You committed the ultimate sin, then you played upon the sympathies of a community that is far too compassionate."

"Nat. Easy. Let it go."

The voice was Nick's. Vaguely, she was aware of his fingers wrapping around her arm, pulling her back. But there was no way she could retreat now that Elliott Ratcliffe had flung open this Pandora's box of pain. She was too angry. In too much pain. She would not let him win this battle, even though she'd long since lost the war.

Shaking off Nick's hand, she stepped toward Elliott. "You don't know anything about me," she said breathlessly. "You're blinded by hatred and bitterness—"

"I know you seduced my son. First with your body, then with a bastard son."

The words echoed like gunshots in her ears. Fury poured through her veins, like a scream trapped inside her body, its shrill ring powerful enough to shatter bone. Her vision tunneled on his face. She could feel her pulse beating inside her head, a giant hammer clanging against her skull until she thought her head would explode. The last of her control fled. "You son of a *bitch*!"

She launched herself at him. A terrible sound that was half scream, half roar tore from her throat. Her first punch went wide and glanced off his shoulder. She heard a shout, then her second blow struck him squarely in the jaw. But his head was as large and solid as a boulder, and the impact barely fazed him.

Dully, she was aware of him stepping back, dodging her blows. His hands flying up to protect his face. "Get her off me!"

She landed another blow to his chin. Pain exploded in her

hand, zinged all the way to her elbow. She could feel her teeth grinding together. Rage igniting into a violent blast inside her. Intent cemented in her brain. She wanted to hurt him. Rip the terrible words from his mouth.

"Call the police!" Elliott said. "She's out of control!"

Strong arms wrapped around her from behind and swung her around. "Knock it off."

Nick, she thought vaguely. But she was beyond reason and twisted away. It was as if all the emotions that had been trapped inside her for the last three years came pouring out in a single, violent rush. "Let go of me!" she screamed and tried to lunge at Elliott again. "Don't you dare speak of my son that way!"

Locking his arms around her waist, Nick pulled her back. "Nat! Pull yourself together."

The elder Ratcliffe raised his hand and pointed at her. "Vengeance is mine; I will repay, sayeth the Lord."

"Dad . . ." Travis stepped between her and Elliott. "Let it go. This has gotten ugly enough."

Nat struggled, but Nick's arms were like steel bands around her. "Let go of me," she choked.

"I don't have the cash to bail you out of jail, *chere.*" Grasping both her arms, he turned her toward him and gave her a small shake. "Get ahold of yourself."

But Nat had already lost her grip. She could feel the last remnants of her control peeling away. She could hear herself sobbing, and the thought struck her that she sounded like a crazy woman. She could hear the shuffle of their shoes against the floor as Nick forced her toward the door.

Travis stood in the foyer with the door open. His hair was mussed. He looked shaken and angry and shook his head at her when she passed. "You'd better not come back," he said.

"Your father is wrong," she choked as Nick muscled her past him. "I'm going to prove it!"

He slammed the door without responding.

chapter
16

NICK WAS NO STRANGER TO UGLY EMOTIONS. IN THE six years he'd spent in prison, he'd seen just about every emotion known to mankind. Hatred. Rage. Grief. Despair. He'd felt varying degrees of those emotions in his own heart. He'd seen those emotions come to fruition in terrible acts of violence, rape and murder and suicide. He'd witnessed almost every vile thing a man could do to another man.

But the ugly scene that had played out between Nat and Elliott Ratcliffe got to him in a way nothing else could have. She'd been like a lioness protecting a dead cub and willing to fight to the death to do it. Old man Ratcliffe had known just where to strike, and in the minutes she'd been out of control, consumed by grief and rage and God only knew what else, the man had seemed to draw some sort of twisted satisfaction from hurting her.

Nick had wanted to deck the son of a bitch. But he knew an assault charge would only land him back in Angola, so he'd settled for getting her the hell out of there.

The tension in the truck was palpable as they sped toward her house. She sat in the passenger seat, her hands in her lap, staring through the window with all the animation of a mannequin. He glanced over at her several times, but she didn't meet his gaze, didn't even acknowledge him. It was as if she'd gone to a place deep inside herself. A place that was quiet and dark where the pain couldn't reach her. He figured she'd spent quite a bit of time there in the last three years.

The need to reach out to her was strong, but Nick resisted. He wasn't quite sure how to do it. He didn't know what she wanted, what she needed. He wasn't even sure what *he* wanted—or if he should risk getting any more involved than he already was.

He parked in the driveway behind her Mustang. He'd barely shut down the engine when she shoved open the door. She was out of the truck and running toward the house before he could stop her. For a moment he just sat there, refusing to take his hands off the wheel, and watched her bound up the steps to the porch. A woman running from her demons, he thought. If his own personal experience was any indication, she would never outrun them. If she was lucky, she might learn to live with them.

He knew better than to go after her. She was hurting; he was feeling a hell of a lot more for her than was prudent. It was a dangerous combination for a man with a weakness for vulnerable, troubled women. But Nick had never been prudent when it came to getting what he wanted, even when he knew it was going to cost him something. At the moment, he wanted Nat.

"Goddamn it."

Rapping his palm hard against the wheel, he shoved open the door and started for the house. She was standing on the porch, fumbling in her purse for the key, when he reached her. He stopped a few feet away, shoved his hands into his pockets to keep them from reaching for her.

"I'm fine," she snapped. But her eyes belied the words; they were haunted and so lovely it hurt to look into them and see the deep well of pain.

"I can see that," he said dryly.

"I want to be alone."

He knew all about being alone, knew it was about as helpful as a bottle of whiskey on top of a broken heart. "Yeah, well, sometimes what we want and what we need are two different things, *chere*."

She tossed him a glare over her shoulder. "I mean it. I need some time. Just . . . go."

Nick held his ground, telling himself for the dozenth time he could handle this. He could handle her and her grief and all the things she was making him feel. "I don't think this is a good time for you to be alone."

"You don't know me, and you don't know what I need."

He watched her grapple in her purse for her keys. Her hands were pale and shaking. He didn't think she was going to find them anytime soon. "Let me."

She shook her head, continued digging in her purse. "I can do it, damn it."

Ignoring her protest, he eased the bag from her hands, gave it a single shake to locate the keys, and pulled them out. Brushing past her, he inserted the house key into the lock, gave it a twist, and opened the door.

Wordlessly, she stepped into the foyer. Nick hesitated an instant before following. The house smelled like a combination of coffee and some soft scent he was beginning to recognize as hers. He watched her walk into the living room and stop. She stood there for a moment with her back to him, her arms wrapped around herself, her shoulders squared, chin high. An odd mix of body signals that told him she was trying hard to get a handle on her emotions. Judging from the way she was shaking, she wasn't succeeding.

"I'm sorry I lost it," she said after a moment. "I don't know what happened. I just . . ." As if not knowing how to finish the sentence she let her words trail.

"He pissed you off."

Slowly, she turned to him. "He had no right to say those things about Kyle."

"No, he didn't."

"Kyle was just an innocent little boy."

"And Elliott Ratcliffe is a coldhearted son of a bitch."

"He wasn't illegitimate," she whispered.

Nick shook his head, felt something go soft inside him when her eyes filled. "Nat, it doesn't matter."

"It matters."

"To Elliott Ratcliffe, maybe." In the back of his mind, he

wondered how a man who called himself a man of God could be so cruel.

A breath that was deep and filled with emotion shuddered out of her. "I'm the daughter of a cotton farmer, Nick. My dad had only a sixth grade education. We weren't poor, just . . . middle class." Her shoulders rose and fell. "When I got pregnant, Elliott accused me of trapping Ward because of the Ratcliffe money."

"Some people have small minds."

"I loved Ward. He was the first man, the only man I ever loved. We were happy."

Nick thought she was trying a little too hard to convince him, but he didn't interrupt. For whatever reason, she needed to say this. The least he could do was listen.

"What's really sad is that Elliott never once had a kind word for his own grandson. He never held him or laughed with him. Ward tried to justify his father's lack of affection by telling me he was a disciplinarian and didn't believe in coddling children. But I knew better." Her expression turned wistful. "Kyle was a happy little boy. He was exuberant and beautiful and loving. I never understood how anyone could not love him, especially his own grandfather." A bitter sound escaped her. "I think when he looked at Kyle, he saw me."

"Elliott Ratcliffe is a hypocrite."

Turning away from him, she bowed her head and put her face in her hands. She didn't make a sound, but Nick sensed the dam was about to break. He didn't know what to do. For several interminable moments he just stood there, wanting to go to her, knowing what would happen if he did.

He didn't like seeing her like this, laid open and raw, like a quivering nerve exposed to air and screaming with pain. There was simply no way he could stand there and do nothing while she came apart right in front of him.

"Nat."

"Don't." She raised her hand as if to stave him off, but she didn't look at him.

He reached her in two resolute steps. She jolted when he wrapped his fingers around her biceps. *"Vien ici."* Come here. He didn't wait for her to comply. Gently, he turned her toward him. She tried to avert her face, but he set his fingers beneath her chin and forced her gaze to his.

"I know it hurts," he said gently. "But you're going to get through this. You're going to be all right."

"I'm never going to be all right. It's been three years since my little boy died, and I still miss him so much I can't bear it."

"It gets easier. You'll have good days and bad days. This is just a bad day."

"They're all bad."

"No they're not." Tucking a strand of hair behind her ear, he offered a thin smile. "The ratio will improve with time."

"Nick, I still see him. I still hear his voice, his footsteps in the house. I smell him. For God's sake, we have conversations inside my head."

For the first time he realized how profoundly bittersweet, how heartbreaking the trance writing was for her. He knew that no matter how hard she tried to heal, it would not let her move on.

"I want my baby back," she whispered.

Lifting his hand, he gently brushed a strand of hair from her face, let his fingers linger against her cheek. "You can't have him back, *chere*. He's gone. You have to let him go and move on with your life."

"I can't. Not when he talks to me."

"He's trying to help you, *chere*."

"It's killing me."

"Maybe you can take some comfort in that with his help we're going to make things right for him."

It was the first time Nick had spoken the words aloud, and even though he'd come to believe Nat was, indeed, psychic, they still shocked him.

"Promise me," she whispered. "Tell me we're going to find the son of a bitch who took our children from us."

Nick stared at the pale frame of her face, aware that his chest was tight, his palms damp. He hurt for her, he realized. He could feel the pain burgeoning inside him, a silent ache that was powerful and cold and squeezed his heart like a fist. "We'll find him," he said. "I promise."

They were standing face-to-face, so close he could smell

the sweet scent of her hair, feel the warm brush of her breath against his face. He knew better than to let the moment go on. But simmering in some shadowy place deep inside him was an attraction he could no longer deny. He knew there shouldn't have been anything sexual about the moment. The last thing she needed in her life was ex-con who couldn't offer her anything but his own troubles. But the need to feel her body against his was as powerful as his need to take his next breath.

Putting his arms around her, Nick pulled her to him. A tremor went through her on contact. The sweet ache that followed went all the way to his core. He set his cheek against her hair, which was like fragrant silk against his skin. Closing his eyes, he breathed in the lemon scent of her shampoo. He was keenly aware of her arms encircling his shoulders, her soft body conforming to his.

It had been six unbearable years since he'd been this close to a woman. His response was instantaneous and base. The rush of blood from his head to his groin made him dizzy. His sex grew heavy and full and strained uncomfortably against his fly.

"I don't usually have emotional meltdowns like this," she said.

He pulled back slightly so she couldn't feel his erection against her, and looked into her eyes. "Don't apologize."

Her eyes filled, and something went soft and warm in his chest. She blinked furiously, but the tears squeezed through her lashes to roll down her cheeks. When her shoulders began to shake, he tightened his arms and set his chin on her crown.

"Go ahead and let it out," he said softly.

The tears came with a vengeance, racking her body with great, shuddering sobs. He held her tightly while she purged the grief that had lain dormant inside her for so many months. All the while he stroked her hair with his right hand, held her against him with his left, and whispered words of comfort into her ear.

He wasn't sure how long they stayed like that, locked in an embrace and standing body to body. It could have been minutes; it could have been an hour. The only thing he knew for certain was that she'd needed to be held. That he'd needed to hold her. And that he damn well didn't want to ponder the significance of either of those things.

When the last of her sobs subsided, she pulled back and raised her gaze to his. "I've cried all over your shirt."

"It's an old shirt."

Nick thumbed a tear from her cheek. Even pale with grief, her eyes red-rimmed from crying, she was lovely. Her mouth was partially open. Her lips were damp. He could feel the need coiling and flexing inside him. He wanted to kiss her. He wanted to do a hell of a lot more than that. He wanted her naked and beneath him. He wanted to sheathe himself inside her heat and pour his seed into the deepest reaches of her body.

Leaning close, he brushed his mouth lightly against hers, testing her, testing himself. Her lips were pliable and soft beneath his. He touched her lip with the tip of his tongue, tasted the remnants of her tears and the fever of his own lust. The quick rise of heat stunned him. He could feel the gallop of blood through his veins. A hot pool forming in his groin to pulse with every frenzied beat of his heart.

Neither of them had closed their eyes, and when he pulled away, hers were wide and puzzled. "Why did you do that?"

"Because I wanted to taste you." Nick stared into the turquoise depths of her gaze, more shaken than he wanted to admit. "Because I'm a fool."

"If that makes you a fool, what does it make me?"

"Vulnerable. Troubled." He scrubbed a hand over his jaw. "A mistake, probably."

"A mistake for whom?"

"You more than me, *chere*." He sighed. "I have to go."

He fully intended to turn around and walk out the door. He envisioned himself walking down the porch steps, getting into the truck, pulling out of the driveway.

But neither of them moved.

Nick wasn't sure he could. He couldn't take his eyes off her. Raising his hand, he brushed his thumb across her lower lip. It was like a rose petal, soft and pale and slightly wet as if with dew. "I don't like seeing you hurt, *chere*."

"I'm okay." She gave him a shaky smile. "Your being here helped. Thank you."

That she would thank him when all he could think about was laying her down and burying himself inside her made him feel like a lecher. He was about to step back when she raised up on her tiptoes and brushed her mouth against his cheek.

Sudden need flared like a thousand matches igniting simultaneously inside him. She must have seen the intent on his face, because her eyes widened. She opened her mouth as if to speak, but before she could utter a protest, Nick leaned close and crushed his mouth to hers.

The kiss wasn't gentle this time, and a shudder ran the length of her body on contact. The snap of pleasure made him groan. It was like an electrical surge that ignited every nerve ending in his body, each of them zinging with a thousand volts. He devoured her mouth, and all he could think was that he wanted more.

Tilting her head for a better angle, he deepened the kiss. She didn't kiss him back, but he didn't care. He penetrated her with his tongue. A groan rumbled up from his chest when she finally responded. It was what he'd been waiting for, and he fed on her mouth like a starving man. A man possessed. A man about to cross to the point of no return.

She made a sound in her throat, but he couldn't tell if it was a protest or sigh. He was too far gone to care. Too far gone to do anything but kiss her and hope one of them came to their senses before things went too far. His intellect made a last ditch effort to stop him, reminding him of the havoc a woman could wreak upon a man's life. But Nick's body didn't give a damn about ancient history. Didn't give a damn about boundaries or right or wrong.

Somewhere in the back of his mind, he could hear his breaths coming short and fast, as if he'd just run a marathon. The blood roaring in his ears was like a raging sea, rising up to crash against a jagged shore. He was painfully aroused, his erection straining against the constraints of his jeans. A sweet agony that tortured him like the keen blade of a knife. A razor edge that cut deeper with every beat of his heart.

Nick couldn't remember the last time he'd been with a woman. Tanya, at some point before he'd begun his prison term. After being alone for so many years, the needs rampaging through him built quickly into desperation.

Nat turned her head slightly, breaking the kiss. He heard his name on her lips, but before she could say anything, he captured her mouth again, coaxed her into submission with his tongue. Pure male pleasure rippled through him when she opened. Growling low in his throat, he went in deep, tasting her, exploring her, encouraging her to enter him as well.

Nick had never been an impatient lover. He preferred to take things slowly, let things build to a natural crescendo. But kissing Nat Jennings was like nothing he'd ever experienced in his life. It was as if he were oxygen starved and no matter how hard or deeply he breathed, he couldn't get enough air into his lungs.

Never taking his mouth from hers, he skimmed his hands downward. She shivered when he ran his fingertips over the outer curves of her breasts. He wanted his hands on her. His tongue in her mouth. Her skin against his. His body sliding into the tight, wet heat of her body . . .

She stiffened when he brushed his hands over her nipples. He felt the tiny peaks harden through her bra. He knew the moment had affected her, and the knowledge drove him a little bit insane. "I've got to touch you," he whispered. "Now."

"Nick . . ."

He was pretty sure she'd been about to stop him. He didn't give her the chance. She arched when he molded her breasts with his hands. When her head lolled back, he kissed her neck. Her shoulders. The tops of her breasts, the valley between them. Desperate to touch her skin, he slipped his hands beneath her shirt. Kissing her, he fumbled for the closure of her bra, located the tiny clasp between her breasts. But his hands were shaking so badly he couldn't manage. Frustrated and a little embarrassed at his ineptness, he took the simpler route and lifted the scrap of silk over her breasts.

He raised her shirt, and the sight of her shook him, awed him, made him realize how desperately he'd missed this, how much this moment meant to him. "Aw, God," he whispered. "You're beautiful."

"Wait . . ."

A sound that was part sigh, part moan escaped her when he cupped her breast. Her flesh was incredibly soft and warm against his palm. Her entire body jolted when he scraped the pads of his thumbs over her nipples.

He skimmed his hands lower, and for the first time felt the

pucker of the scar. It ran from just below her left breast to her
navel. She tensed the instant he made contact, and a slow
wave of anger rolled through him that someone had hurt her,
disfigured her.

Because he wanted her to know whatever scars she bore
didn't detract from her beauty, or make any difference to him,
he traced his fingers over it. "It doesn't matter," he whispered.

"It's . . . ugly."

"It's not."

"Nick, I can't."

"Yes, you can." Lowering his head, he took her nipple into
his mouth. She cried out when he began to suckle, laving the
engorged tip with his tongue. She tasted hot and sweet, and all
he could think was that he would die if he didn't get inside
her. At the moment, he couldn't think of a better way to go.

NAT COULDN'T BELIEVE THIS WAS HAPPENING. SHE
couldn't believe he'd kissed her. That she'd kissed him back.
That she'd liked it, and now the moment was spiraling out of
control. Somehow the grief that had held her in its grip for so
many months had morphed into a need so powerful she felt it
all the way to her foundation.

The sensation of his mouth on her nipple shocked her, sent
hot electrical impulses from her breast to her brain and every
erogenous zone in between. He was making her feel things
she didn't want to feel, making her want things she was a fool
for considering, at a time in her life when she was lucky just to
make it though the day.

But she could feel her pulse hammering. Her breasts
aching, swelling beneath his hands. The wetness hot and pulsing between her legs.

She jolted when the backs of her calves made contact with
the sofa. In some far corner of her mind, she acknowledged
that there was a small, reckless part of her that wanted this.
She was tired of hurting, of being alone. She wanted the pain
to go away, if only for a little while.

But Nat knew sex for the sake of sex wasn't going to pull
all the broken pieces of her life back together. Nick Bastille
might be attractive and sexy and willing to use both of those

things to get what he wanted. But going to bed with him was not the way to healing. She knew it would only interfere with the alliance she'd worked hard to forge. That in the long run a relationship with him would hurt her far more than it would help.

He was so close she could feel the heat coming off his body and into hers. He trailed kisses up her neck. Then his mouth was on hers, tearing down her resolve, stealing the last of her resistance. He'd lifted her shirt and bra. She could feel the wetness of his saliva on her nipples. Her body clenching, releasing. Her control skittering just out of reach.

All the while his mouth worked dark magic on hers. It was as if he'd put her under a spell. She couldn't stop kissing him, accepting him into her mouth. Vaguely she was aware of his hand at the snap of her jeans, the zipper being lowered. An alarm blared inside her head. The words to stop him echoed in her brain.

Then his hand was against her pelvis. She could feel her womb contracting in response. The sensation wrenched a moan from her. Guilt and pleasure screamed through her, but it was now tempered by the need to protect herself.

Nat wasn't sure if her knees buckled or if she sat of her own accord, but the next thing she knew she was sitting on the sofa, and Nick was pushing her back. The breath rushed from her lungs when he wedged himself between her legs and came down on top of her. She could feel the hard ridge of his erection against her belly. He moved against her, and she got the impression of hot steel sliding against her body. She tasted desperation on his mouth, felt it in the way he touched her. He'd braced his arms on either side of her to keep his weight off of her, and she could feel his muscles straining with tension.

The sound of breaking glass came to her as if from a great distance. For an instant she thought the sound was her imagination. Something shattering inside her . . .

Then Nick was clambering off the sofa. "What the *hell*?"

Nat sprang to a sitting position and immediately spotted the cloth-covered bundle on the floor just inside the window. She stared at it, taken aback by the sight of blood, aware that the curtains were billowing in a breeze. Then she noticed glass on the floor and realized someone had thrown the bundle through the window.

"What is it?" she asked, righting her clothes.

"Don't touch it." Giving her a quick look over his shoulder, Nick rushed to the door. "Call the police," he said and was through the door and sprinting across the porch before she could say anything else.

Nat rose unsteadily to her feet and crossed to the window on shaking legs. She pulled the curtain aside and saw that the window had, indeed, been broken. Glass sparkled like ice crystals at her feet. Within the shards lay the bundle. A bundle that looked very much like a newborn baby wrapped in a bloodstained blanket.

The blanket was old and frayed with little blue hippos and yellow giraffes. The colorful print looked macabre spattered with red. Her hand shook when she reached for the corner of the blanket. Pinching it between her thumb and forefinger, she slowly unraveled the bloody mass from within. Nat saw matted hair. Dark smears of blood and tissue. She smelled its horrible, familiar stench.

The mass rolled onto the hardwood floor. Revulsion shuddered through her when the pale, white face came into view. She could hear herself breathing hard. The scent of blood filling her nostrils with its terrible copper stench. Nausea churning thick and hot in her gut.

She put her hand over her mouth to stifle the scream clawing at her throat. "Oh, no." Wrapping her arms around her stomach, Nat sat back on her heels and closed her eyes. "Oh, God, no."

She nearly jumped out of her skin when Nick came up behind her and put his hands on her shoulders. His fingers tightened, digging into her skin, lifting her.

"Come on," he said. "Get away from it. You don't need to see that."

"It's a . . . Oh, God, Nick, it's a baby."

Nudging her aside, he knelt for a better look. "It's a doll," he said. "Some sick bastard's idea of a joke."

Nat forced herself to look. A wave of abhorrence rose inside her at the sight of the blood and staring eyes. But for the first time she could see that it wasn't real. "Who would do something like this?"

Nick grimaced, shook his head. "I don't know."

Sudden rage sent her to the window where she ripped back the curtain and looked at the broken pane. "I'm not going to let them do this to me."

"Nat . . ."

"I'm not going to let them get away with this."

He reached for her, but she danced out of reach. Her heart pounded with fury as she yanked open the door. She heard Nick behind her, heard him call out her name, but she didn't stop. She burst through the front door and hit the porch running. She took the steps two at a time to the sidewalk and ran to the driveway. In the thin light of dusk, she could see the lingering rise of dust that had been kicked up by the tires of the vehicle that had sped away just moments earlier.

"*Bastard!*" she screamed. "Goddamn you! Leave me *alone!*"

For a full minute she stood there, grappling for control. But she could feel her emotions spiraling, a sob clogging her throat. She sensed Nick behind her, watching her, and wondered if he thought she was crazy.

When he came up behind her and put his hand on her shoulder, she didn't shake him off. She closed her eyes and tried to absorb the comfort he was offering, even though she knew it wasn't enough. That it would never be enough.

"We need to call the police," he said.

"I don't want to deal with the police."

"Then I'll deal with them."

She turned to face him. "Did you see the vehicle?"

"By the time I got through the door, they were already too far away." He grimaced. "Are you okay?"

She nodded, but she was far from okay. She was outraged and furious and completely unable to fathom how someone could do something so vicious. "Who would do something like this?"

"It could have been anyone," he said. "Kids. Some misguided jerk who thinks you had something to do with the murders."

Her laugh was bitter. "Half the town."

He thought about that for a moment. "Anyone specific you can think of?"

"Hunt Ratcliffe. Jim Arnaud. Elliott Ratcliffe. Take your pick."

"I don't see Elliott stooping to juvenile pranks."

"He could have hired someone."

"Not his style, *chere*. Men like Elliott Ratcliffe aren't going to bother with some juvenile prank. If he wants to get you, he'll buy a cop or have the district attorney put you in front of another grand jury."

Nat knew he was right. It was bad enough having enemies. But to not know who they were was infinitely worse. "Frankly, I'm surprised he hasn't done more. He certainly hates me enough."

"Or maybe we're thinking about this all wrong. Maybe this doesn't have anything to do with a town blaming you for something you didn't do, and everything to do with your being back and asking questions."

The words chilled her. "You mean the killer."

"Think about it. He was home free. Everyone thought you did it, and you were tucked neatly away in a coma. Three years later, you show up and start asking questions. He's not going to be happy about that."

"A prank like this . . . it seems like an odd tactic for someone brutal enough to kill a child."

"Maybe he doesn't want to alert the police. Maybe he just wants you gone."

"It's going to take a hell of a lot more than some teenage hoax to scare me off," she said hotly.

"Yeah, well, I think it's time we talked to Alcee."

Nat choked out a laugh, but she could feel her hackles rising. "And tell him what? That I'm here to solve a three-year-old murder that I was once a suspect in? Oh, and by the way, something happened to me when I was in a coma and now I'm psychic and communicating with my dead son." She shook her head. "I can do without a one-way ticket to the loony bin."

Nick shot her a dark look. "Don't tell him about the trance writing. But for your own safety, I think you should tell him what you suspect."

"I've already told him that the person responsible for what happened to Kyle and Ward is still free. Here's a news flash for you, Nick. He didn't believe me. If I take it any farther, he's going to have questions I don't know how to answer."

"Yeah, well, maybe that bloody doll in there will help convince him, because I have a feeling the son of a bitch who put it through your window is just getting warmed up."

chapter
17

"YOU DIDN'T FIND ANOTHER DEAD BODY, DID YOU?"
Chief of Police Alcee Martin removed his hat and stepped
into the foyer.

"I wasn't so sure a few minutes ago," Nat said.

His gaze went from Nat to the grotesque bundle on the
floor, then to Nick. "What happened?"

"Some joker tossed a doll wrapped in a bloody baby blanket through the living room window," Nick said.

"Anyone hurt?"

"No, but I'm pissed," Nat answered.

Martin looked pained. "Anyone see who did it?"

Nick shook his head. "They were gone before I could get a
look at the vehicle."

"Sounds like teenagers."

"Or someone with a vendetta." Nick shot Nat a pointed look.

Martin followed his gaze and stared hard at her. Nat knew
that was her cue to tell the chief what she suspected. But she
knew all too well what it was like to tell the truth and not be
believed. She knew that without some shred of proof to back
up her theory, there was no way in hell Alcee Martin would
believe her.

After an uncomfortable moment, Martin walked over to
the bundle and squatted. Removing a pen from his uniform

pocket, he used it to lift the blanket and made a face. "Smells like blood."

"I thought so, too," Nick said.

"Probably animal blood," the chief said. "But I'll go ahead and send it to the lab in Baton Rouge to make sure it's not human."

"Nat thinks this might have something to do with what happened three years ago." Nick gazed steadily at her for the span of several heartbeats. "Tell him or I will."

Chief Martin raised a brow, looked expectantly at Nat. "Tell me what?"

Silently cursing Nick for pushing her into doing something she wasn't ready to do, she shook her head. "I think the person responsible for Kyle's and Ward's deaths might be behind this. I think he's still in Bellerose. And I think he's threatened because I'm asking questions about what happened three years ago."

Martin looked like a stomach cramp hit him. "Nat, you know my take on that—"

"The killer isn't some transient," she snapped. "He's here. In your pretty little town. Hiding behind some face you know."

"I know you want this cleared up, Nat. Damn it, so do I. But pointing fingers at some phantom bad guy isn't the way to do it."

For a crazy instant she was tempted to tell him about the trance writing. The notes. How she'd known where to find Ricky Arnaud's body. There was a part of her that wanted to let it all come pouring out and let the cards fall where they may. But she simply wasn't willing to destroy what little credibility she had left.

"He doesn't want me asking questions, Alcee. In fact, he wants me gone. That's why he did this."

"So he throws a doll through your window?" he asked incredulously. "What's that going to accomplish?"

"Maybe next time it'll be a Molotov cocktail," Nick cut in. "I think she's right."

Martin shot Nick a killing look. "I'm not interested in conspiracy theories." His gaze cut to Nat and his eyes narrowed. "How did you get that bruise on your face?"

"I ran into a cupboard door when I was cleaning."

"Uh huh." He rubbed at his eyebrow. "How the hell do you expect me to do my job when you keep lying to me?"

"I expect you to do your job by finding the bastard who murdered my husband and son."

"I'm a police officer, Nat. I operate on facts. On proof and evidence and the law of the land. You give me something solid, and I'll be the first cop on the scene. If you can't do that, then I suggest you curtail the accusations."

She could feel her credibility slipping, and it hurt. She needed Alcee to believe her. He was a smart man. A good man. A by-the-book cop who was trying to do the right thing. But he was also the product of a small Southern town. There was no way he would believe Kyle had spoken to her from beyond the grave. Most days, she could barely believe it herself.

Nick stepped toward Martin. "At least send a cruiser out this way every couple of hours to check on her."

Martin frowned, his gaze flicking from Nick to Nat. "I'll see what I can do," he said and started toward the door.

NAT KNEW THERE WASN'T MUCH CHIEF MARTIN could do on the information she'd given him. A petty vandalism hardly warranted the expense of police protection or a high tech forensics lab. She figured she was lucky he'd taken enough interest to place the doll in one of her tall kitchen garbage bags to have it checked for fingerprints and the blood tested to see if it was human. But she was disappointed just the same when he left.

"You should have told him everything."

She looked up to find Nick scowling at her from where he'd been holding vigil at the front window. "He wouldn't have believed any of it," she said. "Not without proof."

"What if this guy takes it a little bit farther next time?"

"I don't know," she snapped. "I'll just have to be alert, be careful."

She'd managed to avoid him for all of the twenty minutes it took for him to tape a sheet of polyurethane over the broken pane. Now that he was finished, she was quickly realizing Nick Bastille wasn't a man who could be avoided if he didn't want to be.

She busied herself preparing a pail of detergent and bleach and carried it to the living room to wash away the remaining blood.

"I need to check on Dutch," Nick said. "He's been alone all day." He grimaced. "I don't want to leave you here alone."

"I'll be fine. Don't worry about me."

"Come with me," he said. "I'll introduce you to my father and fix the three of us dinner."

Surprised—and inordinately pleased—by the invitation, Nat looked up from her cleaning to find him staring down at her with an intensity that unnerved. Even with everything that had happened, she found her mind wandering to the intimacies they'd shared in the moments before the window had been shattered. The memory jarred her back to reality, and she shook her head. "I've got things to do here," she said.

"I make a pretty mean gumbo."

"Nick . . ."

"I don't like the idea of your being here by yourself."

"I know Alcee. He'll send a deputy by." But she figured they both knew the chief's deputies hated her as much as everyone else in Bellerose. "I'll be fine."

"The house is secure," Nick said, but he didn't look happy about leaving. "The windows and doors are locked down tight."

Trying hard to ignore the chill that passed through her at the thought of his leaving, she plucked off her rubber gloves and got to her feet. "I'll lock up behind you."

He stared at her long enough to make her uncomfortable, then said, "Nat, about what happened . . ."

For an instant, she wasn't sure if he meant the kiss or the doll incident, and it make her feel foolish.

"I just wanted you to know. I didn't mean for things to get out of hand."

She pretended to wave off the apology as if it were nothing. "We were wound up pretty tight after leaving the Ratcliffes. . . ."

"Adrenaline dump does that sometimes."

She nodded her agreement, but she didn't think either of them believed it. "I don't think either of us is ready for . . ." Because she didn't quite know how to finish the sentence, she let her words trail.

"Ready for what?"

"Each other." She sighed. "I'm a widow, Nick."

Never taking his eyes from hers, he shifted his weight from one foot to the other. "You didn't taste like a widow when you were kissing me. You didn't feel like one when you were pressed up against me."

She tried to deny the quick rise of heat, but couldn't because she'd liked kissing Nick Bastille. For a few precious moments he'd made her feel like a human being. He'd made her feel like a woman. He'd made her feel cherished and alive. Like maybe she had something to live for besides revenge.

"You'd better go check on your dad," she said.

For a moment he looked as if he wanted to say more. Instead, he gave her a look that was half smile, half resignation and turned on his heel and walked out the door.

NICK CURSED HIMSELF ALL THE WAY TO HIS TRUCK, got behind the wheel, and cursed himself some more. Of all the idiotic things he could have done, kissing Nat Jennings was at the top of the list. He had enough problems of his own without getting tangled up with a woman. Of all the women in Bellerose he could have developed a hard-on for, why did it have to be her? Hadn't he learned his lesson with Tanya?

But he knew Nat wasn't anything like Tanya. His ex-wife had brought her troubles down on herself. Nat was a victim of circumstance. Some very brutal circumstances, he thought, and remembering her tears, felt a surprisingly sharp pang of guilt. Guilt for pushing when he shouldn't have. Guilt because she'd been hurting, and he'd taken advantage of the situation. She'd needed a friend, not some sex-crazed ex-con.

Maybe he should take Mike Pequinot up on his offer of a hooker. Maybe sex would get this monkey off his back. But Nick had a sinking feeling that it wasn't going to be that simple. Now that he'd had a taste of Nat, there was no way some woman with a pretty face and the morals of an alley cat was going to do the trick.

Rapping his palm against the wheel, he cranked up the engine and tore out of the driveway. He hit the road doing fifty and didn't slow down until the turnoff for the Cypress Creek

Mobile Home Park on the south edge of Bellerose. He knew he should have driven straight to the farm to check on Dutch, but this was one thing that wouldn't wait.

He pulled up next to the collage of mailboxes and spotted the name he was looking for. He pulled onto the crushed shell lane and idled past a dozen rusty, broken down trailer homes. Halfway down the street, he parked the truck and cut the engine.

The symphony of the swamp met him through the open window. The incessant buzz of mosquitoes. The chirping of crickets. The grunting of pig frogs. The sun had dipped below the tree line, casting the forest in shadows. The bayou seemed to sense the coming of night.

Nick left the truck and crossed to the rusty blue-and-white trailer. The place was worse than he'd imagined, and he felt a hard tug of guilt that this was where his son had spent the last years of his short life. He ascended the metal steps and knocked on the dented aluminum door.

A moment later, the door swung open, and he found himself looking at his ex-wife. She had a beer in one hand, a cigarette in the other. She didn't look very happy to see him. "What the hell are you doing here?"

"Can I come in?"

"Why?"

"Who's there, baby?" came a gruff male voice from somewhere inside the trailer.

"Nobody," she snapped.

Nick looked away, then back at his wife. "I don't care if you have company. I just want to talk for a moment. It won't take long."

"Who the hell you talkin' to out there?" A man with shoulder-length brown hair, a salt-and-pepper beard, and a belly the size of a Volkswagen came up beside her and gave Nick a narrow-eyed glare. *"Quoi tu veux?"* What do you want?

"Jacky, this is my ex-husband, Nick Bastille," Tanya said quickly.

The man belched, his eyes never leaving Nick. "You going to hassle her, or what?"

"I just need to ask her a few questions." Nick turned his attention to Tanya. "It's important."

Scratching his belly, the man turned away and sauntered
back to the living room. Tanya stared at Nick as if she wasn't
quite sure what to do next. "You want a beer or something?"

"No."

"Come on in."

Nick didn't want to go inside. He didn't want to see how
his ex-wife lived, how his son had lived. He didn't want to
know if she'd had men in her bed while his son had lain in his
bed and listened. Nick wasn't a jealous man; he'd long since
stopped caring with whom his ex-wife slept. But it bothered
him that his young son had been exposed to a lifestyle he
should have been protected from. That Nick hadn't been there
to protect him.

Tanya opened the door wider, and he stepped into the
trailer. The night was hot and humid. The air conditioner rattling in the kitchen window did little to cool the interior. The
place reeked of cigarette smoke, cheap carpet, and yesterday's
dinner, heavy on the onions.

Tanya crossed to an ancient refrigerator and bent to retrieve
a beer. "What brings you out here?" She handed him a beer.

Even though he didn't want it, Nick uncapped it and drank
deeply, thankful it was cold. "I need to talk to you about
Brandon."

She stared at him as if he'd plunged a knife into her stomach. After Brandon's death, it had been Tanya who'd needed to
talk about it, and Nick who'd been unable to do so. But after learning that his son's death hadn't been an accident, he
knew there was no way around the subject, and no one to do
anything about it except him.

"What do you want to know?" she asked warily.

"I need to know what happened that day."

She lifted her hand and dragged hard on the cigarette, then
looked at him through the thin cloud of smoke with narrowed
eyes. "Why?"

"Because I'm his father."

"Look, if you're looking to lay the blame—"

"I don't want to lay blame anywhere," he said. "I just want
to know what happened. What you saw. I need to see the place
where he—" *Drowned.* Nick still couldn't say the word. Even
after two years, he couldn't bear to think of his son dying that

way, a thought made infinitely worse by the possibility that he'd been murdered.

She crushed out her cigarette in an ashtray teeming with butts. "Let me get my shoes on."

Nick watched her walk to the rear of the trailer. Slouched on the sofa, watching a small black-and-white television, her lover contemplated him with dispassionate eyes.

"Tough thing losing a kid that way," he said.

"Yeah, it was tough."

"A lot of folks in town blamed her," the other man continued. "Still do, in fact. Saying she was drunk and passed out in her bed."

"Was she?"

"Coulda been. She's been known to tie one on occasionally." He took a long swig of beer. "But she wasn't drunk that night."

"How do you know?"

"I was with her up until almost midnight the night before it happened. We'd been down at The Gator, having us a drink. But I was working third shift at the mill that night, so we came back here around eleven thirty or so. Baby-sitter—Cora Anders from two trailers down—had put Brandon in bed. Tanya herself was in bed asleep and sober as a nun in church when I left."

"She could have gone back to The Gator after you left."

"She didn't."

Nick wasn't going to argue with him. If the other man hadn't figured out by now that Tanya was a liar and an alcoholic, it wasn't his place to enlighten him. The man would find out soon enough.

He looked down at the lock on the door. It was a cheap bolt lock, the kind you could find at any discount or hardware store. The kind a five-year-old would have no problem unlocking if his mom was in bed, and he wanted to go out and play . . .

Tanya came down the hall wearing a pair of sneakers without socks. She looked gaunt and unhappy, and for a moment he couldn't believe she was the young woman he'd married just eight years earlier. Because he didn't want her lover tagging along, Nick made eye contact with her, then walked out the door. He waited on the metal steps for her to join him. She came out a moment later. She'd lit another cigarette, and the beer in her hand was full and cold.

"I want you to tell me exactly what happened, exactly what you saw," he said. "Then I want you to take me through every step of how you think it happened."

"Oh, Nicky, I did that for the cops. I don't wanna—"

"Now you can do it for me." When she didn't say anything, he gave her a hard look. "You owe me that much."

She tilted the bottle of beer and drank deeply, then wiped her mouth on her arm. "I don't like talking about it."

"I don't like talking about it, either. But I need to know what happened."

Cursing beneath her breath, she descended the metal steps. Neither of them spoke as she took him across the crushed-shell street to a wide path cut into the woods. "Brand and I used to walk back here sometimes, just to get out of the trailer, especially when it was hot." She swatted at a mosquito as they entered the woods.

"He ever come out here by himself? Or maybe with another child?"

She shook her head. "There's only one other kid in the trailer park. She's a little older and didn't like playing with Brand."

They walked a couple more minutes. Around them, the bayou teemed with life. Somewhere nearby, an owl hooted. Something rustled in the dead leaves off to his left. The path veered right and took them to a wide pond with a black-glass surface. The bank was muddy but gently sloped. The opposite shore was crowded with reeds as tall as a man.

Nick knew immediately this was where his little boy had died. Such a pretty, peaceful place. He could feel the old pain encroaching, an invading army marching through him, tearing at his insides with steely bayonets.

His heart was pounding when he crossed to the muddy bank and looked out over the water. Beyond, cypress and pine loomed forty feet into the air, blocking the dim light of dusk. Knobby cypress knees jutted from the black water like the legs of old men. For a moment, he could do nothing but stare and try like hell to keep a handle on his emotions.

"Tell me what happened," he heard himself say.

Tanya held her ground behind him, as if she didn't want to venture too close to the water. "I knew something was wrong the moment I woke up," she said. "One minute I was sound asleep. The next I was sitting up in bed. My heart was pounding so hard I thought I was having a heart attack or something."

"What time was that?" he asked.

She looked away, but not before he saw the shame on her face. "Ten o'clock."

Nick held his tongue against the quick rise of anger and tried hard not to judge her. Tanya hadn't been a good mother, and there was a part of him that hated her for that. A part of him that blamed her because she'd let their five-year-old child play alone in a dangerous place.

"I ran out of the bedroom and down the hall. Brand was usually in his room, playing. But he wasn't there that morning. And he wasn't at the table."

"Was the front door locked?"

She shook her head. "Closed but not locked."

"You'd locked it the night before?"

"I always lock it, Nicky. I swear."

"You think Brand unlocked it and went out?"

She nodded. "The chain, too."

"So what happened next?"

"Once I realized he wasn't in the house, I started getting worried. I ran outside and called for him. I swear, I thought I'd find him playing with his little matchbox cars in the driveway. He liked to do that sometimes. When I didn't find him there, I got scared. I ran over to the neighbor's trailer and asked her if she'd seen him. She hadn't, so I started looking for him."

She looked down at the muddy bank. Tears shone on her cheeks, but she didn't bother to wipe them off. "I didn't come into the woods right away. I searched the trailer again, under his bed, in his closet. I looked in the car. I even looked in the crawl space beneath the trailer.

"But he wasn't anywhere. That's when I knew." Tears shimmered in her eyes when she looked at him. "I ran down the path you and I just took. It was raining and muddy, but I didn't care. I knew what had happened even before I saw his little body." A sound that was pure anguish escaped her. It was the sound of a mother's grief. Of self-recrimination because she knew in her heart that an innocent child shouldn't have been left alone.

"He was laying facedown by the reeds over there." She pointed to the far side of the pond. "He looked so little and pale. I don't remember going into the water. You know I don't swim, and I sure don't like snakes. But the next thing I knew I was standing in water up to my chest and holding him in my arms. I tried to breathe into his mouth, to get some oxygen into his lungs like they do on TV. But he was just limp. And cold. His little head kept lolling back. His eyes were only half open, and his tongue . . . oh dear Lord, seeing him like that . . ."

Nick had imagined the scene a thousand times in the two years since it had happened. Times when he hadn't been able to hurt or cry or even grieve. Times when he'd had to rely on an endless supply of anger and outrage just to get him through the day. But hearing the words firsthand, standing in the very place where his little boy had lost his life—possibly at the hands of a killer—was almost too much to bear.

Closing his eyes tightly, Nick put the heels of his hands against his eyes. *"Le bon Dieu mait la main."* God help.

Standing a few feet away, Tanya dropped to her knees in the mud, put her face in her hands and began to sob. Nick knew he should go to her, offer her comfort. But he didn't have any comfort to give. There was too much bitterness inside him. Too much grief. Too much blame. Too little forgiveness.

Instead, he turned away from her and walked to the bank closest to the place where she'd found Brand's body and looked out over the water. He took a deep breath. Another and another and slowly the grief began to recede into its deep, black hole.

"Did you see anyone else here that day?" he asked.

She slowly got to her feet. Her knees were caked with mud, but she didn't seem to notice. The cigarette between her fingers had burned out at some point, but she hadn't noticed that, either. She crossed to him and looked out at the water.

"If there had been anyone around, they would have heard me screaming and come to help."

Nick stared hard at her. "Are you absolutely certain?"

She raised her gaze to his. He saw the question in her eyes, and he knew she was wondering what he was getting at. Her face was wet with tears. A black streak of mascara extended from her left eye to her nostril. The face of grief, he thought. He saw the same thing in his own face. In Nat's. So much grief for one small town . . .

"I didn't see anyone."

"How long before the police arrived?" he asked.

"God, Nick. It could have been five minutes. It could have been five hours." She lifted the cigarette as if to draw on it, realized it had gone out, and tossed it to the ground. "I carried him to shore." Her face screwed up and she began to cry again. "I didn't want to put him down because I didn't want him to get muddy. That's so stupid. He was covered with moss and dirty swamp water. He was wearing the new sneakers I'd just picked up at Wal-Mart. I didn't want him to get them dirty."

"Did you notice anything else about him?"

"Like what?"

"Did he have any bruises? Anything like that?"

She blinked as if the question had surprised her. "I don't think so. I don't know. I was so upset. . . ."

Nick chose his next words carefully. "Did you ever . . . lose your temper with him, Tanya? Maybe grab his arm a little too tightly?"

Her mouth opened. Her eyes widened. She made a choking sound. "God no! Nick, how could you ask such a thing?"

"This is important, Tanya. Are you absolutely certain you never bruised him? Around the throat?"

She stepped back, raised her finger and shoved it close to his face. "I may not have been a perfect mama to Brand, but I swear to God I never hit him! Goddamn you for asking me that!"

Because her voice had risen, Nick raised his hands to silence her. "What happened when the police arrived?"

"Alcee Martin . . . took him from me. Laid him on the ground and tried mouth-to-mouth resuscitation. Even though Brand was blue, I was praying to God he would come around. That he would come to. But he didn't."

"Did any of the deputies look around? Search the area?"

She gave him an irritated look. "How would I know? I was out of my mind with grief! I don't know what the police did. All I knew was that I'd lost the only good thing I'd ever had. My little boy was dead, and he wasn't ever coming back."

TANYA WAS STANDING ON THE STEP OUTSIDE THE front door of the mobile home when Nick left her. She'd gotten herself a fresh beer, lit another cigarette, and asked him to stay for a drink, but he'd declined and was relieved as hell when he finally got in the truck.

For a moment, he sat behind the wheel and tried to decide what to do next. He'd been hoping Tanya would reveal some tidbit of information that would either prove or disprove Nat's conviction that Brandon had been murdered. As much as he hated to think of it, he'd been hoping she would substantiate the presence of bruises about his neck. Only she hadn't, and now he was faced with only one remaining alternative: Alcee Martin.

Nick had gone to school with Alcee but didn't know him well. He sure as hell didn't know him well enough to join him at the diner and announce over Mama Dee's fried okra that Nat Jennings's dead son had told them that Brandon had been murdered. No, he would have to think of another way to approach him. And soon, too. Because Nick had the sinking feeling that that there was a killer on the loose in Bellerose. A killer who would strike again if he wasn't stopped.

chapter
18

NAT SETTLED INTO A CHAIR AT THE DINING ROOM
table with a yellow legal pad and pen in front of her. A candle
flickered in the center of the table, sending a warm bouquet of
vanilla throughout the room. To her right, a manila folder lay
open, the messages from Kyle spread out like the pages of
some mysterious manuscript.

Mommy.
bad man came in ar house n hurted me an daddy.
Kill Branden to...
gona hurt more kidz
Make him stop.
hell hurt you to
monster in the woods
bad man take ricky. kill again. hurry.
Monster has ricky. Wood house
Heaven.
Bad man Took him.
Gatea mud.

Setting her hand against the latest note, she closed her eyes
and conjured the image of Kyle's face. For several minutes,
the only sounds came from the ticking of the grandfather

clock in the living room and the incessant chorus of the woods behind the house.

"Kyle," she whispered. "Help me, sweetie."

She picked up one of the pens, set the ballpoint tip against the paper, and waited. She tried to relax and focused on opening her mind. One minute stretched into five. Frustrated because nothing was happening, she wrote her name on the pad. She wrote Kyle's name and then *Where are you?*

A blast from the doorbell nearly sent her out of her skin. Pressing her hand to her chest, she gathered the notes, put them inside the folder, and closed it. A quick glance into the dining room told her the paint had covered the words she'd written on the wall the night before. At the door, she checked the peephole and was surprised to see Faye standing on the porch, a bottle of wine in one hand, a carryout pizza in the other.

Nat opened the door. Faye didn't wait to be invited inside, brushing by her and striding directly to the broken window, which she had evidently spotted from the front porch. "What in the bejeebers happened to your window?"

"A prank." Nat put her hands on her hips. "What are you doing here?"

"I was hoping to pig out on some pizza." Faye pulled the curtain aside and studied the window. "What kind of prank?"

Sighing, Nat told her about the doll. "If I talk about it, I'm just going to get pissed."

"You called the cops, right?"

She nodded.

"Good." Faye looked down at the pizza box. "Have you eaten?"

Nat breathed in the aromas of yeast dough and pepperoni, and her stomach rumbled in response. The day had been such an emotional roller coaster, she'd forgotten about dinner. "Don't tell me that pizza came from Pepperoni Kitchen."

Smiling, Faye headed toward the kitchen. "I'll get the plates."

"In the cupboard." Nat flipped on the overhead lights, trying hard to get used to the idea of having pizza with a woman whose friendship and loyalty she'd spent the last three years doubting.

"I brought merlot—"

Nat knew it the instant Faye spotted the bruise on her cheek. She'd done her best to cover it with makeup, but beneath the bright lights of the kitchen there was no hiding it.

"Oh, Natty." She looked pained. "Someone hit you."

"I ran into an old friend at The Blue Gator."

"What on earth were you doing at The Blue Gator?"

"Getting into trouble, evidently."

Crossing to her, Faye cupped her chin and tilted her cheekbone toward the light, her expression sympathetic. "Who did this?"

"Hunt Ratcliffe."

"That woman-hitting son of a bitch." Faye's lips thinned, her eyes flashing indignation. "You pressed charges, didn't you?"

"Not exactly . . ."

"You can't let him get away with hitting you."

"I hit him first."

"That doesn't matter. Hunt Ratcliffe outweighs you by eighty pounds. He's a bully and a mean-spirited jerk." Sudden understanding dawned on her friend's face. "He has no right to blame you for what happened to Ward and Kyle."

"I know. And I know I would have been within my rights to file charges against him, but I swear Faye, I didn't want to go through it. He's a Ratcliffe and I'm—"

"You're a woman who's been through a horrific ordeal." Studying the bruise, she shook her head. "Look, my ex is a judge over in Tangipahoa Parish—"

"I thought your ex was a landscaper?"

"My other ex."

"Oh, you got married again?"

Faye flushed. "He had a really powerful energy. But it was a fast marriage, even faster divorce." She shrugged. "But he's strong on crime, especially domestic stuff and women's rights. If you want me to talk to him . . ."

Absurdly thankful there was at least one person in Bellerose who believed in her, Nat had to blink back tears. "No, it's okay. I just want to forget about it."

Determined not to cry, she walked to the pizza box and opened the lid. "If we're going to put a dent in this, we should probably get started."

Faye poured wine while Nat loaded pizza slices onto plates. They settled into chairs at the dining room table and for several minutes the only sound came from forks scraping against ironstone.

"You don't have to bring food every time you come over," Nat said as she reached for her second slice.

"I knew you'd let me in if I had food."

Nat felt a smile emerge, realized it felt good on her face.

Faye grinned back. "So what were you doing at The Blue Gator, anyway?"

Nat scrambled for a lie, but none seemed plausible. When the silence became charged, Faye looked at her over her pizza, her brow quirking. "Now I'm intrigued."

"I went to see Nick Bastille," Nat said.

She stopped chewing. "What?"

"I said—"

"I heard you the first time. I'm just wondering why on earth you went to see him. I mean, he's not exactly your type." Her brows knitted. "Is he?"

Nat ignored the flutter in her stomach and answered her friend's question with one of her own. "Did you know he lost a son?"

"I sure do. It was awful. Poor little kid was only five years old. Slipped out of the house while his mother was passed out. He drowned in the swamp. The whole town was broken up. Bastille was in prison. Jenny Lee told me the warden wouldn't even give him a pass to attend the funeral."

Nat felt a pang of sympathy for Nick. How terrible it must have been, losing his only son while incarcerated and not even allowed to attend the funeral.

"Honey, is there something going on between you and Nick Bastille?"

Nat laughed, but it came out a little too forcefully, as if she were trying a tad too hard. "Of course not."

But, Faye wasn't easily fooled. "Natty, he's not the kind of guy you want to mess around with. I mean, the man did time for murder."

"He told me he didn't do it."

"What else is he going to say?" Faye pursed her lips.

"Look, he might be something to look at, but tread carefully. As far as we know, he could be dangerous."

Nat thought he was plenty dangerous, but not in the way Faye meant. "I can handle Nick Bastille."

"I'm not sure he's the kind of man who can be handled."

Not at all comfortable with the subject of Nick, especially when the memory of his touch was so fresh in her mind, Nat started to rise. But a sudden wave of vertigo sent her back down. In her peripheral vision the walls fluttered. The floor seemed ten feet down as she lost her sense of depth perception. In the last six months she'd become familiar with the sensation, and she knew what would happen next.

Fighting intense dizziness, she glanced at the legal pad next to her plate and watched it fade in and out of her vision, as if she were seeing it through wavering columns of heat. Vaguely, she was aware of the pen in her hand, that she was clutching it the way a child would clutch a crayon.

No, she thought. *Not now . . .*

"Nat?" Faye's voice reached her as if through a thick fog. "Honey? What's wrong?"

Nat heard the other woman's chair scrape against the floor, the rustle of her skirt as she rose. In the back of her mind, she was aware of Faye moving closer, touching her shoulder gently. "Natty? Honey, you're scaring me."

But Nat couldn't answer. She couldn't speak or move or explain herself. It was as if she'd been paralyzed by some insidious drug. As if something—or someone—had taken control of her body. The sensation was utterly terrifying.

The initial wave of energy hit her with the force of an earthquake. The lights seemed to dim, and then she was plunged into darkness. She reached for Kyle, searched desperately for the comfort and goodness he brought her.

But none of those things came, and abruptly, she sensed that something was terribly wrong. Adrenaline spiked, and then fear punched her like a giant, cold fist.

NAT CAME TO ON THE FLOOR. SHE STRUGGLED TO her hands and knees, still clutching the pen, her hair hanging

limply in her face. Her arms were weak and quivering. Her
heart was pounding. Cold sweat slicked the back of her neck.
She was breathing so hard her chest hurt.

"Nat! Honey, what happened? Are you okay?"

Nat looked up to see Faye punching numbers into her cell
phone. "Put down the phone."

"Natty, you just had some kind of seizure. Lie still while I
call an ambulance."

"Don't," she managed, but her voice was weak.

Faye stopped dialing but didn't put the phone down.
"What?"

"No ambulance. Please."

"Why not?"

"Because I'm okay."

"Oh, yeah, I can see that as you bleed all over the floor!"

"I'm not bleeding." Nat started to get to her feet, then spotted the bright red droplets of blood on the tile and realized
with some surprise that she was, indeed, bleeding. "Put the
phone down, Faye. Now, damn it. I mean it."

Faye choked out a sound of pure exasperation as she
dropped her phone onto the table and crossed to Nat. "You
have two seconds to tell me what the hell just happened."

"Where am I bleeding from?"

"Your nose, I think." Faye slid her arms beneath her shoulders. "Let's get you into a chair."

Nat's legs felt like paper, but she made it into the chair.
"It's never happened like that before."

"You mean this isn't the first time?" Faye asked incredulously.

"Unfortunately, no." She leaned back in the chair. "Tell me
what happened."

"You went down like a felled tree is what happened." Faye
tossed a concerned look at her over her shoulder as she
crossed to the counter and yanked a paper towel off the roll.
"You went stiff as a board. Then you started writing, digging
into the paper and tabletop with that pen. The next thing I
know you're on the floor." Her hand was shaking when she
wet the towel beneath the faucet. "Natty, I've never seen anything like it in my life. You scared the hell out of me!"

"You're not the only one I scared."

"Here." She shoved the paper towel at her. "Tilt your head back."

Putting the paper towel to her nose, Nat reached for the legal pad and her blood went cold in her veins.

Going to kill him. In big danger. Help him.
Jason Larue. Find him Mommy. The bad mans
coming.

I'm scared!

She'd used two sheets of paper. The words were written haphazardly, in huge, messy letters. She'd pressed so hard the paper had torn, and she'd ground the tip of the pen into the wood surface of the table.

"Oh my God."

Nat looked up to see Faye staring down at the legal pad, her face the color of paste. "What on earth? Why did you write that?" She raised stricken eyes to Nat's. "What is this?"

Not sure how to answer without revealing something she did not want to reveal, Nat rose on unsteady legs and threw the bloody paper towel in the trash, relieved to find her nose was no longer bleeding.

"Nat? What's going on?"

Feeling steadier, Nat returned to the table and sat down. "You probably ought to sit down for this."

Faye eased into a chair. "Honey, if there's some kind of residual damage from the coma, you should get yourself checked out. Have you had seizures like this before?"

"I have them all the time."

"Okay." Faye blew out a pent up breath, then looked hard at her. "How many times has this happened?"

"I've lost count. Maybe a couple of dozen times in the last six months."

"Does your doctor know you're having seizures? Does he know why? Are you on medication?"

"I saw four neurologists before leaving River Oaks. Two of them finally agreed that these . . . petit mals, for lack of a better term, could be a result of psychogenic epilepsy."

"Would you mind repeating that in English for us laymen?"

Remembering how disheartened she'd felt upon hearing the official diagnosis, Nat frowned. "It used to be called hysterical epilepsy."

Faye gave her a sympathetic look. "They think it's all in your head, huh?"

"Don't get me wrong, Faye. It's a very real disease. But I don't have epilepsy. And what you just witnessed was not a seizure."

Faye choked out a laugh and put her hand to her bosom. "You just scared the living shit out of me and you're trying to tell me there's nothing wrong with you?"

"Not physically."

"What the hell is *that* supposed to mean?"

Nat took a fortifying breath. "Something happened to me when I was in the coma."

"Something like what?"

"When I regained consciousness, I could . . . do certain things I hadn't been able to do before. It's like there was a channel to my brain that had been opened. A sixth sense, so to speak."

"Sixth sense? Natty . . ."

"Have you ever heard of trance writing?"

"Automatic writing? Of course, I've heard of it."

"Faye, you know I've always been a skeptic about any kind of psychic phenomena."

"You laughed at me when I had my palm read that time in New Orleans."

Nat let out a shuddery breath. "Since the coma, I've been able to . . . receive messages. I black out for a few seconds and when I come to, I've written something down."

Nat had only seen her friend truly surprised twice before. The first time was when she told her she'd given Ward Ratcliffe her virginity the night he'd been crowned homecoming king. The second was the night she'd called to tell her Ward and Kyle had been murdered. This was the third time.

Nat felt a moment of panic when Faye only continued to stare at her, her mouth open, her eyes round with shock. "Don't look at me like I'm crazy," she said. "Dammit, Faye, not you. If I can't convince you of what's happening here, I don't have a snowball's chance in hell of convincing anyone else."

"Just give me a minute to digest this, will you?"

But Nat could tell by the look on her face that Faye had a pretty good idea where this was going. Nat looked down at the childlike scrawl in front of her, picked up the paper with hands that were still shaking. Blinking back tears, she said, "It's him, Faye."

For a moment, the only sound came from the hum of the refrigerator in the kitchen. The pizza sat in the center of the table, cold. After a moment, Faye reached across the table and grasped Nat's hands in both of hers. "You are way too grounded to be saying what I think you just said."

"It's Kyle," Nat said. "I don't know how or why, but it's him. I can *feel* him. It's like he's inside my head. I can even smell him sometimes."

"Oh, Natty . . ."

"You don't believe me."

"I didn't say that."

"You don't have to. I see it in your face."

"For God's sake, Nat, you've been through a horrific ordeal. You've suffered severe emotional and physical trauma. You lost your family. You were in a coma for two years."

Reaching for the folder containing all the messages she'd received, Nat slid it across the table to Faye. "Open it."

Faye opened the folder. What little color that had returned to her cheeks drained as she paged through each sheet of paper. She raised her eyes to Nat's. "Do you realize the implications of what you're claiming?"

"Of course, I do. That's what makes this so damn impossible."

Both women jumped when an owl screeched seemingly right outside the window. Faye choked out a nervous laugh and reached for her wine. Nat got up from the table and went to the window and closed it.

Faye was still looking at the messages when Nat returned to the table and sat down. "What do you think Kyle is trying to tell you?"

"I think he's trying to help me solve his murder."

"Oh, Natty—"

Nat cut her off by saying the words that neither of them wanted to hear. "There's a killer living in Bellerose."

Faye looked a little sick. "My God."

"The man who murdered my husband and son is still out there. He's killed before. And he's going to kill again."

"Brandon Bastille," Faye said hollowly. "That's why you've been asking so many questions about his father."

"That child did not drown in that bayou alone."

"But the parish coroner ruled it an accidental drowning. The newspaper was all over that story. How on earth could the police *and* the coroner be wrong about something like that?"

"I don't know. They're human. They make mistakes."

"Honey, if you believe that's what happened, maybe you should involve the police. Tell Alcee Martin everything you just told me." She picked up the notes. "Show him these."

"What would I tell him, Faye? That I hear voices inside my head? That people from beyond the grave send me messages? That I'm communicating with my dead son? Come on. He was there the night I slit my wrists. He already thinks I'm unstable. If I tell him I'm talking to dead people, he'll think I'm a raving lunatic." She picked up the legal pad and turned it so Faye could see it.

Going to kill him. In big danger. Help him.
Jason LaRue. Find him Mommy. The bad mans
coming.

I'm scared!

"Jason LaRue? Jean and Paulette's boy?" Faye raised her eyes to Nat's. "What does it mean?"

"The only way I can interpret this is as some kind of warning."

"You mean Jason LaRue is in danger?"

"How would you interpret it?"

For the first time, Faye looked more afraid than skeptical. "Nat, if there's another child on this killer's list and you know about it, you have to take it to the police."

There was a part of her that knew her friend was right. But Faye wasn't the one who'd spent seven hours being questioned for a crime she hadn't committed. She wasn't the one who'd been locked in a cell like an animal while her mind had slowly unraveled.

"I can't." Rising, Nat strode to the living room and picked up her purse and keys.

Faye trailed her. "What are you going to do?"

"I'm going to warn the LaRues."

"Honey, you don't even know who the killer is."

But Nat was already halfway to the door. "I've got to do something."

"You can't just walk into Jean and Paulette's home and tell them their son is about to be killed. Do you have any idea how crazy that sounds?"

"Of course I do! It sounds insane. But what else can I do? Keep my mouth shut and let it happen? Do I want a child's death on my conscience? Faye, of all the things that could happen, I think that's the one that would push me over the edge."

"Honey, I think we need to think this through."

"There's no time." Nat tried to go around her, but Faye countered and stayed solidly in her way. "Get out of my way, Faye, or I'll go right over you."

"Are you forgetting the history between you and Jean?"

"I haven't forgotten." Nat would never forget. Jean LaRue was a prosecutor with the St. Tammany Parish District Attorney's office. He was the man who'd taken the case to a grand jury and tried to get her indicted for the murders of her husband and son. She'd always suspected he'd done so under intense pressure from the Ratcliffe family—namely Elliott Ratcliffe—but he'd done a damn good job of helping to finish off what was left of her life.

"If you're not going to listen to reason, then I'm going with you." Whirling away, Faye snagged her bag from the sofa.

The last thing Nat wanted to do was to confront Jean LaRue alone. But her conscience wouldn't let her involve Faye any more deeply. "I can't let you come with me."

"Why not?"

"Because if I get arrested, I'm going to need you to bail me out of jail."

chapter
19

THE LARUES LIVED ON A QUIET STREET ON THE NICE side of Bellerose, just two blocks from the historic St. Tammany Parish Courthouse. Nestled among magnolias and live oaks, the stately colonial looked like the feature home in *Southern Living* magazine. Dormant azaleas formed a lush border around the front porch where white wicker furniture beckoned one to sit and drink sweet tea. The ruler-straight row of crepe myrtles that grew along the sidewalk still held their fuchsia blooms left over from summer. In the driveway a big Lincoln Navigator SUV was parked next to a sleek little Lexus.

Paulette and Jean LaRue were Bellerose's crème de la crème of the upper crust. As a prosecutor, Jean had earned a reputation for being tough on crime. Paulette had been a journalist and news anchor in New Orleans before marrying Jean and moving to Bellerose some fifteen years earlier. Last Nat had heard, she was heading up the Louisiana Philanthropic Association, a charity that raised funds to house the homeless in some of the state's most economically depressed areas. They had two children, Jason, six, and Sheralee, who was eight. A perfect marriage, a perfect home, two perfect children.

Four perfect lives about to be shattered.

Nat got out of the Mustang and took the stone path toward

the house. Double gas lamps flickered on either side of intricately carved cypress doors. Through the sidelight, she could see that the lights were on inside. Not giving herself time to debate, she crossed to the doors and rang the bell.

A moment later the door swung open. Paulette LaRue was holding a cordless phone to her ear, smiling at something the person on the other end of the line had said. Wearing cream-colored slacks and a short-sleeved red sweater, she looked pretty and content. A woman without a care in the world. Nat knew firsthand just how quickly the illusion could be snatched away.

Paulette's smile fell the instant she recognized Nat. "I'll call you back," she said into the phone and set it on the console table. Her eyes cooled to just below freezing when they landed on Nat. "What do you want?"

During the short drive from her house, Nat had tried to come up with a way to approach the LaRues without alarming them unduly—or sounding like a lunatic. But for the life of her she hadn't been able to devise a plausible angle that would allow her to save face and still get her message across. The possibility that she had somehow misinterpreted the warning from Kyle never left her mind. Twice, she'd almost turned around and driven home and left things to Fate. Twice, she'd realized there was no way she could turn her back on these people, knowing what could happen if she did.

"Mrs. LaRue. Hi, I'm sorry to bother you so late."

"Just tell me what you want, or I'm going to have to ask you to leave. I don't think it's appropriate for you to be here, Ms. Jennings."

Nat had known she wouldn't be welcomed. The woman standing before her believed she was a monster capable of murdering her own child. Trying not to think about that, she took a fortifying breath. "I know this is going to sound strange, and I do not mean to alarm you, but . . . are your children home?"

"*What?*"

Nat tried to smile to reassure her, but didn't think she managed. "I was . . . just down the street and thought I saw your boy—Jason—talking to a stranger. There was an old car pulled up next to him. I thought the car looked kind of suspicious, so I thought I'd stop in and let you know, so you could check on him and make sure everything's all right."

Paulette's eyes flicked down the front of her, and Nat realized she'd noticed the blood on her T-shirt from the bloody nose she'd had earlier. Her eyes narrowed. "What are you talking about? You saw Jason? When?"

"I think it was Jason. He was right down the street just a few minutes ago. The guy in the car looked a little shady. I just thought you might want to check it out."

For the first time, impatience and annoyance entered her expression. "I don't know what you're up to, Ms. Jennings, but you did not see my son."

"Are you sure? The little guy looked just like him." Nat held her hand up to her chest. "About this high. Brown hair . . ."

"My son is in the hospital. He's having an appendectomy. I stopped by the house to pick up some pajamas and toys for him."

Going to kill him. In big danger.

Nat jolted when the words flickered in her mind's eye. The utter certainty that she was not wrong about the boy being in danger pressed into her like a physical force. But now that she'd been caught in a lie, she didn't know how to get through to this woman without alarming her.

"Look, Mrs. LaRue, I don't mean to alarm you, but I think you ought to check on your son."

"Check on him?" For the first time, the woman looked startled. "What is that supposed to mean?"

"Just to make sure he's safe."

"Safe? What are you talking about? Why are you saying that?" But she was already reaching for the phone.

"Please, don't be upset."

Paulette's face was red, her eyes revealing alarm and anger. She punched numbers into the phone with a shaking hand. "Jean!" she cried over her shoulder. *"Jean!"*

The last thing Nat wanted was a confrontation with Jean LaRue. Three years ago he'd been ruthless in his quest to get her indicted for a crime she hadn't committed. He hadn't pulled any punches in attacking her, and his tactics had played a major role in the ruination of her reputation.

"Mrs. LaRue, please try not to get upset—"

"Don't tell me not to get upset." The other woman began pacing the foyer, clutching the phone, her glare never leaving Nat. "How can I not get upset when you barge in here, intimating that something has happened to my son?"

"What's going on here?"

Nat looked past Paulette to see Jean LaRue striding toward them, his expression leery and decidedly unfriendly. "Paulette, what's she doing here?" he demanded, his gaze sweeping from his wife to Nat.

Paulette clutched her husband's arm. "I'm calling the hospital," she said.

"The hospital? What happened?"

She pointed at Nat. "She claims something happened to Jason."

"*What?*" He shot Nat a killing look, his eyes filled with anger and disdain and maybe even a little fear. "What did you say to her? Why would you say such a thing?"

"I didn't mean to upset her. It's just that . . . I thought I saw your son down the street, talking to a stranger, and I became concerned."

"Is that some kind of sick *joke?*" Jean demanded. "Who are you to be concerned about one of our children?"

"I'm just trying to help." Nat felt sick. This was exactly what she hadn't wanted to happen. All she wanted now was for Mrs. LaRue to reach the hospital so she could be assured that the boy was safe.

"That's bullshit. My son isn't even in the neighborhood." He snatched the phone from his wife. "Hello? This is Jean LaRue." Someone must have answered because he spoke quickly and forcefully. "I need to know where my son is. No, I won't hold on. Check on him. Right now. I'll wait." His lips formed a thin line for a moment as he listened. "He's fine? You're sure?" He nodded brusquely. "No, everything's okay. We just . . . thought something might be up. Can you post a nurse in his room until we get there? I know it's unusual. Yes,

I'll be happy to speak with the hospital administrator. Just do whatever it takes." He glared at Nat. "Under no circumstances is Natalie Jennings to be anywhere near my son. I'll get a restraining order as soon as I can." Sighing with impatience, he spelled her last name. "She threatened him. Yes, you can bill me for private security. Great. His mother and I will be there as soon as we can."

Relief made Nat's legs go weak. The boy was all right. He wasn't in danger. She hadn't been too late. . . .

She started when LaRue slammed the phone down on the console table. The look he gave her was cold enough to freeze steel. "I don't know what in the hell you're trying to pull, but you're not going to get away with it." He looked at his wife. "Call the police."

Dread coiled inside Nat, a rope being drawn into a tight knot. "Mr. LaRue, I don't want any problems. I was just trying to be a good citizen and follow up—"

"A good citizen doesn't waltz into someone's home and start making wild accusations about their children being in harm's way," he said between clenched teeth. "How dare you?"

"I didn't mean any harm."

"Or maybe you just don't like the way I did my job three years ago."

"No, that's not why I came here."

"You implied that our son had been hurt!"

"I implied no such thing. I just wanted to make sure he was okay." Because she couldn't go into detail without opening herself up to questions she hadn't the slightest clue how to answer, she cut off her answer without elaboration. "I was only trying to help."

"The children in this town are better off without your kind of help." His eyes went flat. "Stay away from my kids. Stay away from my wife. And if you want to stay healthy, you had better stay the hell away from me."

Trying desperately not to let his words affect her, Nat raised her hands and backed slowly toward the steps. "Okay, I'm leaving."

Paulette stepped onto the porch, still carrying the phone. "The police are on the way."

Jean didn't acknowledge his wife. Instead, he followed Nat across the porch, then down the steps. On the sidewalk, he grasped her arm hard, jerked her toward him. In an instant, he went from loving father and husband to a man willing to inflict violence in order to keep his family safe. "Listen to me, you crazy little bitch."

Nat gasped when he squeezed, her only thought that she'd never seen a human being make such a profound transformation so quickly.

Out of earshot of his wife, he raised his finger and shoved it in her face. "I'm going to get a restraining order against you, so don't even think about trying to pull this shit again. You got that?"

Nat broke away from him and ran toward her car. Tears stung her eyes as she fumbled with her keys. She told herself she'd done the right thing. She'd had to either act or deal with the consequences. There was no way she could handle having a child's death on her conscience. She couldn't blame the LaRues for being suspicious of her motives, for not believing her. The most important thing was that Jason LaRue was safe.

But the hatred she'd seen in Jean LaRue's eyes hurt. He'd looked at her the same way he'd looked at her three years ago. As if she were a piece of scum. A killer. A woman evil enough, insane enough, to murder her own child.

Nat reached her car and flung open the door. Sliding behind the steering wheel, she stuck the key in the ignition and started the engine. When she looked up, police lights danced in her rearview mirror. Damn. Damn. *Damn*.

For an instant she considered putting the car in gear and driving away. But she knew that would only make things worse. She couldn't escape this. Even though she hadn't done anything wrong, they were going to have questions. Questions she had no idea how to answer.

Heart pounding she sat with her hands on the steering wheel while the deputy walked up to the car. From where she was sitting she couldn't see his face. He was holding his flashlight in his left hand, his right hand hovering above the pistol strapped to his belt. "Evening."

Another layer of dread settled over her when she recognized the voice. Then Matt Duncan leaned close to her and shone the light in her eyes. "Nat Jennings," he said. "I thought it was you."

"Hi, Matt."

"Why don't you turn off the car and step out to talk to me for a moment?"

Even though he'd phrased it as a question, Nat knew he wasn't asking. It was an order. And unless she wanted to spend the night in jail, she'd damn well better comply. Matt Duncan wasn't known for being diplomatic.

"All right."

"Nice and slow." He opened the door for her and stepped back.

Nat rolled her eyes as she slid out of the car. "You want my hands up, too?" she asked dryly.

"That won't be necessary." Just to let her know he was in charge, he shone the light in her eyes. "I want you to walk over to my cruiser with me. Then you're going to stay there while I talk to the LaRues. You understand?"

"I understand," she said. "But I didn't do anything."

"That's the tenth time I've heard that tonight." Taking her arm, he guided her to the rear of his cruiser. "Put your butt on the bumper and don't move it. If you do, I'll cuff you and put you in the car. You got that?"

"I got it." Nat did as she was told and watched Duncan hitch his belt and take the stone path to the porch where Paulette and Jean were standing, looking as if they'd just had a close encounter with a well-armed Bonnie Parker. Nat couldn't hear what they were saying, but Jean motioned in her direction several times. Some of the neighbors had noticed the police lights and ventured onto their porches to see what all the commotion was about. Police lights in their neighborhood obviously meant something unsavory was afoot.

Humiliated and frustrated, Nat could do nothing but stand there and let them speculate. After several minutes, Matt came back down the walk and approached her. "You want to tell me what you were thinking, walking up to those people and telling them their son was in danger?"

"I didn't say that," Nat said.

"That's what they told me." He stopped several feet from her and put his hands on his hips.

"I just told them they should check on their son, to make sure he was okay."

"Did you have some reason to believe either of their children were in harm's way?"

Nat thought about the story she'd devised, and even though it was thin—stupid even, now that she'd had some time to think about it—she decided she was already vested and should stick with it. "I thought I'd seen Jason down the street, talking to some strange guy in an old car."

"A strange guy in an old car, huh?" His tone made it clear he didn't believe her any more than the LaRues had. "Exactly where did you see this strange guy?"

"At the corner of Fifth and Vine."

"A block away?"

"That's right."

"What kind of car was it?"

"An old Chevy, I think. Maybe an Impala."

"Huh. Haven't seen a vehicle like that around Bellerose." He hitched up his trousers again and shot her a sour look. "How did you get that blood on your shirt?"

She glanced down at the dozen or so droplets of blood. "I had a bloody nose earlier."

"How did you get a bloody nose?"

"I bumped it."

"Uh huh." He stared hard at her. "Do you have any idea how much you upset the LaRues?"

"I have a pretty good idea." She rubbed her arm where Jean had grabbed it.

"Jean seems to think you've got some kind of vendetta against him because of what happened three years ago. Is that true?"

"I know he was just doing his job. Honestly, I just wanted to make sure their kids were all right."

"Do you have any idea how strange that sounds, Nat? Considering the circumstances?"

She looked away, nodded.

"Have you been drinking alcohol tonight?"

Her gaze snapped to his. "No!"

"Are you on any kind of medication?"

"No."

"A doctor's care?"

"No." She pinched the bridge of her nose, shook her head.
Jesus.

He sighed. "I'm going to write this up as a neighbor dispute. No citation for you. But you're going to have to stay away from Jean and Paulette. You got that?"

Nat nodded. "Loud and clear."

"He's going to file a restraining order against you. You violate that, and you're going to jail."

"I won't bother them again," she said.

He didn't say anything for a moment. "I don't believe you really saw a guy in a Chevy. I don't know why you'd make up a story like that, but you did, didn't you?"

Nat knew better than to admit to a lie. This was one of those rare moments when a lie—even a bad one—was a better alternative than the truth. "I'm telling the truth," she said.

"Uh-huh."

For a moment she considered asking him to keep an eye on the LaRue children, but she figured such a request at this point would do more harm than good. Besides, Jason was in the hospital for an appendectomy. What harm could come to him there? "Can I go now?" she asked.

"Next time you see something suspicious, call the police," he said.

Nat started for her car without responding. She could feel Matt's eyes and a dozen more follow her as she opened the door and slid behind the wheel. She told herself their disdain didn't bother her; being an outcast was nothing compared to the hell she'd been though in the last few years. She could handle it.

But as she pulled onto the street, she acknowledged the pain. And she vowed that if it was the last thing she did, these self-righteous jackasses were going to know Nat Jennings was not a murderer.

HE SITS IN THE FRONT SEAT OF HIS SUV IN THE parking garage of the hospital, shaking with rage. The window is down and his labored breaths echo off the concrete walls around him. His heart pounds adrenaline and fury through his system.

He doesn't know how she did it, but the bitch has foiled his plans. But how could she have known? He'd been so careful, waiting until just the right moment. He'd been meticulous in his planning, right down to the tiniest detail. Jason LaRue would have been so satisfying, so brilliant. He would have been the one that set him free.

He'd been moments away from killing Jason LaRue when the deputy had arrived with his shiny badge and six shooter. Stupid, stupid cop. He'd listened to the conversation between the cop and the nurse and that was when he'd realized Nat Jennings was behind the added security. That she'd made some kind of weird threat against Jean LaRue's son.

A cold sweat breaks out all over his body. He doesn't like the timing of it. But how could Nat Jennings have known what he had planned? It's as if she's climbed into his mind and stolen his innermost thoughts. His dark, secret thoughts. He knows it's impossible, but still he is afraid.

And very, very angry.

Fury courses through him at the thought of what she deprived him of. The need is desperate and sharp inside him, and he feels it all the way to his bones. The hunger torments him, a starving animal clawing his insides to shreds. He has ached for days now. A terrible pain that never leaves him. An agony that keeps him up nights, like a freshly broken bone screaming to be set.

Opening the small duffel on the seat next to him, he pulls out the towel with a shaking hand and unwraps the knife. The blade gleams, and his blood begins to pound. He knows better than to do this here. The last thing he needs is for someone to walk by and see him. But this won't wait. Urgency and anticipation coil and snap inside him. Oh, sweet Jesus, he needs this.

He can hear himself breathing heavily as he unbuttons his shirt. Glancing down at his chest and stomach, he sees that the old wounds are healing nicely. All but the deepest cuts are nothing more than tiny pink lines. The rest are scabbed over. He stares at the raised pink slashes of scar tissue crisscrossing his abdomen. Most people would think the scars are hideous. But they don't understand that he needs to do this. That it brings him pleasure and comfort. That the sight of blood welling on his own skin feeds something twisted inside him.

Light flickers on the blade as he picks up the knife. His palms are so sweaty he can barely grip it. Leaning against the seat back, he sets the blade against his flesh. Pain flares as he draws the knife across his chest, from nipple to nipple to naval. Red blooms in its wake, and a rush of pleasure engulfs him.

"Ah . . . God . . ." His voice echoes eerily in the garage. A weak, feminine sound that shames him, reminds him of what he is.

But the sight of his own blood excites him. His penis is hard and aching between his legs. He can't look away as the blood drips toward his belt. He runs his fingers through the brilliant red streaks, slippery and wet between his fingers. He can feel his heart beating. Lifting his hand, he opens his mouth and touches his tongue to the blood.

So good, and yet it shames him because he knows it is wrong. He knows they will never understand.

"Goddamn it." He closes his eyes against the sudden rush of tears. "Fuck. Fuck! Goddamn her. Goddamn them all."

They will never understand. But they don't know about the terrible things that were done to him. Things that made him want to die. Things that made him what he is.

Tasting bile at the back of his throat, he throws open the door and retches. Vomit spews onto the concrete, and all he can think is that this is her fault. For coming back. For interfering. This should have been perfect. Perfect! And she ruined everything.

He wipes his mouth on his sleeve, aware that his penis has gone flaccid. He shudders uncontrollably. Sweat slicks the back of his neck. His stomach cramps. His bowels feel loose, and he realizes with dismay that he is about to soil his pants.

Once again he has been reduced to a shaking, sniveling nothing. A coward who throws up and soils his pants. Just like when he was twelve years old. Locked in that room. Alone in the dark with things crawling all over him . . .

He has been humiliated for the last time. He is going to show them just how powerful he is. He is going to show all of them.

Using the towel, he blots the blood from his chest. His hands tremble as he buttons the shirt. The need recedes back into its deep, dark hole. Once again he is in control.

Putting the SUV in gear, he heads toward the exit.

chapter
20

Nat made it two blocks before the shakes hit her. She didn't know if it was the result of anger or relief or maybe a combination of both, but she was shaking so hard she didn't trust herself to drive. She pulled over in the parking lot of Manchac's Burger Villa and waited for the worst of the shaking to subside.

It took her nearly ten minutes to get herself calmed down. The worst thing that had happened was that the police had been called and that Jean LaRue was going to get a restraining order against her. A small price to pay, she thought, considering she'd probably saved a child's life. For now, that had to be enough.

Feeling steadier, she went through the drive-through and bought a chocolate shake, then headed out of town toward home. The night was mild and humid, so she rolled down the window and sang aloud to the Wallflowers' "One Headlight." For just a little while, she wasn't going to think about the past or the state of her life.

A few miles out of town, she passed Pelican Island Road—the road to hell according to her mama when Nat was in high school—and found herself thinking about Nick Bastille. She'd relived the incident between them a dozen times in the hours since it happened. She recalled with perfect clarity the heat in his eyes when he'd looked at her. The way he'd trembled when he held her. The gentle touch of his hands against her body. The pressure of his mouth against hers . . .

He might be an ex-con living on the edge of the bayou in a dilapidated house on a run-down farm, but Nat knew there was more to Nick than met the eye, even if you had to look closely to see it. She sensed something decent and good beneath that hard facade. What kind of man put in endless hours of backbreaking work on a farm, spent his evenings working a second job, all the while caring for his father, who was afflicted with Alzheimer's disease? A man with character, she thought. A man who cared about all the right things. And for the first time in what seemed like an eternity, she allowed herself to feel the barely familiar stir of feminine interest.

She'd long since given up on the notion of happiness. In the last three years, it had taken every ounce of determination she possessed just to get through the day. She'd learned to simply exist and not expect too much from anyone, including herself. Slowly but surely, Nick was changing that. Today, in the short minutes he'd held her in his arms, Nat had felt something that went deeper than mere sexual arousal. After everything that had happened in the last three years, that she was capable of feeling something so fundamentally human— so fundamentally female—shocked her.

Nick Bastille hadn't just touched her. He'd moved her. He'd given her back something she'd thought was gone forever. He'd given her hope. Hope for the future. Hope that someday she would be whole. That life didn't have to be about pain and loss. That happiness wasn't just for other people.

Suddenly ridiculously anxious to see him, she slowed the Mustang and turned around. Gravel spewed when she hit the gas. Turning up the radio, she turned onto Pelican Island Road, where The Blue Gator would just be winding into high gear. Smiling, she picked up the shake and, for the first time in months, she actually tasted food. The ice cream was rich and cold and suddenly she was famished. Not just for food, but for life.

She was midway to the bar when headlights appeared in her rearview mirror. "Go around if you're in such a hurry," she muttered, checking her speed. In the next instant the headlights loomed dangerously close. She had a split second to brace before the vehicle slammed into her rear bumper hard enough to bang her head against the headrest.

"What are you doing?" she snapped. But she heard the fear in her voice. It was too dark for her to see the vehicle, the headlights too bright, but she knew it was an SUV or truck because it rode higher off the ground than her Mustang.

She slowed, but the SUV zoomed up beside her. She caught a glimpse of tinted glass and a black side view mirror an instant before the vehicle slammed into her car.

Steel ground against steel as the Mustang fishtailed. Gasping, Nat gripped the wheel with both hands, turned into the skid, and managed to regain control an instant before the wheels would have gone off the shoulder.

She hit the brake, then glanced over to see the SUV fall back. Relieved, she slowed to forty miles per hour. An instant later, headlights flashed, and the SUV crashed into her rear bumper. The impact was violent and sent the Mustang into a slide.

She took her foot off the brake, but the SUV threatened her bumper again, so she hit the gas. Simultaneously, she reached for her cell phone, which was clipped inside her purse. In the instant she took her eyes off her rearview mirror, the big vehicle came up beside her. Metal screamed when the SUV slammed into her door. The Mustang skidded right. Nat cut the wheel and would have regained control, but the SUV banged into her a second time. She stomped the brake, but it was too late. The rear tires lost purchase, and the Mustang went into a spin.

Nat screamed as her headlights played wildly over the tall grass and billowing dust. She lost sight of the SUV. The Mustang flew by a tree, missing its massive trunk by inches. Reeds exploded off her front bumper as the Mustang careened down an embankment. A scream tore from her throat when the headlights glinted off black water. An instant later, the car hit the surface. Nat was jerked hard against her safety belt. The airbag exploded with the force of a bomb, striking her in the chest and face hard enough to daze her.

For several heartbeats she sat there unmoving. The radio was still blaring. She could see the glow of her headlights through water the color of strong tea. She smelled the stink of mud. The sensation of cold water on her feet jerked her back. The car was in the water and nosing down. She saw moss against the windshield, water gushing in through her open window.

Panic struck with a vengeance. A scream poured from her throat. Frantically, she fought away the remnants of the airbag. The radio had stopped playing, and she could hear the roar of the water rushing in, ragged breaths tearing from her throat. Her heart exploding in her chest.

The car shifted, nosed down at a steeper angle. She was still strapped in. The steering wheel was directly below her. The water was up to midthigh now, edging over the steering wheel.

"Oh, God! Oh, *God! Help meeeeeee!*"

But Nat knew there was no one around to hear her.

She fumbled for the latch on her harness. But she was disoriented and couldn't remember if it was on the left or right. Another surge of panic crashed through her. She'd once read about a driver whose car had plunged into a lake. An expert swimmer who'd become disoriented and drowned because he couldn't get out of the car. She wasn't going to let that happen to her.

She located the latch on her harness, released it. Gravity sent her plunging down. The steering wheel struck her in the chest, knocking the breath from her. An instant later cold, black water enveloped her like an icy cloak. She tried to suck in a breath, took in water, and began to choke.

She managed to get her feet on the steering wheel, then used her legs to push herself upright. Suddenly she felt air on her face. She opened her eyes to find her head in the back window. Through the dirty glass, she could see a small stretch of night sky. She could hear herself choking and sobbing. Panic was a scream inside her. She struck the glass with her fist, but couldn't get enough momentum to break it.

"*Help me!*"

Realizing her only escape was through one of the open windows, that she didn't have much time, she sucked in a deep breath, then ducked into the water and began feeling her way toward the window. She hit her thigh on the driver's-side headrest. She grasped the seat belt with her left hand and used it to pull herself down. Her ears hurt. She needed to take a breath. Just a little farther . . .

She reached out and felt glass, then her hand plunged into mud. For an instant she feared that maybe the car had rolled onto its side and that she was trapped. Then she thrust both hands through the window and felt open water.

Blind, desperate for oxygen, Nat thrust her body through the window and began to kick. But she was disoriented and couldn't tell up from down. All she knew was that if she didn't get a breath, she was going to pass out.

She opened her eyes, but the water was pitch black. She could feel the darkness and cold edging in. She kicked her feet, hoping what little oxygen she had left in her lungs would float her to the surface. But she could feel her strength waning. Her lungs seized, and Nat sucked in water. She began to choke, her entire body convulsing.

Oh, God, I'm drowning. . . .

But Nat didn't stop kicking, and an instant later, she broke the surface. She could hear herself coughing and retching. Her legs felt as if they had been set in concrete, but she continued to tread water. She looked around but couldn't see the bank, didn't know which direction to swim.

Then she spotted the cattails against the night sky and began to dog paddle toward them. She was cold and fatigued and coughing so violently she thought she would be sick. But she was going to make it.

Then she was going to make the son of a bitch in the SUV pay for trying to kill her.

IT WAS TEN P.M. ON A THURSDAY, AND THE BLUE Gator was just winding into high gear. Nick Bastille stood behind the bar, listening to the Red Hot Chili Peppers lament the City of Angels as he wiped the rack of mugs Rita had brought to him from the dishwasher in the rear. Working on thirty-six hours without sleep, he was bone tired. After leaving Tanya's trailer, he'd gone home, prepared dinner for Dutch, then hauled himself off to bed. But even exhausted, he hadn't been able to sleep. Between his visit to his ex-wife's trailer and the time he'd spent with Nat Jennings, his mind had been as revved up as a 747 barreling down the runway for takeoff.

Seeing the place where his son had drowned added a cruel twist to the old pain. It had made him ache in a place so deep there was nothing on this sweet earth that could reach it. For the thousandth time he had questioned God, asking Him why He'd taken his sweet little boy, an innocent child who'd done nothing to deserve such a terrible fate. But Nick knew it was a question that would never be answered.

And then there was Nat Jennings. She was heat and ice and sharp edges rolled into one very intriguing package. A beautiful woman with haunting eyes and a broken heart. A vixen with the kind of body that would never give a man any peace. She was all the things he didn't need in his life.

But she was exactly what he wanted.

Nick hadn't intended to kiss her. He sure as hell hadn't expected the explosion of heat that followed. He knew that kind of heat could burn a man to embers if he wasn't careful. He wasn't looking to get burned again. All he wanted were a few laughs and some no-strings-attached, sweaty, raunchy sex.

Lots and lots of sweaty, raunchy sex.

But he knew Nat Jennings wasn't a no-strings-attached kind of woman. She was complicated and troubled and dealing with the kind of grief that would have crushed a lesser person. While Nick could sympathize, he wanted no part of it.

He'd just finished drying the last mug when a commotion at the door caught his attention. He looked up to see Andy Hobbs rush in looking like he'd just had a close encounter with Bigfoot. A cane farmer, Andy was tall and thin with mussed red hair and skin the color of a cooked shrimp.

Nick watched him approach the bar, searching his memory for the man's drink of choice. "Bourbon straight up?"

"Make it a double." Andy raked his hand through his hair. "I'da been here twenty minutes ago, but there's a accident a couple of miles down the road."

Nick poured bourbon from the bottle and tried to look interested. "Anyone hurt?"

"Doggone car went down the embankment straight into Miller's Pond."

"Deep pond." Nick knew because he'd skinny-dipped there as a teenager. "Any idea who it was?"

"That woman who kilt her kid. Drove her Mustang right into the water. Car went down like a goddamn tank. They got a wrecker out there, trying to get it out, but it's muddy as hell. Gonna need a winch." He leaned close, his eyes glinting with some forbidden knowledge. "Probably some kind of weird suicide thing. You know, she slit her wrists right there in the jail cell after killin' her husband and baby. I swear to the good Lord, I don't know why they didn't string that woman up when they had the chance."

Nick's heart was pounding when he shoved away from the bar and started toward the kitchen. He worked off the apron as he passed by the ice machine, then hit the double doors with both hands. Rita looked up from where she'd been loading mugs into the dishwasher. Mike Pequinot made eye contact with him from his office where he was at the desk, counting cash.

"I have to go." Nick tossed the apron at Rita. "Take over for me."

She caught the apron with one hand. "Sure."

Mike hobbled out of the office. "What's up?"

"Accident. Car went into Miller's Pond."

"Know who it was?"

Nick could hear his pulse pounding in his ears. He could feel his breaths coming too fast. Disbelief and a terrible ache grinding his guts into pieces.

Pequinot was looking at him oddly.

"Nat Jennings," he heard himself say.

"She okay?" Rita asked.

"I don't know," Nick said and started for the door.

chapter
21

NICK PUSHED THE TRUCK TO A TREACHEROUS SIXTY
miles per hour on the narrow gravel road. All the while, Andy
Hobbs's words rang in his head like some terrible mantra.

*"That woman who kilt her kid . . . car went down like a
tank . . . some kind of weird suicide."*

His only thought was that Nat couldn't be dead. There was
too much life inside her. Too much determination to bring a
killer to justice. There was no way he would believe she'd deliberately driven her Mustang into the water.

The accident had occurred just two miles from The Blue
Gator. There was one police cruiser on the scene, its red-and-
blue strobe flashing off the tree branches and shaggy Spanish
moss. Nick brought the truck to a skidding halt behind the
cruiser and jammed it into Park. Ahead, Bill Beamer's old
pickup was blocking the road, its diesel engine rumbling and
filling the air with exhaust. Two other cars he didn't recognize
were parked haphazardly along the muddy shoulder.

Nick left the truck and hit the gravel running. There was no
ambulance. No paramedics. A cruel voice inside his head reminded him that ambulances and paramedics didn't show up
if the victim was dead. . . .

Cutting the thought off cold, he looked around and spotted
Bill Beamer standing on the shoulder of the road. He was

holding a flashlight, its beam illuminating the small body of water fifteen feet down the embankment.

"Where is she?" Nick demanded.

Bill shook his head, and for a terrible instant, Nick thought he was going to tell him she was dead. "I swear anybody can get outta that water has nine lives." He pointed toward his truck, where a small figure was leaning against the fender, huddled in a blanket.

Nick had never been an emotional man. He'd learned at a young age that it was better to feel nothing than to feel too much. As a man, he'd learned that emotions were his enemy. That they made a smart man do stupid things, a strong man weak. But seeing Nat standing against that car safe and alive yanked those emotions out of their deep, dark cave. They burgeoned inside him until he thought he would choke on them. Relief. Gratitude. All of it laced by the cold, hard knowledge that at some point he had begun to care for her.

Unable to think about the repercussions of that now, he left Bill and jogged across the road. Even from several yards away he could see the dark stain of blood on her forehead. She was trembling violently, her clothes soaked and dripping.

"Nat. Are you hurt?"

She looked up at the sound of his voice. The sight of blood on her face jolted him, scared the hell out of him. But he was even more frightened by her lack of color. She looked like a ghost. Her eyes were large and dark and seemed too big for her face. He could hear her teeth chattering, see her arms and legs shaking.

"My car is totaled," she said.

Shock, he thought, and went to her. "Cars can be replaced." He stopped just short of touching her, knowing if he did, he might not be able to stop. "Where are you hurt?"

"J-just c-cold."

"You were inside the car when it went into the water?"

She jerked her head once.

Shaken by the knowledge of what could have happened, he let his gaze skim over her, looking for torn clothes, bruises, any sign of pain. "Has anyone checked you out? A paramedic? EMT?"

"No."

"Are you in any pain?"

"My head. My knee. Come to think of it, everything hurts except my teeth." She touched her left temple, then stared at the blood on her fingertips as if surprised. "I'm bleeding."

Setting his hands gently on her shoulders, he turned her to face him. Her entire body was vibrating. In the light of the headlights, he could see the gash on her left temple. It was deep and bleeding freely. "You're cut."

"I must have hit the side window." She gave him a weak smile. "My mama always said I had a hard head."

"I don't think she meant that literally." Reaching into his pocket, he withdrew the bandanna he'd taken out of the dryer just that morning and folded it into a small, fat square. She winced when he pressed it against the cut. "You want to sit down?"

"No. I'm okay." But the way she was clutching the blanket around her shoulders belied the words.

"Were you unconscious at any point?" he asked.

She shook her head. "No. Just scared shitless."

Reaching out, he lifted the blanket, set it higher on her shoulders. But it was too wet to be of much help, so he used it to pull her to him. "Let's see if we can get you warmed up."

"People will think we're embracing."

"We are." Wrapping his arms around her, he pulled her flush against him, hoping to use his body heat to stave off hypothermia. He could feel water soaking through his shirt and the front of his jeans, but he didn't care. At the moment all he cared about was holding her, feeling the strong thrust of her heart against his. He wanted to kiss her, too, but he didn't think that was what either of them needed at the moment, so he didn't.

"I'm glad you're okay," he said.

"Me, too."

"What happened?"

"Someone forced me off the road."

Shock rippled through him. He eased her to arm's length and searched her gaze. "Deliberately?"

She explained how the SUV had crashed into her car. "The next thing I know I'm going down the embankment and heading straight for the water—"

"Or maybe you had a little bit too much alcohol down at The Gator."

Nick looked up to see Matt Duncan walking toward them and felt his hackles go up. Of all the cops that could have been on duty, Matt was the most likely to cause problems. He had a small mind and a mean streak, and the uniform gave him a free pass to exercise both of those things at will.

"She wasn't at The Gator," Nick said. "She needs an ambulance."

"Step away from her, Bastille."

"She's nearly hypothermic," he said. "Going into shock."

"Or maybe she got drunk and ran off the road and you don't want me finding out about it."

Nick took a step toward him. "Look at her. Damn it, her face is cut."

Duncan held his ground. "This is a police matter. Get the fuck away from her, or I'll cuff you and haul your jailbird ass into town for interfering with an accident investigation."

"Nick. It's okay." Nat moved between the two men, then turned to Duncan. "I haven't been drinking, Matt. I swear. Someone forced me off the road. An SUV. Dark. Big."

Nick's hands clenched into fists when the deputy's gaze slid down the front of her. Her clothes were soaked and clinging, outlining every curve. The blanket she'd had over her shoulders had slipped, and her nipples were visible through her bra and T-shirt.

Matt Duncan licked his lips. "Yeah, we get wrecks out on this road every weekend when some idiot gets drunk and drives his truck into the ditch." He ran his eyes over her again. "I swear I smell alcohol on you."

Fury coursed through Nick at the thought of Duncan abusing his position as a cop. The urge to put the other man on the ground was powerful. But six years inside Angola had taught him to choose his battles carefully when it came to law enforcement types, and he knew this was a battle he would lose.

"She's injured and needs an ambulance," Nick said. "She needs a blanket."

Duncan eyed Nat. "Are you injured?"

"Just the cut on my temple," she said.

Rage coiled inside Nick when Duncan removed his cuffs from his belt. "Why don't you turn around for me nice and easy, Miss Jennings."

She gaped at the cuffs. "Why are you cuffing me? I didn't do anything wrong."

"This is for my protection and yours." Amusement glinted in his eyes. "Now turn around and give me your hands while I investigate this situation and make sure there was no traffic infraction or DUI involved."

Nick shot her a hard look. "Where's your phone? This jackass is out of control."

Nat closed her eyes. "It's in the car."

Cursing beneath his breath, Nick looked around. Most of the onlookers had gone down the embankment to have a look at the accident site. He needed a phone but didn't want to leave Nat alone with Duncan. He didn't trust the other man not to cross a line.

"Looks like you've got people walking all over your crime scene, Duncan," Nick said.

"It'll keep." Duncan took Nat by her biceps and turned her so that her back was to him. "Now give me your hands."

Nat's gaze warned Nick to stay away as Duncan cuffed her. But Nick could feel the rage and frustration building into something ugly and huge. He'd known too many men like Duncan in his lifetime, and he knew if he turned his back, Duncan would be all over her. Nick swore that was the one line he wouldn't let him cross.

"Can't you see she needs an ambulance?" Nick said.

Duncan pointed at Nick. "You keep your distance."

"You have no cause to cuff her," Nick said.

Duncan looked from Nick to Nat and then grinned. "Well, if I didn't know better, I'd say you had a thing for her, Bastille." He skimmed his finger over her shoulder. "She is kind of hot, isn't she?"

"Cut it out," Nat snapped, but Nick's voice dwarfed hers.

"Get your goddamn hands off her."

"Watch your mouth, farm boy. I'm the law in this town and if you give me any lip, I'll kick your hick ass from here to Sunday. You got that?"

"You lay a hand on her, and I'll make you regret it."

Duncan laughed, but it was an ugly, humorless sound. "How long were you in for, anyway, Bastille? Six years? That how long it's been since you had any pussy? I hear most guys give it up after that long. They get desperate and give someone their ass. Did you give it up, Bastille? Huh?"

Nick knew Duncan was baiting him. He knew if he lost his temper and went after him, he would go to jail and ultimately wind up back in Angola. He was on parole, and Duncan knew it. Because he had been a model prisoner, Nick had only served six years of his twelve-year sentence. One of the conditions of parole, however, was that he not be arrested for any reason.

But he could feel the fury coursing through his system, dumping adrenaline until he was shaking with it. His muscles twitched as he envisioned himself grabbing Duncan by the lapels, slamming him against the car, and pounding his face into hamburger until his own fists were bloody.

"Fuck you," Nick said.

Grinning, Duncan took Nat's arm and forced her toward his cruiser. Nick trailed them, his heart pounding. With her hands cuffed behind her back, she was completely vulnerable. He knew if Duncan put her in his cruiser, things were going to get ugly. He knew it would cost him. But there was no way he could let the other man assault her. It would be her word against his. With Nat's reputation, Nick figured Duncan would probably get away with it.

"You got your driver's license and proof of insurance?" Duncan asked Nat.

"They're in my purse, still in the car."

"Well, you're just chalking up charges left and right, aren't you, sweet thing?" Duncan tsked. "It just so happens that I'm feeling charitable tonight. Maybe we can work something out."

He was gripping her arm too tightly, but Nat let him take her to his cruiser. At the rear of the car, he pushed her against it. "You got anything on you I ought to know about?" he asked. "Weapons? Drugs?"

Nat shook her head. "Of course not."

"I'm just going to have a look-see."

She jolted when he put his hands just below her armpits,

and skimmed them down her sides, brushing the outsides of her breasts. He paused at her hips, his eyes meeting hers. Nat saw the glint of cruelty, and it chilled her. She couldn't believe this was happening. Couldn't believe Matt Duncan would take advantage of his position as a cop—or be so blatant about it. Out of the corner of her eye, she saw Nick a few feet away. Even in the darkness, she could see that his face was dark with fury, his hands clenching into fists. She didn't know what was going through his mind, but he looked as if he were on some very steep edge and about to jump. She didn't want him doing something stupid.

"Nick, I'm okay," she called out to him. "Go get Alcee."

Duncan finished patting her down, then turned toward Nick. "Don't get any closer, Bastille, or I swear to Christ I'll arrest you for interfering with an investigation. You got that, convict?"

Nick held his ground ten feet away, but he didn't look as if he were going to stay. Nat caught his stare and shook her head. "Don't give him a reason."

Duncan grinned. "Yeah, Nicky, because I'll do it." He hitched up his belt and turned to Nat. "I smell alcohol on your breath."

"I haven't had anything to drink."

He leaned close as if to smell her breath, lingering with his mouth just a few inches from hers. "Do you have any idea how often I hear that?" he whispered.

Nat turned her head. "I don't care. Someone tried to run me off the road tonight. You should be out looking for them, not hassling me."

"Yeah? And an hour ago you were standing on Jean and Paulette LaRue's front porch swearing up and down you'd seen their son a block away when all the while he was safe and sound in the hospital."

She closed her eyes for a moment. "That has nothing to do with this."

"A lie is a lie. You ever see that movie *Conspiracy Theory*? The crazy guy kept telling people everyone was after him?"

"Once my car is pulled out of that pond, the damage will tell the story." Nat tried to make her voice strong, but her teeth were chattering. She couldn't stop shivering. She didn't know if it was from being cold or shaken up in the wreck or having to deal with a bastard like Matt Duncan. But she couldn't stand the way he was looking at her, as if he were a moment of bad judgment away from touching her.

She started to push away from the car, but Duncan hooked his finger in the belt loop of her jeans and yanked her back. "Where do you think you're going?"

"I'm c-cold. My head hurts."

"You should have thought of the consequences before you got drunk and drove your car into that pond. You looking for a little attention, or are you just fucking crazy like everyone says?"

"I-I need to sit down."

He locked her against the car with his body, then leaned into her. Nat could feel the hard ridge of his erection against her belly and cringed. She could hear him breathing hard. She knew it was only a matter of time before the situation exploded. "Don't do this, Matt," she said.

"You think anyone in this town is going to listen to you if you cry foul and accuse one of Bellerose's officers of misconduct? Do you think anyone will believe you? A woman cold enough to kill her own fuckin' kid?"

All the breath left her lungs at his words. She could feel her heart hammering like a piston in her chest. "I didn't. You know I didn't."

"Here's a news flash for you, Nat. No one believes you."

"You have no right to do this to me."

"I'm a cop." His gaze dipped to her breasts, his tongue flicking over his lips like a snake's. "I can do whatever the hell I want, including putting my hands on those sweet little titties of yours."

Nat closed her eyes, mentally bracing for what she knew would happen next. She told herself it didn't matter. She could get through this; she'd gotten through worse.

In the next instant, Duncan's hands were ripped off her. She opened her eyes to see him flying backward, his face a collage of shock and fury. She saw Nick hauling him back by his shirt collar. Duncan reached for his expandable baton. But before he could slide it from its holster, Nick spun him around, fisted his collar with both hands and slammed him against the car hard enough to dent metal.

"You just assaulted a cop!" Duncan screamed.

"And you were two seconds away from crossing a line." Grinding his teeth, Nick pulled him away from the car and slammed him back.

Duncan jerked like a rag doll. "You're going to jail, Bastille."

"No I'm not, you little pumped-up prick." Nick slammed him against the car again. "Because you're going to keep your mouth shut about this."

"Why would I do that?"

Nick leaned close until his face was an inch from Duncan's. "Because I'll kill you if you don't," he said menacingly.

A chill went through Nat at his tone. She'd never seen this side of Nick, but she could tell by the fury on his face that he meant what he'd said, that he would make good on it. Evidently, Duncan believed him, too, because his face went pale.

An instant later Duncan's hand dove for his service revolver. But Nick was faster and snatched the weapon from its holster. Stepping away from Duncan, Nick drew back and hurled the weapon into the pond.

"Why did you do that?" Duncan jumped away from the car.

Nick shoved him back against the car. "You have two seconds to get those cuffs off her," he snarled. "Then you're going to get on the radio and get your boss out here. Or I swear to Christ I'll put you in your car and drive you into that pond myself."

"ANY IDEA WHO MIGHT HAVE BEEN DRIVING THE SUV?"

Alcee Martin looked as if he'd been torn from his bed and thrown into yesterday's clothes before he was fully awake. His usually impeccable uniform was wrinkled, and the cowlick at the back of his head was sticking up like a rooster tail. He looked none too happy to be out on a call at midnight. Especially a call where nobody wanted to tell him what the hell was going on.

Duncan hadn't mentioned Nick's so-called assault. Not to protect Nick, but because he didn't want to have to explain to his boss how Nick had disarmed him, tossed his side arm into the pond, then forced him to call his superior. Nick in turn hadn't mentioned Duncan's treatment of Nat. But he would, first chance he got.

Nick knew he was treading on thin ice. One wrong step and he would end up in prison again. All he could do at this point was tell Martin the truth and hope the other man believed him. If the chief of police wanted some incompetent yahoo cop working for him, there wasn't a damn thing Nick could do about it.

Nat shook her head. "No."

"Color? Make?"

"Dark, I think. Blue or black." She lifted her shoulder and let it fall. "It happened fast, and I was just trying to keep my car on the road."

"Hunt Ratcliffe drives a blue Suburban," Nick put in.

"Jim Arnaud drives an old black Bronco." Alcee scraped his hand over his face. "Shit."

"Either one of them might think he had reason to hurt her."

"I'll talk to both of them." Alcee snapped his notepad closed, then shot Nat a pointed look. "I reckon you're not exactly one of Bellerose's most favored citizens these days."

"I have no control over what people think of me," she said.

"Yeah? Well, Matt filled me in on what happened at the LaRues' earlier. You want to tell me what that's all about?"

Nat looked away.

Alcee looked at Nick. "Either of you?"

Since Nick had no idea what Nat had been doing at the LaRues', he had no problem looking confused. But he wasn't completely innocent; he knew enough about what was going on in her life to realize it probably had to do with her search for a killer.

Alcee divided his attention between them. "I don't know how you expect me to get to the bottom of this if I don't know what the hell is going on. Both of you are skating a thin line." He frowned at Nat. "You show up at the LaRue house again, and I'm going to have to arrest you. Jean filed a restraining order."

"I understand," she said.

"Good." Alcee shook his head in exaggerated disgust, then turned his gaze on Nick. "And you stay the hell away from my deputy."

Nick met his gaze steadily, lowered his voice. "If you hadn't gotten here when you did, Duncan would have been all over her."

Anger flashed in the other man's eyes, but he quickly masked it with a scowl. "Why should I believe you over what my deputy told me?"

"Because I think you're smart enough to know what kind of man he is."

Martin didn't have anything to say about that, but Nick saw the truth in his eyes. Alcee Martin knew exactly what kind of cop Matt Duncan was. "I'll take care of it."

"What about my car?" Nat asked. "There's probably paint on it or something. Dents. Evidence."

"We're going to have to get a diver to go down to get the winch hooked up. I know a guy works for the sheriff's department in Baton Rouge. I'll give him a call and see if I can get him to drive up first thing tomorrow morning."

The lawman's gaze slid from Nat to Nick. "In the interim, I suggest you two stay the hell out of trouble."

chapter
22

NICK KNEW IT WAS SELFISH, BUT HE DIDN'T WANT to be the one to take her to the hospital. He knew that made him a son of a bitch. But the truth of the matter was he didn't want to spend any more time with her. Damn it, he didn't want to *care* about her. He was in no position to care for a woman. Especially tonight when he was wound up so tight he could feel the tension all the way to his spine.

There was something about Nat Jennings that brought out his protective nature with a vengeance. And even though she would argue to her dying breath that she didn't need someone looking out for her, there was no way Nick could walk away.

"You didn't have to do this."

On the passenger seat next to him, Nat huddled in the blanket, shivering so hard he thought she might just vibrate right out of the truck.

"How else are you going to get there?" he asked. "Take a taxi?"

"I don't need some doctor to tell me I have a headache. I already figured that out all by myself."

"I hate to break it to you, Miss I-Figured-It-Out-All-By-Myself, but you need stitches."

"What I need is to find the son of a bitch who tried to kill me."

Nick didn't want to think about how close she'd come to dying tonight. He would never forget the stark terror he'd felt in the seconds he'd thought she was dead. Or the relief that was so powerful his legs had gone weak when he'd realized she was not.

"Any ideas?" he asked.

"Half the population of Bellerose." She shook her head. "I guess the question is, which one of them hates me enough to want me dead."

St. Tammany Memorial was a sixty-seven-bed hospital located off Interstate 12 in nearby Covington. At just before one A.M., Nick and Nat walked into the emergency room where a sour-faced nurse with salt-and-pepper hair took her information, then ushered them into a curtained examination room.

"Let me get you a gown so you can get out of those wet clothes." Digging into a cabinet, the nurse turned to Nat, brandishing a wrinkled gown. "Put it on and have a seat on the exam table. Doc will be with you shortly." She shoved the gown at Nat, then with a swish of white nylon she was out of the room.

Nat frowned at the gown in her hand, then raised her eyes to Nick. "I can't believe I let you drag me here."

"You let me drag you here because your head is laid open."

"I hate hospitals."

"Put on the gown, Nat, and stop complaining."

"How the hell am I supposed to get home with my butt hanging out of this thing?"

"I'm sure you'll manage." Not wanting to think of her in terms of her butt, Nick turned his back and stared at the wall. "Put it on or I'm going to sic Nurse Ratched on you."

He heard the rustle of clothes, then a clipped, "You can turn around."

Nick turned slowly and had to steel himself against a quick slice of lust. He knew this was neither the time nor the place to ogle. But she had absolutely no right to look so damn good sitting on the examination table in a wrinkled gown, a cut on her forehead, and damp hair tangled around her shoulders. She looked good enough to eat, and it took every bit of control he could muster to keep himself from reaching out to touch her just to make sure she wasn't some figment of his imagination.

She'd taken advantage of a disposable paper blanket and draped it over her legs. But it only reached to her ankles and he found himself staring at pretty feet with toenails painted the color of hibiscus. He'd never been unduly interested in female feet, but hers were small and pretty and sexy as hell.

Tearing his gaze away, Nick shifted his weight from one foot to the other to accommodate his swollen member and sighed unhappily. Vaguely, he was aware that she was staring at him, that his heart was pounding, that he was going to do something really stupid if he didn't get the hell out of there pronto.

"I'll see if I can round up the doc."

He'd just turned toward the door when it swung open. Surprise jarred him when Travis Ratcliffe breezed into the exam room with a clipboard in one hand, a stainless steel tray in the other. He looked up and stopped abruptly, his gaze darting from Nat to Nick and then back to Nat. "Oh." His brows snapped together. "Nat? What are you doing here? What happened?"

Nick could see the other man struggling not to show his surprise. But not even a man of Travis Ratcliffe's training and education could hide good, old-fashioned shock.

She paled all the way to her mouth at the sight of Ratcliffe. For an instant, Nick thought she was going to bolt. But she stayed on the exam table, clutching the paper draped over her, staring at Ratcliffe as if he'd just announced he was Dr. Hyde. "I-I wasn't expecting to see you here."

"I do my time here in the emergency room once a week." Grimacing, he turned his attention to Nick and stuck out his hand. "I didn't properly introduce myself last time. Travis Ratcliffe."

Nick gripped his hand, all the while searching the other man's gaze, gauging his sincerity. "Nick Bastille."

Looking more than a little uncomfortable, Ratcliffe dropped Nick's hand and squinted down at the clipboard. "If I had been able to make out Margaret's writing, I would have known it was you in here and not Nate Jenkins." Giving a self-deprecating shake of the head, he forced a smile. "I'm afraid her writing is worse than mine."

"Travis, if I had known you were here, I wouldn't have—"

"Nat, come on." He cut her off by raising his hand. "I'm a professional. I'm not going to let anything personal between us interfere with my work here at the hospital. Okay?" He studied her a moment, his eyes narrowing. "Besides, from the look of that cut on your forehead, I'd say you need about four stitches."

"That's what I thought, too," Nick put in.

Regaining his composure, Travis looked down at the clipboard. "You were in a car accident this evening?"

Nat nodded. "Out on Pelican Island Road."

"Narrow road. Parish needs to get it asphalted and put up a guardrail." Travis addressed Nick. "Were you in the car with her?"

"She was alone."

He looked at Nat. "How did you get wet?"

"The car went into the water," she said.

Ratcliffe made a doctorly sound of distress. "Damn. You're lucky it wasn't worse."

Pulling a small penlight from the pocket of his lab coat, he set his hand against her forehead and shone the light into first her right eye, then her left. "Were you unconscious at any time? Any headache? Confusion?"

Nat shook her head adamantly. "No. None of those things."

"Good."

She flinched when he probed the cut.

"Hurt?" he asked.

"Only when you stick your finger in it."

He chuckled. "Four stitches ought to do the trick." He gave her a reassuring smile. "Let me numb you, and we'll have you out of here in no time. Okay?"

Nat felt incredibly vulnerable sitting on the examination table in nothing but a flimsy hospital gown and wet panties. Her heart pounded in her chest as Travis donned a pair of examination gloves and prepared the needle and syringe for anesthetizing the gash.

The tension in the room was palpable. She was keenly aware of Nick standing by the door, watching them like a hawk. Travis made small talk and did his best to pretend that she was just another emergency room patient. He told Nick he could leave if he wanted to, but Nick opted to stay. As much as Nat didn't want to admit it, she was thankful.

"Lie down please." He moved the small pillow to the head of the examination table and patted it. "There you go."

The last thing she wanted to do was lie down, but she knew there was no way around it if she was going to get herself stitched up, so she complied.

"Cold?"

"No."

"You're shaking." He smiled down at her. "You're not afraid of needles, are you?"

"I don't like doctors."

He laughed, a practiced sound that might have put her at ease if she wasn't hopelessly tied up in knots. "Relax. Just a little pinprick, then you won't feel a thing. I promise."

Nick came up beside the table and surprised her by taking her hand. Nat looked over at him and tried to smile, but failed. Being treated by Travis Ratcliffe when there had been so much hostility between them was just too weird. She closed her eyes while he injected the numbing medicine into the wound.

"There. Should be completely numb in just a sec. Better?"

"All things considered."

"Good. Here we go."

While there was no pain, it was disconcerting to feel the tug of the needle as he sutured her skin.

"Nat, I know this may not be the most opportune moment, but I feel the need to apologize for the things my father said to you."

"Travis, you know I didn't hurt Ward or Kyle."

"I believe you. I've believed you from the start. It's just that Dad . . . Well, he hasn't been the same since losing them. He's bitter and angry and—"

"All of us are bitter and angry," she said. "The last three years have been hell. Elliott's blaming me is only making things worse."

Nick spoke up. "Elliott Ratcliffe is probably part of the reason some son of a bitch tried to run her off the road tonight."

Travis's hand paused an instant before tying off the final

stitch. "Someone deliberately tried to run her off the road?" He made eye contact with Nat. "Is that true?"

She nodded.

"Any idea who did it?"

"Maybe it was your old man," Nick said.

Travis made a sound of annoyance as he set his tools on the tray and lifted a sterile gauze to the newly sutured wound. "You can't possibly believe my father would do something like that."

"I don't know what to believe," she said. "An hour ago I couldn't believe someone was trying to kill me."

"My father might have said some terrible things to you in the past, but he would never harm another human being."

"He harms her every time he shoots off his mouth," Nick said. "It would go a long way in this town if he kept his trap shut."

Travis's mouth formed a thin line. "Look, Nat, there are any number of people in this town who don't like it that you're back. My father might be one of them, but he would never resort to violence."

Nick laughed. "Oh, that's rich. If we hadn't intervened yesterday, your old man would have torn into her like tornado through a mobile home park."

"He's never harmed anyone in his life." Snapping off his gloves, Travis tossed them into the biohazard receptacle with a little too much force. "He's sure as hell never killed anyone."

"You sure about that?"

Travis looked at him sharply. "What the hell is that supposed to mean?"

Nat's heart began to hammer when Nick crossed the room. "Nick, don't."

Ignoring her, he got in Travis's face. "That means keep your family away from her. You. Your old man. And Hunt. You got that, Doc?"

Travis took a swift step back, his eyes darting to the door as if he thought he might need a quick route of escape. "I think you had better leave." He looked at Nat. "Both of you."

Nat could see Nick reining in his temper, and for the first time she realized just how angry he was about what had happened to her. While it was good to know he cared, she didn't think he was being fair to Travis. "Wait a moment—" she began.

Travis cut her off by raising his hand. "It's okay. Just go."

Sliding from the table, Nat scooped up her wet clothes and left without looking back.

IT HAD BEEN ALMOST A YEAR SINCE HUNT RAT-cliffe had been frogging. He loved getting out in his sixteen-foot mud boat at night with a six-pack of Budweiser and some Acapulco gold. He'd grown up eating frog legs and considered them a delicacy. Bernard, the butler at Ratcliffe Plantation, had always fried up the best frog legs in the whole freaking world. But Bernard was too damn old to frog these days, and so the Ratcliffe men went without. Hunt figured he'd remedy that tonight.

Mort Cooper was supposed to go with him but begged off at the last minute. Mort had said it was because he wasn't feeling well, but Hunt knew better. That wife of his probably had him doing laundry or something. Nina Cooper had her husband pussy whipped so badly he would cower at the sound of her voice. Jesus H. Christ. It was getting to where a man couldn't even be a man anymore without some bossy bitch telling him what to do. That wasn't going to happen to Hunt Ratcliffe. He'd spend his days jerking off before he let some mouthy female tell him how to live his life.

The moon illuminated black water that was as smooth as glass and teeming with duckweed. Mosquitoes and water gnats flew frenziedly around the light. Along the shore he saw the glowing eyes of the gators, heard the occasional slap of a reptilian tail. Maybe he'd nab a gator with his .22 while he was out here, too. Even if Bernard didn't cook it up fresh, Hunt could dress and freeze it for later.

Hunt motored down the shallow channel until he reached his destination, Edward Bayou, and shut down the engine. He scooted onto the rowing thwart and reached for his bag of weed, tapping a small amount onto a paper. He rolled the joint by the light of the moon, taking care not to drop any into the boat. The weatherman was calling for thunderstorms later, but Hunt didn't see any lightning. Hopefully, he'd be long gone before the skies opened up. Freaking mosquitoes were eating him alive, anyway.

He sat on the thwart and smoked the joint, watching the glowing eyes of a gator move slowly along the muddy bank. He thought about picking him off; he had a nice little Kimber semiauto in his tackle box. But Hunt was pleasantly buzzed and feeling lazy.

"Lucky bastard," he muttered.

When the joint was spent, he tossed the roach into the water. Standing, he bent to retrieve a Budweiser from the cooler, popped the tab, and drank deeply, enjoying the cold rush down his throat. He set the can on the rowing thwart, then bent to pick up the gig.

When he'd been a kid, his daddy had brought him and Ward and Travis out here frogging. He and Ward had had a blast catching frogs with their hands and tossing them into the bag. Travis had been afraid of them. Hunt and Ward had teased him mercilessly, but Travis had never so much as touched a frog. He'd always been a pantywaist faggot about things like that. Hell, he was probably *still* afraid of frogs. The thought made Hunt laugh aloud.

He'd always thought it was a little spooky that Travis had grown up to become a doctor. As far as Hunt was concerned, some of the shit doctors did was a hell of a lot more disgusting than picking up a frog. He'd been doubly surprised when Travis ran for parish coroner. The position wasn't busy in St. Tammany Parish, but just the thought of cutting up some poor dead bastard gave him the heebie-jeebies.

Rising, Hunt started the motor. He took anther swig of beer, then picked up the gig. He'd fastened the pronged spear to a long cane pole, which made it perfect for spearing frogs. Carefully, he maneuvered the boat through the shallow water to just the right place, then turned on the light clipped to the bow. Sure enough, right there in front of the boat a little pig frog's head was sticking out of the moss, looking at him. Grinning, Hunt drew back the gig, then slammed it down just behind the sacral hump on the frog's back.

"Gotcha, you little fucker."

He hauled the frog into the boat, then tossed it expeditiously into the bag. In the darkness he didn't see the approaching boat until it was practically on top of him. He straightened to have a look, but the powerful spotlight snapped on and shone right in his eyes. Raising his hand against the glare, he tried to identify who'd approached.

"Hey, cut the light, will you?" he said. "I can't see shit."

"Sorry." The spotlight blinked out.

Surprise rippled through Hunt. "What the hell are you doing out here?"

"Same as you, I guess. Looking for something to kill."

Hunt laughed. "Want a beer?"

"Sure."

Still laughing, Hunt bent to retrieve another Budweiser from the cooler. When he straightened, the spotlight was on again and drilling into his eyes. "Turn off that fucking thing, will you?"

He heard a resonant click an instant before a .22 caliber bullet plowed through his forehead and lodged in his brain.

NICK'S TEMPER WAS STILL PUMPING WHEN HE parked the truck in the driveway and shut down the engine. He knew better than to lose his cool, but he'd never had much tolerance for self-righteous jackasses like Travis Ratcliffe.

"You shouldn't have spoken to Travis that way," Nat said from her place on the passenger seat.

"Ratcliffe is a two-faced son of a bitch."

"He's been decent to me."

"Yeah, well, since he's such a sweetheart, maybe he'll go the extra mile and get his sanctimonious old man off your back."

Shaking her head, Nat opened the door and slid to the ground.

Nick sat behind the wheel and glanced over at her through the open door. "We need to talk about what happened to you."

She slammed the door in his face.

Muttering beneath his breath, he got out of the truck and followed her inside. The house smelled like her. Sweet and warm with a hint of spice. He wondered how she could have such a profound impact on a house after only a few days. How she could fill it up without changing a thing. How she could make it feel like a home with nothing more than her presence.

Without speaking, she left him to take a shower. Nick knew he'd pissed her off, but there was nothing he could do about it, so he resolved to let it go. He wandered to the kitchen and checked the locks on the door and window. He found tea bags and put a kettle on the stove to boil. He heard the shower come on and tried hard not to picture hot water and fragrant soap sluicing over soft flesh. But his willpower failed, and he found himself remembering their encounter earlier in the day.

Her mouth had been wet and hot and full of promise. He remembered the way her breasts had molded beneath his hands. The soft hiss of her sigh in his ear. The tight buds of her nipples against his palms . . .

His response was powerful and primal and stopped him dead in his tracks. He went hard, then stood there wondering what the hell he was going to do about it. Not a damn thing, he assured himself. For now, he needed to focus on keeping her safe. On getting to the bottom of his son's death.

But Nick could feel the reckless need pumping inside him, taunting him, making him want things that would only bring him heartache. "Damn it."

Cursing the discomfort in his groin, he walked to the dining room. He glanced down at the legal pad on the table. A chill passed through him when he saw the childlike scrawl.

Going to kill him. In big danger. Help him.
Jason Larue. Find him Mommy. The bad mans
coming.

I'm scared!

The message made the hairs at his nape stand up.

"I see you found the latest note from Kyle."

He turned at the sound of her voice to find her standing a

few feet behind him, staring at him with eyes that were huge and shadowed with fatigue. She'd changed into a pair of faded jeans and an oversize Tulane sweatshirt. Even from a few feet away, he could smell her. A sweet, ripe scent that reminded him of some exotic tropical fruit. She'd dried her hair, but the ends were still curly and wet. Her complexion was as flawless as porcelain and so pale it was almost translucent.

"How are you feeling?" he asked.

"Better." She gave him a small smile. "Warm."

Even though the sweatshirt was loose, he could see that she wasn't wearing a bra. That made him remember touching her breasts earlier in the day. The memory made him hard again. Made him mad because he knew he wasn't going to do anything about it, and the frustration was starting to make him cranky.

Her sweatshirt was cropped. Not short enough for him to see her navel—which was probably a good thing at this point—but the curves of her hips were visible. He could make out the slight gap between slender thighs. The cleft between her legs. Even her damn feet were sexy.

Nick knew he shouldn't be staring. He sure as hell shouldn't be wondering what it would be like to cross the few scant feet between them, peel away all that denim and cotton and lose himself in the beauty of the flesh beneath. But he was aching like he'd never ached before, and for several long moments he couldn't take his eyes off her.

As if realizing where his thoughts had ventured, she wrapped her arms around herself in a protective posture. He cleared his throat, shifted his weight from one foot to the other in an effort to hide the effect she was having on him. "I made tea."

"Oh." She looked flustered for a moment, and he found himself a hell of a lot more charmed than he should have been. "Thank you."

"I figured you could use something hot." Nick walked to the counter and retrieved the cup, then carried it to the kitchen table. "Sit down."

Her gaze went wary as she sank into the chair, and for a moment the only sound came from the grandfather clock in the living room, and the chorus from the bayou coming through the kitchen window.

"Thank you for stepping in when you did earlier," she said. "I mean, with Duncan. You took a huge risk. I don't know how far he would have taken things if you hadn't stopped him."

"He would have crossed a line. He's dangerous. Stay away from him."

"I didn't exactly have a choice tonight."

"You did earlier, when you went to see the LaRues."

Her gaze skittered away. "That couldn't be helped."

"You could have come to me."

"There wasn't any time."

Nick gestured toward the tablet. "I take it you had another trance writing session earlier this evening?"

She nodded. "There was something different about this one."

"How so?"

"It was more intense. And I got a very strong sense that Kyle was afraid."

"Afraid of what?"

"I'm not sure, but I felt it strongly. He seemed utterly certain that Jason LaRue was in imminent danger. I felt it strongly. That something terrible was about to happen."

"So you went to see Jean and Paulette."

She closed her eyes briefly. "I rushed to the rescue like an utter fool. Nobody believed me, of course. And I can't blame them."

"What happened?"

He listened intently as she explained how she'd approached the LaRues with a warning that their son could be in danger, only to find that he was safe and sound in the hospital waiting for an appendectomy.

"They thought I was a lunatic."

"Duncan showed up?"

She nodded. "It was a bad scene. I knew better than to rush over there. But I was terrified if I didn't something terrible would happen."

Nick understood why she'd done it. There was a part of him that admired her for being so willing to put herself on the line. But he didn't like the way any of this was playing out.

"You can't do that again," he said.

"If I hadn't acted and something terrible happened to that child, I'd never be able to live with myself."

"The children in this town are not your responsibility."

"How can you say that? That's exactly the reason this is happening to me. Think about it, Nick. I've been given the opportunity—the responsibility—to protect children who may be at risk."

"You've accepted a huge responsibility for something you have no control over. That's a losing proposition, *chere*."

"No it's not. I have control as long as I act—"

"How much control did you have when your car was plunging into that pond?" Angry, Nick rose and strode to the French doors. He hadn't intended to lose his temper, but he couldn't stop thinking of the terror he'd felt at the accident scene when he'd thought she was dead.

Shoving the thought to the back of his mind, he turned back to her. "Okay, so we know Hunt Ratcliffe drives a blue Suburban. Jim Arnaud drives an old black Bronco. What about Elliott Ratcliffe?"

"I don't know." She sighed. "What about the Wileys?"

"Reno drives an old Ford truck. I don't know about Sara."

"Nick, there are seven thousand people in Bellerose. In case you haven't noticed, a huge percentage of them think I murdered my husband and son. Any one of them could have convinced themselves they were ridding the town of a child killer and run me off the road."

"Or maybe someone thinks you're a threat."

Her face went pale. "The killer."

"It's an angle we've got to consider."

The possibility that the killer had his sights set on Nat made him break a cold sweat. Fate had taught Nick to be cautious when it came to the people he cared about. He wasn't happy about it, but he definitely cared for her. Too damn much, if he wanted to be honest about it.

Raking a hand through his hair, he returned to the table and sat down. "We need to tell Alcee Martin everything."

She choked out a laugh. "There's no way he's going to believe us without some kind of proof."

"Then we give him proof."

"How do you suggest we do that?

"We start by laying out the facts. We know someone tried to kill you tonight. We know the person who killed Kyle and Ward is still out there—"

"Nick, Alcee is sold on the theory that the murders were committed by a vagrant who rode in on the railroad."

"Theories can be disproved."

"Two witnesses placed this vagrant in town that night."

"That's hardly open and shut."

"I agree with you, but it isn't going to matter to Alcee." She bit her lip. "There's no way we'll be able to convince him I'm receiving messages from the dead via trance writing. I can barely believe it myself!"

"If you proved it to me, we can prove it to Martin."

"In case you've forgotten, you were a hard sell, Nick. I'm not sure I want to risk what little credibility I have. If we had some hard evidence—"

"We can't put this off in the hope of getting our hands on proof. If Kyle's messages are accurate, there's a child killer out there. He's already murdered at least three children. Who knows how long this guy has been—" The next thought that struck him stopped him cold, sent an oily wave of nausea climbing up his throat.

"What?" she asked.

"We don't even know how long this guy has been operating."

Nat pressed her hand to her stomach. "When I researched what happened to Brand, I didn't think to look into previous deaths."

Nick let the information roll around in his brain for a moment. "Why the hell haven't the police been able to put this together?"

"Maybe the killer is a cop."

The thought gave him a sick feeling in the pit of his stomach. If the killer were a cop, it would explain a lot of what had been going on. "What makes you think that?"

She studied Nick intently for a moment, and for the first time he got the distinct impression she was keeping something from him. "I'm not saying he's involved in any way—"

"Who?"

"Matt Duncan," she said.

"Matt Duncan?" He knew he was gaping, but couldn't

seem to help himself. "What do you know about Duncan?"

"I went out with him a couple of times back in high school." She let out a self-deprecating laugh. "He was this big football star. I was a naive sixteen-year-old farm girl with an awful lot of silly dreams."

"Let me guess. Duncan wasn't the nice guy everyone thought he was."

"He didn't like to be told no, especially by someone he deemed lower than him on the social ladder."

"Did he . . ."

She shook her head. "No. But he's definitely got a mean streak."

"We got a glimpse of that tonight." Nick thought about what had happened between her and Duncan earlier and felt a quiver of relief that things hadn't gotten any uglier than they had. "You think he's capable of murder?"

"I don't know. I can't see him killing children. But I think he's capable of running me off the road."

"Do you know what kind of vehicle he drives?"

"A big four-wheel drive job. Dark."

"It could have been him?"

She nodded. "It's possible, but it happened too fast for me to be sure."

Anger ground through him at the thought of a bully like Duncan hurting Nat. She'd already been hurt enough. "I should have decked that son of a bitch when I had the chance."

"Nick, we need to stay focused on the killer."

He knew she was right, but it enraged him that Duncan had come within an inch of putting his hands on her. That he may have been the one to run her off the road . . .

"We need help from the police," she said. "Alcee."

He shot her a canny look. "That brings us back to getting proof." Rising, he began to pace, his mind jumping. "We need to find out if there were any suspicious deaths previous to Brand's."

"The library," Nat said. "There are computers there with access to the Internet."

"And the newspaper. There will be archives."

"The *Bellerose Daily Advocate* is across from the post office."

"We'll start there first thing in the morning. We'll search the news reports for accidents in which children have died. We'll also need to search for missing children, going back five or ten years. We need to talk to the parents. Becky and Jim Arnaud to start. Maybe they know something or saw something that could help."

"Nick, I could invite another trance writing session. It's a tool we haven't really tapped into."

He stopped pacing and looked at her. "You mean ask Kyle a direct question and see if he can answer?"

Nat stared back at him, a small but determined warrior willing to face her worst nightmare to get this done. "It's worth a shot."

"Are you up to it?" he asked.

"I'll do whatever it takes to keep this bastard from killing another child."

chapter
23

NAT'S HANDS WERE COLD AS SHE SAT AT THE DINING room table and stared at the blank legal pad in front of her. Nick was sitting across from her, and even though her eyes were closed, she sensed him watching her. She could feel the power of his gaze, touching her like the soft trace of a fingertip.

They'd been sitting in silence for nearly twenty minutes, but nothing was happening. She tried to concentrate on channeling energy into her mind the way she'd done in the past, but she couldn't seem to focus. The gash on her temple was beginning to throb. She was exhausted. She was starting to get frustrated.

The yawn took her by surprise. She looked over at Nick and smiled. "Sorry."

"Would it help if I left the room?" he asked.

She shook her head. "If it's going to happen, it will happen, no matter what I'm doing or who I'm with. If not . . ." She shrugged. "Let's give it a few more minutes and see what happens.

"Sometimes it helps if I write questions." She picked up the pen and wrote, "Kyle, are you there?" Closing her eyes, she waited a full minute before adding, "I need to know if there were any other children besides you and Brandon and Ricky Arnaud who were hurt by the bad man."

Holding the pen ready, she closed her eyes. She breathed deeply, willing her mind and body to relax. She visualized her son's sweet face. She conjured his little-boy scent. *Come to me, baby. . . .*

The dizziness descended like a fast-moving vortex that spun her violently and hurled her into a free fall. Too fast, she thought, and a frisson of fear flashed through her. Then she was tumbling end over end through a tunnel that was filled with color and light and shadow.

Kyle?

As if through a kaleidoscope, she saw her left hand moving over the paper in an awkward dance. Pressing too hard. Tearing the paper. Her knuckles white and trembling. She couldn't see the words, but she could feel the warm pulse of them inside her head. She tried to speak, but her voice was mute. She tried to move, but her body seemed paralyzed.

As quickly as the episode had begun, it stopped. Nat felt herself sagging in the chair. Strong hands on her shoulders, holding her upright. Nick's voice in her ear. Sharp with concern. "Nat. Nat!"

For an instant she didn't want to open her eyes, but she did, and slowly the kitchen came back into view.

"Nat? Can you hear me?"

"I'm okay." She looked up to see Nick staring down at her, his expression dark with concern.

"Easy," he said. "You passed out."

Shaken, she looked around to get her bearings. "How long was I out?"

"Two minutes maybe."

"Seems like an instant. I lose track of time." She tried to rise, but her knees refused the command. Nausea roiled in her stomach. She would have collapsed if he hadn't scooped her into his arms.

"Don't try to stand. I've got you."

"I'm . . . okay. Just a little woozy."

She let him carry her to the living room and lay her on the sofa. Concern was etched deeply into his features when he knelt beside her. "Jesus, you're shaking all over."

"That happens afterward." She scrubbed a hand over her forehead where a headache pounded. "Give me a few minutes, okay?"

He reached out and smoothed the hair back from her face. "You keep scaring me."

"What did I write?"

"Just a few words. I was paying closer attention to you than what you were writing." Rising, Nick crossed to the dining room table and picked up the pad. Even from ten feet away, Nat saw his jaw tighten.

"What does it say?"

He carried the pad to the living room and handed it to her.

Eddy Flatter. Ron Wily. Murdur.

A shiver went through her as she read the words. "Ron Wiley was Reno and Sara Wiley's son. He was hit by a car and killed five, maybe six years ago."

"An accident?"

"Hit and run. The driver was never apprehended. The entire town was in an outrage. The police speculated someone had been drinking. The boy was playing on the road in front of his house. It was dusk. The driver didn't see him." She sighed. "Ronnie died at the scene."

Shuddering inwardly at the thought of a child being purposefully mowed down by a car, Nick looked down at the paper. "What about Eddie Flatter?"

"I don't know the name."

"Me, neither."

She looked down at the paper. "This means the killer has been operating for at least five or six years."

"Longer if Eddie Flatter was a victim and killed before the Wiley boy."

"God, Nick, two more children dead, and we're still not any closer to finding the murderer." Frustrated by their lack of progress, Nat put her feet on the floor and rose. The dizziness had subsided but she was still nauseous. Her head was pounding. She felt his eyes on her as she crossed to the dining room table and put the newest note in the folder.

"We're missing something," Nick said.

"What?"

"I don't know." He shook his head. "Why is he targeting kids? Why *these* kids? Were they random? Or did he choose them for a reason?"

"You're wondering if there's a common denominator?" She hadn't thought of that. The situation was so emotionally devastating for her, she was having a difficult time being analytical about it. "So far it seems like he's only targeted boys."

Nick nodded. "Right. And all of them have been between the ages of five and nine years of age."

"It seems like that's where any similarities end. All the boys were so different. Different social and economic backgrounds. Different personalities. Even though Kyle had asthma, he was active and played—"

Nick's gaze snapped to hers. "Kyle had asthma?"

She nodded. "We managed it, but—"

"Brand had asthma."

"I don't see how that could make them the target of a killer." But her heart had begun to pound.

"What about Ricky Arnaud?" he asked.

"I don't—" She bit off the words, greasy nausea spreading through her. "Faye once told me the Arnauds' boy had childhood-onset rheumatoid arthritis."

"And Ronnie Wiley?"

"He was autistic."

"Jason LaRue?"

"He's . . . obese. Some kind of thyroid disorder."

"Jesus. That's too coincidental."

"Why would somebody . . ." Unable to finish the thought, Nat pressed her hand to her stomach. She knew it was stupid at this point, but she felt like crying. For the children who'd been killed. For the families that had been devastated. For her own shattered life. "That's incredibly evil."

"Or insane." He raised his gaze to hers. "But I think maybe we've found The Why."

"Now we just need to figure out who could be so utterly . . . demented."

Nick raked his fingers through his hair. "First thing in the morning, we dig up anything we can find on Eddie Flatter. See if there's some detail that might point us in the right direction."

"Even knowing what kind of children he targets, how is it going to help us find the killer?"

"It's all we have. Let's pursue it, see where it takes us."

"I don't want to wait until tomorrow." Wishing for a laptop, she began to pace. "Damn it, there's got to be something we can do tonight. Maybe we could drive to Baton Rouge or New Orleans and find a coffee shop with computers and Internet access. Maybe we could talk to somebody here in Bellerose—"

She started when Nick came up behind her and put his hands on her shoulders. "It's two o'clock in the morning," he said. "You're so wiped out you can barely stand upright. There's nothing we can do tonight."

She knew he was right. But even though she was so exhausted she could feel it all the way to her bones, it didn't make the waiting any easier.

Turning to Nick, she realized she wasn't the only one who was tired. He looked as exhausted as a man could be and still be standing. His dark eyes were shadowed. The grooves on either side of his mouth seemed deeper. Even his broad shoulders seemed bowed.

"If you want to sack out here, you're welcome to the sofa," she said.

"I wasn't planning on leaving you."

"What about your father?"

"I'll give him a call, let him know I'm tied up."

While Nat carried sheets and a pillow to the sofa, Nick called Dutch. She was in the process of unfolding the quilt when he walked into the living room.

"Your dad okay?" she asked.

"Fine. He was in bed. Cussed me out for calling."

She gave him a sympathetic smile over her shoulder. "Sorry."

"It's okay. That's just how he is."

She finished with the quilt and started toward the linen closet in the hall. "I've got an extra pillow—"

"Nat . . . wait."

Something in his voice stopped her, and she halted midway to the hall and turned back to him. "What is it?"

"There's one more thing we need to talk about before we call it a night," he said.

She could tell from his expression it was a subject she wasn't going to like. "What?"

"I want you to tell me what happened that night three years ago."

She felt the words like an open-handed slap, painful and unexpected. She couldn't believe he wanted her to talk about the night Kyle and Ward had been murdered. The night her life had been torn apart and she'd begun a slow spiral into hell. She knew it was a cowardly reaction, but she didn't want to discuss it. Not now. Not ever.

"I can't talk about that," she heard herself say.

"I know it's difficult." He crossed to her, his eyes direct and earnest, as if he'd somehow looked inside her head and knew exactly what she was thinking, what she was feeling. "Of all the murders we've looked at, Kyle's and Ward's stand out as different. They could never be explained as accidental. I think that could be significant."

"Significant how?"

"I don't know, but I think it's something we need to talk about."

Nat raised her hands as if to fend him off, but she knew it wasn't going to help. She was going to have to tell him what happened whether she wanted to or not. "I've spent the last two and a half years trying to forget. I don't want to remember."

Turning away from him, she walked to the dining room table and lowered herself into a chair. The tea he'd made for her earlier had gone cold, but she picked it up and drank anyway, desperately needing that tiny act of normalcy.

She didn't want to remember that night. Didn't want to relive the hell of seeing her husband and son lying dead on the floor. But she knew that no matter how horrific the memory, she was going to have to relive it one more time. A child's life could very well depend on it.

Vaguely, she was aware of Nick taking the chair across from her. She didn't look up. Didn't even acknowledge him. She didn't want to do this. She was angry at him for suggesting it, shaking inside because her memory was already taking her back. Back to a place she didn't want to go . . .

"I'm sorry," he said. "I know it's hard."

"It's worse than hard," she snapped.

"If it wasn't important, I wouldn't put you through it," he said. "But I think it's important. Nat, I don't know how, but I think what happened to you that night is somehow related to what's happening now."

A full minute passed before she spoke. When she did, her voice was so low, she could barely hear it over the thrumming of her heart. "It started out like any other night. I put Kyle to bed around nine. Ward and I went to bed around eleven. I don't know what woke me a few hours later. I thought it was thunder. It was two fifty-three A.M., and Ward wasn't in bed.

"When I checked Kyle's room and saw that he was gone, too, I figured they were downstairs, raiding the refrigerator." She closed her eyes briefly, remembering with such clarity that her heart was pounding. "I thought it was strange that they hadn't turned on the lights. But there was enough light for me to see, so I went downstairs. I was going to surprise them.

"I saw Kyle first. He was lying on the floor, on his stomach. He was still wearing his pajamas. The yellow ones with little hippos. He looked so little and . . . broken." She closed her eyes against a hard punch of grief, the rush of tears, blinked them away.

"I went to him. I thought, this can't be happening. Not to my baby." A sob bubbled up, but she put her hand over her mouth, forced it back down where a thousand more lay in waiting. "His throat had been cut. There was so much blood. It was like a terrible nightmare. I kept hoping I would wake up, but I didn't and it seemed to go on forever.

"Ward was slumped against the cooking island. I remember staring at him, willing him to get up and help me because our little boy needed to be rushed to the hospital. At that point, I was utterly certain that they couldn't possibly be dead.

"But Ward didn't get up." She looked at Nick. Staring into the depths of his gaze, she saw the endless black chasm of grief mirrored in his eyes. She recognized it and wondered if he saw the same thing when he looked at her. A woman whose soul had been hollowed out and would never be whole again.

"Then I heard a noise and realized the intruder was still in the house. I tried to get to the phone, but he came at me with the knife. I fought him, but I couldn't get away. I remember pain and blood. I remember horror. I remember thinking I was going to die. . . .

"I picked up the gun—Ward's revolver—but there were no bullets. I threw it at him. We struggled and I ended up falling. I don't know why he didn't kill me. He had every opportunity. But he just . . . ran. Somehow, I made it to the phone and called the police. I remember looking at my husband and son and thinking if the ambulance arrived fast enough they would be okay. I remember hearing screams. Terrible, blood chilling screams. It wasn't until the first police officer arrived on the scene that I realized those screams were coming from me."

NICK WANTED TO GO TO HER. HOLD HER. DO SOMEthing, anything to stanch the flood of grief he saw in her eyes. But he knew if he touched her now she would shatter into a thousand pieces. Looking at her, he didn't think either of them could put all those pieces back together.

He could only imagine the hell she'd gone through that night. Even though his own son's death would forever stand in his memory as the blackest day of his life, he knew it would have been infinitely worse to see it happen. Nat had experienced the horror firsthand. She'd been injured herself. Putting himself in her place, he thought it would be too much for his mind to absorb. The pain too deep for his heart to endure.

"Did you see the killer's face?" he asked, surprised by the roughness of his voice.

"He was wearing a ski mask."

"Ward had been stabbed? Same as Kyle?"

"Ward had been shot. It wasn't until later that I realized the gunshot is probably what woke me."

Nick raked his fingers through his hair, surprised to see that his hand was shaking. "Did the cops think it was a home invasion? A robbery? Did Ward walk in on something? What?"

"The cops think I killed Ward for the insurance money. They think I didn't want my child or the life I'd made with them."

"Did they have secondary theories?"

"Just Alcee's vagrant."

"But you don't believe it."

She met his gaze steadily, but her eyes were so haunted it was impossible to look at her and not ache. "I think the killer was after Kyle. I think he was trying to lure him from the house. I think Ward walked in on them and tried to stop it."

"Were there any prints on the gun?"

"The gun was never found."

"The cops looked?"

"Thoroughly. They tore up the backyard. They trampled through the woods behind the house. They searched the vehicles. Every inch of the house. The flower beds. They even had a couple of divers search the river behind the house."

"What about the knife?"

"It was left in the kitchen sink. Covered with blood. My prints were all over it."

Jesus. "How did your prints get on the knife?"

"I don't know. I don't remember picking it up, but I must have at some point. I barely remember those moments after finding them."

"Why were the police so certain that you had done it?" he asked. "Surely the people who knew you spoke out in your defense."

"Some did. Some were so intent on getting justice for a horrendous crime . . . I think they needed someone to blame. It didn't matter that that someone was me."

"What about the evidence?"

"I told you about the screen."

Remembering, Nick ran the scenario through his mind. "The screen had been cut with your knife from the inside."

"So it would appear as if I'd cut the screen to make it look as if someone had cut the screen and come into the house through the window."

"What else?"

"There was some blood spatter. On my nightgown. Kyle's blood." She let out a shuddery breath. "The police sent the gown to the lab and had some blood spatter expert look at it. He ascertained that, judging from the direction of the spatter, it allegedly came from my knife as I was supposedly stabbing . . ."

"It was later disproved?"

"By a second expert witness during the grand jury stage."

Nick contemplated her, hurting for her, outraged and saddened by what she had been put through. "Do you think someone tried to frame you?"

Her expression turned fierce. "I know they did. It's the only explanation that makes sense."

"Any idea why someone would do that?"

"I don't know. To protect themselves by diverting suspicion onto me. To get back at me for some perceived wrong. Because they're insane. All of the above."

"Did you have any enemies at that time? Did Ward?"

"No." But her gaze skittered away, and for the first time Nick got the feeling she hadn't told him everything.

"Nat, if you're holding something back . . ."

She stared at him for an uncomfortable moment, then lowered her head and pinched the bridge of her nose. "I dragged you into this. I guess I owe you the rest of it."

"Rest of what?"

The silence weighed heavily for several seconds. Nat fiddled with the folder, looking everywhere but at him. "Ward and I . . . we'd been having some problems."

"What kind of problems?"

"Marital. There was a distance between us I didn't understand."

"Did you argue?"

"No, we just . . ." She sighed. "It was like we were going through the motions. We didn't talk. We didn't share. We didn't . . . connect the way I thought a husband and wife should. It was like there was a distance between us I couldn't seem to gap no matter how hard I tried."

"Do you have any idea why?"

She shook her head, looked away. "No."

But Nick sensed there was more. "Nat, talk to me," he said gently. "Get it out. It's okay."

When she raised her gaze to his, there were tears in her

eyes. "We hadn't . . . been intimate for almost a year. He . . . he'd had some sexual problems. It only happened a couple of times. I just figured it was stress. I mean, it happens. We were busy, and we just didn't talk about it." She lowered her head and rubbed the place between her eyes. "God, Nick, this feels wrong, talking about him like this. He was always a very private man."

"If he were here now, do you think he'd want you to get to the bottom of what really happened that night?"

Raising her head, she blinked away tears. "He was having an affair."

"With whom?"

"His administrative assistant at the church. Sara Wiley."

Nick shouldn't have been shocked. He'd known for a long time that people weren't always what they appeared. But Ratcliffe had been a minister. A man with a squeaky-clean reputation. Nick had always assumed Nat's marriage to him had been solid. Until now, she'd never given any indication that the relationship was troubled.

"Did the police know?" he asked. "Did they talk to her?"

"After the fact."

"Was she ever a suspect?"

Nat shook her head. "From what I understand, she was questioned, but never a viable suspect. I've met her several times. Nick, she's no killer."

"People have been known to snap."

"Not in this case. I think she loved him."

"What about her husband? Could he have done it?"

"Maybe. He has a temper. But I don't know. . . ."

"At the very least, both Sara and Reno are worth talking to."

Rising abruptly, she walked to the kitchen to stare through the window above the sink. Her shoulders were square, her chin high. But Nick could see it was only a facade.

He knew better than to go to her. He knew touching her now would bring into the moment something neither of them wanted. But she was hurting in the worst possible way a human being could hurt. There was no way he could stand there and do nothing while she came apart right before his eyes.

Shoving away from the table, he walked to the kitchen and stopped several feet from her. "Nat."

She didn't turn to him. "Even after three years it still hurts," she whispered.

"Healing from that kind of grief takes a long time."

Slowly, she turned to him. She hadn't turned on the light, and even in the dim light from the living room he could see that her eyes were ravaged. She wasn't crying, but he saw the bottomless well of grief. And because he understood all too well what that kind of pain could do to a person, he crossed to her and pulled her to him.

"I don't want to hurt anymore," she said.

"I know, *chere*."

"Make it stop."

She laid her head on his shoulder. He tightened his arms around her and stroked the back of her head. "I don't think I'm the right man to heal you."

She shouldn't have felt so good in his arms. Not when she was hurting and vulnerable and his own need for her was a sweet ache that grew with every beat of his heart. He was aware of every inch of her against him. The soft curve of her breasts against his chest. The solid press of her cleft against his pelvis. The sweet scent of her hair titillating his senses. The warm caress of her breath against his neck.

He was already hard, but it was a response he could no more control than he could the beat of his heart. Because he knew she could feel his shaft against her, he tried to pull back, to put a few inches of space between them, but she tightened her arms around him.

Nick closed his eyes and tried not to think about where this moment could lead or what it was doing to his resolve to stay away from her. She was everything that was decent and good in the world. A woman who'd been shattered by grief. Betrayed by a man she should have been able to trust and a town that should have stood by her. A woman who wanted to heal and was now reaching out to him . . .

Only Nick didn't have anything to offer. He was flat broke and hollowed out by injustices and betrayals he hadn't been able to fight. But his need for her was insane and pounded through his body like a sledgehammer driving a nail. He wanted badly to believe the sensations coursing through him were about sex. That all he needed was one good fuck and he would be able to walk away and not look back.

But he knew his feelings for her went deeper than physical. He knew if he gave in to those feelings, they would cost him. He knew it was a price he didn't want to pay. Intellectually, he knew Nat was nothing like Tanya. But the grief would not let him forgive. The bitterness would not let him forget.

"Being with me isn't going to make the pain go away," he said.

"This doesn't have to be about pain."

Heart raging beneath his ribs, he grasped her arms and shoved her to arm's length. "I'm not what you need right now," he ground out. "I can't help you heal. I don't have anything to give you. I'm hollow inside, Nat."

Her eyes were huge and fraught with all the things he didn't want to see. Pain. Need. The hope that one would assuage the other. She was standing so close he could feel the puffs of her breaths against his face. "If you were empty, you wouldn't hurt, Nick. I see you hurting as clearly as I feel my own heart beating."

Never taking her eyes from his, she stood on her tiptoes and brushed her mouth against his. Nick stiffened, ready to pull back. But the quick shock of pleasure was like a bolt of electricity that shot through his body and exploded in every nerve ending. His control shattered. Making a low sound in his throat, he put his hands on either side of her face and tilted her head to him.

"It's been six goddamn years since I've been with a woman," he growled. "Don't expect me to stand here and tell you I don't want you."

"Then don't."

He took her mouth with a violence that wrenched a gasp from her, but Nick didn't stop. He didn't think about consequences or right or wrong. It was as if a starving beast had been unleashed inside him. A beast that had been beaten and deprived, and then given a bounty so lush and rich he would never be able to consume all of it.

He kissed her hard and long. When that was no longer

enough, he used his tongue and kissed her some more. She made a sound in her throat at the intrusion, but he didn't give her the chance to change her mind. For the first time in a long time, Nick didn't think. He crossed the point of no return at the speed of light and didn't look back.

He could only hope this moment didn't cost both of them something they couldn't afford to lose.

chapter
24

THE KISS WAS RAW AND PRIMAL AND BLATANTLY sexual. It took her breath away. It told her things about Nick Bastille that he didn't want her to know. Things that, until now, she'd only been able to guess.

He wasn't a tentative kisser. He wouldn't be a tentative lover. He knew what he wanted and made no bones about taking it. Right now, he wanted his mouth on hers, his hands on her body. He was bold and sure of himself, and all Nat could do was kiss him back and hang on for the ride.

His body was like carved granite against her. She could feel the hard shaft of his erection against her belly, her womb fluttering in response. That she was capable of feeling something as complex—as simple—as sexual arousal surprised her. For months, she'd been certain that that part of her was as cold and empty as the rest of her. But Nick had proved to her that she wasn't dead inside. That she was very much alive and every bit as capable of feeling joy as she was pain.

She opened to him, let him inside her mouth, and her tongue warred with his. He groaned, a sound of pure male need, and a surge of feminine power engulfed her. His hands slipped beneath her sweatshirt. A gasp that was part shock, part pleasure escaped her when he cupped her breasts. Her back arched when he took her nipples between his thumbs and forefingers and gently squeezed.

The pleasure was maddening. Nat could feel the heat of desire between her legs now. Blood pounding like a drum in her womb. Her panties were wet, and she realized with some surprise that even though he hadn't touched her there, she was already on the verge of orgasm.

When she'd initiated the kiss, she hadn't been sure where it would lead. In the back of her mind, she'd thought she would stop before things went too far. She hadn't expected his kisses to sweep her away. Or his hands to set her body on fire.

He lifted her sweatshirt. His mouth left hers. She opened her eyes, and then his mouth was on her breast. She cried out when he began to suckle, first her left breast then her right. She could feel her body responding, softening, weeping for the release only he could give her.

She closed her eyes against the burst of sensation. Her head lolled back. The ache in her breasts was almost painful in its intensity, building to a crest, taking her to a very sharp edge, but never over.

He moved lower, pressing his hand flat against her stomach. His palms were warm and rough against her skin. Then he was unfastening the button of her jeans. Nat knew she should stop him before things went too far. She wasn't ready for this. Wasn't ready for the things she knew he would make her feel, both emotionally and physically. But the need was ripping through her, tearing down her resistance, her control.

All the while he made love to her mouth with his, dazing her senses so that she couldn't think. Vaguely, she was aware of him lowering her zipper, her jeans being tugged downward.

Turning her head slightly, she broke the kiss. "I-I don't think I can . . . do this," she panted.

His eyes glittered with intensity when he looked at her. "Your place is with the living, Nat, not with the dead."

When she tried to look away, he put his hand beneath her chin and forced her gaze to his. He was breathing hard, as if he'd just run a mile. She could feel the tension humming through his body and into hers. A current that flowed like electricity between them.

"Life doesn't have to be about pain," he said.

The words brought tears to her eyes. More than anything, Nat wanted the pain to stop. She wanted to move forward with her life. She wanted a future. "Show me," she whispered.

Leaning close, he kissed her like she'd never been kissed in her life. Nat let him explore her with his tongue. She jolted when she felt his hand against her pelvis. Never taking his mouth from hers, he tugged down her panties, and she kicked them off. She whimpered when his hand moved over her mound. She opened to him, and he slipped two fingers between her folds. Nat cried out, but he swallowed the sound.

Pleasure zinged like a bullet inside her brain when he began to stroke. Waves building and threatening to crest. Nat hadn't wanted their first time to happen this way. She was traditional when it came to lovemaking. She wanted to make love to him in the bedroom under cover of darkness. She wanted him on top of her, their completion to happen simultaneously. "Wait," she said between breaths. "Together."

"Next time," he said.

She caught a glimpse of his eyes, dark and shuttered. An instant later his fingertip found the small kernel. She tried to resist, but the high wire pleasure wrenched a cry from her. Vaguely, she was aware of her legs opening. Her body going liquid around his fingers. Those fingers taking her to a precipitous edge and a fall that would be fatal.

"Let go," he whispered.

She wanted to say something that would let him know she was in control of the situation. But Nat knew she was only fooling herself. She hadn't been in control of a damn thing since the moment he'd touched her.

The pleasure burgeoned to a sweet ache that left her insides quivering. A knot drawn to an inexorable snap. She could feel her entire body shaking. Sweat heating her skin. His kisses were like an addictive narcotic, one she would never get enough of. All the while he stroked her with those magical fingers. She moved with him, curling her spine to take him more deeply.

And then suddenly her body was no longer her own. It moved independently of her brain. She could feel herself coming apart, her hips moving quickly. A long, slow cry tearing from her throat as the pleasure burst and scattered inside her.

"Nick! Oh, God!"

Her body was still spasming when he gripped her hips and swung her around and onto the counter. He stepped between her knees. Her gaze snapped to his, and for the first time since she'd known him, his eyes were unshuttered. Within their depths she saw the breadth and width of his feelings for her. The deep well of vulnerability. The heat of a passion she'd never before known. The reflection of her own heart.

"In the bedroom," she whispered.

"Here," he said. "And the bedroom."

Never taking his eyes from hers, he unfastened his jeans. Nat gasped at the sight of his jutting sex. Ward was the only man she'd ever been with. He'd been a gentle lover. . . .

"Don't think about him," Nick ground out. "This is about us. Only us."

He didn't ask for permission when he pulled her to the edge of the counter. She could feel the tension winding up inside her. The need building to a crescendo. Moving closer, he put his hands on either side of her face and kissed her deeply. Nat felt herself begin to free-fall. Vaguely, she was aware of his hands sliding down, over her shoulders to her waist, her hips.

"Open to me," he whispered.

But she was already opening to him, and in one smooth motion he slid into her and went deep. He was thickly built, and for an instant discomfort overrode pleasure. But she was well lubricated and within a few seconds her muscles relaxed enough so that she could accommodate him.

"Ah, sweet Jesus." Nick went perfectly still, his body rigid, and he simply held her for the span of several heartbeats.

"Nick . . ."

"Don't move."

Understanding dawned, and it sent a small thrill through her to realize he was struggling to hold back, to prolong the pleasure of the moment. "It's okay," she whispered and put her arms around his shoulders where his muscles were coiled and tight. She could feel sweat coming through his shirt. Even though he wasn't yet moving within her, she could feel her muscles beginning to contract around him, the waves beginning to build.

"This isn't going to wait," he said.

"I think you're right." Tilting her pelvis, she took him more deeply inside her.

"Nat . . ." Closing his eyes, he put his hands on her hips in an effort to still her.

But the waves were breaking, swamping her with sensation. As if realizing this was a battle he was destined to lose, he began to move, slowly at first and then at a frantic pace.

She had never seen Nick Bastille unshielded. Since the day she'd met him, he'd kept his thoughts, his emotions locked down tight. But as she accepted him into the deepest reaches of her body, she saw the man behind the hard facade. The man who had been hurt and betrayed. A man who'd had six years of his life stolen. A man who'd lost his only son.

A good man who'd been to hell and back and survived.

Looking into the depths of his eyes, she knew this man who made love to her with such utter tenderness would never hurt another human being. That all the things she'd read about him in the newspaper, heard about him from the town gossipmongers, were not true. And the truth of that devastated her.

His arms tightened around her. A powerful shudder racked his body as he poured his seed into her. And, whispering her name, he held her like there was no tomorrow.

NICK HAD KNOWN SEX WOULD BE GOOD AFTER SIX years of celibacy. But he hadn't expected it to move him so profoundly he couldn't speak. Or to touch him so deeply he had to close his eyes and take a few moments to get a grip on his emotions.

He'd missed sex desperately when he'd been in prison. For six unbearable years he'd harnessed his frustration, turned it into positive energy. He'd used that energy to beef up his body, running nearly ten miles a day and working out in the weight room when he had the freedom to do so.

Tonight, everything he'd missed poured over him in a torrent that was as powerful and bittersweet as the promise of a first kiss. The realization that he was still human enough to

want with such desperation made him more than a little uneasy. He knew firsthand that wanting was a dangerous thing
for a man who couldn't have.

After making love in the kitchen, he swept her into his
arms and carried her upstairs. By the time they made it to the
master bedroom he was hard again and aching with an intensity that bordered on pain. But if he'd thought the physical release of an orgasm would ease the sharp edge of need that had
been driving him crazy for days now, he'd been wrong. Making love to Nat made him even more desperate to have her
again.

They made love a second time on the bed. It was slower,
not as frantic. Somehow he managed to make it last long
enough to bring her to peak. And as he'd listened to her cry
out his name, he swore to himself this would have to be
enough.

But he knew it wouldn't.

"Hey."

Something went warm and soft inside him when Nat offered him a sleepy smile. She was incredibly lovely in the dim
light slanting in from the window. And even though his
thoughts were troubled, he found himself smiling back at her.
"I didn't mean to wake you."

"You didn't," she said. "I'm just . . . not used to this."

"Neither am I. But I think I like it."

She laughed and Nick felt a hard squeeze of emotion. He
liked the sound of her laughter. Loved the feel of her against
him. He was lying on his back. Her head was resting on his
shoulder, and she was snuggled against him with her leg
thrown over his. He wondered what he'd done to deserve this
little slice of heaven.

She propped herself up on an elbow. "Do you always brood
after sex?"

"Only when it's over too quickly." Embarrassed because
that much was true, he smiled. "I'm a little rusty."

Grinning back at him, she tsked. "Maybe we need to keep
working and see if we can sharpen up your skills a little."

Nick threw his head back and laughed. At the same time he
felt the same weird squeeze of emotion in his chest. Tightening his arm around her, he pulled her back down and kissed

her temple. "I'm a slow learner, *chere*. But with enough practice, I'm betting I'll eventually get the hang of it."

She raised her gaze to his. "Nick, being with you like this . . . I didn't think I'd ever feel like this again. I thought that part of me had died."

"That part of you is alive and well, *chere*. It's been there all along. But I'm glad I could help you find it."

She traced her finger over the tattoo of a dragon on his shoulder. It was a large, intricate design. The work of an artisan with imagination and an eye for color and scale.

"Where did you get the tattoos?" she asked.

He glanced down at the dragon and gave her a half smile. "Guy by the name of Sanchez. He owned a tattoo parlor in New Orleans, made the mistake of thinking he could make more money dealing dope. Not a bad cell mate once I got to know him."

She thought about that a moment. "Prison must have been incredibly difficult."

Nick didn't want to talk about it. Invariably, it made him feel like a fool. But he saw the way she was looking at him. The questions in her eyes. After everything they'd just shared, he figured he at least owed her an explanation.

"What happened?" she pressed.

"I was stupid. Blind. Naive." He smiled, but it felt false on his face. There was nothing even remotely humorous about the hellish years he'd spent behind bars. "Just the kind of guy you want to get tangled up with, right?"

"Nobody knows better than I do that things aren't always as they appear." When he didn't continue, she reached out and touched his face. "What happened, Nick?"

Over the years he'd trained himself not to think about the turn of events that had ultimately landed him in prison. During those first unbearable months, the injustice of it had nearly driven him over the edge. It had filled him with rage and bitterness. Turned him into a man he didn't want to be. Because he hadn't had a choice, he'd learned to live with it, but the story would never be an easy one to tell.

"I had a lot of big ideas as a kid," he said after a moment. "Dreams, I guess."

"Dreams are a good thing for a young person," she said.

Drawing her against him, he pressed a kiss to her temple. "Sometimes dreams just breed discontent." Remembering, he sighed. "My mama died when I was sixteen. Pop was pretty broken up. We both were. But once she was gone, he got bitter. We fought a lot. I didn't want to be in Bellerose. I didn't want to end up like my old man. Don't get me wrong; I've got nothing against hard work and I'm sure as hell not afraid of it. But I didn't want to spend my life breaking my back and barely eking out a living only to have Fate snatch it away one piece at a time when I got old.

"By then, I'd met Tanya. She was from a poor family. Her old man was a mean drunk and liked to beat on her. I figured it wouldn't be long until he started doing more. So I asked her to leave with me, and she said yes. I was seventeen."

"So, you ran away?"

"We went to New Orleans. We rented a dumpy little apartment near the French Quarter. I landed a job at one of the upscale restaurants. Cleaning toilets, I think." He gave a self-deprecating laugh. "But I liked the sparkle of the place. I liked the people. The music. The glitter." He shrugged. "I worked two jobs and went to school at night. My second job was as bartender in a five star hotel. I was good and moved up fast. I took classes at night. I was arrogant and ambitious and a little bit reckless; I wanted it all, and I wasn't afraid to go after it.

"That's when I met Race Roberson. He was managing a club on Bourbon Street. He was from Australia and wore two thousand dollar suits. He tossed around a lot of cash. Drove a fancy car. Let me tell you, this farm boy was impressed as hell. We became friends. We partied together. Eventually, he hired me to manage his club. A few months later, one of the historic buildings down the street came up for sale. The owner had filed for bankruptcy and the place was going at a steal. It was the perfect location for a restaurant. I had the experience. Race Roberson had the capital."

He sighed. "We became business partners. Had an attorney draw up a simple partnership document for us. We bought the building and began renovating it. Three months later, we opened The Tropics. It was a jazzy club and restaurant. Lots of dark wood and palms. We hired the best chefs in the city.

The best bartenders. The place was going to be a huge success. I was working a lot, maybe eighty or ninety hours a week. But I loved it. I was in my element. I knew Tanya wasn't happy about my being gone so much, but I always figured once the place was running smoothly, I could hire an assistant manager and cut back on my hours.

"Race took care of the books. We had a CPA, and it wasn't until after the place was open for six months that I was told we hadn't yet turned a profit. I was stunned. Race had called a meeting with me and the CPA. I couldn't believe we weren't making money. The place was doing a great business. Sure, labor and food costs were high, but not *that* high.

"Race and the CPA and I sat in the office above the restaurant and came up with a business plan. Ways to cut costs and increase profits. Once the CPA left, Race and I had a few drinks. He sat down at the desk and asked me if I wanted to burn the place and collect the insurance money. I didn't consider myself naïve, but I couldn't believe he was asking me that. The Tropics was my dream. I told him I could make it work. I just needed more time. I told him not to bring it up again."

Lying back on the pillow, Nick looked up at the ceiling, surprised that even after so many years, talking about it got his heart rate up. "I should have stopped trusting him at that point. Race Roberson was a little too slick. Instead, I went back to my routine of eighty hour weeks. I started watching the costs a little more closely." He ground his teeth. "Two weeks later the restaurant burned to the ground."

"Oh, Nick."

"Tanya and I had a nice house in the Garden District. I got the call at five in the morning and rushed over. But the place was fucking gone. I couldn't believe it. I suspected Race had something to do with it. I went over to his place in Metairie ready to knock his head off. But he swore to me he hadn't done it. He said the place was old. The wiring was probably bad. He was a damn good liar.

"The next day I found out one of the cleaning crew had died in the blaze. A guy with a wife and two kids, for God's sake. The police had a lot of questions. The ATF got involved. I cooperated fully, but I never mentioned that Race had suggested we torch the place for the insurance money. I didn't want to cast any suspicion.

"A few days later the fire marshal ruled the blaze arson. Some type of accelerant had been used. Two weeks later, two detectives came to the house with a warrant for my arrest. They searched the house. Cuffed me while Tanya screamed her head off. They took me down to the station. I knew I was in trouble. But there was no doubt in my mind it would be cleared up. I wasn't too worried. I made the mistake of thinking all I had to do was tell the truth. I spent the night in jail. I hired a lawyer.

"But Race Roberson was one step ahead of me. He'd already given the police a sworn statement telling them I had suggested we torch the place for the insurance money. Then I found out the police found a container of naphtha paint thinner at my house—the same kind of accelerant that had been used to start the fire. By the time I realized what was happening, it was too late."

Nat stared at him, her chest tight with outrage. "But you had the truth on your side. You had a lawyer. Didn't the truth come out during the trial?"

He closed his eyes briefly, then continued without looking at her. "I'd been incredibly blind," he said. "It wasn't until the trial that I found out Tanya and Race had been together."

"Oh, no . . ."

"She and I had been having problems. Serious problems. Brand was only two years old. I'd been working a lot of hours, leaving her alone all hours of the day and night. . . ."

"But you were working to make your dream come true. To make her dream come true. She was your wife. Your partner."

"Not her dream, Nat. Mine. And I was blinded by it." He grimaced. "That made Tanya an easy mark for Race Roberson. All he had to do was flash a little cash, take her for a ride in his Jaguar, pour on the charm, and he had her eating out of his hand. So, while I was working like a fool, he was coming on to my wife. He convinced her I was sleeping around with one of my waitresses. He told her she deserved better, that I was going to leave her. Then he seduced her."

Nick let out a breath, surprised that even after all this time the betrayal hurt. "He told her I'd approached him about torching The Tropics. He said if the restaurant burned, she should tell the police the truth. That she shouldn't feel any loyalty to me. He told her he was going to Los Angeles to start over. He promised to take her and Brand with him. By then, she was crazy in love with the guy."

"During the trial, she sat in the witness box, crying her eyes out, and told the court Race had told her I'd approached him about torching the place for the insurance money. Her testimony and the accelerant that had been found in my garage pretty much sealed my fate. She had no idea she had been manipulated. Two days later, I was convicted of arson, conspiracy to commit insurance fraud, and manslaughter."

Nat felt gut punched. "I'm sorry."

"I swear, I couldn't believe it. I was in shock. My wife. My goddamn best friend. I knew I was in deep trouble, but it was too late. My lawyer did her best, but she wasn't very experienced. Two weeks later, I was sentenced to twelve years in Angola."

It made her sick to think this man had had to endure something so brutally unjust. "I can't image how awful that must have been."

"Twelve years seemed like an eternity to me. They cuffed me in the courtroom. In front of my wife and son. I couldn't believe that was the end of it. That I was going to prison for twelve years when I hadn't done a goddamn thing to deserve it.

He turned tortured eyes on her. "I swear, I thought that sentence was going to kill me. I was outraged and furious and I didn't have anyone to blame but myself."

"What about an appeal?"

"My lawyer went through the motions and filed an appeal, but it was too little too late."

"For God's sake, Nick, you were innocent."

"That's what every guy in that prison was saying, Nat. I was just another con running his mouth. Pretty soon, I just stopped saying it."

Outrage was like a giant hand squeezing her chest. "There wasn't anything anyone could do?"

"Nope. I got put into the population two days later." As if remembering, he closed his eyes briefly. "It was tough. The things you hear about prison . . . I can tell you that being there was a hell of a lot worse."

"I can't imagine."

"The adjustment was the hard part. There's an entire underground society inside a prison. People fucking with you twenty-four hours a day. No privacy. The isolation. The humiliations. Always having to watch your back." He shook his head. "Don't get me wrong. Most of the guys there deserved to be there."

"Not you."

"Not me. And I let them know it at every turn. I was filled with rage and bitterness. I got into fights. Just about got myself killed a couple of times."

"You had every right to be angry. What they did to you was unspeakable."

"Yeah, well, what could I do? That ten-by-ten cell was going to be my home for the next twelve years. I could either make the best of a bad situation, or I could keep going like I was and end up dead." He glanced down at the tattoos. "I was two years into the sentence before I finally accepted the reality that I wasn't going to be getting out anytime soon. I'd made a couple of friends by then. Guys I could count on to watch my back. I got into a routine. I worked laundry and spent the rest of my time pumping iron and running laps at the track. I finished the degree I'd started.

"Tanya came to see me a few times. She brought Brand. But, God, it was hard. I was furious with her. I hated her for what she'd done. But she had been manipulated by the same man who'd manipulated me. What could I say? She was the mother of my son. My only link to Brand. I didn't want my boy in that prison, but Nat, I swear to Christ I didn't have the strength to tell her not to bring him. He was the only thing that kept me going most days.

"The last time she came to see me was the day she told me she was filing for divorce and moving back to Bellerose. I was three years into my sentence. Nine more to go, and it felt like a million. Tanya was broke. The house had been repossessed by the bank. Race Roberson had long since gone to Los Angeles. She walked into the visitor room and just laid it out for me.

"It didn't hurt because I loved her. I hadn't loved Tanya for a long time. But it killed me because somehow I knew I wouldn't be seeing Brand again. I don't know how I knew that, but I did. He was five years old, and I loved him more than my own life."

Closing his eyes, he scrubbed his hand over his face and blew out a breath. "A year later, two corrections officers and the chaplain came to my cell. It was late, after lights out, so I knew something had happened. I had always figured it would be Tanya. Or maybe Pop. They took me into an interview room, and the chaplain told me Brand had drowned."

chapter
25

EVEN THOUGH IT HAD BEEN MORE THAN TWO YEARS since that terrible day, recounting it made him break into a cold sweat. Nick had relived that horrific moment a thousand times since. His mind could conjure up the same brutal punch of shock. The way the chaplain's eyes had skittered away. The corrections officers shifting uncomfortably and wishing they were anywhere but in that tiny room with a man who was about to come apart at the seams.

"Just like that, my beautiful little boy was gone," he heard himself say. But he could hear the change in his voice. The black grief, the residual bitterness, the sharp edge of hatred that had darkened his heart for so long.

"I felt like a part of me had died. The only part of me that was decent and good."

Pulling the comforter to her breast, Nat sat up and turned to him. He saw tears on her cheeks, realized he'd made her cry. Raising her hand, she touched the side of his face. "I'm so sorry," she said softly. "About Brand. About your having to go through that."

He pressed his cheek against her hand, liking the way her palm felt against his face. "I didn't mean to lay this on you tonight."

"I asked. As terrible as it is, I'm glad you shared it with me."

He smiled and thumbed away a tear. "I wanted you to know I'm not a criminal."

"What happened to you is heartbreaking and incredibly unfair."

"Life is heartbreaking and unfair sometimes. I mean, one moment we're at the top of the world, cruising, on autopilot. The next, Fate steps in and just sucks the air out from under our wings and we crash and burn."

"You survived."

"I was still alive—at least on the outside. But I'm not the same man I was the day I walked into Angola. I'm not the same man I was before I lost my son." Taking her hand, he lowered it from his face and looked at her. "I'm bitter, *chere*. I have a lot of hate inside me. I don't think I'm the right man to heal you."

"I'm not looking for someone to heal me," she said.

"We're all looking for someone to heal us. At least all of us damaged souls." He smiled in an effort to soften what he had to say next, but wasn't sure he managed. "I'll never trust another human being. I'll never give my whole heart. I'm not even sure I'm capable of loving anyone."

"You've been hurt. Betrayed—"

"You deserve a man who can give you everything," he said firmly. "I don't have anything left to give."

"You're kind and generous. You have dreams—"

"I let go of those dreams a long time ago, *chere*."

They were propped against the pillows, facing each other. The bedroom was dark, but light from the window offered just enough light for him to see the hurt in her expression, the sheen of tears on her cheeks.

"Being with you," he whispered. "Like this. It was incredible. Better than I can ever make you believe. But I don't want it to change the way you feel about me."

"You can't tell me what to feel."

"Nat, I'm broke. The farm is in a shambles. I work in a goddamn bar half the night. Pop's Alzheimer's is getting bad."

For the first time, she looked angry. "Why are you telling me this?"

"Because I know you're not the kind of woman who sleeps with a man on a whim. Because you're vulnerable, and I'm a son of a bitch for taking advantage of that."

"Would it be such a bad thing if I admitted to caring about you?" she snapped.

"I just told you I will never trust you. I will never love you."

"I don't believe that."

"I'm a convicted felon. I spent six years in prison. I saw things I don't let myself think about. I did things I'll never admit to. Those years tainted me, Nat. They took away my decency. My humanity. They made me dirty."

"You're wrong."

"You've already had your life torn apart. You deserve a good man. A whole man. Nat, I'm trying to be kind by telling you this before things go too far. You don't want to get tangled up with me."

"You don't get to choose who I get tangled up with."

"Once we find the person responsible for these murders, whatever you and I have . . . we've got to let it go. Believe me, it's the kindest thing I can do for you."

"You think running away from your feelings is somehow *noble?*" she asked.

"Noble is the last thing I am, *chere,* but five years from now, you'll be thanking me."

"You don't know what you're talking about." She started to rise, but Nick was across the bed and grasping her hand before her feet hit the floor.

"Wait," he said. "Don't be angry."

"I want you to leave." She shoved at him, tried to shake off his grip.

But Nick was ready. Grasping both her wrists, he rolled her onto her back and came down on top of her. For a moment the only sound came from their heavy breathing. Her eyes were large and dark and filled with hurt. Hurt that he'd put there. Of all the things that had happened between them, that was the one he was the most sorry for.

"I'm the worst thing that could happen to you right now," he heard himself say.

Her hair was fanned out on the pillow behind her. It looked like silk in the dim light. At some point she had stopped struggling. She was staring at him, her eyes wide, her mouth partially open. He knew it was wrong, but he wanted her. That need was like a thousand needles pricking his skin.

"Who are you trying to convince, Nick? Me or you?"

The heady pull of lust taunted him, made him want things he was a fool for considering when she was so close he could see the sheen of moisture on her lips. Grinding his teeth against the unwanted emotions exploding inside him, he sat up and peeled the comforter off of her. She tried to cover herself, but he didn't give her the chance. Bracing his arms on either side of her, he lowered his weight onto her and crushed his mouth to hers.

The need to possess was more powerful than his need to protect. He knew he was a bastard for giving in to those needs. But Nick had never claimed to be a saint. He had never even claimed to be a good man.

He knew this would hurt her. Knew it would hurt him, too, if he wanted to be honest about it. But it wouldn't be the first time he'd sold his soul to get what he wanted.

He kissed her long and deep and hard. She didn't struggle, but she didn't kiss him back, either. He wanted her to kiss him. Damn it, he needed her to want this.

Wedging his knees between hers, he parted her legs. A sound escaped her when he moved against her. His penis nudged her opening. She was wet, but he felt her body go rigid beneath him.

"If you want me to stop, you had better say so right now," he ground out.

Surprising him, she began to move against him. Her arms went around his shoulders, her nails raking down his back. She opened her mouth and let his tongue inside, returning his kisses with equal ferocity.

Closing his eyes against a barrage of emotions he didn't want to feel, he slid into her heat and tried not to think of anything at all.

NAT JOLTED AWAKE TO THE PEAL OF THE DOORBELL. She sat bolt upright, her heart pounding. Beside her, Nick was already out of the bed and stepping into his jeans. A glance at the alarm told her it was almost four A.M. The time of night when a knock at the door could only mean bad news.

"Are you expecting someone?" he asked as he zipped his fly.

Nat slipped into her robe and belted it at her waist. "No."

His gaze lingered on hers a moment too long. "If it's someone looking for trouble, I'll be right behind you, out of sight, okay?"

She walked into the hall and took the stairs to the living room. The first thing she noticed was the flicker of police lights coming through the front window. A surge of worry sent her running to the door. Flipping on the lights, she flung it open, found herself staring at Alcee Martin and Matt Duncan.

"What's wrong?" she asked. "What happened?"

"Is Nick Bastille here?" Alcee said.

Nat's heart began to pound. "Why? What's happened? Is it his father?"

Alcee gave her a dark look. "Nat, answer the question. Is he here?"

"I'm right here."

Nat spun at the sound of Nick's voice and watched him descend the steps, his expression taut and wary.

She heard the slide of steel against leather as both Duncan and Alcee drew their weapons. "Stop right there, Bastille. Put your hands up where we can see them," Alcee said.

Nick stopped in the center of the living room and raised his hands to shoulder level. "What's this all about?"

"We have a warrant for your arrest." Alcee nodded at Duncan. "Cuff him."

Nat couldn't believe what she was hearing. "Arrest for what?"

Nick stood quietly with his hands raised, his expression totally devoid of emotion. Knowing he'd spent six years in prison for a crime he hadn't committed, she could only imagine the thoughts running through his mind.

Chest puffing out like a mean little rooster, Duncan crossed to Nick. "Turn around. Nice and easy. And give me your wrists."

Nick was a good three inches taller than Duncan, so the other man had to look up slightly to make eye contact. Taking one long last look at Nat, Nick slowly turned and offered his wrists. "What's the warrant for?" he asked.

Duncan tugged the cuffs from his belt. Once the bracelets were in place, he faced Nick and proceeded to pat him down. Since Nick was only wearing jeans, it didn't take long. But Duncan was thorough and purposefully rough, pulling his pockets inside out and leaving them that way.

Humiliating him, Nat thought, and anger surged through her. Adrenaline sent her across the room where she got in Alcee's face. "Why are you arresting him?" she demanded.

Alcee looked pained. "He's wanted for questioning in connection with the murder of Hunter Ratcliffe."

She felt the words like a punch. Hunt. Dead. She couldn't believe it. "My God. How? When did it happen?"

"I can't get into the details with you, Nat." Alcee looked at Nick and sighed. "We're going to take him to the station. If you want to help, I suggest you make sure he gets a good lawyer."

"He didn't do it," she said.

For the first time, Nick looked directly at her, his expression, hard. "I don't want you alone. Call Faye Townsend to stay with you."

She stared at him a moment, then crossed to Alcee. "He was with me all night."

The chief glared at her. "Nat, don't say anything you're going to be sorry for later. This is a serious matter."

"I'm telling the truth," she said. "He was with me. All night."

"We'll take a statement from you later," Alcee said. "Right now, all I've got to go on is a dead body and a dozen witnesses telling me Nick threatened him. I'm bound to take him in."

She glanced at Nick, but his eyes were already on her. She thought she'd never seen a man look so cold, so emotionally dead. "As soon as bail is set, I'll get you out," she said.

"Be careful," he said.

The phone clipped to Alcee's belt chirped. He glared at it for an instant. "'Scuse me," he said and walked out the door and onto the front porch.

The instant Alcee was out of earshot, Matt Duncan drew

back and rammed his fist into Nick's stomach. A quick, brutal punch to the solar plexus. She heard the sickening whoosh of air from Nick's lungs, then he bent forward and his knees hit the floor.

"That's for throwing my revolver in the pond, you fuckin' convict."

"Stop it!" Glaring at Duncan, Nat crossed to them and dropped to her knees at Nick's side. But he didn't look at her as he tried to catch his breath.

"Why did you do that?" she asked Duncan.

"He deserved it. Now get out of the way, or we'll take you in, too, just for being stupid enough to go to bed with this piece of convict scum."

Nat knew better than to get into a confrontation with the police. But she had no respect for cops like Matt Duncan. Getting to her feet, she stepped between the two men. "I'm going to make sure Alcee knows what you did."

Nick got to his feet. "Nat. Damn it. Back off."

Duncan's expression flashed mean. "If I were you, I'd worry about getting my own alibi in order. Your convict here wasn't the only one who argued with Hunt the other night at The Blue Gator."

The words frightened her more than she wanted to admit. Not for herself, she realized, but for Nick. A dozen or more people had seen him argue with Hunt Ratcliffe. Now they were taking him to jail, and there wasn't a damn thing she could do about it.

"Then why not arrest me?" she asked.

Duncan sneered. "Because we found Dutch Bastille's rifle at the scene."

Nick sent Duncan a hard look. "That rifle was locked in the gun cabinet."

"Save it for the judge, lover boy."

Nick ignored him, his expression growing concerned. "Has anyone checked to see if Dutch is all right? If that gun was used, that means someone broke into the house and stole it."

"Alcee talked to him, but that crazy old man of yours don't know nothin' about no gun." Pushing his cuffed hands up between his shoulder blades, Duncan shoved him toward the door. "Let's go."

"I'll check on Dutch," she called out to Nick.

He looked at her over his shoulder. But the eyes that met hers were not the eyes of the man who'd made love to her so tenderly just a few short hours ago. They were the eyes of a stranger, cold and hopeless and as hard as stone.

She wanted badly to go to him, to tell him this wasn't going to be like before. But everything about him screamed for her to keep her distance. She'd never seen him look so detached. So distant. So utterly dangerous.

"I'll meet you at the police station," she said.

"I don't want you alone," he said. "I mean it."

"What about a lawyer?"

"I'll take care of that when I get my phone call." He gave her a meaningful look, and she realized he didn't want to talk in front of Duncan. "Nat, damn it, be careful."

"I will," she promised.

"Someone tried to kill you last night." He lowered his voice. "Maybe that same person found a way to get me out of the picture."

Realization dawned, bringing a rise of gooseflesh to her arms. Before she could say anything more, Duncan shoved him out the door.

chapter
26

THE FIRST RUMBLE OF THUNDER SHOOK THE WIN-
dows as Nat dashed up the stairs and into the bedroom. No
time for a shower, so she quickly washed up, then darted to
the closet and chose jeans and a short-sleeved blouse. She
couldn't believe Hunter Ratcliffe was dead. She couldn't believe Nick had been arrested for his murder.

But she knew Alcee Martin well enough to know he
wouldn't have done such a thing unless he thought he had just
cause. Nick's being an ex-con combined with the argument
he'd had with Hunt was bad enough. But the real problem was
the rifle that had been found at the scene. What if Nick's prints
were on the gun? Even if he'd handled it during a routine
cleaning, it could spell very bad news for him.

The image of the way he'd looked at her when Duncan
cuffed him struck her like a blow. She could only imagine
what had been going on inside him. He'd spent six years in
prison for a crime he didn't commit. He'd been branded a
murderer. His life and reputation had been ruined. His dreams
had been crushed, six years of his life stolen. He'd lost his little boy while he'd been locked away. Now, it seemed the
nightmare was happening all over again.

She desperately wanted to believe she would be able to
get things straightened out. To consider the alternative was

unthinkable. But Nat knew from experience that Fate didn't always play fair. She knew that sometimes innocence and truth were not enough. She was Nick's alibi. But there was a small part of her that was terrified no one would believe her, that the gun and Nick's reputation were enough reason for the charge to stick, for a jury to deem him guilty and send him away for the rest of his life.

Slipping into her shoes, she took a final glance in the mirror and dragged her fingers through her hair. A swirl of vertigo sent her back a step. The glass rippled like water. A stone being dropped into a well . . .

Dear God, not now . . .

She lost her sense of depth perception, and for a moment felt as if she were tumbling into a well a hundred feet down. The ensuing dizziness hit her with the force of a sledgehammer. In her peripheral vision, the furniture began to spin, as if it were being sucked into a giant vortex. She was aware of her body going rigid. Her balance toppling. She grasped the edge of the dresser for support.

Words and dark emotions whirled inside her head. Vaguely, she was aware of her left hand grappling with something rigid and cold. In the last weeks she had trained herself to mentally reach for Kyle when the trance descended. She tried to do that now, tried to draw him inside her mind.

Come to me, baby. . . .

A hundred emotions struck her at once. Violent blows that dazed and confused and left her shuddering with horror. An animal sound tore from her throat as she descended into the turmoil of a terrified mind. And then her left hand was moving quickly, frantically. Words pouring like blood. Red on her fingers. Darkness closing in. Time running out.

Nat came to on the floor in front of the bureau. She was lying on her side with her knees drawn up to her chest. She was choking back sobs, her entire body trembling. A headache hammered behind her eyes. Nausea roiled in her gut. She could hear the rain pounding outside, thunder rattling the windows. The bedroom was dark, and she realized belatedly the storm had taken out the electricity.

Scrubbing her hands over her face, she grasped the bureau and pulled herself to a sitting position. Lightning flashed,

reflecting light in the mirror. She saw red on the glass and
gasped.

Uncle Travis. Mad. Danger.

A chill swept through her at the sight of the words written
on the mirror in bright red letters. She glanced around, saw
the tube of lipstick lying on the floor. She must have pulled it
out of her purse.

"My God." Reaching out, she set her fingertips against
Kyle's second-grade handwriting. She didn't know what to
make of the message. Was he trying to warn her that Travis
was in some kind of danger?

Rising unsteadily, she stumbled to the bed and sat down,
her mind reeling. There was no love lost between her and the
Ratcliffe family. But if for some reason the murderer had targeted Travis, she needed to warn him. Not just to keep him
safe, she realized, but because she knew this might be her best
chance of catching the killer.

A crack of thunder made her jump. She could hear the
sharp tap of hail against the roof. The howl of wind through
the trees in the front yard, the branches clacking together
like bones. A glance at the alarm told her it was almost four-
thirty A.M. The dead of night. But she knew Travis would be
awake. Everyone at Ratcliffe Plantation would be awake because the mansion would be filled with the grief of losing a
loved one.

Taking a deep breath, Nat reached for the phone beside the
bed and dialed the number from memory. She held her breath,
dread building inside her with each ring. On the sixth ring, the
butler answered.

"Bernard, this is Nat Jennings."

"Ms. Jennings . . ." His cultured voice was hushed as if to
keep someone nearby from hearing with whom she was talking.

"I heard about Hunt," she said. "I wanted to say I'm sorry."

"Thank you. I'll pass along your condolences to the Ratcliffe family."

Knowing he was about to hang up, she spoke quickly. "I
need to talk to Travis."

"I'm afraid he's not here."

"Can you tell me where I can reach him?"

"He's gone to the hospital in Covington, where the police . . ." He sighed. "Where they took Hunter."

She didn't have Travis's cell phone number and didn't think Bernard would give it to her, but she had to ask. "Can you give me Travis's cell phone number?"

"Ms. Jennings, I don't think that would be appropriate—"

"This is an emergency, Bernard. I think Travis might be in some kind of danger."

"*Danger?* What kind of—"

"Look, I can't say. It's just . . . really important that I talk to him."

The ensuing silence lasted so long that for a moment she thought he would hang up on her. "Bernard?"

"It's 884-5667," he said. "I didn't give it to you."

"Of course."

He hung up.

Sighing, Nat set the phone in its cradle. She looked at the alarm clock and thought about Nick. "I'm not going to let you go to jail for something you didn't do," she whispered.

Grabbing her bag, she started for the stairs. The house was dark as she crossed through the living room. The silence seemed to enhance the tempo of the storm raging outside. Trying to ignore the uneasiness tugging at her, she walked into the kitchen and unplugged her cell phone from the charger. She grabbed her keys from the hook above the desk and started for the door, dialing Faye's number as she went.

Faye picked up on the fifth ring with a groggy. " 'Lo?"

"I'm sorry for waking you." Fumbling with her keys, Nat opened the front door. "Nick's been arrested. I was wondering if—"

Shock flashed through her at the sight of Travis Ratcliffe standing on her porch. His clothes were soaked. Rain streamed down his face to drip off his nose and chin unnoticed. He looked as if he were in shock.

"I'll call you back." Nat hit the End button on her phone and shoved it into her bag. "Travis . . . what are you doing here?"

"Hello, Natalie. I figured you'd be awake. It seems like most of Bellerose is awake tonight, doesn't it?"

"I'm sorry about Hunt," she said.

He looked away, but not before she saw the emotion slash across his face. "God, I can't believe it. Shot dead. Jesus."

A pang of sympathy went through her. No one knew better than she did the agony of losing a family member. She started to step back to let him inside, but something in his eyes made her hold her ground. "Are you holding up all right?" she asked.

"For the most part I just feel numb. I can't believe this happened."

"How is Elliott?"

"Inconsolable. Angry. Ranting. You know how he is."

Remembering Kyle's warning that Travis could be in danger, she took a deep breath. "I tried to call you earlier."

"Yeah? What about?"

"After hearing about Hunt, I just . . . wanted to tell you to be careful."

He gave her a wry smile. "You think some madman is picking off us Ratcliffes one by one? God, it seems that way, doesn't it? First Ward. Then Hunt. You think I'm next?"

"Just be careful, okay?"

He was studying her closely now. A little too closely, and an uncomfortable silence ensued. Nat felt guilty for wanting him to leave, but she needed to get to Nick. "I was just on my way to the police station."

"So you're aware that they arrested Nick Bastille."

She nodded. "Travis, I know you don't like him, but he didn't do it."

"The police found his father's rifle at the scene. Hunt and Bastille argued. He was in prison for murder."

"He was in prison for manslaughter, and he was innocent."

That wry smile again. "Ah, Nat, you put way too much faith in people."

"He didn't kill Hunt."

"How do you know?"

"He was with me." Realizing she'd probably said too much, that this was a conversation she didn't want to have with him now, Nat glanced at her watch. "Look, I'm sorry, but I've got to go."

"All right." He shoved his hands into his pockets. "I have to get back to the house, anyway. I was going to the hospital to . . . see what's happening with Hunt. But the police are having to call in the coroner from Tangipahoa Parish, since I'm related . . ." Sighing, he let his words trail. "I'll walk you out."

Leaving him standing on the porch, she crossed to the coat closet for a light jacket and umbrella, her mind already jumping forward to Nick.

"I just can't figure out why you came back, Natalie."

She jumped at the closeness of his voice and spun to see that he'd followed her into the living room. The coat closet was recessed in an alcove. He was standing too close, crowding her, blocking her in. Lightning flashed, and for the first time she saw his face in full light. The strangeness in his eyes and the utter blankness of his expression sent a chill through her.

"I always figured Bellerose was the last place you'd want to be after what happened to your husband and son," he said.

Nat stepped back, something terrible niggling at the back of her mind. "What are you doing?"

"Protecting my interests."

She tried to step around him, but he blocked her way. That was when she spotted the club in his hand. It was fashioned from wood and shaped like a miniature baseball bat. "I think you should leave."

"I'm afraid I can't do that." He shook his head. "Why couldn't you just stay gone? Why did you have to come back and start asking questions? Digging up things that shouldn't be dug up?"

Realization poured over her in a vicious rush, as cold and shocking as a plunge into ice water. Her heart was like a battering ram against her ribs. Her throat was so tight she could barely speak. Never in a million years would she have suspected Travis. . . .

"You . . ." she choked, but her throat was so tight she couldn't finish the sentence. Her heart was pounding so hard she could barely hear him.

"Yes," he whispered. "Me. Isn't that a shocker?"

She glanced to her left. If she could get by him, she might be able to make it to the kitchen, then to the back door.

"Don't even think about trying to get away." He raised the baton, studied it with a fondness that chilled her. "It might look small, but it will stop you cold. Just ask my old man. He used it on me plenty when I was a kid." He slapped it against his palm. "It will break a bone, but it's not nearly as messy as a gun or knife."

The words rang hollowly in her ears. "Travis, for God's sake, what are you doing?"

"Come on, Nat. You know exactly what I'm doing. I see it in your eyes. I don't know how you figured it out. It was so fucking perfect." His smile raised gooseflesh on her arms. "It's almost as if you've been talking to the dead. But we both know that's not possible, don't we?"

"Tell me you didn't . . ." All the oxygen left her lungs in a rush. "God, Travis, tell me you didn't hurt Ward and Kyle."

His silence was all the answer she needed. Tears of rage and grief welled in her eyes. She choked back the sob that had climbed up her throat. She couldn't believe he could do something so vile. Travis, the gentle doctor. The healer. Her only ally in the Ratcliffe family. A psychopath . . .

Uncle Travis. Mad. Danger.

Suddenly she realized Kyle hadn't come to her to warn her that Travis was in danger but to warn her that Travis was a danger to *her*.

"You killed them," she choked.

He laughed, but it was a maniacal sound with the rain pounding the windows and roof. "He was just like me, Nat."

"Who?"

"Kyle. Your bastard son. The sniveling little asthmatic. Do you think he ever would have lived up to my father's expectations? Hardly. He would have disappointed all of us. And he would have suffered so much for it. You should be thanking me. I saved him from a life of pain and humiliation."

The words struck her brain with the violence of a bullet. She couldn't believe he was talking about her son. Her sweet, innocent little boy.

The fury and pain that had been festering inside her for so many months took control of her body. With an animalistic scream, she launched herself at him. Her lips peeled back in a snarl. Then her hands were on his face. Her fingernails digging into flesh. Her thumbs searching for eye sockets.

"How could you?" she screamed. "You coldhearted son of a bitch! I'll kill you!"

Travis raised his hands to protect himself. She saw the baton flash and tried to duck, but she wasn't fast enough. The wood connected solidly with her cheekbone, hard enough to crack bone. Pain exploded beneath her skin. She reeled backward, streamers of light shooting behind her eyes. Her back hit the closet door. She would have fallen, but she managed to grab the knob and brace herself against the door.

Blinking back tears of rage, she looked at Travis, felt a hot rise of hatred. "How could you?" She was sobbing, her voice breaking. "A little boy . . . Your own *nephew!* God, Travis, why? *Why?*"

"Because he was like me, Nat. Didn't you see it?"

She stared at him, confusion and utter disbelief welling inside. "He was nothing like you."

"He never would have measured up. He was a mirror image of me when I was his age. Chubby and shy. He wore those thick, stupid glasses. He even had asthma. Just like me. Do you know what all the kids say when you can't run and play like the rest of them?"

"Travis, my God, do you know what you're saying? Do you know how crazy that sounds?"

"I'm not crazy!" he shouted. "This hasn't been easy for me!"

Nat stared at him, her mind reeling.

"I don't expect you to understand," he said. "You have no concept of what it's like." His laugh was a hoarse, bitter sound. "I *know* it's a sin to kill. But what nobody seems to understand is that what I do is bigger than God. It's bigger than the laws of man."

She was still leaning against the door. Her cheek throbbed, the pain radiating from her temple to her jaw. It felt like he'd shattered her cheekbone. She could feel her face swelling, the skin getting tight, her jaw stiffening.

But watching Travis, she knew the injury to her cheek was the least of her worries. He meant to harm her. Kill her, if she let him. She didn't plan on giving him the chance.

He yanked her bag from her shoulder. Snarling a profanity, he reached inside and withdrew her cell phone. "You won't be needing this." He dropped the phone to the floor and crushed it beneath his heel.

She glanced from the ruined phone to the baton in his hand. He was holding it so tightly his knuckles were white. She knew it was only a matter of time before he used it again. Before he incapacitated her. Or worse.

"Put the club down, Travis," she said. "We'll talk about this. Just you and me."

"Don't play me for stupid, Nat. It's insulting."

"I'm not—"

"Shut up! I need to think!" He rapped his fist against his head. "I've worked too hard to let you ruin everything."

"Travis, you don't want to do this." Realizing she might be able to use the umbrella in the closet as a weapon, she edged closer to the door and slowly twisted the knob. "You have to let me go."

"I wish it were that simple," he said. "Unfortunately for you, it's not."

Facing him, she eased open the door one centimeter at a time. "What are you going to do with me?"

"I've got a special place for you, Nat. The same place I took the others."

The others.

She could barely absorb the meaning of the words. Sickened by the thought of what this man had done, she closed her eyes, fighting the images prying into her brain. "How many?" she whispered.

"Counting the one when I was fifteen?" He shrugged. "Six. Spread out over seventeen years. I was very selective. It was a huge responsibility. And I took that responsibility very seriously."

Shock and disbelief took turns punching her. How could a man kill six children over a seventeen-year period and not get caught? Her mind voiced the question, but deep inside Nat already knew the answer. Travis Ratcliffe was not only a doctor—he was the parish coroner. He'd performed the autopsies himself.

"Why? How could you hurt innocent children?"

"I know it's hard for you to understand," he said. "But, Nat, they had to die. Don't you see? They were inferior. All of them.

Eddie Flatter had a terrible speech impediment. Kyle and Brandon Bastille had asthma. Ricky Arnaud had rheumatoid arthritis. Ronnie Wiley was autistic. Do you know what happens to children like that? Do you know how much they suffer when the other kids make fun of them? Call them names? Hurt them?"

She thought about Kyle, her beautiful, smart, exuberant son, and a fresh flare of hatred erupted inside her. "You sick bastard."

"That's me. Travis Ratcliffe, the sick bastard." His smile chilled her to the bone. "It was tough making each death look like an accident. I had to get damn creative to pull it off, you know?" Something she could only describe as evil glinted in his eyes. "I only wanted Kyle that night, Natalie. I lured him from his bedroom to the kitchen by telling him we were going to take a little drive. Children are so trusting. I was seconds away from having him in my car. But Ward came downstairs with the gun and ruined everything."

A sob tore from her throat at the thought of this man hurting her son.

"I'd wanted to see Ward suffer the pain of losing his son. But it was surprisingly satisfying to put a bullet in him. Then you came along and just about blew it. I almost killed you, too. Then I realized you'd be a hell of a lot more useful as a suspect. It was common knowledge you and Ward weren't getting along. I'm an expert in forensics. With a little ingenuity, I set up the crime scene." Tsking, he looked at her and shook his head. "If only you'd stayed in that coma."

Nat stared at him, hatred and disbelief pounding through her. "You took my child from me," she choked. "You had no right."

"My father gave me the right. Ward and Hunt gave me the right. And they never let me forget I wasn't good enough."

"You're not making any sense."

His lips twisted. "You didn't know I was adopted, did you, Nat? Not the sort of thing a man like Elliott Ratcliffe likes to broadcast, I guess."

"There's nothing wrong with adoption." When the door was open enough for her hand to slip inside, she began to feel along the wall for the handle of the umbrella.

"There is if you adopt a kid like me." His mouth stretched

into an ugly, bitter smile. "But then you know the Ratcliffes, don't you, Nat? You have a pretty good idea what it's like to be an outsider in that family, don't you? Think about what that would have been like for a fat, stupid child like me."

Nat heard the words, but her mind simply couldn't absorb what he was telling her. Her only thought was that six children had died at the hands of a man who'd taken an oath to heal. A man she'd cared for and respected.

"Everyone in this town thinks the great Elliott Ratcliffe is a man of God," he said. "Some kind of goddamn saint spreading the gospel and protecting all the poor, helpless sheep from their sinful ways. You know what he really is, Nat? A fucking tyrant. A man who terrorized and demoralized. That's why mother left him. He made up the story about her having a lover. She didn't have a lover. She simply couldn't take the abuse anymore. And so she left. And my fate was sealed."

Nat nearly sobbed with relief when her fingers made purchase with the wooden umbrella handle. It wasn't much of a weapon, but it might buy her some time. If she could get to the phone in the kitchen . . . "Travis, I know Elliott can be a hard man. But he would never hurt his children."

"Not his children. Just me."

"No, Ward would have told me."

"Ward didn't tell you because he was every bit as guilty as his old man." Hatred burned in his eyes. "Let me tell you, they did a hell of a lot more than hurt me."

"Travis, what are you talking about?"

"I spent my entire life hearing, 'Why can't you be more like Ward?' Ward the football star. Ward the scholar. Ward the fucking prom king. Ward the minister."

Nat didn't know whether to believe any of what he was telling her, but she didn't argue. There was no way to reason with someone who'd lost touch with reality. All she could do was try to keep him talking and hope for an opportunity to escape.

"What about Hunt?" she asked. "He wasn't as successful as you. He worked at the mill. He drank heavily. He certainly wasn't perfect."

"Ah, but Hunt was Father's most virile son. A man's man. Hunt the warrior. Hunt the ass kicker. Elliott would never admit

it, but he was secretly pleased with that." His mouth curved.
"And then there was me."

"But you're successful. A doctor—"

"Do you think that mattered to him?" he shouted abruptly.
"All Elliott Ratcliffe ever saw was the fat, stupid boy he'd
adopted. I didn't even know I was adopted until I heard them
arguing one night. Elliott actually wanted to nullify the adoption and send me back to the agency." He threw his head back
and laughed. "Of course, that was after I'd started the fire in
the church." His eyes blazed with insanity when he looked at
her. "Do you know what he did to me for that?"

Nat vaguely remembered the incident. She'd been in grade
school at the time. There'd been a fire at the church. No one
had been hurt, but there'd been some minor damage. She'd
heard later that Travis Ratcliffe had been playing with
matches. "It was an accident."

"It was no accident, Nat. For God's sake get a clue. None
of the fires were accidental." He raked his hand through his
hair. "He put me in the storage room at the church to punish
me. A tiny room with no windows. He beat me with this." Lips
peeling back, he slapped the baton against his palm. "Then he
shoved me inside and locked the door. He told me I needed
time to think about what I'd done and ask God for forgiveness.
I was only twelve years old. I begged him not to. I was afraid
of the dark, and he knew it, so he unscrewed the bulb and took
it with him. Do you have any idea what that did to me?"

She stared at him, keenly aware of the baton in his hand
and that he had begun to shake. She sensed he was on some
steep precipice and about to slide. "I'm sorry—"

"It was pitch black in that room. I couldn't even see my
hand in front of my face. I could hear things scurrying around,
cockroaches and rats. I was so fucking terrified, I soiled my
pants." He fell silent, his face twisted into a mask of pain, as if
he were twelve years old and reliving that terrible moment all
over again.

"He left me in there for three hours. When he finally
opened the door and realized what I'd done, he had Ward and
Hunt drag me to the backyard, strip off my clothes, and hose
me down like I was some kind of dirty animal.

"Ward and Hunt were just as bad as Elliott. They never let

me forget what happened that day. They *laughed* at me. Made fun of me because I'd soiled my pants. Do you have any idea what that does to a kid?" His eyes hardened, blazed. "My own father couldn't stand the sight of me. I'd embarrassed him."

"You were just a kid. . . ."

"That didn't matter," he spat.

She waited, her fingers wrapped around the wood base of the umbrella, and watched his eyes glaze.

"After that, except for some teasing, Ward and Hunter left me alone. I had asthma and couldn't play with other kids, so I turned inward. I started reading a lot. Eating a lot. Gaining weight.

"But I had friends, Nat." Smiling, he tapped on his head. "Only they were up here. And every time my old man put me in that room, my friends came out to play. After a while, I wasn't even scared anymore. I *liked* going into that room by myself."

"Travis, I can't imagine Ward not trying to help you."

"You think that husband of yours was such a saint," he hissed. "Do you want me to tell you about Ward the Saint? Do you want me to tell you what he did?"

Nat didn't want to hear more. All she wanted was to get away from him. Away from the terrible things he was saying. But he was blocking her way to the kitchen. She gripped the umbrella and waited for an opportunity to rush him.

"I got put in that storage room a lot. You see, I'd realized I *liked* to set fires. I burned the shed in the backyard. The cabana by the pool. The gazebo in the garden. Every time I got put in the storage room. Every time my friends came out to play. When I was fourteen, I set the kitchen on fire. Elliott put me in the storage room, and I must have fallen asleep, because the next thing I knew Hunt and Ward came into the room. They didn't turn on the light and started making fun of me. Ordering me around. Pushing me. Hitting me. Calling me names. And then it was like someone flipped a switch. Something happened to them. They got *really* mean. Looking back, I know it has something to do with that primal, pack mentality." His voice broke, his words trailing. "They told me to take off my clothes. When I said no, they started punching me, mostly in the gut, because they never messed up my face. When I couldn't take any more, I took off my clothes. Then things got really bad because they . . . they made me . . ." He made a choking sound, squeezed his eyes closed for an instant.

"They did unspeakable things. They made me do things to them. Vile, nasty things. They told me I was fat and stupid and I deserved it. They called me a fat, little sow."

Nat stared at him, her heart pounding. She gripped the umbrella handle, but her palm was slick with sweat.

"There was a hand broom in the closet, and Ward the saint, the minister, your perfect fucking husband . . ." His voice broke. "He sodomized me with that broom," he whispered. "He stuck it in me and made me want to die. Then they laughed at me. Do you have any idea what that did to me?"

"Travis," she said, struggling to keep her voice level, "It's not too late to stop this. I'll help you. Just let me go."

"I don't want to go to prison, Nat."

"You were abused as a child. Psychologically. Physically. Your brothers sexually assaulted—"

"Shut up about that!" Spittle flew from his lips as he snarled the words. "Don't say it! Don't ever bring that up!"

She measured the distance between them, wondering if she could slam the umbrella into his temple and run past him before he hit her with the baton. "Those are extenuating circumstances, Travis." Knowing this could very well be her only chance to talk him down, she laid it on thick. "You were just a boy. The police and the courts will take that into consideration. They'll make sure you get the help you need. Counseling. Medication. They'll see to it that Elliott Ratcliffe is punished."

"No one will understand, Nat. If the police find out what I've done, I'll never see the light of day. We both know that."

"Travis, you have to let me go. Alcee is expecting me at the police station."

"The only person expecting you is Bastille, and nobody in this town gives a shit about him."

"I care." She glanced at the baton, saw his fingers flex. "And I care about you, too."

He looked at her as if the words had startled him. "You're lying. You don't give a damn about me."

"That's not true. Think about all the years we've known each other. You were kind to me." She held his gaze, but it was difficult with her mind scrambling wildly for just the right thing to say. "It's not too late to fix things."

He looked at her as if seeing her for the first time, his eyes filling. "You'd help me even after everything I've done?"

Seeing the opportunity she'd been waiting for, Nat jerked the umbrella from the closet. Swinging it like a bat, she slammed the handle against his forehead. His hands flew up to protect himself, but he was already reeling backward.

The force of the impact knocked the umbrella from her hand. Knowing she only had an instant to escape, she bolted past him and tore around the stairway.

"*Bitch!* I'm going to make you pay for that!"

She hit the dining room at full speed, made a hard left, barely missing the table. Behind her, she heard his footfalls pounding the floor. She saw movement in her peripheral vision. Air *whooshed* as he swung the baton and missed. Too close, she thought, and dove for the phone on the counter.

Before she could punch in the numbers, pain exploded the right side of her head. The violence of the blow snapped her head to the side. White light flashed in front of her eyes. The phone clattered to the floor. Then she was falling into space. The counter crashed into her chest as she went down. Her knees hit the floor. Then she was lying on her side, the tile cold against her cheek.

This is what it feels like to die, she thought.

She saw blood on the floor and realized her nose was bleeding. It was on her hands. Dark and sticky between her fingers. Dizziness assailed her. The room began to spin as if she were being sucked into a vortex. Not from the blow, she realized, but her son . . .

Kyle?

The words inside her head were disjointed and rushed. She sensed his fear, knew it was being augmented by her own. Vaguely, she was aware of her finger moving over the tile. Red letters written in blood on the floor.

And then the world faded to black.

chapter
27

NICK HAD BEEN IN ENOUGH TROUBLE IN HIS LIFEtime to know when it was bad. As he stood in the jail cell of the Bellerose Police Department and watched the jailer lock the outer door behind him, he figured this qualified and then some.

It had been two hours since Alcee Martin and Matt Duncan had dragged him away in cuffs from Nat's house. They'd questioned him for an hour, in which time he'd found out that Hunt had been out in his mud boat frogging when he'd been shot in the head at point blank range. Dutch's rifle had been found at the scene, conveniently dropped into Hunt's boat. Alcee had already questioned at least two people from The Blue Gator, and both of them had mentioned the argument between Hunt and Nick a few nights earlier.

The situation wasn't looking good for a parolee with a murder conviction on his record.

Nick was counting on Alcee Martin being smart enough to look beyond the obvious. Nick hadn't shot Hunt. He hadn't been anywhere near Edward Bayou. The problem was proving it when someone had gone to great lengths to make it look like he had.

Nick had used his phone call to contact his lawyer in New Orleans. But the man had a court date the following morning and wouldn't be able to drive up until afternoon. Unless some-one was able to rouse a judge—or conjure a miracle—Nick was stuck.

He looked around the small cell and tried not to feel claus-trophobic. As far as jails went, Bellerose was top of the line. At twelve feet square it was roomy and clean with a single ground level, barred window that looked out over the parking lot. The mattress on the bunk was unstained and fresh as the day the citizens of St. Tammany Parish had paid for it.

But Nick could feel the glossy tiled walls closing in on him. Six years in prison had left him with a bad case of claus-trophobia. The day he'd walked out of Angola, he'd sworn no one would ever lock him in a cage again. He hadn't counted on someone putting a hole in Hunt Ratcliffe's forehead. Sweat-ing, his heart pounding, he sat down hard on the bunk. Who the hell had done it? Dutch? Nick didn't think so. His old man might have Alzheimer's and a mean streak as wide as the Mis-sissippi, but he wasn't violent. Dutch was a hunter and had al-ways been a responsible gun owner. He was obsessive about gun safety. So then how the hell had Hunt ended up shot with his old man's rifle?

Nick didn't have the answer. The only thing he did know was that if he didn't get out of this cell, he was going to go stark, raving insane.

Struggling to stay calm, he bent his head and put his face in his hands. He'd been trying not to think of Nat, but every time he closed his eyes, he saw her face. He saw the way her eyes had glazed when he'd been inside her. The way her body had shuddered when he'd moved within her. The sweet cries she'd uttered when he'd brought her to peak. Making love to her had been one of the most erotic experiences of his life. She'd been responsive and loving and more passionate than he ever could have dreamed. She was decent and good and de-served a man who could give her his trust, his whole heart. As desperately as he wanted to be that man, Nick knew he wasn't.

He glanced at the clock above the jailer's desk. Two hours and ten minutes had passed since he'd left her. She'd volun-teered to check on Dutch, then come to the station. Nick had been trying not to consciously think of it, but she should have been here by now. Where the hell was she?

The question hit a nerve and out of the dark recesses of his mind, a terrible new worry began to eat at him.

Rising abruptly, he cursed and began to pace. Why hadn't she come? Had something happened to her? He could feel his heart beating heavily in his chest. A sheen of sweat slicking his back beneath his shirt. He didn't know if it was claustrophobia or fear for her safety, but it had clamped down on him like the teeth of a steel trap. He could feel panic edging in. The utter certainty that something had happened to her. That he wasn't going to be able to protect her the same way he hadn't been able to protect Brand.

Nat, where are you?

A door clanged. Nick rushed to the bars, hope jumping through him that she had finally come. Instead, a large woman with a mane of wild red hair and a flowing maroon cape strode toward him like a battleship gliding out to sea. Behind her, one of Alcee's deputies and a skinny man in a dark suit rushed to keep up with her.

What the hell?

"You Nick?" she asked.

"Who wants to know?"

She stopped outside the bars, bringing a wave of some exotic perfume with her. She stuck her hand through the bars. "Name's Faye Townsend, but that's not important. What *is* important is that I think Nat's in trouble. I just came from her house and she's not there. This here's my ex-husband, Judge Tommy Doyal from Covington. You just made bail."

NAT WOKE TO DARKNESS AND PAIN ON TOP OF PAIN. Nausea ebbed and flowed in her stomach, so she closed her eyes and concentrated on taking slow, deep breaths. There was a roaring in her ears. Vibration all around. She was lying on her side with her knees drawn up to her chest. She tried to shift, only to realize her hands were tied behind her back.

Confusion swirled; then the memory of everything that had happened came rushing back. Nick being arrested. Her struggle with Travis. A terrible blow to the head . . .

Panic sliced her cleanly, and for several unbearable moments she struggled mindlessly against her bindings. Her heart was like a piston in her chest. She could hear her breaths tearing from her throat, too shallow, too fast. The smell of exhaust told her she was in the back of a moving vehicle. Another wave of panic threatened, but she fought it back, willed her muscles to relax.

"Calm down," she whispered. "You're going to be okay."

Taking a deep breath, Nat looked around, but the back of the vehicle was completely dark. The carpet smelled like motor oil and dust. She tried to stretch out her legs, but the space was too small. She tested her bonds, found them secure, her hands already growing numb.

Where was he taking her?

The vehicle stopped abruptly, and the engine went silent. Every nerve in her body went taut when she heard the door slam. An instant later, the back opened. Fresh air and rain and the soft black light of night poured in.

"You're awake." Travis smiled down at her. "I was hoping I wouldn't have to carry you."

Nat raised her head and looked around. She saw trees and misty rain and the utter darkness of the woods. "Where are you taking me?"

"You'll find out soon enough." He reached for her arm. "Come on."

She struggled to a sitting position. Then he was pulling her roughly from the vehicle. She barely managed to get her feet beneath her when he slammed the door closed.

He'd stopped the SUV on a dirt road surrounded by thick woods. He was holding a powerful spotlight and was using it to illuminate his face. A ripple of satisfaction went through her when she saw the raised bruise on his forehead where she'd hit him with the umbrella.

Taking her arm, he pulled her away from the SUV, then used the spotlight to indicate the path cut into the woods. "Start walking," he said.

Nat started toward the path, but kept her pace slow. She didn't know where he was taking her, but knew it was a place she didn't want to go. Once they arrived, she was pretty sure he was going to kill her.

She could feel the fear bubbling inside her. Panic nipping

at its heels. "Travis, it's not too late to stop this," she said. "It doesn't have to end this way."

"Shut your mouth and walk."

"What can you possibly hope to accomplish by killing me?"

"Killing you will keep me out of prison, Natalie."

"I promise not to tell anyone what you've told me."

He laughed. "You think I'm pretty stupid, don't you?"

"I think you need help."

"Walk." Putting his hand between her shoulder blades, he shoved her hard enough to make her stumble. "We don't have much time."

Because she didn't have a choice, Nat obeyed. But her thoughts were already jumping ahead to escape. If she could find a way to distract him, she could make a run for it. If she could put some distance between them, maybe she could find the highway and flag down a motorist.

She thought of Nick and wondered if they'd put him in a cell or if he was still being questioned. She wondered if he'd realized she was missing. But even if he had, she knew he was in no position to help her.

Her thoughts shot to Faye. Nat had been on the phone with her when Travis showed up at her door. Nat had told her she would call her right back. Had Faye become worried when the call didn't come? Or had she gone back to sleep, totally unaware that Nat was in trouble?

Another layer of fear settled over her when she realized there was no one she could count on to help her. Nat was alone and at the mercy of a madman with no one to rely on but herself.

The rain was little more than a drizzle, but the foliage was dripping, and within minutes she was soaked. The air had grown cold, bringing a rise of fog. At some point she had begun to shiver, great shudders that racked her body from head to toe.

Around them, the bayou sang a soulful predawn chorus of frogs and crickets and the cadence of water dripping onto leaves. Mud sucked at her feet as she continued down the path. She was aware of Travis behind her, holding the spotlight steady on the path ahead. She wondered what he had planned for her. Was he going to beat her to death with the baton? Tie her up and leave her to die like an animal?

She slowed her pace slightly, all the while watching the shadows along the path for a trail she could dash into and run. She was in good physical condition. It was still dark. She had the element of surprise on her side. If she could get a head start, maybe she could put some distance between them and hide.

The thought had barely formed in her mind when she spotted the fork in the trail ahead. The main path went right, but there was a vague impression of a narrow, overgrown trail to the left. Praying she wasn't making a mistake that would only hasten him to kill her, Nat started to go right, then dodged left at the last second and leapt into a dead run.

chapter
28

ARRANGING FOR BAIL SEEMED TO TAKE FOREVER, and by the time Nick and Faye arrived at Nat's house, he was climbing out of his skin. Faye had tried to call Nat four times in two hours, but had yet to get an answer. When they pulled into the driveway and found the house dark, Nick got a very bad feeling in the pit of his stomach.

Where the hell was she?

Faye had barely brought her Volkswagen to a halt when he swung open the door and sprinted to the house. He took the steps to the porch in a single leap, crossed to the door. His heart began to pound when he found the door unlocked. And he knew they weren't going to find Nat inside.

He shoved the door open. *"Nat!"*

The house was eerily silent and dark as a cave. Nick felt around for the wall switch, but when he flipped it, nothing happened. "Damn it."

Faye came in behind him. "Storm must have taken out the electricity."

"I'm going to see if I can find a flashlight."

"I think there's one in the kitchen drawer." She pushed past him and headed toward the dining area. "Candles, too."

Nick trailed her to the kitchen and watched as Faye went to a drawer and began to rummage. An instant later, a light flicked on. He reached for the flashlight. "I'm going to check the rest of the house. Light some candles, will you?"

"Sure thing."

He was halfway through the living room when she screamed. He found her in the kitchen, kneeling, a candle in her hand. "What is it?" he asked, but even from where he stood, he could see the primitive words scrawled onto the tile. He shone the beam on the floor.

Travis. Office. Map.

"Oh, my God." Faye's gaze met Nick's. "That's blood."

He knelt, touched the grotesque letter with his fingertip. "Still wet."

"What does it mean?"

"It means she's in trouble." Stepping over the bloody letters, he started toward the living room. "Stay put."

He took the stairs two at a time, then moved silently down the hall, calling out her name, shining the light in each room as he passed, finding nothing. He entered Nat's room. He could still smell her. He shone the light on the bed where the sheets were still rumpled from their lovemaking. The memory of everything they'd shared flashed in his mind's eye. The wave of emotion that followed made his chest so tight he could barely draw a breath. She had to be all right. God would not take something precious from him twice in his life. . . .

"Did you find anything?"

He started at the sound of Faye's voice, turned the beam of light to see her standing at the doorway. "She's not here," he said.

She stepped into the room and looked around. "Any idea where she might be?"

Because he didn't have a clue, Nick directed the flashlight beam around the room, looking for anything that might tell him where she'd gone or who she was with. Something out of place on the dresser mirror caught his attention. He steadied the beam on the mirror, and the hairs at his nape stood straight up.

Travis. Mad. Danger.

"What the hell?"

"Blood?" Faye asked.

Nick walked to the dresser, touched the red letters with his fingertips. "Lipstick."

"She must have had two seizures before she left. What do you think it means?"

He glanced at Faye. "In the past, almost every trance writing incident has been focused on protecting someone from harm."

"You think Travis Ratcliffe is in some kind of danger?"

"Maybe." But that didn't feel right. Nick studied the words on the mirror. "Or maybe it's a warning."

"Travis?" Faye whispered.

Cold, hard fear pounded through Nick at the thought. Ratcliffe was one of Bellerose's most upstanding citizens. He was the son of a renowned televangelist. A doctor. The parish coroner. All of those things would be the perfect cover for murder.

The realization struck him like a punch. Reaching out, he leaned against the dresser, bile flooding his throat, his mind reeling. "She's with Travis," he said.

Faye was already digging her cell phone from her bag. "You don't think he'll hurt her, do you?"

"Call the Ratcliffes," Nick said. "Find out if Nat is there."

Her hand shook as she punched numbers and put the phone to her ear. The seconds ticked by like hours. Nick felt as if he were coming apart inside. He couldn't image Travis Ratcliffe hurting children or wanting to hurt Nat. Surely they were wrong about this.

"Hello? Bernard? Hi, this is Faye Townsend." She looked at Nick. "Yes, I was very sorry to hear about Hunt. Can you tell me if Nat Jennings is there? No?" She grimaced. "Has she been there?" Her brows rose. "She called? When?" Faye looked at her watch. "Okay. Um . . . is Travis there?" Even in the dim light from the flashlight, Nick saw her expression change, her complexion go pale. "No one knows where he is? How long has he been gone?" She nodded. "I see. Thank you. And please give my best to Elliott."

She clicked off the phone, giving Nick a knowing look. "Nobody has seen Travis for a couple of hours."

The words shook Nick, drove home his worst fear. Taking Faye's arm, he guided her toward the door. "Listen to me. I want you to call Alcee Martin. Tell him everything. About the trance writing. About what we found here. Tell him we believe Travis killed Hunt. That he is a murderer and he has Nat."

Breaking away from her, Nick started down the hall at a jog.

"Where are you going?" she called out.

"I'm going to find her before Travis kills her."

NAT RAN BLINDLY THROUGH THE DARKNESS AND rain, bursting through wet foliage and brush at a reckless speed. Branches tore at her face and clothes, but she didn't slow down. She could hear Travis behind her, cursing and screaming at her, terrifyingly near. But running with her hands tied behind her back had proven a lot more difficult than she'd imagined. Her balance was off. She couldn't seem to get up her speed. One wrong move, and he would be upon her.

"Don't you run from me you fucking bitch!"

Travis's voice sounded maniacal in the dense silence of the forest. If there had been any doubt in her mind that he was insane, this moment put that doubt to bed. Travis Ratcliffe was an out-of-control madman. And if he caught her, he was going to kill her.

"I'm going to get you. I'm going to make you pay."

Choking back a sound of pure terror, Nat left the trail. She plowed through brush and tangled vines. Branches slashed her face as she plummeted down a small incline. Too late she realized she'd entered some sort of bog. She sank into mud up to her ankles. She lost a shoe, but she muscled her way through the bog and up the opposite bank. She'd just reached the top when her foot caught on something. A root growing out of the bank. She was running so fast, her own momentum slammed her facedown hard enough to take her breath.

Expecting Travis to fall upon her at any moment, Nat rolled, then raised her head just enough to see over the top of a fan palm. Less than ten feet away, he stood motionless as if listening. She could see his breaths puffing out as he swept the surrounding area with the spotlight.

"Come out, come out, wherever you are," he called.

Nat squeezed her eyes closed and tried desperately to control her labored breathing. Sinking into the grass, she pressed her face to the ground. But she knew it was only a matter of time before he spotted her.

Oh, dear God, help me.

The rain was coming down in earnest now. She was soaked to the skin. Mud covered her clothes, but she barely noticed the cold or wet. Hoping the tempo of the rain would help conceal any noise, she began to inch toward a thick briar patch. If she could reach it before he found her, she might be able to hide.

The beam of the flashlight played over the dead trunk of a tree less than a foot away from her. Nat froze, terrified he'd spotted her. But after a moment the light continued on. She could hear him screaming incoherently. She tried to block the sound of his voice. She did not want to think about what he was capable of. Or what he would do to her if he got his hands on her again.

"Natalie! You bitch!"

She was less than two feet from the relative safety of the briar patch when the beam from the flashlight fell upon her. The sound of heavy footsteps pounding through mud sent her bolt upright. Out of the corner of her eye she saw Travis running toward her. She caught an impression of murderous eyes. Lips peeled back in a snarl.

This is it, she thought. *He's going to kill me.*

She tried to scramble to her feet, but her bound hands hampered her, and by the time she got to her knees he was upon her. "I'm going to make you pay for doing this to me!" he roared.

She didn't see the blow coming. Pain like she'd never felt before exploded at the small of her back. She felt her right leg give. A scream tore from her throat as she fell forward. The son of a bitch had hit her with the baton. He was going to do it again if she didn't stop him. Twisting onto her back, she lashed out with both legs.

"Get away from me!" she screamed.

Her foot connected solidly with his groin. He doubled over, but Nat knew the pain wouldn't stop him for long. She lined up for another kick. But before she could nail him a second time, he raised the baton and brought it down with bone-crunching force against her right shin.

Nat felt the bone crack. A scream of agony burst from her throat. She forgot about getting away from him and closed her eyes against an undulating shock wave of pain that rolled through her body. She tried to curl, but it was difficult with her hands tied. And so for several unbearable seconds she lay on her side, her uninjured leg drawn up to her chest, the other stretched out in front of her.

"I told you what would happen if you crossed me."

Nauseous from the pain, Nat opened her eyes and looked up at him, hatred and pain choking her. "Stay away from me."

"Get up."

"Travis, for God's sake . . . I think my leg is broken."

He stared down at her, his face dispassionate. "You should have considered the consequences before you ran away, Natalie. Now get the fuck up, or I swear I'll break the other one and drag you."

Knowing he was demented enough to do it, she rolled onto her side and struggled to a sitting position. Travis leaned over and grasped her beneath her shoulders. She tried not to jar her injured leg as he pulled her to her feet, but it was impossible. A cry of pain escaped her when her foot touched the ground.

"Put your weight on it," he said.

She glanced over at him. He was staring at her leg, the flashlight in one hand, the baton in the other. Fearing he would hit her again, she eased some of her weight onto her foot. The ensuing pain wrenched a groan from her. "It's broken," she said. "I can't walk."

His eyes were alight with an emotion she couldn't begin to understand. It was as if he were drawing some sort of twisted satisfaction from her pain and fear. And for the first time she seriously considered the possibility that her life would end here and now, and there wasn't a damn thing she could do about it.

Hopelessness pressed into her. She could feel her heart bucking and leaping in her chest. Trembling uncontrollably, she looked around. They were surrounded by trees and the thick tangle of undergrowth. The urge to run was strong, but she knew she wouldn't make it two steps before he stopped her.

She jolted when he came up beside her and pulled her arm

around his shoulder. "Put your weight on me," he said. "Let's walk."

Fearing he would explode into violence if she refused, Nat obeyed. She hated being close to him. Hated the smell of his wet hair and expensive cologne. But she endured it, and for several minutes the only sound came from their feet against the wet ground as they struggled through the forest. The pain in her leg was bad, like a chisel clanging against her bone. Even though she was soaked to the skin and shivering with cold, she could feel sweat breaking out on her neck.

"Are you familiar with the history of Gautier Mud Flats?" he asked abruptly.

She looked at him, wondering if she should go along with him. If she should try to talk him, try to convince him to let her go.

"Paul Willis Gautier and a team of four men disappeared without a trace while mapping the area, in 1918. Legend has it that a tropical storm had flooded the area and the four men became lost. One by one, they perished in the quicksand pits."

"I've heard the legend," she said.

"Some of the old-timers tell stories about full grown cattle being swallowed whole in a matter of minutes." He glanced at her, his eyes glinting with insanity. "Do you believe that, Natalie?"

"I think it's folklore."

"A horrific way to die, don't you think?"

She didn't answer.

"Most people think a man can step into quicksand and be swallowed alive. What most people don't realize is that the human body is mostly water. It has a density of sixty-two point four pounds per cubic foot and will float on water. Quicksand is denser than water. So a human being will simply float. So much for those Hollywood dramatizations." He smiled, his expression intensifying. "A human body must be *weighted* in order to become fully submerged in quicksand."

The words filled her with such horror that for a moment she couldn't catch her breath. "Travis, let me go. Please."

"Natalie, I can't let you ruin my life."

Nat couldn't believe her trip back to Bellerose had culminated in this moment. That she was in the middle of nowhere, facing the man who'd murdered her husband and son. That he was probably going to kill her, too, and there was nothing she could do to stop him.

"We're here," he said.

They stopped in a small clearing surrounded by trees and heavy brush. A few yards away was a stand of cattails and what looked like a shallow pool of water. "I won't tell anyone," she said. "I promise. I'll do whatever I can to help you."

"Sit down, Natalie."

Her heart was pounding so hard she could barely hear him. She could feel her entire body shaking. Her blood pumping adrenaline to every muscle. "You won't get away with this."

His hand snaked out. She succeeded in dodging the punch, but when she lunged back, the motion jarred her leg, sending lightning spears of agony through her body. Nat went down, landing on her side, gasping.

He tsked. "See what happens when you don't listen?"

Lying on the ground, she watched him cross to a pile of dead brush and begin to clear it away. In a matter of seconds a large plastic bin came into view. It was muddy, but intact. He opened the bin and pulled out a coil of nylon rope. Setting the rope aside, he tugged a concrete block from beneath the brush. Every muscle in her body tightened when he turned to her. "This is my burying ground, Natalie. The quicksand here is almost twelve feet deep. It takes a while, but a body will eventually end up at the bottom. Pretty goddamn brilliant way to hide a body, don't you think?"

"Stay away from me." Using her good leg, she inched away from him. "Stay the hell *away!*"

"Don't make this any more difficult than it already is." Malice gleamed in his eyes as he picked up the rope and started toward her. "Lie still for me, and I'll make sure you're unconscious before I toss you into the pit."

Nat had known terror before. But she had never felt the kind of raw, wild horror that rose inside her at the thought of drowning in quicksand. She knew struggling was futile; she would never be able to escape him, but her will to survive would not let her submit. Rolling quickly, she scrambled, made it to her knees.

Snarling a profanity, Travis put his foot between her

shoulder blades and shoved her to the ground. "Don't fight me, Natalie."

She screamed in rage and terror when he put his knee at the small of her back. She lay there like a beaten animal while he secured the weight to the bindings at her wrists.

She hadn't wanted to break down in front of him, hadn't wanted to give him the satisfaction. But the thought of such a horrific death at the hands of this evil, soulless man left her bereft. Closing her eyes tightly, she began to cry.

As the tears ran unchecked down her cheeks, she found herself thinking about Nick. The last hours they'd spent together. She wondered if he'd realized she was in love with him. If he saw it in her eyes. Felt it in the way her body responded to his. And even though he'd told her he would never give her his whole heart, she wondered if he would have eventually loved her, too.

That she would never get the chance to find out broke her heart.

chapter
29

NICK BROUGHT THE TRUCK TO A SCREECHING HALT in the alley behind Travis Ratcliffe's office near downtown Bellerose. The doctor shared the two-story brick structure with a dentist, a pediatrician, and the law offices of Henson, Bain and McFarland.

He left the truck at a dead run and crossed to the back entrance where a steel door was set into an alcove. He tried the knob, but found it locked. Heart pounding, he looked around for something to pry it open with, but the alley was damnably clean.

Feeling the seconds tick by, he went to the truck and quickly searched the bed for a crowbar or shovel—anything he could use to break into the building. But the only items in the bed were a five-gallon bucket and a rusty chain he'd used to pull down an old toolshed the week before.

"Damn it!"

He knew in his heart that Nat was with Ratcliffe. He knew if he didn't find her quickly, Ratcliffe was going to hurt her. Kill her. The thought that he may already be too late ate at him like acid . . .

Climbing behind the wheel, he started the engine and backed to the door. Ramming the shifter into neutral, he hauled the chain out of the bed and carried one end to the door. He

wrapped the rusty links around the knob and secured them
with the hook. Dragging the other end of the chain to the truck,
he hooked it to the undercarriage and tried hard not to think
about the consequences of what he was about to do.

He slid into the truck and jammed the shifter into first gear,
then edged the vehicle forward until the chain went taut.
Slowly, Nick let out the clutch, giving the truck just enough
gas to power it forward. Metal groaned as one and a half tons
of steel tugged at the door. An instant later the door flew from
its hinges and landed fifteen feet into the alley.

The security alarm began to wail, but it didn't keep him
from going inside. Knowing he only had a few minutes before the police arrived, he sprinted down the main hall, reading the names on each office door as he passed. The last door
was the one he wanted: Travis Ratcliffe, M.D.

Not considering the consequences, he stepped back and
rammed the door with his shoulder. The door flew open and
slammed against the wall. He burst into a tastefully deco-
rated waiting area. Ahead, a sliding window opened to a reception desk. To his right, a door with a small rectangular
window led into the interior office. Grabbing a lamp from
the nearest end table, he shattered the window, then thrust
his hand inside and unlocked the door.

He found Ratcliffe's inner sanctum at the end of the
hall. Nick turned on the light and looked around. He saw expensive furniture. A wall covered with framed certificates and
plaques. He strode to the credenza behind the desk and tried
the drawer. Locked. Feeling the press of time, he tried the desk
drawer. Frustration burst through him when he found it locked.

Spotting a letter opener on the desk, he snatched it up and
jammed it into the locking mechanism hard enough to split
wood. The drawer rolled open. Time ate at him as he paged
through the files. Finding nothing, he went to the second
drawer.

Travis. Office. Map.

The words written in blood flashed in his mind's eye. Her
blood, he thought. What the hell did it mean? Did Travis have
some kind of a map? A map to what?

Nick had no idea what he was looking for, but he methodically went through every file, desperate for any clue that would tell him where Travis had taken her. If he didn't find it here, he would have no recourse but to go to Ratcliffe Plantation. If Elliott Ratcliffe got in his way, Nick swore he'd go right through him.

He was about to close the last drawer when he spotted a folder at the very back with the word *Gautier* written in red ink on the tab. "Bingo." He snatched the folder from its nest and found himself looking at a crude map.

The paper was yellowed and worn, with trails marked in blue highlighter. Gautier Mud Flats was a vast area, but Nick recognized it immediately. A red X marked a spot not far from where they'd discovered Ricky Arnaud's body. Something pinged in his brain. He knew in his heart that was where Travis had taken Nat. He knew it was where he'd taken more than one of his victims in the years he'd been killing.

And he knew that if he didn't get there soon, he was going to be too late.

Stuffing the map into his waistband, he left the office and sprinted down the hall toward the rear door. He barely noticed the pouring rain as he crossed to the truck and started the engine. His only thought was that he had to reach Nat. He couldn't bear the thought of losing her. In the few short days he'd known her, she'd come to mean more to him than he ever could have imagined. She'd proven to him that not all people were bad. She'd given him hope when he'd been hopeless. She'd made him feel when his heart had been frozen. Made him laugh when he wanted to cry.

Against all odds—against all hope—he'd proven himself wrong and fallen in love with her.

His heart pumped ice through his veins as he left Bellerose and headed toward the river road. He glanced at the map on the seat next to him. He had no idea what to expect when he got there. Maybe he was wrong and nobody would be there. Or maybe he was about to walk into his worst nightmare. Unarmed, he wasn't sure what the hell he was going to be able to do about it.

Praying he wasn't too late, he pushed the accelerator to the floor and the truck spun into the night.

* * *

THE PRIMAL SYMPHONY OF THE BAYOU EBBED AND flowed, an ocean of life in the midst of death. Rain pounded the foliage and muddy ground. Mist swirled like restless ghosts among the cypress and reeds and fan palms.

Nat lay on her side, taking it all in through the dull haze of shock and pain. Vaguely, she was aware of Travis securing the concrete weight to the rope at her wrists. Her heart beating heavily in her chest. The pain in her leg throbbing with every beat.

She couldn't believe she was going to die like this. Like an animal in the bayou with no one but her killer to hear her screams. That she'd failed to vindicate her son's death filled her with outrage and pain.

She thought about Nick, and a different kind of pain engulfed her. He'd made her believe that there was more to living than revenge. That life didn't have to be about pain. That the future was hers for the taking if she was brave enough to take that first, faltering step. That one day she might even be happy.

Oh, how she'd wanted the chance to love him. . . .

"Get up."

Blinking rain from her eyes, she looked up at Travis. He was leaning over her, rain dripping from his hair into his face.

"Don't do this," she said.

"It's either you or me, Nat." Tightening his grip on her arm, he pulled her to her feet. "I choose me. It's that primal will-to-survive thing bred into all of us, you know?"

She knew what would happen next, and the horror of it was too much for her mind to absorb. She could see the surface of the quicksand fifteen feet away. She knew he was going to push her into it. She wasn't going to go without a fight, even if it was a fight she couldn't win. With her hands tied behind her back, she fought the only way she could. Bending, she went in low and butted him with her head. An instant of satisfaction zinged through her when she heard his teeth snap together. He reeled backward, landed hard in the mud on his backside.

Unable to run because of the concrete block tethered to her wrists, she gripped the rope and tried to swing the block, use it as a weapon. But the piece of concrete was too heavy and she only succeeded in dragging it.

Then Travis was upon her. His mouth snarling expletives. His eyes furious and cruel. "I was going to knock you unconscious for this. But now I think I'll watch you die."

The next thing she knew, she was being hauled toward the quicksand pit. Nat lashed out with her uninjured leg, but lost her footing and went to her knees. He continued dragging her toward the mud pit. She fought him, twisting and throwing her weight in an effort to free herself. But he was stronger, and her struggles were in vain.

"Help me!" she screamed. "Someone *please!*" She heard panic in her voice. Felt the terror grip her, shake her like a giant beast.

At the edge of the pit, he shoved her hard. "See you in hell, Natalie."

"No!" Off balance, she reeled backward. Another scream burst from her throat when she sank into mud up to her knees. She could feel it closing around her thighs like a giant, sucking mouth.

For an instant, she didn't think she was going to sink any deeper. Then she saw Travis pick up the concrete block and toss it into the pit beside her. Mud splattered. The weight sank quickly. Blinking rain and mud from her eyes, Nat went still. An instant later, she felt the weight of the block tug against her bound hands, pulling her down.

Panic exploded in hot, undulating waves. She struggled against her bonds. Screams ripped from her throat, animal sounds of pure horror. "Help me! Oh, God! Oh, *God!* Help me, *pleeeeeease!*"

But the more she moved, the deeper into the mud she sank. Vaguely, she was aware of Travis moving into her line of vision. She felt the cold, wet pressure of the mud moving steadily over her legs to embrace her hips. She tried to move her legs, to kick her way free, but they were frozen in place.

This can't be happening, she thought. *I cannot die like this. Oh, dear, God, not like this!*

But the water and mud and decaying leaves crept steadily over her hips. Choking back sobs, she looked at Travis.

Another layer of horror crashed over her when she realized he was enjoying himself.

"You sick bastard!" she cried.

He moved to the edge of the bog and squatted, his eyes alight with excitement. "Don't fight it, Nat. You can't beat death."

She threw her head back and screamed. The mud was up to her breasts now, pressing against her, as cold and black as death. She thought about Kyle. Wondered if he would be there when she crossed over. If she would be able to hold him in her arms. Hear his laughter. See his smile. Smell his little boy scent. Feel the goodness of his child's soul.

Closing her eyes, she tried to picture him. But it was Nick's face that came to her. It was Nick she wanted. Nick who represented life. And it was Nick who made her want to live with such utter desperation.

"Nick!" she cried.

"Nick!"

chapter
30

NICK TOOK THE MUDDY ROAD AT A DANGEROUS speed. Rain and hail pounded the windshield, but he didn't slow down. The tires plowed through water and mud and sand. The truck bounced wildly, veering dangerously close to the trees that grew along the narrow shoulder, but he wrestled it back onto the road. He was beyond the point of considering his own safety. Beyond logic or reason or sanity. The only thing that mattered was finding Nat.

The rain and condensation made it difficult to see through the windshield. Nick glanced away for an instant to flip on the defrosters. When he looked back at the road, a huge tree lay in his path. He stood on the brake, but the truck slid sideways and slammed into the massive trunk.

The force of the collision threw him hard against his safety belt. The motor died, and for several seconds the only sound came from the hiss of steam from the engine and the pound of rain on the hood. Knowing the truck wasn't going to do him any good, he stumbled from the vehicle. Within seconds he was soaked. He was in the process of stepping over the fallen tree when he heard the first scream.

"Nick! *Niiiick!*"

Everything inside him froze into a solid block of ice at the sound of Nat's voice. For several endless seconds he stood motionless, his heart pounding, trying to discern from which direction the screams were coming.

"Help meeeee!"

Nick left the trail and cut through heavy brush, following the sound of her screams. All the while his mind took him through the horrors of all the things Ratcliffe could be doing to her.

He fought through a hundred yards of heavy briar, mindless of the scratches on his face and arms. The brush opened to a large clearing that was part pond, part bog. Through the driving rain he saw a four-wheel drive SUV, the engine running, the vehicle's headlights on. Travis Ratcliffe was squatting at the edge of the bog, watching something that was partially submerged.

What the hell was he doing? Where was Nat?

Nick wiped the rain from his eyes and squinted, trying to make out the object in the bog. Realization struck him with the violence of a bullet slamming into his body and going deep. The object in the bog was Nat. She was in quicksand up to her chest. And Travis was sitting on the bank, watching her sink.

Outrage and fury slashed him cleanly. No time to think this through or plan some elaborate rescue. If he didn't get her out of the quicksand swiftly, she would be sucked down to the most horrible death imaginable. . . .

Nick left the cover of the brush. Staying low, he started toward Travis, his vision tunneled on the other man's back. Nat's voice had gone hoarse from screaming. The mud was nearly up to her shoulders. A few more minutes and the earth would swallow her whole.

Hang on, Nat. I'm coming for you.

He was ten feet away when Ratcliffe turned and spotted him. For an instant the other man's expression was utterly surprised. Then, as if realizing he wouldn't survive an encounter with Nick Bastille, Ratcliffe reached into his slicker and leveled an ugly-looking semiautomatic at Nick's chest.

"Stop right there, Bastille."

NAT COULD FEEL THE MUD CONSUMING HER. IT ENcompassed her torso. She could feel its deadly weight against her chest. Mud creeping over her shoulders . . .

She tried to scream, but the terror had sucked the last of the oxygen from her lungs. She could hear her pulse thundering in her ears. Her breaths tearing from her throat. Rain and tears wet on her face.

Movement to her left caught her eye. She squinted through the rain, spotted Nick's tall form striding toward Travis. At first she thought she was hallucinating. Then she heard him speak, and she knew the image was no hallucination. Against all odds, against all hope, he'd found her.

Relief and horror tugged her in different directions. At the rate she had been sinking, she didn't have much time left before she became fully submerged. Travis was armed with a pistol. Chances were, Nick was not.

"Nick!" she choked. "He's armed!"

Travis fired two shots in quick succession. An instant later, the two men became a single, tangled form. Nat stared in horror. She screamed at them, but the sounds tearing from her throat were little more than choking gasps.

All the while she continued to sink. Dried leaves scratched at the tender flesh of her neck. She struggled against the weight tugging her slowly down, but her efforts were fruitless.

"Nick! Oh, God, Nick! I'm *sinking!*"

Mud leaked into her ears, plunging her into utter silence, trapping a scream inside her head. She tilted her head back, praying for a miracle, one more breath, one more minute of life.

She opened her mouth to scream. Mud rushed past her lips. She tasted grit and the sour tang of her own terror. She spit, but the mud was in her mouth, cutting off her scream. She looked at the night sky above. The rain slashing down. Her final glimpse of life.

She took one last breath, and the mud closed over her nostrils like a giant, smothering hand.

THE FIRST BULLET WENT WIDE. THE SECOND TORE into his neck like a hot cane knife. But Nick didn't let the pain or the knowledge that he'd been shot stop him. The way he saw it, he had two choices: Stop Travis Ratcliffe or let Nat die. His own safety never entered the picture.

He went after Ratcliffe with everything he had. The two men hit the ground with bone-crunching force. Nick reached for the gun. Blue steel flashed. The ensuing gunshot deafened him. He felt the hot zing of a bullet open his cheek. He saw the bright red surge of blood. But the knowledge that Nat was seconds from suffering an unspeakable death numbed him to the pain.

Travis Ratcliffe had control of the gun, but Nick was in better physical condition. He was faster and desperate and well schooled on fighting dirty. He used his knee. Bellowing a curse, Ratcliffe twisted, tried to bring up the gun for another shot. But Nick grasped the other man's wrist, slammed it against the ground. Once. Twice.

"Drop it, you son of a bitch."

The pistol flew from Ratcliffe's grip. Both men dove for the weapon. Nick's hand closed around the grip first. He was on his belly. He could hear Ratcliffe behind him and twisted onto his back. The other man charged. Raising the pistol, Nick pulled off a shot.

Ratcliffe's body jerked. The impact of the bullet sent him reeling backward. Blood bloomed vivid and red on his slicker. His arms flailed, and then he plunged into the bog ass first.

"Help me."

Ignoring him, Nick shoved the pistol into the waistband of his jeans and sprinted to Nat. Terror screamed through him when all he could see of her was the top of her head.

Oh dear God. No!

Panic screamed through him. The urge to go in after her was powerful. But he knew enough about quicksand to realize that would be a fatal mistake. Instead, he darted to Travis's SUV and began tearing the vehicle apart, looking for anything he could use to get her out.

In the rear of the vehicle, he came across a length of rope and what looked like a wooden shelf from a bookcase. Tossing the rope and shelf onto the passenger seat, he got behind the wheel and backed the vehicle to the bog, then put it in Park and got out.

"Bastille! I'm bleeding out. You can't leave me like this!" Ratcliffe was in mud up to his hips. He was bleeding badly, the water and foliage bright red against his yellow slicker.

Nick barely spared him a glance. Tying one end of the rope to the bumper, he picked up the shelf and carried both the rope and the shelf to the bog. He dropped belly down on the shelf and plunged his hands into the quicksand.

He found her submerged just a few inches beneath the surface. Fresh terror flooded him when he realized she wasn't moving. That her body was limp and cold to the touch. Shaking inside, terrified that he was too late, he quickly looped the rope around her torso. The shelf had begun to sink. He used it to get back to the bank, then began the agonizing process of pulling her from the bog.

Aware of the panic tearing at his control, he pulled long and hard and steady. Every second ticked by like a death knell. It took every bit of strength he possessed, but slowly the quicksand released her from its death grip. By the time Nick dragged her onto the bank, he was shaking so violently he could barely function.

He fell to his knees beside her and rolled her onto her back. Fresh horror cut him when he realized she wasn't breathing. Clearing her airway with his fingers, he set his mouth against hers and began mouth-to-mouth resuscitation. He gave her six breaths, then switched over and gave her several chest compressions.

"Nat . . ." Emotion constricted his throat so that her name came out as little more than a croak. "Jesus, come on. Don't do this to me."

She was covered with mud and as still and cold as death. Once more, Nick set his mouth against hers. Tilting her head back, he pinched her nose and breathed life into her lungs.

"I'm not going to let you go," he choked. "Breathe. Damn it, *breathe!*"

An instant later, she coughed. Her arms and legs began to thrash.

"Easy, honey. Slow breaths. Not too deep." Gently, he helped her to a sitting position.

Her body shuddered as she coughed up water and mud. Then her eyes fluttered open, and she focused on him. "Nick . . ."

"I'm here," he whispered. "You're going to be all right."

"He was going to . . . Oh, God, Nick, I was drowning. The mud . . . it was in my mouth. I couldn't . . . He was going to—"

"Shh. Don't try to talk." He brushed mud and wet hair from her face. "You're okay now."

Nick wasn't sure who reached for whom, but in the next instant she was in his arms. She was shaking and sobbing, and he felt his own emotions rise dangerously to the surface. "I'm not going to let anything happen to you," he said.

"You saved my life."

After a moment, he eased away from her. She was covered with mud and soaked to the skin, which made it difficult to assess her for any injuries. "Did he hurt you anywhere else?"

"My leg . . . I think it's broken."

Outrage that Travis had hurt her made him grind his teeth. "Ah, honey, I'm sorry—"

Her gaze sharpened on his face. "You're bleeding . . ."

"It's just a graze."

"Nick, you need an ambulance."

"I figure both of us could use one about now. Let me just sit here and hold you for a moment, okay?" As soon as he trusted his legs—as soon as he could make himself let go of her—he would walk over to Ratcliffe's SUV and use the phone he'd spotted in the console.

"What about Travis?" she asked.

Nick glanced over his shoulder toward the bog to see that the other man had sunk into the quicksand to his chest. He was slumped over, semiconscious. "He'll keep until the cops get here."

"How did you know where to find me?"

"I had a little help." He pulled away just enough to make eye contact with her. "Kyle," he said.

"Kyle?"

"He left a note at the house."

Nat put her hand over her mouth, but it wasn't enough to stifle the sob. "I don't remember writing anything."

"It was on the kitchen floor. Three words telling me where to find the map in Travis's office. If it hadn't been for Kyle, I wouldn't have found you because that map led me directly here."

"Such a brave little boy . . ."

"His mom's pretty brave, too." Putting his arms around her, he closed his eyes and held her tightly. "Do me a favor and thank him for me next time you talk to him, okay?"

"I will," she said and began to cry.

chapter
31

Three Days Later

"YOU SURE YOU WANT TO SELL THIS PLACE?"

Nat leaned on her crutch and watched Joe Strickland of Strickland Real Estate drive the new For Sale sign into the ground with a nifty little hammer he'd pulled from his trunk. "I'm sure," she said.

"It's a buyer's market right now. You could hang on to the place for a while . . ."

"I don't think so. I've hung on to it long enough. I think this house needs a family."

"Well, it certainly is perfect for a growing, young family. Nice big backyard. Good school system, too. With that new medical center going up in Covington and some new blood in town, it shouldn't be too long before someone snatches it right up." Finished with the sign, Joe straightened and stuck out his hand. "I'm sure glad everything worked out for you, Ms. Jennings. I saw the story in the newspaper the other day."

"Thank you."

"I'll let you know when we get that contract."

She watched Joe walk to his Cadillac and slide behind the wheel. With a wave, he turned the car around and pulled onto the parish road.

Nat stood in the front yard and drank in the sights and sounds and smells around her. She couldn't have conjured a more beautiful day, even in her imagination. An afternoon breeze rustled the leaves of the magnolia and live oak standing solid and tall. She was keenly aware of the cool breeze on her skin. The warmth of the sun on her back. The song of a mockingbird calling to a prospective mate. The earthy scent of the river behind the house.

Life, she thought, and smiled.

If the last three years had taught her anything, it was to never take the small things for granted. As she stood in the driveway and studied the pretty house that had once been filled with so much life, with so much hope, she tried not to feel melancholy about selling. It was time for her to let go of the past. Time for her to move on with her life, start thinking about the future.

It had been three days since the terrible ordeal she'd gone through at the hands of Travis Ratcliffe. She couldn't believe the man she'd known most of her life was responsible for the deaths of his own brothers and at least six children over a fifteen-year period. A doctor who'd taken an oath to heal, then used his position to get away with murder.

The question of what had really happened between Ward and Hunt and Travis all those years ago would probably never be answered fully. But Alcee Martin was convinced Travis had killed them for what they'd done to him in that storeroom. Nat had relayed to him everything Travis had told her the night he'd tried to kill her. Alcee had dutifully put it in the report. The rest would be up to the St. Tammany Parish District Attorney and a jury of Travis's peers.

The sound of tires crunching gravel drew Nat's attention. She looked up to see Faye Townsend's Volkswagen pull into the driveway. Nat smiled at the sight of her friend's car and watched as she parked and crossed to her.

"Think it will sell this time?" Faye was wearing a flowing red dress with orange flowers that fluttered gauzily around her ankles as she approached.

"Mr. Strickland seems to think so."

The other woman looked at the house and nodded. "The place has a real positive energy about it now, honey. I think you're doing the right thing."

"It feels right," Nat agreed.

"How's the leg?"

"Hurts."

Faye gave her a sympathetic smile before turning serious again. "Are you dealing with everything else okay?"

"As well as can be expected." Nat was still having nightmares, but her therapist in Covington had told her that was to be expected after going through such a horrific ordeal. "I'm pretty good at healing."

"If there's anything I can do . . ." Faye said.

"I know. Thank you."

For a moment the only sound came from the mockingbird scolding them from the chimney. "I miss Kyle," Nat said.

"You haven't heard from him?"

She shook her head. "I sat at the dining room table for an hour last night with paper and a pen, waiting for something to happen."

"Nothing happened?"

"I know it sounds crazy, but I miss communicating with him. I miss him so much."

"Of course, you do, honey. You're his mom. You're always going to miss him." Faye crossed to her and pulled her into an embrace. "It's going to be okay."

Nat closed her eyes against a sudden rush of tears. "You know I cry when you hug me."

"You're entitled, sweetie."

Forcing a smile, Nat pulled away and wiped the tears from her cheeks. "I won't hear from him again, will I?"

Faye shook her head. "Probably not."

"That hurts."

"I know, sweetie. But I think maybe this is his way of telling you to move on with your life. Maybe even try to find some happiness."

Nat smiled at the notion of happiness and found herself thinking about Nick Bastille. "I'm not sure I know how to do that."

"If you can solve a three-year-old double murder, you can do anything, including finding a little bit of happiness for yourself. You just have to put your mind to it."

Intellectually, Nat knew her friend was right. The problem

was, she didn't know how. For three years, she'd geared her life toward one single-minded goal: Bring Kyle and Ward's murderer to justice. Now that Travis Ratcliffe was in jail facing a multitude of serious charges, she felt oddly adrift.

The sound of a vehicle pulling into the driveway caused both women to look up. A warm emotion Nat couldn't quite identify jumped inside her at the sight of Nick Bastille's pickup truck. She hadn't seen him since the night he'd saved her life. But she'd spent plenty of time thinking about him. The nurse at the hospital had told her she hadn't been breathing when he pulled her from the quicksand, that Nick Bastille had breathed life into her body and brought her back from the edge of death.

"Honey, I think this is one of those times when three's a crowd."

Nat glanced over at Faye to see her grinning from ear to ear. For a moment, they stood there, both sets of eyes on the tall man moving toward them with long, confident strides.

"He sure is something to look at," Faye said wistfully. "The man wears a tattoo the way a tattoo ought to be worn."

"I hadn't noticed," Nat said, and both women broke into laughter.

"Liar." Faye took her hands and squeezed them. "Tell your mama I said hello," she said. "And be careful on your way to New Orleans, okay?"

"I will."

Nick had reached them, his dark gaze flicking from Faye to Nat.

Flipping her hair over her shoulder, Faye started past Nick, then paused to pat his cheek. "I was beginning to wonder if you were going to show."

"Wouldn't miss it for the world," he answered, but his eyes were on Nat.

Vaguely, Nat was aware of Faye crossing to her Volkswagen. Of the engine turning over and the vehicle pulling out of the driveway. But her every sense was homed on the man standing close enough for her to smell the tangy scent of his aftershave. She watched as his dark eyes swept from her, to the For Sale sign, to her suitcase on the sidewalk near her car.

"Going somewhere?" he asked.

"New Orleans." Nat took a deep breath to steady her nerves.

"I haven't seen my mother yet. I thought I'd take some time to visit her and try to figure out what comes next."

"How long will you be gone?"

"I'm not sure."

A heavy silence fell as he digested that.

Because she couldn't stand the way he was looking at her—like she'd just sucker-punched him—she asked, "How did your parole hearing go?"

"Alcee Martin spoke to the parole board on my behalf. He explained to them that Travis Ratcliffe tried to frame me for Hunt's murder. He added that I was instrumental in Ratcliffe's arrest. Even though technically I had violated parole, the board wiped the slate clean, so to speak. I won't be going back to Angola."

Relief flooded her. "That's great news, Nick. I'm glad it worked out. It would have been incredibly unfair for you to be sent back for what you did."

He shifted his weight from one foot to the other. "I wanted you to know . . . I spoke to Tanya this morning. If she can get immunity for herself, she's willing to give a statement to the court, telling them what she knows about Race Roberson framing me for arson and insurance fraud."

For a moment, Nat wasn't sure she'd heard him right. "You'll be cleared?"

"All charges will be expunged from my record."

A quick burst of joy shot through her. Before even realizing she was going to move, she closed the short distance between them and threw her arms around his shoulders. "I'm happy for you. Congratulations."

She felt him stiffen; then an instant later, his arms encircled her, and he pulled her close. "If all goes well, the district attorney's office in New Orleans might be able to get an arrest warrant issued for Race Roberson."

"That's even better." Tears stung her eyes. "You'll finally have justice."

She tried to look away, but Nick raised his hand and put his fingers under her chin, forcing her gaze to his. "That's supposed to cheer you up," he said. "Not make you cry."

Nat choked out a laugh, but it sounded more like a sob. "I was just thinking about dreams."

He didn't give her any warning that he was going to kiss her. One moment he was holding her at arm's length, the next his mouth was on hers, and the earth was quaking beneath her feet. The quick shock of pleasure stunned her. She could feel his heart thrumming against hers, her blood beginning to heat. She wasn't sure where this moment would take them. The only thing she knew for certain was that being held by Nick Bastille felt right in a way that nothing else in the world could.

She was dizzy when he finally released her. His eyes were dark and intense when he gazed down at her. "I almost didn't come here today," he said roughly.

"Why?"

"Because I don't like good-byes." He shot a look at her suitcase. "How long are you going to be gone?"

"I don't know. I need some time to get my head together. Figure out what to do with the rest of my life." She shrugged. "I'm selling the house."

"I sort of gathered that from the For Sale sign."

She laughed, but the sound was fraught with emotion. "What about you?"

"I thought I might spend some time getting reacquainted with Pop. I found a nice retirement home in Baton Rouge, but he's not quite ready. I've got some crops to put in before the season is over." He rolled his shoulder. "I'm still thinking about the long-term stuff."

"I hope it works out for you, Nick. You're a good man. You deserve good things to happen in your life."

He stared at her, astounded by the unexpected emotion twisting him into knots. "Nat . . . what you said about dreams . . ."

She stared back at him, her eyes so clear and bottomless he thought if he got any closer he might just tumble into their depths. "There's an old warehouse for sale in Baton Rouge. It's in an historic district and going for a steal. I think it would be the perfect place for a restaurant."

Her eyes widened then filled with tears. Unable to speak, she started to put her face in her hands, but he gently took her hands and forced her gaze to his. "It would be a new start. A new life. There's some risk, but I've never let that stop me."

"I'm glad you haven't given up on your dreams."

"I haven't given up on a lot of things." He squeezed her hands. "I was wrong when I told you I could never give you my whole heart," he said. "I haven't been able to get you out of my mind, and it's killing me because I have no idea how you feel or where I stand."

She searched his gaze, her eyes luminous and so filled with emotion it took everything he had not to pull her to him. "You told me you weren't the kind of man I needed in my life."

He blinked, his jaw flexing. *"Chere . . ."*

"You were wrong, Nick." Standing on her tiptoes, she brushed her mouth across his. "You're exactly the kind of man I need in my life. It just took you a little while to figure it out."

"In that case," he said, crushing her against him. "I'll be waiting for you when you get back from New Orleans."

"I won't be long," she said and kissed him back.

Turn the page for a special preview of
Linda Castillo's next novel

DEAD RECKONING

Coming soon from Berkley Sensation!

Monday, January 23, 7:25 A.M.

THE CITY OF DALLAS ROSE EARLY ON MONDAY
morning. By six thirty A.M., Central Expressway, the Dallas
North Tollway, and LBJ Freeway were packed with tens of
thousands of commuters, each determined to get to work on
time despite the miles of construction, the endless congestion,
and the simple fact that there were more cars than roads.

Part Southern belle, part cosmopolitan metropolis with a
little bit of the wild west thrown in, Dallas was a city of stark
contrasts. A city caught in a perpetual identity crisis. It was a
place where gracious old mansions battled for space among
the glass and steel skyscrapers that had been born during the
oil boom of the 1980s. A city where the slow pace of the old
south clashed with the high-tech scramble of urban America.
A place where lush southern magnolia trees shivered in the
wicked winds that whipped down from the high plains during
the short, but cold winters.

But despite its quirks and growing pains, Dallas was home
and Kate Megason loved it with a passion. She loved the excitement of big city living. The restaurants and shopping, parks and
cultural events. She loved the interesting mix of cultures that
made Dallas one of the most diverse cities in the United States.

But like all big cities, Dallas had a dark side and more than its share of violent crime. Averaging more than two hundred murders a year, the city was one of the nation's most violent. As a Dallas County assistant prosecuting attorney, Kate took those statistics as a personal affront.

She'd graduated magna cum laude from the University of Texas at Austin. For her law degree she'd chosen Southern Methodist University over Northwestern. And at the ripe age of twenty-six, she'd passed the Texas State Bar exam and become a lawyer. That same year she landed a job with the Dallas County District Attorney's office. Two years later she became one of the youngest ADAs in the country's one hundred and fifty year history.

Now, at the age of twenty-eight, Kate had one of the highest conviction rates in the county. Whether it was the vehemence with which she argued every case, or the meticulousness of her research, no judge or jury had ever found one of her defendants not guilty or even dismissed one of her cases.

Kate was good at what she did—damn good. One of the best prosecutors Dallas County had ever seen according to her boss, District Attorney Mike Shelley. Kate believed staunchly in the criminal justice system. She believed just as staunchly in the judicial system upon which she had devoted her professional life. She enjoyed the challenge of her work. She craved the satisfaction that came with knowing she'd put a dangerous criminal behind bars where he couldn't hurt anyone else. She liked knowing she made a difference. Maybe even helped make the world a better place to live.

It was just after seven A.M. when she turned off Industrial Boulevard and swung her BMW into the parking garage of the Frank Crowley Courts building in downtown Dallas. She entered the building and flashed her ID badge at the police officer stationed at the front entrance the way she had every day for the last two years.

"Morning, Ms. Megason."

"How's it going, Sam?" she asked as she set her briefcase on the belt and walked through the metal detector. "LaShonda have that baby yet?"

He grinned. "Going to be any day now."

Kate smiled back, liking both the routine and the man. "Number three?"

"Four."

"Give her my best, will you?"

"Sure will. You have a nice day now."

She picked up her briefcase. "You, too, Sam."

Her Italian boots clicked smartly against the tile floor as she crossed to the bank of elevators and rode to the eleventh floor. The doors opened to a wide hall with tiled floors and walls covered with an industrial blue fabric some well-meaning interior designer had installed the year before when the offices were being remodeled. Next to two double-glass doors, a bronze wall plaque proclaimed the office of Mike Shelley, Dallas County District Attorney.

Swiping her security card in the proximity reader, Kate used her key to open the door and stepped into the outer office. The familiar smells of paper dust, old books, and new carpeting greeted her as she passed through the main lobby. Even though the operator didn't come in until eight, the switchboard was already lit up like a Christmas tree. It was going to be another wild day at the Dallas County District Attorney's office.

Kate turned left and entered the small break room. Setting her briefcase on the table, she quickly made a pot of coffee, then picked up her briefcase and headed toward her own cubbyhole office at the end of the hall. She unlocked the door, shoved it open with a booted foot, and went directly to her desk. Taking the chair, she opened her briefcase, pulled out her Palm Pilot, and checked her schedule for the day. Conference call at ten o'clock. Lunch at noon with one of her paralegals, who would be expecting a positive review and a raise and was going to get both. Court at two o'clock where she would give her opening statement on an armed robbery felony case. Back to the office in time to meet with a potential witness in a vehicular homicide case. By then it would be well after six o'clock. If her phone wasn't ringing, she might just be able to get some work done.

Kate was a creature of habit and thrived on routine. A workaholic by nature, she lived by her schedule, however stringent, and drove herself relentlessly. She was up before dawn and at the office until long after dark six days a week. Aside from the occasional dinner or lunch or happy hour with coworkers and the occasional Sunday visit with her parents, she didn't have much of a personal life. Kate preferred it that way.

The smell of dark roast wafted into her office, telling her the coffee had brewed. To save time, she dug the case file she was working on out of its brown expanding folder and read as she headed for the break room.

Ricky Joe Paulsen was a repeat offender with a cocaine habit and a penchant for violence. He'd gotten off easy twice in the past. Probation for possession of marijuana six years ago. Then a five-year sentence on a burglary conviction. He'd been released after only eighteen months due to prison over-crowding. A week after his release, he'd walked into a liquor store, shoved a .357 Magnum into the clerk's face and asked for money. He hadn't expected an off-duty police officer to walk in for a bottle of 1991 sauvignon blanc.

Ricky Joe Paulsen had been caught red-handed, and Kate was going to do her utmost to make sure the son of a bitch didn't kill someone the next time he decided he'd rather steal his money than earn it.

She poured coffee into a Lawyers Do It Better mug and carried it to her desk. She would outline her strategy this morning while her mind was fresh, then try to squeeze in the rest of her caseload between court and meetings.

Pulling a legal pad from her drawer, she scribbled the points she wanted to make in her opening statement. Repeat offender. Violent. Potential for extreme violence. No deals.

"Kate?"

She looked up to see District Attorney Mike Shelley standing at her office door, watching her as if she were his favorite child and had just ridden her bicycle without training wheels for the first time. The image made her smile. "You're in early this morning," she said.

"Says one workaholic to another."

"I prefer to think of it as dedicated."

"Sounds healthier if you say it that way. But if you're angling for a raise . . ."

"I already got my raise." Kate jotted a final note on the

pad and set down her Mont Blanc. "And it was a good one. Thank you."

"Make it last. Both the mayor and city manager are screaming about budget again." Mike Shelley was a large man with direct, square features and a mouth that was too big for his face. He wore a custom black suit and the requisite conservative tie over a crisp white shirt. His graying hair gave him a distinguished air without making him look older. His forthright expression revealed little of what he was thinking. A trait Kate admired in an attorney even though it invariably made her just a little bit nervous.

"Can I see you in my office for a moment?"

Surprise rippled through her at the request, and it was quickly followed by curiosity tinged with a low-grade uneasiness. Lunch meant a raise. Dinner meant a promotion. The conference room adjacent to his office was usually reserved for ass-chewings. In the six years she'd worked for Mike Shelley, Kate had never been called into his office. He was a hands-off manager and trusted his people to do the work and keep him apprised. The only time an ADA was called into the DA's office was when something big was going down.

She wondered if this was something big.

"Of course." Closing the legal pad, she rose.

He smiled as if trying to put her at ease, but it didn't work. Mike Shelley might have the face of someone's favorite uncle, but Kate knew a shark with very big teeth resided beneath his benevolent facade. He hadn't gotten where he was by being a nice guy. At least not all the time.

"Sorry for the short notice," he added. "I know you're busy."

"No problem." Plucking a fresh legal pad from her drawer, she rounded her desk.

Mike motioned for her to precede him and they walked side by side toward his office. "This shouldn't take long."

Several paralegals and administrative assistants had arrived to start their day, and Kate was keenly aware of her coworkers' eyes following them as they passed by the break room and cubicles. The District Attorney's office was no different than other offices and had a healthy grapevine; it didn't take much to get tongues wagging.

Mike's corner office was the largest on the eleventh floor and offered a stunning view of downtown Dallas. His rosewood desk was huge and as glossy as a new car hot off the showroom floor. It was stacked with the requisite expanding legal folders and a smattering of photographs of his wife and three children. But Kate knew most of what he did was political. And she'd always thought Mike Shelley was too good of an attorney to spend so much of his time smoothing feathers.

Another layer of surprise settled over her when she entered the office and noticed the other three people already seated. Barbara Pasquale was a high-level ADA who'd been with the DA's office for going on twenty years. Kate guessed her to be in her mid-fifties. She was attractive in a red power suit and conservative strand of pearls. She was sitting on Mike's black leather sofa, a legal pad in her lap, her legs crossed. She made eye contact with Kate and gave a small nod in greeting.

The man sitting on the opposite end of the sofa was Alan Rosenberg, who was also a high-level ADA. Thin and balding, he had a boisterous personality and was one of the best lawyers Kate had ever met. Every time she heard him argue before a jury, she was invariably relieved that he worked for the DA and not the private sector because there would be a hell of a lot more felons on the street if he did.

"Alan," she said with a nod. "Haven't gone over to the dark side yet?"

He grinned. "The thought of facing you in court keeps me here."

She snorted just enough to let him know she didn't buy a word of it, and her gaze went to the third man sitting at the small conference table. Kate knew immediately he wasn't a lawyer. He wore a store-bought suit that was too tight in the shoulders and a hideous tie with a soup stain in the center. He had steel gray hair and jowls that hung like strips of meat off each side of his face. But it was his direct stare that gave him away. She'd been a prosecutor long enough to spot a cop on sight and this man had detective written all over him.

"Kate, thank you for meeting with us on such short notice." Mike motioned toward the two ADA's seated on the sofa. "You know Alan and Barbara."

"Of course."

He motioned toward the man sitting at the table. "This is Detective Howard Bates with the Dallas PD."

Kate nodded at the detective. "Hello."

"Ms. Megason."

"Okay." Mike rubbed his hands together as if he were about to dig in to a hearty meal, then motioned toward the table. "Have a seat and we'll get started."

Kate wasn't easily intimidated, but she didn't like surprises, especially when it came to her job. She didn't like the idea of walking into a high-level meeting without knowing the agenda. She had a sinking feeling she *was* the agenda. "What's this all about?" Never taking her eyes from Mike's she took the chair opposite the detective.

Mike slid behind his desk, slipped his bifocals onto his nose, and picked up a file. "I'm sure you're aware of the Bruton Ellis case."

Kate nodded. "The convenience store double murder."

"The grand jury indicted on Friday. It's an open-and-shut case. Two women gunned down. A mother of four and a grandmother with her first great-grandchild on the way. Two nice people with families just trying to make a living." Mike looked at her over the tops of his glasses. "One of the women was sexually assaulted *after* she'd been shot in the back."

Kate wasn't exactly sure why he was telling her all of that. She'd heard of the case, but hadn't followed it closely. She didn't know the particulars. She hadn't known about the sexual assault. But at some point her heart had begun to pound.

The DA continued. "Ellis is a repeat offender. Robbery. Drugs. Assault. He had enough crystal meth in his system at the time of his arrest to send an elephant to the moon. Shot out the security camera, but he didn't know there was a second camera, so the entire crime was caught on video."

"That will definitely help convict," Kate said, her lawyer's perspective coming automatically.

"We're counting on it." Mike took off his glasses. "I want you to prosecute the case."

The initial zing of adrenaline hit her blood and Kate's heart pounded harder. Most cases with a true bill of indictment handed down from the grand jury were randomly put on the docket. Whichever prosecutor was assigned to a certain district court would get whichever cases went to that particular district. Occasionally a prosecutor would be handpicked to handle a specific case, but the practice was unusual.

"Why me?"

Mike laughed, a hearty belly laugh that told her he was truly amused. "Several reasons, actually. First and foremost because you're a damn good prosecutor. You're thorough. Low key. Juries love you. Judges love you. But most importantly I chose you for this case because I know you'll get a conviction."

There was more coming. Kate could see it in his eyes. She could see it in the faces of the other three people in the room. That she didn't know what it was irked her, made her suspicious, gave her a prickly sensation on the back of her neck.

"This defendant is a repeat offender, Kate. He committed a double murder and a rape while in the commission of a felony."

Realization flashed an instant later, but the excitement was quickly followed by a quiver of nerves that was powerful enough to make her hands shake. "You want me to try it as a capital case?"

Mike nodded, then looked at each of the other three people in the room. "The three of us met over the weekend and discussed the case at length. We've got legal sufficiency and adherence to statutes any way you cut it." He looked at the detective. "We looked at the evidence. The statutes of the state of Texas are clear. We believe the cold brutality of this crime calls for the most severe of punishments applicable by law."

Kate didn't know what to say. It would be her first capital case. The kind of case most prosecutors would give their right hand to try. It was the kind of case up-and-coming ADAs dreamed of. The kind of case that could make a career. Or maybe even put a young prosecutor on the political map and give her a shot at the judgeship she'd always wanted.

But while the challenge of prosecuting her first capital case appealed to her immensely, she couldn't help but wonder why Mike had handpicked her when there were a half dozen other prosecutors in his office with just as much experience.

Leaning back in his black leather chair, Mike Shelley fiddled with his glasses, but his gaze never left hers. "Next year is an election year. It could help with the judgeship you've been aiming for."

Kate tried not to react, but she was flattered. She'd never been one to talk about her dreams. She liked to keep them close to her chest, in case she fell flat on her face no one would know.

"I can give you until tomorrow morning to make up your mind," he added.

"That won't be necessary," she said. "I'll take the case."

Monday, January 23, 8:58 A.M.

THE SUN WARMED HIS BACK AS HE SAT AT THE BRISTO TABLE and waited for her to arrive. The aromas of smoked fish and grilling vegetables filled the air. The cafe was crowded with the noontime business crowd, couples having lunch, students laughing over hafuch, the local version of cappuccino. The leaves of the olive trees that grew along the boulevard shimmered silver and green in the breeze coming in off the sea.

It had been two days since they'd been together, and he couldn't wait to see her again. He couldn't wait to see her smile. To touch her skin. To hear her voice and the music of her laughter.

Setting his hand over the tiny velvet box in his pocket, he grinned like an idiot. But he didn't care. The diamond wasn't much—less than half a karat and flawed to boot—but he knew it wouldn't matter. She was going to say yes. And when she did, he was going to be the happiest man in the world.

His heart swelled with pleasure and anticipation when he spotted her on the other side of the cafe. Smiling, he waved and motioned her over. "Gittel!"

She met his smile with a dazzling one of her own and waved back. He couldn't take his eyes off her as she worked her way around the smattering of tables and colorful umbrellas. She was wearing a pale blue dress with matching sandals. Her legs were bare and sexy and she was so lovely it hurt just to look at her. And he wondered what he'd done to deserve her in his life.

He'd already told his parents he was going to marry her. It didn't matter that she was from a wealthy Israeli family and he was a hell-raising Catholic boy from Texas. They were in love

and he knew with an optimism he'd never before experienced
that everything would work out as long as they were together.

"Frank!" Waving her arms, she laughed as the crowd jos-
tled her about. "Sorry I'm late!"

He couldn't wait to get his hands on her. A need that was
part emotional, part sexual sent him to his feet. He wanted to
cross to her, put his arms around her, and take her down right
there on the cobblestone walk.

For an instant time stood still. He watched her approach,
liking the way the fabric swept over her body. He felt the
warmth of the sun on his back. He heard the din of voices
punctuated by the traffic that ran along the thoroughfare. Anticipation pumped through him with every step she took, with
every beat of his heart. So much to look forward to . . .

The blast struck him like a speeding, burning car. One moment he was standing, the next he was airborne and careening
through space. Agony ripped through his lower body as a thousand missiles penetrated skin and muscle and bone. Pain tore
through the right side of his head as his eardrum burst. His
world went silent and white, and he was tumbling in a void of
shock and pain and confusion.

The next thing he knew he was lying on the ground. He saw
black smoke billowing into a perfect blue sky. Around him,
people were running, their faces covered with blood and soot,
their eyes filled with horror. Raising his head, he looked
around for Gittel, but all he saw was smoke and the twisted re-
mains of a table and umbrella. He called out her name, but he
couldn't hear his own voice and he realized the blast had
deafened him.

Gittel! Gittel!

He didn't know if he was screaming her name or if he was
only thinking it. Panic and horror swept through him as realization settled into his brain, as the amount of damage registered in his brain. And he knew people had died.

Oh, dear God, no . . .

Pain zinged up his left leg all the way to his hip as he struggled to his hands and knees. When he looked down he saw that
his jeans were soaked with blood. His stomach pitched when he
saw the shrapnel jutting from his thigh. His leg was broken; he

*could see the bone fragments in the blood. But he was alive.
He could move. He had to find Gittel.*

*He looked around wildly. A patch of blue snagged his eye.
He recognized the fabric. Gittel, he thought, and his heart began to hammer when he realized she wasn't moving. Groaning
in pain, choking on smoke, he began to crawl toward her.*

Please, God, let her be all right. . . .

*It was as if he were crawling through a tunnel that was de-
void of sound and light. He saw mangled bodies and parts of
bodies and twisted heaps of metal and blood. In all the years
he'd been in the military, he'd never seen so much blood. The
cobblestone was slick with it. A red river that ran like death
into the street. He could smell it, sickly sweet and mingling
with the stench of the dead and dying.*

*The wail of an ambulance sounded in the distance. Hope
bubbled up from somewhere deep inside him. The paramedics
would arrive quickly. Gittel would be taken to the hospital and
everything would be all right.*

*But he knew the instant he saw her that nothing would ever
be all right again. She was lying on her back in a pool of
blood that glimmered like red ice. Her eyes were open as if she
were looking up at the sky. Even torn and bleeding, she was
beautiful. So innocent and decent and good.*

*"Gittel." He reached her, ran his hands over her torso.
"Aw, God. Honey, it's me. Wake up."*

*Her dress was blood soaked, burned in places, and had
been nearly torn from her body. Shoving a fallen chair out of
the way, he tried to assess her injuries. The world crumbled
beneath him when he saw her legs. Both had been severed from
the knee down. . . .*

*Denial and rage rose in a violent tide inside him. "Aw, God
no." He pushed himself onto his elbows and put his arm
around her, shook her gently. "Gittel. Oh, God. Oh, baby, no."*

No!

No!

Frank Matrone sat up abruptly, his heart pounding, his mind
raging at the horrors trapped inside it. He could hear himself
breathing hard. Feel the cold slick of sweat covering his body.
The scream in his throat receding back into the deep, black hole

it had burst out of where a thousand more lay in waiting.

He jolted when a knock sounded at the door. Scrubbing his hand over a day's growth of beard, he threw his legs over the side of his bed. Pain streaked up his left leg and exploded brilliant and red inside his head.

"Goddamn it." Face contorted, he sat down hard on the bed and waited for the muscle cramp to pass.

The bell rang four times in quick succession, an annoying buzz that drilled a hole straight to his brain, and he wanted to kill the bastard standing in the hall, gleefully pressing the button.

"Can it, damn it. I'm coming."

Hefting himself off the bed, he limped to the doorway, trying hard to shake off the dark press of the nightmare, knowing that was the one thing that would never really leave him no matter how many shrinks he saw or how many pills he took. God knew he'd had his share of both in the last year.

He glanced at the clock as he crossed through the living room. "Shit," he muttered, wondering who the hell would be dragging him out of bed at nine o'clock on a Sunday morning.

Twisting the knob, he swung open the door. "This had better be good," he growled.

"I guess that's going to depend on your perspective." Sergeant Rick Monteith didn't bother with niceties as he brushed past Frank and entered the dimly lit living room. "Jesus, Frank, you look like shit."

"Thanks." Frank closed the door, cringing when the sound slammed into his brain. For the first time he realized how shaky he felt. That his head was fuzzy. To top things off his leg was hurting like a son of a bitch.

Rick crossed to the patio door and pulled the cord to open the heavy drapes. Frank lifted his hand to shield his eyes from the sudden light. Christ, he felt like a vampire. That the light was going to send him up in flames.

Shaking his head, Rick looked around the cluttered living room. "This place looks like a freaking pig sty."

"You should see it on a bad day." Scrubbing his hand over his face, Frank started toward the kitchen, trying hard not to favor his leg. "What the hell are you doing here this early on a Sunday morning, anyway?"

Rick looked to the heavens as if to ask for patience. He looked military neat in his blue uniform and spit-shined shoes. It was a uniform Frank himself had worn a lifetime ago. But he'd sell his soul before ever admitting he missed being a cop.

"It's Monday, you asshole," Rick said.

That surprised him, and for an uneasy moment Frank tried to remember what had happened to Sunday. Or maybe it was Saturday he'd lost. . . .

"You were supposed to be at Mike Shelley's office at seven thirty this morning."

The words stopped him cold. Frank was well aware that he'd been on a downward spiral for the last year. He thought he'd hit rock bottom a couple months ago. Now he wasn't so certain because he'd sure as hell hit a new low this morning. Missing a job interview, for chrissake. And he'd never lost entire days before.

"Aw, Christ," he said. "Sorry . . ."

"Don't apologize to me, partner. I don't want to hear any more of your excuses. I've done what I can and the rest is up to you. If you want to fuck up what's left of your lousy life, then go for it. Just don't expect me to stand around and watch. I can't stomach it."

"I'll call him."

"If I were Shelley, I'd tell you to get screwed."

"Maybe he will."

"I doubt he'll make it that easy for you, partner. You're going to have to do some creative fucking up to get out of this one." Rick stood in the middle of the living room looking exasperated and more than a little angry. "Shelley's a sap. Somehow he got the idea that you're some kind of a goddamn war hero."

"I don't know where he got that idea," Frank said dryly. But for the first time in a long time, he was ashamed. Ashamed for what he had done. For what he had become.

"The ball's in your court, buddy. If you want the job, you're going to have to do some damage control and see if you can salvage the offer."

Frank didn't know what to say.

Rick made a sound of disgust. "I watched you throw away fifteen years with the police department. Don't expect me to watch you throw away another opportunity—"

"I didn't throw it away," Frank snapped with sudden anger. "The department tossed me and you know it."

"They offered you a desk job and your ego wouldn't let you take it." He looked around the littered living room. "You'd rather wallow in this shithole like some kind of a drunken pig. I've had it with you and your bingeing and self pity."

Self-pity. Jesus.

Furious because it was true, Frank spun away and limped to the patio door and looked out at the gray morning beyond. But he could feel his friend's words crawling inside him, like a bundle of worms in his gut, taunting him with a truth he didn't want to face.

"So you got a rough deal. We both know it could have been a hell of a lot worse."

The image of Gittel's torn and bleeding body flashed grotesquely in his mind, and Frank could feel the old rage building into a storm he wasn't certain he could contain if it broke free. "Shut the fuck up about that," he said darkly.

Rick didn't look away. "Some of our guys were brought back in body bags. You could have been one of them. Think about that next time you pick up that bottle."

Frank's hands curled into fists, but he didn't move. Rick was his best friend. They'd been rookies together some twelve years ago. It didn't matter. Frank didn't trust himself not to knock the other man flat, even though he knew everything the other man had said was true. And he would never reveal that there had been times in the last year when he'd thought coming home in a body bag would have been better than coming home alone and torn to pieces inside and out.

Behind him he heard Rick walk to the door and yank it open. "Pull yourself together, Frank. I'm sick of watching you self-destruct." He waited a beat, as if expecting a rebuff. But Frank didn't have a rebuttal. There were no words left inside him. Nothing left to say. Nothing left to feel.

Just a big black hole that had blown through him that day in Jerusalem.